RAIN FOR THE WICKED

Tomer Benito

BOOKSURGE
AN AMAZON.COM COMPANY

BookSurge Publishing

An imprint of BookSurege, LLC.

Rain for the Wicked. Copyright © 2007 by Tomer Benito. All rights reserved. Printed in the United States of America. No part of this book may be used or reproduced in any manner whatsoever without written permission from the author.

Library of Congress Control Number: 2007901979
Publisher: BookSurge, LLC
North Charleston, South Carolina

Benito, Tomer, 1973

Rain for the Wicked / Tomer Benito. –1st ed.
ISBN 1-4196-6367-4
EAN 9781419663673

For more information about this book, its source, and morals please visit
www.rainforthewicked.net

First Edition: March 2007
Cover designed by Moshe Hacmon

For mom and dad,

without you it would have never happened.

Regarding Persons and Places

The major characters in this novel are fictional. Actual persons of public prominence have been included within the story in appropriate settings. Most of the events, methods, and backgrounds are factual. Some of which were never brought to the attention of the public in order to avoid panic and its consequences. This book is dedicated to the public who can and should be an integral force to assure its self-security.

This work is the culmination of almost a lifetime of data gathering, research, surveillance, articulation, and training others. As such, it would be impossible to list all of the people who influenced this work. I'd like to thank Maya Imberman, Amy Bryman, Rosemary Shufeldt, and anyone who took part in supporting, revising, suggesting, assisting, and approving this project. Thank you all!

"For he makes his sun to rise on the evil and the good, and sends rain on the just and the unjust."

(Matthew 5:43-47)

Chapter 1

It was a bomb. Even a child would know that. The stainless steel cylinder was spotless. Its shimmering surface was unstained; not even a fingerprint could be seen. On the side of the cylinder, displayed in a large square, red digits counted down to zero. An annoying electronic beeping sounded with the descending seconds.

Two hands reached down and unhooked the screws that held the square onto the cylinder. Visible now inside the container, one could see that the mechanism was connected to the cylinder with two colored wires—blue and red.

"Yeah, right. Blue and red. Aren't they tired of that fallacy already?" The man spoke from his sofa, his mouth filled with potato chips. His blue dress shirt was unbuttoned, and his thick glasses reflected the picture from the television screen.

The view showed hands holding a pair of pocket-sized folding scissors. The background music was now dramatic and suspenseful. The bomb's timer showed only six seconds to go. The camera switched to a man whose forehead was covered in sweat, then quickly panned back to the descending digits on the timer. The protagonist's hesitation was visible; which wire should he cut first?

Five ... four... three...

The doorbell rang just as the hand was about to cut the red wire. The man on the sofa kept watching while buttoning his shirt. When the timer stopped at the point all four digits showed zero, he muttered, "Of course," and propelled himself up from the sofa: not an easy task. By the time the doorbell rang again, he was glancing through the peephole.

"Okay, okay, I'm coming," he called and threw open the door.

The deliveryman wore a familiar red-and-blue outfit and held a large square pouch in his hands. "Did you order a pizza, Mister, Umm ..." He opened the larger pouch and looked at the ticket inside. "Ah ... Mister Just Joe?"

"Yes," Joe said, keeping predatory eyes on the steaming food boxes. "How much do I owe you?"

"Medium, two toppings, and buffalo wings. That'll be sixteen dollars and ninety-nine cents, sir. Ah ... Joe."

Joe took the boxes inside and put them on the tiny apartment's coffee table. While he did, the deliveryman glanced around the room, spotted the television and edged forward to stand just inside the doorframe. "Hey, you watching *CTA*?"

"Huh? Yeah, I do. I mean, I am." Joe handed the man a twenty-dollar bill and put his hand on the door, fighting the urge to shove the man back into the hallway so he could slam it closed.

"That's my favorite show," the deliveryman announced. "Never miss an episode. I've learned a lot by watching it too. Like ... I'm only the pizza guy, but I can tell a lot just by looking around a person's living room when I'm delivering an order."

Joe's face stilled. "Oh? Like what?"

"A lot of things. If a person's married. Even how much money they make. Lots of stuff." He glanced around again. "Like you, for instance. Single professional in your forties, I bet. You're still in a dress shirt, so you left your office early today and decided to chill out for a while. And I bet you do that most every day. You wear glasses, but there are no bookshelves around. So you're not into reading or any of that educational stuff. Middle class. Bearded, so you've got something to hide. Not too much into fancy parties either, if you know what I mean." He grinned. "And you've got the right TV channel on. Like I said, I never miss an episode of *Counter Terrorism Agency*."

"Well, you probably missed this one," Joe said, and jerked a thumb over his shoulder in the set's direction. He started closing the door, hoping the man would back up on his own. Simpler that way.

Thankfully, he did. "Actually, I'm not missing it. I bought a TiVo too. Never miss an episode." He gave Joe a victorious smile and nodded toward the TiVo unit on Joe's television.

There was only a crack now between the door and the doorframe. "Well, enjoy watching the show then."

"Thanks. And enjoy your pizza."

The man turned around and began walking down the hallway. Joe closed the door, reopened his button-down shirt, retrieved the boxes, and returned to the recliner. "TiVo for a pizza deliveryman who hardly earns a living," he said, chuckling. Just another example of America's tainted values.

But he didn't want to waste anymore energy thinking. It was showtime. He leaned back in the recliner and focused on the screen.

The hero's unshaved face perspired. The sweat looked real, as did the purposeful strain on his face. His eyes moved in their sockets like wild predators in a small cage, while an electronic ringing could be heard from somewhere off the screen.

Joe swallowed a bite of pizza and flushed it down with a long gulp of Coke, following the sequence closely.

The TV-hero reached into his pocket and dug out a cell phone. "Chuck," he said into the receiver then, "I'm waiting. Get me the info as soon as you can."

On tonight's episode, Chuck wore khaki cargo pants and a plain black shirt. Aside from a slight bulge on his right side, nothing about him appeared unusual or suspicious. He brought a tiny, yet powerful monocular to his eye and aimed it toward the valley below the hill he was using as a cover. The monocular focused on a gate about five hundred yards from him. Behind the gate were sliding doors, partly hidden by weeds growing wild on the surrounding hills. Closed-circuit TV cameras, mounted at each side of the doors, circled the area sporadically.

The sound of an electric motor followed the sudden movement of the gate, which opened to reveal a concrete entrance. Two men in dark suits stood on either side of it. Dark sunglasses hid their eyes; their right hands rested on the trigger guards of Russian AK-47s. Joe sucked the buffalo sauce from a chicken wing, shaking his head in disapproval. Few organizations in America, be they terrorist or criminal, would use a Russian-made gun when there were so many great American-made brands. Yet Joe knew why whoever produced these TV shows used AK-47s. Since most terrorist organizations in the Middle East and Asia use AK-47s, they'd become a terrorist trademark.

The guards' bulldog-like faces turned toward the area outside the gate, then one of them spoke into his left wrist. Within seconds, a motor-like humming announced the arrival of a truck from somewhere beyond the trees.

Chuck narrowed his eyes to thin cracks and took off his backpack. Without disengaging his eyes from the sight, he opened it. In record time, he had assembled an intimidating-looking rifle from items he retrieved from his backpack. A buzz sounded as he completed the assembly. Moments later, he was viewing a small LCD screen he hooked up to his cell phone.

"Go ahead, transfer it to me," he whispered in a raspy voice.

A massive black Dodge Ram SUV was idling at the concrete platform by the gate. The passenger's tinted window rolled down. The buffalo wings were tasty. Joe licked his fingers, then picked up another slice of pizza and chewed with delight.

"Black-tinted windows," he mumbled while chewing. "Might as well yell out, 'I'm a bad guy. Come and arrest me!' Better an old van. Better yet, a ten-year-old sedan. Idiots!"

The SUV's passenger barked commands to the guard at his side. Chuck's tiny screen began to display a picture. With a hint of excitement, he spat into the mouthpiece "I have a visual on the target. I repeat—visual on the target."

The television's speakers vibrated with pounding drumbeats while the clock digits on the wide screen indicated three more seconds before turning blank. Suddenly the TV played a commercial for a new car. Groaning with a combination of disgust and an overfull stomach, Joe put the empty cardboard boxes in the tiny kitchen, returned, reached for the remote control and brought it close to his face. Peering at the buttons through the lower part of his bifocals, he found what he was looking for and turned the television off, then patted his exposed potbelly with his sticky hand. "Chuck Tower, another stupid American hero."

Despite his opinion of the hero, he loved *CTA*. It mastered everything Hollywood had to offer—good actors, great special effects, and a quick, clip-like pace. But the plot ... the plot. Unrealistic, woefully so. Like this episode, where the exact image of the bad guy had arrived at Chuck's portable device in perfect timing.

But if it was *realistic, we would be in deep shit,* he thought. And watching the show helped him kill a little time anyway.

After a long stretch of his chubby arms, he yawned and looked around, tried to reorient himself to the here and now. His wireless phone was underneath the now-empty potato chip bag. He grabbed it, held it so the buttons were easier to see through his bifocals, dialed a number and scratched his side, waiting for an answer.

"Hello?" asked the hesitant voice on the other end.

"It's Joe," he said, and before the listener could reply, added, "I'm ready for another round."

He listened for another two seconds, then said "Okay, bye." He held the phone close to his eyes and squinted to find the off switch, turned it off and threw it on the couch.

"*Imshy*," he mumbled while walking to the bedroom. Then he caught himself. "Not *imshy*, it is 'move,' you idiot."

He sat down next to the nightstand where another telephone rested, picked up the receiver and dialed a number from the open Yellow Pages next to the phone. After three rings, someone growled on the other side.

"I'd like to order a pickup from Westwood, for one hour from now. 2160 Bentley Avenue."

The dispatcher confirmed Joe's address and phone number. When both sides were satisfied, the line went dead and Joe searched again for the strength to get up.

In his walk-in closet, he took out two hard-sided Samsonite suitcases. Into each, he threw a few of the Yellow Pages that were stacked on the floor by the closet. He closed the first suitcase, lifted it with his right hand to check its weight, reopened it and threw two more books inside. This time, it passed the test. He headed for the bathroom.

The shower was steamy; soothing and reviving at the same time. But he never spoiled his rotund body with too much time in the shower. Seven minutes later, he wrapped a towel around his large waist and wiped the condensation off the mirror. Then he studied his face, remembering what the delivery driver had said.

I don't look 45, he thought while rubbing his chin beneath his six-month-old full beard.

Then, he sighed. "No, you look 55, *Ya Chetyar*. An oldie." He smiled weakly and took a razor from the medicine cabinet.

Another twenty minutes and Joe was waiting outside his apartment building, dressed in a gray suit and holding a briefcase. The full beard was now a goatee. The two Samsonite suitcases were beside him. As he squinted at his watch, a white Toyota Camry pulled into the driveway and stopped. A handsome young man with a hesitant grin greeted him, then hurried to relieve him of the suitcases and placed them in the trunk.

They drove silently, both driver and passenger occupied with their own thoughts. When the young man stopped at a light that had just turned yellow, Joe nodded with approval at the extreme care to follow the laws governing automobiles in this city.

The driver looked at Joe and said softly, "The new look fits you, Joe."

Joe glanced at him for a second, then smiled and touched his goatee. "Like a businessman, ha?"

Smiling back, the young man turned left onto Bentley Avenue and stopped by number 2160. He shifted the gear to park, got out, opened the trunk and pulled the suitcases outside. He shook Joe's hand and said, "See you."

Soon after the Toyota turned the corner and merged into the main road, sooner than Joe had expected, a yellow taxicab drove down the peaceful street. While the driver loaded the suitcases, he asked "Where to, sir?"

From his looks and faint accent, the driver was perhaps Egyptian, but had been in the United States for several years. Joe observed the quiet neighborhood, making sure nobody was watching the scene in front of the house that had been deserted for months now.

"LAX," he finally said, and positioned his girth in the taxicab's backseat, placing the briefcase on the seat beside him.

* * *

Contrary to popular belief, the traffic on Los Angeles' surface streets was less hectic than the freeway. The taxi driver, whose permit identified him as "Muhammad Abu Ali," was in a chatty mood.

"Where are you flying, Brother?" he asked a few

moments into the silent ride.

"Tokyo," Joe replied, hoping it would be the end of the conversation.

It wasn't. "Is it your first time traveling to Japan?"

"No, it's not." Joe replied, and then, to change the subject, "Muhammad Ali? Are you a relative of the great boxer?"

The driver burst out with a rumbling laugh. "No, no. Actually, Muhammad Ali couldn't be *my* relative. He wasn't born Muslim." He checked the rearview mirror to see whether he had Joe's full attention. "He was born as Cassius Clay. He converted to Islam and changed his name only when he was 24 years old or so. He must have discovered who I was, and wanted to assume the same name." The driver cracked up at his own joke, then said, "Where're you from?"

"What do you mean?"

"You're not American, so where're you from?" Muhammad raised two questioning eyebrows at the rearview mirror.

Joe coughed once and said calmly, "You're wrong. I am American. My father was a diplomat for the State Department, so I grew up in Europe. That's why I have a slight accent."

Muhammad nodded, but clearly didn't believe the answer. "Not a big deal, like they say here. This is LA after all." He chuckled. "Everybody here has something to hide, eh?"

Unmindful of Joe's eyes on the back of his neck, Muhammad navigated the car onto Sepulveda Boulevard, one of the longest streets in the world. Except for the air conditioner's hum, the taxi was quiet. Joe played with his cellular phone, now a bit nervous.

"Thanks be to the Prophet, I picked the surface streets this time," Muhammad said, using his free hand to point up to the backed-up I-405 freeway. The signs for LAX were visible there, along with its parking lots, rental car and hotels.

Two police officers on motorcycles blocked the ramp leading to the airport. They signaled for Muhammad to slow down. One of the officers looked at him briefly. After less than three seconds, the officer waved his hand to indicate that Muhammad could proceed.

Muhammad muttered softly "Security, my ass!" and merged into traffic leading to the departure terminals, then spotted an opening near the entrance to Tom Bradley International Terminal and quickly parked the cab. By the time Joe exited the cab, Muhammad had his luggage at the curbside waiting for him.

"That will be thirty-three dollars, sir."

Joe gave him one twenty-dollar bill and three fives, and released a Marlboro cigarette from its pack. "Keep the change."

Muhammad nodded and returned to the driver's side, casting a quick glance toward his passenger, who was now holding the lit cigarette in his mouth but not really smoking it. As he pulled away, he risked another glance. Still, the man wasn't puffing on the cigarette.

"*Allah yisaadac*—God help you," he whispered while pulling away to the lower level to wait in line for newly arriving passengers. The blessing was one his grandmother used to say to him when he was young and did stupid things. "Something isn't right about you, my friend," he muttered.

Chapter 2

Michael eased his pace across the wide lawn, his sneakers making a squishing sound on the grass. The sun was setting behind the trees, as if eager to deepen within the calm ocean and paint Westwood's sky in purple and red. He passed the international student center, only glancing at the building where he'd enrolled at the University of California, Los Angeles almost half a decade ago.

There'd been an enormous number of forms to fill out to acquire his I-20 visa. But it wasn't hard, he thought while nodding to a pretty Asian student who greeted him with a smile when he passed her. *A mere $30K in the bank and the willingness to pay the tuition, and voila! Anyone can be a Bruin.*

He climbed the gothic stairs to the science building, his slim figure drawing a grotesque silhouette on the building's wall. The vibration of his cell phone brought him from his reverie and back into alert mode.

"Hi, babe," he said nonchalantly into the receiver, his accent embodied the clipped wording of the British. He listened, then said, "I'll pick you up in about two hours. ... So do I. See you soon. Ciao."

Maintaining the same pace up the stairs, he punched some keys, sent the text message to its electronic destination, and entered his classroom.

There were ten other students in the laboratory. Two Asian girls sat in the front row, conversing quietly. In the last row, four American males sat together, laughing. They stopped when they saw Michael, but then continued. Michael remembered the days when he was sure every laugh around him was actually *about* him, and the bitter desire to punch the daylights out of the ones laughing. It took him a long time to believe nobody cared about the way he looked or dressed, or even his origin.

Well, that wasn't entirely true. After September 11, 2001, a few classmates had studied him with condemning eyes. One of them even spat something nasty at him. But, looking back on the memory now, he couldn't even recall the words. That brief period didn't last more than a week. After all, both UCLA and Los Angeles was a melting pot of cultures, nationalities and people. Michael blended easily into these heterogeneous seas. It helped that he carefully maintained himself as a role model for not drawing attention. As always, he positioned himself near the middle of the lab.

Professor Vinitzky, escorted by two devoted students, entered and began passionately explaining a complicated process. It seemed as if the two devotees understood every word he said. Michael envied their ease. For him, the chemistry class had been a rare struggle.

When he finished speaking, Vinitzky asked the whole class, "Any questions?" When there was no answer, he said, "All right. Then I have one. What did you all learn from the sublimation experiment that you conducted in our last class?"

Nobody answered him. He abruptly addressed one of the Asian girls in the first row. "Joanne?"

The fragile-looking girl blushed, lowered her head and almost whispered, "We learned that there are materials that change their chemical states from solid to gas by skipping the liquid state."

Vinitzky watched her, waiting for more. When he realized she wasn't going to continue, his voice boomed, "People, we are in an Advanced Chemistry lab, not a high-school cafeteria!" He paused, allowing his words to register before exclaiming, "I want to hear from you what the rapidity of iodine sublimation is. I want to hear you say 'solid carbon dioxide, and not dry ice.' I want you to experience the change of states. Are you with me?"

The students all nodded, but Michael's nod was vigorous. Perhaps a bit excessive even; he felt his dark forelock jumping up and down. But being part of this lab, and the knowledge it contained, was what he had wished and planned for since his first day at the university. This was *his* mission, and he wouldn't let anyone down.

He followed the complicated equations Professor Vinitzky wrote on the board. He'd been doing fine thus far in his program—after which, he planned to push toward a master's degree in science. But he felt the pressure and tension weighing him down now, in his senior year. He'd even come close to changing to a math major. Brilliance with numbers was in his genes. His father was the best mathematician he'd ever known. Michael had once overheard someone say that Iraqis were good bankers because they were so good with numbers. Yet since following his father's career wouldn't forward his plan, he decided to stick with his science program.

His difficulty in mastering chemistry was an unfortunate anomaly for him. From a young age, the processes and analogy of science always intrigued him. And memorizing chemistry's complex formulas shouldn't have been a problem for him. His father, Habib Siluan, whose name fitted him perfectly—*Habib* meant "loveable" in Arabic—used to challenge him with a riddle almost every night. He remembered the long nights looking through his window at the Baghdad sky, waiting for the answers to appear from space. In the mornings, over strong mint tea and *sumboossek*—crispy, cheese-filled pastry—he would solve the riddle for his father. Habib listened to him while reviewing the financial newspapers. If the answer wasn't adequate, Habib would guide him onto the right path until Michael fully comprehended the answer. Yet his other abilities, while exceptional, didn't seem to extend to this particular science course.

Professor Vinitzky scribbled numbers on the board. This time, Michael was in luck. The formula was one he easily recognized, and he solved the equation even before Vinitzky finished writing. He thanked his father silently, and for perhaps the thousandth time, longed to thank him personally.

That would never happen, of course. When he was five years old, Michael and his father moved to Kuwait, where Habib became the manager of the Gulf Bank, an institution owned by oil-rich people. Back then, Michael's name was Mustafa.

Michael especially missed the mornings, when the chauffeur took them to the bank's headquarters to drop his father off. There was always a guard on a motorcycle riding in front of their Rolls Royce. When young Mustafa asked who the man was, Habib told him, "Oh, he is just leading our convoy to announce our arrival at the bank."

Mustafa never bought the story then, and certainly not now. The biker had a gun across his chest, not a megaphone. Even more, when they arrived, two guards stood by the bank's handcrafted wooden doors and watched for something Mustafa couldn't understand back then. His father would give him a farewell kiss on his forehead, and then enter the bank, followed by the biker. Mustafa was then driven to his private school.

"This is the main formula," Professor Vinitzky said while drawing, pulling Michael back from the past. "And this is its wife," he added, chuckling while he drew two shorter equations on the board. "And these are their kids."

His classmates laughed at Vinitzky's unaccustomed humor, but Michael felt a pinch in his heart. Something so common and easily understood by his classmates, but something he'd never known. His and Habib's luxurious lifestyle in Kuwait was a lame attempt to overcome the absence of Mustafa's mother, who'd died during the birth of his younger brother. While the doctors focused on the stillborn baby, they failed to notice his mother had lost consciousness.

By then it was too late; she had already joined her second son.

Mustafa didn't know any of this until he was almost five years old. Several years later he understood that this tragedy was why Habib doted on him, to the point of avoiding the many social gatherings his position afforded. Although Mustafa recognized the huge gap in his father's life, he loved being spoiled by him. Habib had little motivation in his world except for his work and his son. Life was good.

And then Saddam Hussein decided to conquer Kuwait.

Chapter 3

Joe stood on the curbside, waiting as he had twice before, pretending to smoke the disgusting cigarette. One of the skycaps, trailing an oversized cart and a willingness to take anyone's luggage inside the terminal in exchange for a few dollars, approached him.

"Do you need a hand with your luggage, sir?" he asked with a broad grin displaying uneven teeth.

"Sure, why not?" Joe replied calmly, as if they were old pals.

The slim porter made to pick up one of the suitcases, but Joe stopped him and pointed to a label on both cases. "Watch out. There are fragile items inside. Valuable."

Nodding, the porter continued with his task, placing the suitcases carefully side by side on the cart.

"Why don't you go inside to the Asiana counter?" Joe said. "I'll just finish this cigarette and be right behind you."

The porter smiled again. This time, his smile was uncertain.

"Don't worry," Joe said, and pushed a five-dollar bill toward the man. "Remember, what's inside these cases is worth more than you are. No way I'll stiff you on the rest of your tip." He punctuated his assurance with a chuckle.

Somewhat mollified, the skycap took the bill and pushed the cart toward the terminal's sliding doors.

Joe glanced at his watch, noting the exact time. He pulled his cell phone from his pocket and checked the signal bars. All of them showed. He couldn't ask for better reception. Squinting through his bifocals, he dialed a number and checked the time again. Thirty seconds since the porter had entered the terminal.

Joe couldn't see him from where he stood, but he was pretty sure the man had already trundled the suitcases to the Asiana Airlines counter. He pressed the phone's send button, raised the phone to his ear and listened for the ringing to begin, counted three rings, then shut off the phone and threw the cigarette butt in the ashtray by the sliding doors. He didn't dare throw it on the ground and risk one of the hundreds of bored airport officers giving him a ticket. It was a risk he didn't want or need to take.

He set his foot on the doormat, triggering the sliding doors, and enjoyed the sight of the terminal unfold before him. As he expected, the skycap waited impatiently at the Asiana ticket counter. He gave a friendly wave and covered the distance between them in several rapid steps.

"I'm sorry," he said to the anxious skycap, and gave him a ten-dollar bill. The man nodded and unloaded the cart, placing the suitcases onto an abandoned pushcart. This time he had forgotten about, or was purposely ignoring, the "fragile" labels on the suitcases.

Joe smiled to himself and chuckled as he nonchalantly checked their surroundings. *If he only knew*.

A man approached, the patch on his uniform identifying him as a Transportation Security Administration official. "You should scan your luggage first over there," he ordered, pointing toward the middle of the terminal.

Joe thanked the TSA operator and rolled his cart toward the big screening machine and the duty-free shops. There were already a dozen passengers waiting in line for a screening check. He didn't stop, just kept walking and turned left behind the machine's area, as if he was going to visit one of the shops. Instead, he arrived at the elevator and entered. Another fifteen seconds, and he was upstairs at the food court, pushing his cart and suitcases along the marble floor, passing signs that pointed to the nearby bathrooms.

Inside the men's restroom, he went inside a handicap stall and locked the door behind him, then opened his briefcase, took out a notebook and sat on the toilet. The notebook's title read "Sudoku."

The notebook was almost entirely filled, but Joe now scribbled some letters by the numbers written inside—not trying to arrange correct sequences in the Sudoku puzzle boxes, but as codes for the existence of law enforcement, TSA personnel, number of passengers, and the number of undercover security agents if he could spot them. Even if he were caught, nobody would be able to make out the codes he used for his surveillance drills. Worst-case scenario, someone would think Joe was a really bad Sudoku player. But he was good at all other games.

The squeal of rubber on marble caught his attention. He bent forward to peer underneath the stall door, and saw the lower portion of a wheelchair at the same instant someone began yanking on the door handle.

"Shit," he murmured, and then, in a louder voice, added "One second, I'll be right out."

He closed his notebook and returned it to his briefcase, then hurriedly opened the door. A young man sat in his wheelchair, looking with angry eyes at Joe, who obviously wasn't handicapped.

"I'm sorry," he said, not looking at the man's eyes. "All of the rest were taken." He hurried to roll his cart out of the man's way.

The young man followed Joe's retreating form with curious eyes, then rolled his wheelchair inside the stall, wondering what the guy was even doing in there. He'd never even flushed the toilet.

* * *

Muhammad sat in line to pick up passengers at the

international terminal's arrival level. If he was lucky, he could take passengers to the Valley, or better yet, to one of the towns up north, such as Santa Barbara or Ventura. That kind of ride was profitable. On prior occasions, he'd waited in line for half an hour or more just to take passengers, mostly females, from the terminal to the long-term parking lot. Those passengers didn't want to carry their luggage on and off the parking lot shuttles, so they used Muhammad as their porter.

He listened to the radio, to a program he liked on National Public Radio—*All Things Considered.* The topic today was the national threat level ratings, a joke in Muhammad's opinion.

Michele Norris, the host of the show, said, "Today we'll discuss a question many of our listeners have asked: How can anyone make sense of the threat levels, and what do the colors really mean?"

Muhammad chuckled and said to the radio, "Yeah, how? Nobody I know can make sense of them either, Ms. Norris."

As if she'd heard him, she explained, "As most of you know, the system was created in response to September 11. The goal, of course, was to use a higher level, or different color, to indicate a higher threat of terrorist acts. But, is it working as it was intended? One problem I've heard a great deal about is that we aren't always made aware of what the government's actually doing when the threat level changes. We're aware that police and other security agencies' presence increase at several landmarks and other high-profile targets. And no doubt, at certain level, every governmental agency, including the National Guard, are on standby."

"So what?" Muhammad barked at the radio. "That's just the government talking. What do the colors *mean*? If it's green, does it mean there is no threat? Or if it's green, there is no threat they're willing to tell us about?"

The taxi in front of him moved forward, and he followed. Ten more cabs to go before he could pick up a fare.

Michele kept talking about threats and risks. Muhammad felt his mind go fuzzy. He'd heard the word "risk" too many times in the last couple of minutes.

But when Michele said, "Risks are calculated based on vulnerabilities," Muhammad blurted, "Nonsense! Risk is based on past events and statistics only!" He'd learned that last year when his son, Ali, got his driver's license. Muhammad's car insurance doubled, and all of his protests to the insurance company remained unheard. They said youngsters are involved in more car accidents than adult drivers, which automatically put *every* young driver in the high-risk group.

Michele Norris kept talking, but his mind wandered—until he heard the word "LAX."

"Our guest, Kevin Altman of the Rand Corporation, known for its research publications, is an expert in homeland security and strategic studies. Kevin, can you tell us why LAX has been selected as the most vulnerable facility in California?"

Muhammad's brows arched. "What? *Right here?*" With great surprise he actually glanced around while Altman responded.

"LAX has been a target for terrorists for a long time, Michele. Terrorists attempted or actually attacked the airport twice recently. The first time was in late 1999, when Ressam Ahmad tried to get into the United States through Washington State with a car full of explosives. If you'll recall, he admitted his target was LAX. The second time was in 2002, when a terrorist managed to enter the international terminal armed with a handgun."

"Yes, I remember that," Michele said. "Tragic. He made it all the way to the El Al counter—that's the Israeli airline—and just ... started shooting. He killed two people before El Al security brought him down."

"Exactly, Michele," Altman said. "These recent events show that the airport was and still is a target for terrorists."

The fellow had a pleasant voice, Muhammad gave him that much. But he said very disturbing things. Despite this, he felt his tension about sitting in front of LAX right now give way, remembering the police officers who'd stopped him on the way in.

There are nuclear facilities in California, he thought. *And refineries. Big ones. Ha! One can blow up half of the city by just throwing matches in them. Why aren't you mentioning them?*

He shook his head and muttered to the radio, "I'm not an expert like you, Mr. Altman. But if I *were* a bad guy, I would go to a place where I could avoid all of these policemen and guards!"

He intended to say more, but the cab ahead of him pulled away, and he was finally first in line. He turned the radio off and got out of the car, prepared to discuss this foolish so-called news with his next passenger. Within moments, he could regale his passenger with, "Can you imagine? LAX is probably the most secure place in this country, and that fellow thinks it's the most vulnerable. Some researcher *he* is, ey?"

Fighting a chuckle, he stretched his long arms and made an ambling circle of the taxicab. As he completed the circle, he had to fight a gasp as he saw who was waiting for him on the curb.

Chapter 4

Professor Vinitzky shifted his glasses on his nose and winked at the class. "My son can solve this equation in no time, and he isn't even twelve. Get to work, ladies and gentlemen."

He plays riddles with his son too, Michael thought bitterly. Soon after the rumors of an invasion began, the father-son ritual of nightly riddles ended. Instead, young Mustafa saw Habib spend more and more time on the phone in the evenings, in hushed conversation with callers he never knew. Mustafa didn't know the reason for these changes, but as children sometimes do, he blamed himself for not being smart enough, or maybe his father, the only family he had left on earth, had tired of him.

The car rides to the bank were quiet now, and only deepened the loneliness he felt. The atmosphere, as at home, was tense. With his father emotionally absent, Mustafa turned to the bodyguards. Their offhand comments, combined with overheard conversations at school, told him of the growing tension in Kuwait. Before long, he could see it for himself.

One day when he was out of school with a minor case of sniffles, Habib arrived home at noon, right after lunch. Mustafa never saw his father at home before dinnertime. Habib stormed in and barked orders at the house servants and the men who accompanied him. Except for the bodyguards, Mustafa didn't recognize any of them. One unfamiliar man carried a small bag, from which he extracted a camera. Habib walked past Mustafa to the wall behind him, took down the painting there, and ordered Mustafa to stand in front of the blank wall and hold still while the man took his picture. Fear silenced Mustafa's questions, and he obeyed.

The stranger disappeared. Shortly after, his father left. That night, Mustafa lay in bed, staring at the nighttime sky and waiting for dreams of better days and nights to lull him into a peaceful sleep.

"No, Joanne," Professor Vinitzky said flatly. The man's stern voice startled Michael, who listened as the professor continued.

"You shouldn't even look at the A here. What are we looking for?"

Joanne didn't even raise her head when she whispered, "The X." The wrong answer. Michael felt almost sorry for her.

"So look for it where it should be," Vinitzky said and tapped his marker on the board, marking the equation. "Like my late father used to say, 'Where there is no scent of oil, nobody wants to dig.' Any questions?"

Michael didn't have any questions. He understood those particular equations very well. Even if he hadn't, he'd already returned to that terrible, fateful night, when he sensed the presence of someone entering his room and opened his eyes to see his father's towering figure.

"There are some problems," Habib said in a soft voice. Mustafa sat up in bed, instantly alert. His father hadn't spoken to him for weeks.

"Iraq will conquer Kuwait soon. Saddam wants access to the wealth Kuwait has in its oil wells."

Even in the dim light, Habib looked pale and tired. Out of respect, Mustafa nodded as if he understood. And in a way, he did. When Mustafa asked him about a rumor he'd heard at school, that Saddam Hussein had massacred the Kurd insurgents, Habib just said the world was full of conflicts, and he should avoid involvement in any of them.

But now he said, "You must leave Kuwait. It is not safe for you to stay here."

Mustafa felt the room spinning, as wet, salty tears ran down his cheeks.

Habib held his damp face with a loving hand. "I'm sending you to England, to study in a wonderful private school. Remember when I told you to avoid conflict? Well, this is one of those times."

Mustafa didn't know how to respond, even when Habib kissed his head. He squeezed his eyes shut, wiped his tears, and looked at his father. "I have to go. All right. Now what?"

Habib managed a weak smile and picked up a blue binder from the bed. "That's my boy. What we have here are your travel documents. This is your passport." He handed him a blue passport.

This wasn't his passport. It couldn't be. The passport he'd used in the past when traveling with his father was deep green. And besides, this passport had the word "Kuwait" on the front. He opened it, and saw the picture taken earlier that day. And instead of his real name, the name under the picture was "Michael."

He looked up at Habib, who nodded and explained, "It will be much easier for you to blend in with an English name."

Mustafa glanced again at the passport. "But this says 'Kuwait.' That isn't true, Father."

Habib sighed heavily. "If Saddam and the Iraqis plan to capture Kuwait ... it is better you have a Kuwaiti passport than an Iraqi one."

Michael nodded again. "But ... Father, how did you get it?"

Habib smiled. "When you have the money and the right connections, my son, you can get anything."

Michael would never forget this simple statement. As he tightened his free hand into a fist he felt the pain as his fingernails pierced his skin. No, he wasn't dreaming. Not then, and not at the end of the next day, when he was escorted off the airplane at Heathrow by a disinterested attendant who introduced him to Ibrahim Sarhan, the family friend who would take care of him in London. Until sleep finally took him, Mustafa had spent the entire flight rehearsing his new name in his mind. *Not Mustafa, but Michael.*

When he tired of that, he tried to memorize the man's name he was to meet. Of him, his father only said, "Ibrahim Sarhan is a wonderful man, and I trust him. You will come to love him too."

"If there are no further questions, I suggest that you start working on the sublimation formula," Professor Vinitzky bellowed, ending the class.

You will come to love Ibrahim too. He could still hear his father's voice in his head.

If he only knew, Michael thought.

* * *

He left the science building and headed down the long flight of stairs, on his way to the parking garage, missing his father badly. An airplane crossed the sky above, heading to LAX. Michael looked at it and remembered the morning before he left Kuwait, never again to be called Mustafa.

Before the light of dawn appeared through the window curtains, he trudged downstairs for breakfast. The servants had taken extra care to serve all of his favorite dishes: *falafel* balls, *labni* cheese, and *sa'chlabb*—a dairy pudding with the scent of roses—for dessert. The food tasted like sand in his mouth.

He felt two hands on his shoulders and looked up to see his father. Habib was smiling, but his eyes were bloodshot, surrounded by dark circles, just like a panda bear. He'd never seen his father look so old.

Habib took the seat across from him, ignoring the newspaper beside his plate. "Well, Michael, are you ready? You are about to begin a new chapter in your life."

For the first time Mustafa could remember, his father spoke to him in English. He'd studied some English at school, but never took it as seriously as he did his other subjects; his teachers never missed an opportunity to remind the students that English was the language of infidels.

His surprise was instantly replaced by cold fear. How would he get along in a place where everybody spoke only English?

His eyes must have reflected his fears. Habib raised his hand and said, "Don't worry. You'll pick it up quickly. Ibrahim will help you."

Mustafa wasn't convinced. "How do you know English, Father?"

Habib smiled. "If I conducted business only with people who spoke Arabic, I would be trading with camels, not money." He sipped some coffee and continued. "There is a lot of slang in English that even I don't understand. Take 'okay,' for instance. Do you know what it stands for?"

This was one word Mustafa *had* learned in school. He nodded and said, "Everything is all right."

Habib smiled. "Yes. But do you know the origin of the word 'okay'?"

Mustafa shook his head.

"Americans played a lot of word games when the country was still new, before there were televisions and video games. They wrote a riddle of phrases by taking the first letter of each word in an expression and mixing it up. They used to write the letters in the newspaper and the readers had to guess what the acronym stood for. In one newspaper, they muddled the phrases badly. Originally, the phrase in the game was "All Correct," meaning, everything is all right. So they changed the A of the 'All' into O, and the C of the 'Correct' into K. I have no idea how. But since then, 'Okay' has been accepted as meaning 'All right.' There are other explanations, but I like this one."

He leaned forward over and spoke softly. "The main point is, everything has an explanation. Knowledge will help you to overcome fear, Michael. Fear is a reaction to something we don't know. The more knowledge you have, Michael, the more immune you'll be to fear."

Mustafa tried to produce a smile. His father had called him 'Michael.' The name he'd be known by from now on. And he suspected his father's explanation of what "Okay" meant was to shift his focus from the unknown future both of them faced.

"Michael!" a female voice shouted from the general direction of the Business building. Startled, he searched for the source and saw an attractive girl running down the stairs toward a blond guy, the total opposite from Michael's dark hair and olive skin. *Will I ever get used to this name?* he asked himself.

He heard another airplane overhead and glanced up. Someday soon, rather than making him sad, the sound of an airplane overhead would bring him joy.

Chapter 5

Muhammad's passenger wasn't prepared for this kind of chance encounter either, apparently. "Umm, well, I forgot my passport back home, and I couldn't fly without it," he said quickly.

Muhammad waited for more, but Joe was neither willing nor able to provide him with more details. He simply opened the passenger's door and slid inside. Muhammad loaded the two suitcases back into the trunk, several thoughts racing through his mind—and the off-kilter feeling he'd had the last time he saw the man resurfaced.

Ever since he told me he was an American, I felt something.... Something about this man isn't right. But what?

It doesn't matter, he thought. There was a time when he drove long-distance trips every day in his cab. He took his wife's suggestion and borrowed books on tapes from their local LA Public Library branch. As someone who rarely read anything, he really enjoyed listening to someone else read to him. It took him back to his childhood in Alexandria, Egypt, when his grandfather used to tell him stories, tales he came to know by heart. Some months back, Muhammad had listened to *Blink* by Malcolm Gladwell. The author had explained that the first second with someone is the most crucial one. It takes the subconscious a mere split second to determine something that takes the conscious mind much longer to process and articulate.

That's how Muhammad felt at this moment, that his conscious mind was still catching up. By the time he was behind the wheel, though, he was able to start processing the last hour's events. He didn't ask his passenger where he'd like to go; he'd been there before. He released the brake, shifted into gear, and off they went.

All the while, his mind was racing a million mile per hour. *If he really did forget his passport, why didn't he take a taxi from the departure level, where I dropped him off? And why was he so nervous when he saw me? Why did his answer seem like he thought of it* after *he recognized me?*

A chill crept up his spine. *Because he never intended on flying anywhere today. His excuse was a cover. But a cover for what?*

He couldn't force his mind onto the right track. He turned right from Century Boulevard to the Sepulveda intersection, heading north. His keychain, with a small picture of his wife, hung from the ignition switch, and began clinking against the steering column as the car turned into the intersection. He focused his gaze on the picture.

He dared to look into the rearview mirror. His passenger sat motionless and stared out of the window. He seemed very relax for someone who had just missed an international flight. Surely he had a cell phone, but why wasn't he calling anyone to notify them of the change in plans?

He didn't know what this man was up to. But instinct told him that he couldn't let his passenger know that he suspected he was up to anything at all. Suddenly, he knew what he needed to do. Muhammad mustered up a friendly tone and asked, "Are we returning to Bentley Avenue, sir?"

Joe turned his face slightly toward the driver, but kept his eyes on the window. "Where? Oh, yeah, Bentley Avenue, Number, ah, 2160."

Muhammad was desperately looking for a way to melt the lump in his throat. He pressed his index finger against the radio's power switch, but withdrew it. The terrorism program on NPR News would still be on. Definitely not a good idea. Instead, he ventured a comment about the weather. "It's a beautiful day today, isn't it?"

Joe looked puzzled, but he played along and replied, "Yes, indeed. Much better than it would be in Tokyo."

Both of them snorted a short, nervous laugh. A laugh that made Muhammad's nerves worse, not better. *He knows I suspect something,* he thought, fighting panic.

Deciding silence was the best course—if he said nothing else, there was less chance the man would become alarmed—he put all his focus on his driving. The rest of the ride was quiet, with no sound from either one, except for an occasional cough from Joe.

Finally, they arrived at Bentley Avenue. The street was just as peaceful as it had been when they first departed a little less than two hours ago. More cars occupied the driveways, though, a sign that many in the neighborhood were at work or school in the daytime. Muhammad pulled over to 2160, a nice one-story, single-family house. He didn't want to seem nosy, but he gave it more attention this time. The lawn needed some attention from a gardener, but so did his. No lights were on inside the house. But the homeowner was still in his cab.

So he lives alone in this big house?

Forcing his face to become a nonchalant mask, he got out of the car and pulled the suitcases from the trunk. Joe met him there. He cleared his throat and said, "That'll be forty five dollars, sir."

Without even asking why the fare was twenty percent higher this time, Joe nodded and pulled his wallet from his pocket. While he waited, Muhammad raised his head and looked at the house entrance. On the left side of the wooden door, three white notes were stuck to the frame. The familiar green-and-purple note signified delivery notices from FedEx.

Three in just a couple of hours? Why would a FedEx courier post three notes at once? It also didn't make sense that FedEx would deliver packages so late in the day. Unless he knew he wouldn't be gone for very long. *Or unless he doesn't live here at all.*

But none of these thoughts made sense either.

Joe handed him a fifty-dollar bill, and Muhammad searched his pockets for change.

"It's okay," Joe said, waving his hand.

"Do you need a receipt?" Muhammad asked.

"No, it's fine." Now, the man seemed impatient, as though eager for him to get into his cab and leave.

Muhammad nodded and entered the taxi, adding one more item to his list of suspicions. If he worked for a company, he would need a receipt for his transportation. Even if he were self-employed, he would want a receipt for tax purposes. Yet he refused the offer of one.

Muhammad didn't even turn on the taxi's on-duty light. He was too distracted to keep working. He turned onto Olympic Boulevard, but couldn't concentrate on the road. He turned right on Veteran Avenue, pulled over and shifted into park, alarm bells continuing to ring in his head.

The cigarette the man didn't really smoke. The switch he made to the arrival level, as if he was an arriving passenger when he wasn't. The surprise he expressed when Muhammad saw him, surprise that switched quickly, too quickly, to calm. Calm that continued while he sat in the car for the entire trip and didn't inform anyone about the change in his travel plans.

If that weren't enough to trouble him, there was the house that seemed deserted, with FedEx notes that had to have been stuck there for over three days at the very least. The receipts the man didn't request on either leg of the trip. Yes, something was wrong.

He thought about the NPR radio show he'd been listening to. Could the man be ... a terrorist? Muhammad had to say no. Terrorists were young, passionate. This man was his own age, maybe older, and everything about him screamed "mild-mannered businessman." No, the passenger did not fit the perception he had of a terrorist.

But still, something was wrong.

He shifted gears, turned off Veteran Avenue, and

stopped right before the road crossed Bentley, a block away from the place where he'd dropped the man off. To his astonishment, the man was still standing there, his suitcases next to him, holding a cell phone to his ear.

"Now what, he lost his house keys?" Muhammad asked out loud. He played with the idea of calling the police, but abandoned it. "What would I say? That he missed his flight and didn't want a receipt for his ride?"

His foot had started releasing the brake pedal when a white Toyota Camry passed him and continued on Bentley toward the man's direction. He pressed the brake pedal again and looked ahead in time to see the car stop near the man. A young man got out, and without talking to his passenger, started loading the suitcases into the car.

Muhammad scratched his bald head, his eyes locked on the white Camry. Then he grabbed his notepad and scribbled the car's license plate number: 4RCA606.

"Now I got you," he said, but felt no victory, only the fatigue that came from working so hard to find answers that weren't there.

As the Camry pulled away from the curb, he grabbed his cell phone from the armrest and dialed a number. After a couple of rings he said, "Hi honey, I'm coming home a little early. Shall I pick up anything on my way?"

He listened for a second then replied, "Nothing happened. I think. I'll explain when I get home."

Chapter 6

By the time Muhammad arrived home, it was already dark outside. His wife's face revealed her concern. "Are you okay?" she asked the moment he walked in the door. "You look so tired."

"Yes, I'm fine, Fahima," he said, and sat down heavily in his favorite recliner. "It's just that ... today, I had a very weird passenger." Many men of his culture would never consult their wives, but in their long marriage, he respected Fahima's intelligence and insightful nature. He moved to the sofa to sit next to her. When he was finished telling her his odd encounter, he said, "Well, any ideas?"

She looked into his eyes as if she were seeking for answers in them. "Are you sure you want to get involved in this?" she asked softly.

"Look, they tell us to be vigilant. You see slogans saying 'If you SEE something, SAY something' everywhere. What I saw today was suspicious. Yes, I think I ought to let the authorities know what I saw."

She inhaled deeply. "All right then. Vicky next door? Her sister is an important person at the FBI. In Washington DC, no less. She'll know what to do." She stroked his grizzled cheek. "*Allah Ma'ak*—may God be with you."

* * *

The Abu Ali family lived in a quiet neighborhood. Not as well-to-do as the neighborhoods in West LA, but with only moderate levels of crime. As he walked, Muhammad chuckled. In LA, it was easy to tell the good neighborhoods from the bad. One need only look for the bars on the windows. If you saw them, the neighborhood wasn't too good. Muhammad didn't have bars on his windows. Neither did Vicky Woodman, his neighbor. He'd only met her once or twice, waving at her as they came and went. Fahima had told him Vicky was a psychologist, also that Vicky had plenty of money, but lived in their neighborhood out of some sort of idealism. He had to admit the exterior of her house was nicely decorated, her lawn immaculately mown.

He crossed the manicured lawn and knocked on the door. The eye looking at him through the peephole reminded him that no neighborhood was truly safe. *Not in this day and age, as they say.*

A moment later, the door opened. Vicky was tall, almost as tall as him, and her short red hair complemented her attractive face and smart green eyes. He guessed she was in her early or mid-thirties. It was hard to tell; she clearly took great care of her appearance.

"What's up, neighbor?" she asked with a cheerful voice.

"I need your help, Vicky. My wife said ... your sister is with the FBI?"

Her face showed the same instant concern Fahima's had. "Yes, she's the head of a task force. Something to do with fighting terrorism, I think." She reached for his shoulder. "Come on in."

Her house was nicely decorated. She led him into the large kitchen and gestured towards one of the stools at the counter, beneath track lights that lent a soft glow to the entire room. He told her the story for the second time, cautious not to skip any details, welcoming the glass of ice water with a slice of lemon she offered.

"So, what do you think?" he asked when he finished.

She nodded and picked up the telephone from the wall holder next to them. "Definitely something fishy. And sure, it could be nothing, but why take the chance?" As she spoke, she dialed. "It's kind of late in DC now, but I don't think we should wait. The way you described that guy, it's just too weird."

Muhammad stared at the water glass, then up at her when she smiled into the receiver and said, "Hi, Amanda. I know it's late, but this is important." She introduced him before handing the phone to him, and he unfolded his afternoon's adventures once again, this time finishing by saying, "I have the car's license plate number, if it helps."

He retrieved the carefully copied number from his jacket pocket, prepared to recite it to her. But then, he heard a yawn over the phone, followed by, "What you need to do is to contact your local FBI office. They'll know how to handle it."

Muhammad felt as if he'd just sucked the juice out of the lemon slice in his glass. "But ... can't you take the information to the authorities in Washington?"

Slowly, as if speaking to a child, Amanda repeated the same words, but added, "The office in Los Angeles can better handle your tip."

Feeling annoyance rising, he laid the slip of paper aside, and worked to keep a polite tone. "Do you know anyone in the LA office to refer me to?"

"Log onto www.fbi.gov, submit your concern, and an agent will call you."

He closed his eyes and muttered, "Thank you, Amanda."

"You're welcome," followed the cool reply.

* * *

Vicky and Amanda exchanged a few words before

ending the call. But as soon as Vicky hung up, she dialed another number.

"Hi," she said into the receiver in a low, husky voice. "I think I have something that might be a great interest to you. How about meeting at the usual place in about half an hour?"

A few moments later, she hung up the phone and smiled. *Amazing. How often does the fly come to the spider like that?* She grabbed her purse and car keys, turned the lights off and left. The small square of paper fluttered in the breeze as she passed by.

Chapter 7

Michael entered the cafeteria and stood in line. Some football players wearing UCLA Bruins jerseys stood in line before him, talking about the latest game. The tables around were occupied with people using laptop computers or textbooks, or just chatting. A voice came over the speaker system to announce that an order was ready. It sounded like an airport call for passengers.

When his turn came, he took his order and turned to leave, almost bumping into a huge basketball player, attention he didn't want or need. As he walked away, he opened the cup lid and inhaled the aromatic Earl Grey tea. The smell brought back a distinct memory. He could almost *feel* the overstuffed sofa he was sitting in when he drank Earl Grey for the first time in his life, and for the only time with his father. A sudden tear formed, and he blinked it away.

"When will I see you again, Father?" They were sitting in the airport's VIP lounge, awaiting his flight. Michael was first to break the silence.

"*Inshallah*—if God wishes, when things clear up here," was the reply, not the specific date or time Michael had hoped for.

Too soon, it was time to board the plane. He walked with Habib to the gate, holding his hand, fighting tears. His father noticed, stopped and knelt beside him.

"Don't suppress your tears, my son. If you want to cry, just let it go. Consider it like a wave in the ocean. Think of all of the breakwaters we saw on the beach at Dubai, and what the waves did to them. Remember the cormorants floating on the waves? They didn't resist, and nothing happened to them. Let the tears cleanse your soul instead of weighing you down."

Michael gazed at his father, still doubtful. "Arab men shouldn't cry," he murmured.

Habib held him tight, assuring him with his words. "Even grown Arab men cry sometimes."

Michael could fight the tears no longer, tears that Michael-the-adult fought now at the next memory. Habib's hand was replaced by the flight attendant's, and his father gazed at him with a mixture of love, care, concern, and ... something else. Something he'd never seen on his father's face before—a tear....

But it was as though this memory had made him more determined. He felt even stronger proceeding with what he'd come to California to do. Michael kept walking toward the parking lot to his car.

The Camry seemed untouched, but he couldn't take any chances. He never could. He walked past it and found a spot from which he could observe anyone passing by. When he was certain no one showed any interest, he felt safe enough to use the remote control to disarm the alarm and then approach the car. Before getting in, he checked the interior. Everything seemed fine. He sat behind the wheel, placed the half-empty cup into the cup holder, and turned the key in the ignition. In the rearview mirror, a scantily clad coed walked past, likely on the way to her own car. And he remembered.

"What bothers you, child?" The British Airways jet had been comfortable, and the man's face was caring. But how could Michael put words to his shock when he saw the passengers around him, donned in traditional Muslim clothing, actually accepting the flight attendant's offer of wine or liquor?

"Nothing's wrong," he managed to reply. "Well ... I just thought we weren't supposed to drink alcohol."

The man laughed. "We shouldn't be ashamed of who

we are, but we should enjoy this lifetime even before we get to paradise." He handed Michael the tiny, half-empty bottle from his tray. "What's written there?"

Michael read the English letters on the label. "Shiraz." He looked at the man with widened eyes. "It sounds ... Iranian?"

"Exactly! The world's best grapes are harvested in southwestern Iran. Have been, even before the prophets' days." The man sipped from his glass in apparent pleasure. "Today they produce this wine in France, in the America, and even in Australia. It seems the western world knows how to appreciate good wine much better than we do."

Stunned, young Michael couldn't even reply. He'd never heard someone willingly say anything good about the West. He was still amazed at how irritated he felt, even here in Los Angeles, whenever someone praised "the American way." The wide Los Angeles streets accepted Michael and his Camry indifferently, as though he was just one of many worker ants in the gigantic anthill that was America.

But not for long, he thought while signaling his intent to change lanes. *Soon enough, no one will be able to stay indifferent.*

A billboard featured some women's fashion magazine, declaring, "It's hot in LA." His attention was on it, so he didn't see the car that passed him until it had bullied its way into his lane, ahead of him. Any other driver would have blown his horn. Michael didn't. He would do nothing to attract attention.

He turned the Toyota's radio on and listened to a talk show. It was essential for him to listen to news programs, even when the news didn't seem to matter. *"Know the enemy,"* he could almost hear Ibrahim whispering to him. The newscaster said that tomorrow would be another sunny, dry and warm day in LA. He thought of his first day in London, of riding in Ibrahim's funny European car with the steering wheel on the wrong side. It was raining that day, and the sky was gray. He could count on one hand the number of rainy days in Kuwait.

And even then, it was warm rain. But in London, the rain became an incessant theme in his life.

The sleep on the plane had done little good. It helped, a bit, that Ibrahim had seemed so happy to see him. Ibrahim's apartment wasn't even half the size of Michael's house in Kuwait, and contained wall decorations Michael had never seen before; axioms from the Koran covered the walls.

"Do you want to call your father?" Ibrahim asked after showing him to his room.

"Yes, please," he replied, fighting tears of exhaustion and homesickness.

Ibrahim dialed numbers from a card and listened, then handed the phone to him. Habib's warm greeting unleashed his tears. They chatted for a too-short minute before his father asked to speak with Ibrahim. Michael didn't know what they were conversing about, but the expression on Ibrahim's face was very serious. He heard him blessing his father as they said goodbye.

"*Goodbye*," he muttered, steering the Camry onto the exit ramp. "And *Farewell*, and *So long*. And they don't even know what they're saying!"

His cell phone rang. With his free hand, he pulled it from his pocket and looked at the number on the screen, and then hit the talk button.

"I'm on my way," he said.

"I'm waiting," was the short reply.

"We could just talk tomorrow," he said, teasing.

He heard, "I dare you," and then the line went dead.

"He said you can talk tomorrow morning," Ibrahim had informed him so long ago. *"Now it's time for evening prayer."* Without waiting for a reply, he unrolled a small rug beside the dining table.

Michael smiled and said, "Uh ... Ibrahim? I don't practice."

Ibrahim fixed him with a harsh look. "It's about time you start, then."

He taught Michael how to bow and what to say, and although Michael thought it was amusing, he didn't like being forced to pray. Yet for the first time, he got the sense that what he liked, or didn't, wasn't taken into consideration anymore.

The next morning, Ibrahim repeated the ritual of connecting with Kuwait. After a moment, he pressed the button to disconnect, and said, "Humm. Odd."

"Is something wrong?" Michael had asked.

"The line is disconnected. I'll try his study." He started dialing again, again with no success. A third number got the same result.

Ignoring Michael, he placed the receiver back in its cradle and went to the television in the living room, switched channels until he found CNN. The bottom of the screen read, "CNN Breaking News," Red letters declared, "Iraq invades Kuwait." The images were of tanks and troops crossing some kind of border. Michael watched the images, unable to speak.

"What is 'invades,' Ibrahim?" he whispered at last. His English wasn't perfect; perhaps he wasn't translating the word right.

"It means Iraq has attacked Kuwait," Ibrahim said quietly. "What your father feared has come true."

The date was November 2nd, 1990.

From the Camry's radio, he heard the newscaster saying something about a revolution in Central Africa. Her voice was infused with concern and alarm, but Michael doubted she'd remember any of it later that day. Passiveness, it seemed, was the American way. He parked the car and looked around the big parking lot. His Toyota looked like any other car there. Nobody was paying attention to him. He ambled between parked cars toward the grocery store, looking at the reflections behind him in the store's big front windows. Nobody followed.

One of the lessons his father taught him was to avoid ignoring things in his life, to instead act with purpose. Despite this, he feared passivity was taking over his life after that day in November of 1990. It wasn't his choice to be passive, true; as a child, he could do nothing to find out what happened to his father or their beloved servants. Yet even Ibrahim, an adult, seemed helpless. In one of their conversations, when Michael's eyes started to swell up with tears, Ibrahim said, "I think the whole situation is good. Now Iraq will have access to Kuwaiti oil. That will give Iraq great power."

Then, Michael remembered his father's lesson. If there was anything he could do to fight the passivity overtaking him, was to accomplish this goal his father had set by sending him to London. He sniffled back his tears and said, "Ibrahim, when do I begin to study English?"

Ibrahim looked at him with questioning eyes. Michael explained, "It's my father's wish."

Ibrahim gave a solemn nod. *"Okay, let's go."*

That day, as they traveled in Ibrahim's car, Michael had asked about the strange way in which the vehicle's components were set up. Ibrahim laughed and replied, "That's how it is with the British. In fact, it's that way everywhere they had colonies. Australia, India, China, even South Africa. The British systems in those countries are the same as in England."

Michael consumed the new information. "So why wasn't it the same in Iraq? My teacher told me that Iraq was also occupied by England a long time ago."

Ibrahim glanced at him. "A good question, Mustafa. Maybe because the British interest in Iraq was only for our oil, not for our people." The last part of his reply held a great deal of bitterness.

Michael cleared his throat and said, "Meaning no disrespect, Ibrahim ... Father wanted me to go by the name 'Michael'. He thought it would help me to ... to *assimilate*."

Ibrahim nodded but didn't reply. The repetitive sound of the windshield wipers took over. After a while, Ibrahim said, "It bothers me that you want to give up your heritage and tradition. And for what? For the infidels?"

Michael remained silent, intimidated by Ibrahim's

passion. He didn't want to have this argument with the man who was supposed to be his host.

Ibrahim noted his silence and added, "I have no problem calling you Michael, or Mickey, or Muky. I just want you to remember that we are heirs to the Prophet Muhammad. He endowed us with the holiest book of all—the Koran. I can't remember who said this, but for those who don't remember their past, have a weak present, and their future is dim in the fog."

Michael repeated that statement over and over in his head. It seemed so ... *powerful*.

Ibrahim turned abruptly and then slowed down just before a building with a sign that read: "Palingswick House." Michael's questioning expression warranted Ibrahim's swift answer "This is where we get together, the Iraqi immigrants. This is where I work. It's a ... think of it as a charity organization. We can work here because of donations. People like your father allow us to be here and to take care of our Iraqi brothers in England...."

"Will that be all for you?" The cashier asked.

Michael nodded. *To take care of our brothers. What a joke,* Michael thought while he paid for his groceries. *At least it provided us with enough money to send me here.*

A bit later, he parked the Toyota in the semi-deserted parking lot and killed the engine. He always felt uneasy before meetings like this. He inhaled deeply and waved away his bad thoughts, as he'd done so many times before. Like on his second day in London, when Ibrahim parked and they got out of the car, and Michael felt the sudden, bitter cold outside, so different from his home. On the sidewalk, a few people gathered under black umbrellas. Some of them held video cameras. "BBC" and "CNN" were printed in bold letters on the vans behind them.

"That's not good," Ibrahim muttered, and steered Michael to an alley next to the building. Michael struggled to keep up with Ibrahim's long legs. Instead of entering the building as he expected they would, he followed Ibrahim to what he later learned was a subway station. Michael repeatedly asked, "Ibrahim, what's wrong?" Ibrahim only shook his head and said, "Not now."

Soon after they emerged from the subway, his first subway ride ever, he saw a minaret he easily recognized. When they passed Regent's Park, he could see an equally familiar golden dome. He felt his heart expand. Although he barely practiced Islam in Baghdad or in Kuwait, the sight made him feel connected to his tradition and heritage.

The mosque was huge, and there were hundreds of people inside, people who looked and spoke just like him. Ibrahim introduced Michael as a relative from Baghdad. The invasion of Kuwait seemed to be the highlight of the day. Most of the worshippers praised Saddam for the annexation of Kuwait's wealth. The *Imam*—the Islamic head of the congregation—opened the prayers with many mentions of Kuwait, some bellowed, some in a tremulous but passionate tone that made his heart swell even more. This was the first time in his life he was truly excited to pray.

After the prayer was over, Ibrahim approached the *Imam*, an old man with a long white beard wearing traditional white garb. Ibrahim introduced Michael, then said, "We need to bring this child back into the religion."

"*Inshallah*, we'll do just that." The man's eyes pierced through him, but he felt only warmth emanating from them.

When they left London Central Mosque, Michael was a different person. His doubts about Ibrahim had changed to complete trust. His father had sent this man everything he had—his beloved and only son. From that day forth, Michael considered Ibrahim his role model.

In the days after the invasion, when CNN and BBC brought the war into every household, Michael's passion to act was laced with longing. Every phone call to Ibrahim's apartment ignited new hopes in his heart, hopes that turned to disappointment each time.

His ambivalence continued and deepened. Over time, Ibrahim and his friends kept mentioning how all of the sicknesses in the world had been caused by the infidels. He believed them. By then, his regard for Ibrahim and his friends was near-worshipful. Yet each day, he encountered well-mannered infidels who were willing to help him despite his origin or religion. At first, he couldn't understand Ibrahim's loathing. *If it is so awful here, why do you live here?* he wondered more than once. But of course he didn't dare ask Ibrahim or his friends during one of the many nights they came to play *Tawla*—backgammon—and smoke the hookah.

He had adopted everything else Ibrahim had taught him, and Ibrahim's beliefs sank in a little deeper every time. He even started to believe the infidels were the reason he couldn't find his father.

He kept up his religious practice every day at London Central Mosque, and when he was a bit older, he was allowed into the debates they had over Great Britain's diplomacy in the Persian Gulf.

Those discussions prepared him to meet new challenges, to deal with people who didn't share his higher purpose. Like those in Los Angeles, his home for the time being.

You belong to a higher purpose, he reminded himself while he got out of the car and walked the short distance from the parking lot to the unimpressive building of the Los Angeles Public Library. He'd repeated this ritual many times before, but the nervousness he felt in his chest was still new and chilling, almost the same as he felt that day in the mosque.

He stood by the wide entrance and noted only a few people inside. Two librarians stood behind a counter and conversed quietly. On the wall above them was the American flag, a symbol of the infidels' world. He looked at it with disgust, hearing Ibrahim and his friends cursing the Americans and their allies for interrupting Saddam from doing justice.

When he saw her blonde head through the library's

front window, weaving between the bookracks inside, he rehearsed his greeting. He didn't want to go in. He would wait outside. She was about to finish her shift anyway. He liked talking with her, and felt very comfortable doing so. She had sometimes complimented him on his English, and this made him proud, thinking that he'd accomplished his father's last request—to learn English and to excel at school. He succeeded on both fronts. The beautiful girl inside was an unexpected gift. In a country he could never call his real home, it gave him a feeling of stability.

When the girl returned to the counter, her arms filled with books, he smiled at her through the window. She smiled back, dropped the books on the counter and rushed outside to greet him.

There are some beautiful sides to the infidels, he thought, admiring her loveliness. Then he said, "Hello, Dianne. I'm glad we didn't wait to talk 'til tomorrow, after all."

Chapter 8

Muhammad entered his house quietly, and was instantly flooded with the aromas of his wife's home-cooked cuisine. At this point, he didn't know whether he was angry, frustrated, depressed, or all of the above.

"What happened?" Fahima asked. "Why do you look as if all of your fleet sank into the sea?"

He lifted the cover of one of the pots on the stove and took a deep breath, then turned to the sink and washed his hands. Fahima handed him a towel, waiting for his response. He was silent as he went to the refrigerator and returned to the table with a pitcher of lemonade with mint leaves floating inside. He poured himself a glass and said, "I don't know why we pay taxes in this country."

She rolled her eyes to the sky at the familiar words she'd heard many times before. "Now what?" she asked, handing him a *malfoof* on a napkin.

Muhammad believed Fahima's *malfoof* was the best on the West Coast, perhaps even the entire continent. It wasn't easy to choose baby cabbage with the perfect leaves: thin and flexible, yet durable, and the delicious mixture of lamb meat, rice, herbs, pine nuts and olive oil baked inside the oven so the ingredients could blend in great harmony. He devoured the delicacy with delight, then licked his fingers and began to relate what had just happened.

"You were right about Vicky's sister," he said. "She's the head of some anti-terror task force in Washington. She probably even dines with the President every now and then. I told her the entire story, every detail. Do you know what she said?"

Fahima smiled. "That she wants to hire you?"

He smirked. "Yeah, right. With my name, I wouldn't get too far, unless they wanted to assemble a *terrorist* task force."

Both of them laughed heartily, but then his face became serious. "She invited me to contact the local FBI office here. It was like she was saying 'This isn't *my* job.'" He searched Fahima's face, unable to tell what she was thinking.

"And who is our local FBI contact?" she asked finally.

"That's where it gets even better," he muttered, angry. "She advised me to post my story ... no, my *tip* ... on their *website*. I'm lucky she didn't send me to find a carrier pigeon!"

Fahima was silent while she went to the stove. Moments later, she placed two plates on the table, one with *bamiah* and another with a few slices of fresh bread. *Bamiah,* an okra dish, was one of Muhammad's favorites. When she cooked it with tomato sauce and garlic, even the Prophet Muhammad would have paused his holy work to attend her table.

"So ... why *don't* you put it on their website?" she said.

He stopped eating and looked at her closely. "Don't you think she insulted us, the good citizens who are trying to help?"

"Yes, I agree. However, this issue is bothering you so much, you returned home from work early today. Why not go ahead and do what she said? Then you will have done your duty."

He studied her face. "You might be right." Then he looked behind his shoulder to the silent house. "Where is Ali? I need him to help me."

She smiled and patted his arm. "He's supposed to return from his friend's any minute now ... Finish your food, and then we can take a walk outside to calm you down. Then you can save the world."

* * *

By the time they returned home from their walk, their teenaged son's old Mazda was parked in the driveway, behind Muhammad's Ford. A plate with nothing but crumbs was abandoned on the kitchen counter, and music was pounding from somewhere in the house. Muhammad walked to Ali's room. The sign on the door said "Al's Room," with warning bold red letters: "Keep Out!"

It used to bother him that his only child insisted on assuming an American profile, preferring to be called "Al," and not "Ali." When his friends came over, he introduced his parents as "Mo and Pam," as if doing so would convince everyone they were born with these names. Although Ali liked his mom's traditional cooking—how could someone dislike it?—he kept his distance from any tradition that might identify him as an heir to Egyptian immigrants. He didn't practice any aspect of the religion, and probably didn't believe in any god, except for a few American rock and movie stars. Woven into his angst about their son was pride that Ali had so many more chances for success in America than he, his father, ever had.

He knocked loudly on the door, hoping Ali would hear him over the music. Even this annoyance made him smile. Growing up in Egypt, he'd shared his room with four brothers and sisters. He could never close the bedroom door, simply because there weren't any doors in the house.

When he heard the yelled-out, "Come in," he turned the knob and entered a typical young American's room. CD covers strewn all over the floor, a few rock-star posters hung on the walls, and on the desk, a lava lamp was placed beside the room's core—the desktop PC.

"Hi, Dad, what's going on?" Ali greeted him, then rose from his chair and hugged him. "You're home early today."

"Nothing's wrong, *Ya Ibni*," Muhammad said. He

referred to Ali with the Arabic expression for "my son"—the same way his own father used to refer to him when he was a young man. "I was on a call to pick up a passenger at the airport today," he began, and unfolded the story for the fourth time today.

Ali watched him tentatively while he spoke, his look wavering between curiosity and a dubiousness that Muhammad was used to—he'd seen that look on Ali's face since he was twelve years old.

"What do you think?" he asked when he finished.

"I'm sure there must be a good explanation for all of this weird behavior," Ali said.

"That might be the case, but I have a bad feeling about it," he replied. "I tried to contact the FBI through the next-door neighbor's sister, but all she recommended was to post my story on their website. That's where I need you," he said, and patted Ali on the shoulder.

Ali snapped his fingers. "FBI.com?"

Muhammad shrugged. "How should I know?"

The address "fbi.com" didn't work, but Google soon revealed the right one, www.fbi.gov. "Here we go," Ali proclaimed, and clicked on the first link. The blue webpage opened to show many links, including the FBI's Most Wanted List with Osama Bin Laden as the #1 criminal, as well as some more information about corruption.

"Here's the link to submit a crime tip," Ali said, then looked at Muhammad. "Are you sure there was a crime?"

"No, but let's post it anyway," Muhammad replied.

Ali clicked on the link and typed fast, transcribing the story his father had just told him. But he paused when got to the last part, about his passenger being picked up in a white car.

"Do you know what make it was, Dad?"

"A Toyota Camry. I even have the license plate number." He searched his pockets several times, but came up empty. "I must have left it in the kitchen. Hang on."

But the paper wasn't there, or in the living room either.

And then, he remembered. He left the house but returned a few minutes later, telling Ali, "Vicky probably went out. We can submit it without the number for now."

Ali finished composing the message, then placed his index finger over the Enter key and glanced at his father, waiting for approval. Muhammad nodded once, and with the click of a button, Ali sent the message to its electronic destination.

* * *

The alarming ring of the telephone surprised both of them, especially so late. "It can't be Ali, he's home," Fahima said, even as she reached out her hand to answer it.

"Hello?" She listened for a few seconds, and handed the receiver to Muhammad. "It's the FBI," she whispered in awe.

He checked his watch, noting that it wasn't even half an hour since he posted the tip on the FBI website. Feeling proud, though a bit sheepish for his earlier criticism of the government, he cleared his throat and said, "This is Muhammad Abu Ali."

"Good evening, Mr. Ali. I'm Special Agent Smith, from the Federal Bureau of Investigation."

Muhammad suppressed a laugh. *Agent Smith, huh? And your first name is John,* he wanted to say, but restrained himself.

"I'm following up on your tip," the voice continued. "Can you give me the details again?"

Muhammad sighed. Smith heard and said, "Is everything all right?"

"Oh, it's fine," he replied with a nervous chuckle. "It's just that, counting you, this will be the fifth time I've repeated the story today. But here goes. I'm a taxi driver, and I picked up a fare this afternoon...."

Agent Smith asked several questions, and Muhammad could hear scribbling noises, like the man was taking notes. He also asked Muhammad about his background—when and why he arrived in the United States, how devoted he was to certain organizations, and who were his friends. Muhammad saw exactly where these questions were leading, and couldn't help the growing pounding sensation in his chest.

Tell me something, Agent Smith, does my Arab name automatically turn me into a possible terrorist? The words were on the tip of his tongue, but he didn't dare release them. Instead, he mustered all his patience and answered the questions politely.

When the interrogation was over, there was silence. Agent Smith then asked, "Did you see the suspect conducting any illegal activity?"

He thought about it for a second and said, "No."

Another silence, then, "Well, we appreciate your awareness and vigilance. I'll look into the matter and make sure the local police assign a cruiser to patrol the neighborhood around Bentley Avenue. Is there anything else you'd like to add?"

By then, Muhammad just wanted to end this dead-end conversation. But then, he remembered. "Do you want the vehicle license number?"

The man's interest raised his voice an almost imperceptible notch. "Well, sure, if you've got it."

"Um, I don't have it at the moment. I can get it later from my neighbor."

"I see. We'll contact you if we need further information." This time, the tone returned to the former polite but not-terribly-interested tenor.

When Muhammad hung up, Fahima rubbed his neck gently and said, "I'm sorry."

He waved his hand. "It's not your fault the man didn't take it seriously. As you said, we did our duty."

The rest of the evening passed with neither of them

saying a word, but the silence was as deafening as though a thunderstorm raged inside their small living room.

Chapter 9

The bar Vicky stepped into was shadowy and dimly lit. She took a booth at the far end of the room, where nobody could see her from the entrance, then checked her watch. When the waitress approached her, she said, "Johnny Walker on the rocks, easy on the ice."

She checked her make-up in the compact mirror she retrieved from her purse before looking around, hoping she hadn't drawn too much attention to herself. It might have been fun ten years ago, but considering whom she was meeting tonight, she wasn't in the mood.

She called the waitress over again and ordered another drink, this time Jack Daniels and Coke. *If he doesn't show up, at least I'll have a Plan B*, she reassured herself.

At the same moment the waitress placed two cardboard coasters on the table, a man slid into the booth facing her. Vicky smiled openly in welcome.

"What's up, Pumpkin?" he asked, pulling out a ten-dollar bill to hand to the waitress who placed their drinks on the table. "Put the drinks on my tab. This is for you. If you can, please bring us your fabulous calamari cocktail."

"What was the ten for?" Vicky asked as soon as the waitress left.

The blue eyes sparkled when he smiled again, "Tips."

"Huh? At the beginning of the meal?"

"Not *tip*—TIPS. It's an acronym for 'To Insure Proper Service.' The way I see it, a tip should be rendered at the beginning of a meal, so the waitress will work hard to prove she's worth it."

He finished his sentence just as the waitress brought their table silverware and a tray of olives, chips and salsa. Vicky's handsome companion smiled and winked at her. She smiled back and nonchalantly brushed a strand of her hair behind her ears. In spite of her sudden jealousy, she felt a familiar warmth spreading throughout her limbs from the core of her body.

The moment the waitress left, Vicky said, "I have something for you, Rich. Something you'll like. Some information." She accompanied the announcement with a seductive smile.

Richard leaned back in his seat, his smile never leaving his face, and raised his eyebrows. "In exchange for...?"

She laughed, perhaps too loud, and turned her eyes to the ceiling. "Oh, I have a payment in mind," she said, winking back at him and raising her glass in a toast. "Here's to an enjoyable evening."

The calamari arrived, and Richard took one piece of the squid between his fingers, dipped it in some sauce and munched on it with apparent joy. "So ... what do you have for me?" he asked, wiping his fingers on a napkin.

She couldn't reply right away. She was too busy watching the way he carefully wiped each finger, licking his lips as he did, recalling one researcher's correlation between the way a man eats and the way he handles his business between the sheets. How true it was in Richard's case. She sipped her whiskey, feeling it numb her mind. She loved that feeling. The alcohol gave her the chance to ignore her profession and class, even her polite manners. She looked at the man sitting across from her and searched for the same attraction. When she thought she'd found it, she leaned forward and lowered her voice. "Did I ever tell you I have an Arab neighbor?"

Richard's face turned serious for the first time. "He

giving you problems?"

"No, no. Nice fellow, totally harmless. Been in this country for thirty years. Wonderful wife, nice son. He's not a problem whatsoever. But tonight, he came over to the house, asking for my sister's help."

Now it was his turn to lean forward with hungry eyes. "Amanda?"

She couldn't resist. She leaned forward and met his lips. He kissed her back, not passionately, but enough to prove he wanted her too.

But first he wanted to hear the story. He leaned back in the booth and said, "Well?"

She muttered a sigh that was part frustration, part contemplation. "I'll tell you exactly what happened, and you can make whatever you want from it. I'll try to avoid any self-interpretation. Don't want to bias you."

Richard smiled again. "Don't you know? For a journalist, there's no other way. Go ahead."

"Muhammad's a taxi driver, and he believes he came across something suspicious today." Taking occasional sips of her drink, she relayed the rest of Muhammad's story, ending with, "Muhammad left the experience with a very uneasy feeling about the man."

Richard didn't speak right away. Not out of doubt, though. He'd known Vicky for some years now. She wouldn't have called him for something trivial. But her story touched on something that had been bothering him for a while. Her neighbor's experience might put a human face on an article he'd been wanting to write.

He pulled out a small notepad and pen from the inner pocket of his blazer and started to write. "So this Muhammad said the passenger wasn't American, but insisted he was?"

She nodded. "Something else I forgot. The passenger left the taxi holding a lit cigarette in his mouth, but he wasn't really smoking. Just held the cigarette between his lips."

Richard glanced at her glass, wondering how much

alcohol she'd consumed already. Perhaps he'd misjudged the value of her information this time.

"But that's not the only thing," she continued. "Remember that part about where he picked the man up the second time on the *departure* level? A passenger who'd told him he was on his way to *Japan?* I mean, I've been to LAX fifty times. There's no chance of that. And besides, who goes all the way to the airport, then suddenly changes their mind about a flight halfway around the world?"

She sipped her whiskey. This time, she saw his growing skepticism. "Look, I feel the same way. Taken separately, these things wouldn't be a big deal. But all together? I mean, when Muhammad asked him what happened to his flight, the passenger practically stammered through the entire 'lost my passport' explanation. And he didn't take a taxi from the arrival level, even though that would have been easier and cheaper for him.

"But you know what really convinced me? When Muhammad took him back to the same address where he'd picked him up, but the man *didn't go into his house*. And just minutes later, Muhammad saw a white Toyota picking the man up. So if that was his house, wouldn't he have at least dropped off his luggage before going anywhere else?"

Richard leaned back in the booth. "Where does Amanda come into the picture?"

Vicky shrugged. "She doesn't. Not really. Either Muhammad's story sounded too lame, or she can't deal with something like that on top of all of the other things she's had to handle lately. For whatever reason, she brushed the poor guy off."

Chuckling, she held up her empty glass and shook it. "Hey, maybe that should be the lead for your column. 'FBI ignores citizen complaints for the millionth time.' Something like that."

He measured her for a long moment, determining how sober she was, decided she wasn't at all. "Well, that's always an interesting slant. But other than that—and believe me, *that* subject's been done to death—I'm just not hearing anything to write about. We're talking about the feelings of some taxi driver, who might have been behind the wheel so long, he can't tell the difference between a cow and a dog."

He raised his hand in the air to signal the waitress for the check, pulled some bills from his money clip, then looked at Vicky, who was pouting now. "Let's go to my place. I have a free evening. Tomorrow's column's already done. And I promise, even if it's just a filler piece, I'll think of some slant to write up this fellow's story, okay?"

She gave him a drunken smile. "As long as you give me my, ah ... payment, you can do anything you like."

* * *

The noises in her head were unbearable. Like her brain was being squeezed in a vise. When Vicky finally managed to open her eyes, the brightness was like a lightning flash on a dark night. She cursed and shielded her face with her arm. Minutes later, when she dared to open her eyes again, she blinked several times but managed to keep them open.

The objects around her started to become familiar. She recognized her bed, her dresser, her pillows, and the object producing those blaring noises—her alarm clock. She gathered all her strength, leaned forward and struck the horrible device with her hand, almost knocking it off the nightstand.

When she was able, she sat on the edge of her bed and looked at her clothes strewn across the floor, clothes she didn't even remember taking off. The clock she'd nearly smashed read 7:05 a.m. She stood up, making every effort to keep her balance. She hated hangovers as much as she liked being tipsy. At least when she was drunk, she could revel in the ease with which she allowed her body to do things her brain would never have allowed had she been sober. Waking up after a night of drinking had nothing good to offer.

She staggered to the bathroom and into the shower. Her body ached. All over.

"Richard the incredible," she moaned, and reached for a washcloth.

She thought about him while the hot water brought her body back to something near normal. She'd always been attracted to his enigmatic personality, and to that handsome face that held a perpetual hiding-something expression. They'd met at a mutual friend's birthday party, at the bar. She remembered how good he smelled, and of thinking if she closed her eyes, she'd be carried away by his scent.

After their first night and a quick Internet search on his name, she learned he was a respected reporter, working freelance for all of the major newspapers, but mostly for the *LA Times*. In their next few months of occasional sex—occasional sex was all he seemed interested in—she became certain of two things: he wasn't ready for a commitment, but that was something she was more than eager to have with him. All she had to decide was if it was worth the risk to push him about it, and when.

She stepped out of the shower, leaving puddles on the floor, dried her short hair with a fresh towel and glanced at the clock sitting by the sink. When her eyes settled on the toothbrush holder, she smiled. She remembered little from the night before, except that she'd brushed her teeth. "Probably flossed too," she whispered, chuckling.

Hair and makeup done, she donned a charcoal-gray pinstriped suit to match her dark pumps and a cream-colored blouse. From the medicine cabinet, she retrieved two Advils to ease the lingering pain in her head. The to-go coffee mug was ready by then. A glass of orange juice, and she was hurrying to her purse. It was 7:55 a.m. when the doorbell rang.

She greeted her visitor with genuine surprise. "*Hola*, Nelva. *Como esta?* I forgot you were coming today."

Nelva smiled, confused. "Do you want me to come

some other time?"

"No, no, today's perfect. I just need to leave, and I have a huge headache. I drank too much last night."

Nelva smiled with patient understanding. "I'm sorry."

"I'm not," Vicky replied while digging for her wallet. She found it and placed a few bills on the counter. "It was great, he was great, I was great, everything was great."

Nelva gave her a small, embarrassed laugh but didn't reply. She'd been cleaning the senorita's house for over two years now. She'd seen her most intimate drawers' contents and sexy underwear. But she still didn't feel comfortable hearing her employer speak so freely about sexual matters that, in Nelva's opinion, should remain private.

"Oh, you're right, he's not worth talking about," Vicky lied nonchalantly. "If you find him, take him out with the trash." Chuckling, she passed Nelva and headed out the door.

* * *

Nelva smiled openly now while she placed her purse in the kitchen and immediately began straightening. She had always dreamed of being a princess, with many servants. She didn't know how she ended up as a maid, especially for someone like Vicky Woodman. But, she was grateful for the job—it was so difficult to find work if one wasn't in the country legally. Still, she couldn't help recalling her mixed feelings when she first arrived in Los Angeles. She'd been disappointed with the city's fake glory. The famous Hollywood Boulevard and its bums didn't appeal to her at all. On the other hand, she could speak Spanish fluently and freely here, since her language was spoken by more than half of the sprawling city's population.

She cleaned the kitchen counter, clearing the glasses left there. By one coaster she saw a sticky note with a number written on it.

"4-R-C-A-6-0-6. Humm."

She thought for a moment. *If you find him, you can trash him too*, Vicky had said. Could this be something to do with her male visitor? But her employer often said things that weren't serious. Just as obviously, it wasn't a phone number, the kind of thing one might want to refer back to. She threw the note into the garbage bag and continued into the den.

Chapter 10

Richard had almost decided that his story idea wasn't such a great one after all. In a city where there were thousands of politically connected nonprofits, no one seemed willing to speak on the record about nonprofit organizations that had been caught fronting as money laundering machines. Most everyone he'd contacted was "too busy" to even return his calls. In the mid-70s, when he graduated from journalism school, the world was still reeling from Watergate, and reporters were considered almost godlike. Just about anyone was willing to talk to him, about anything. Nowadays, researching any story was an uphill slog. More and more, he looked forward to retirement.

At least Vicky turned last night around, he thought, smiling.

He'd just hung up another pointless conversation with a source, deciding to call it a day and head for the bar in the corner of his living room, when his cell phone buzzed. He looked at the familiar number and accepted the call. "What waves did I stir up this time?" he asked by way of greeting.

"Richard, John Carroll here."

"Yeah, I know," he replied casually to the *Los Angeles Times* city desk editor.

"No tsunamis that I can tell," John said with a chuckle. "But I'm short an article for tomorrow's edition. Got about seven hundred words you can spare?"

Seven hundred words. Any other time, he'd be thrilled to be allotted that much space in the *Times*. Not today. "I'd love to help you, but my idea file's a little sparse right now, if you know what I mean."

John sighed. "I can't use any more ads, or readers might mistake the *Times* for *The Penny Saver*. And my filler file's empty right now. What can you give me?"

He could visualize John glancing at his watch, desperately wanting to send Murphy and his law back to the place they came from. He did too.

And then, he remembered the taxi driver. "Okay, I might have something. It's totally raw, and I'll need to check my sources. I'll get back to you within an hour."

"As long as it's more newsworthy than *Miss Millie the Cat Lady*, you're in."

Richard hung up and smiled. "Perhaps it's time to stir waves after all."

* * *

Vicky had just emerged from the shower when she heard her cell phone ringing in the living room. Yelling "Drat!", she raced for it, rubbing her hair with the towel. It stopped ringing well before she got there. But then the kitchen phone range. Racing there, she checked the Caller ID. It was Richard. Smiling, she pressed the talk button.

"It's not even 24 hours since I left you panting," she said teasingly without saying hello.

"Yeah, I know. But that's not the reason I'm calling."

"No? So what *is* the reason you're calling all my phones?"

He sighed. "That story you told me last night ... about your Arab neighbor and the strange passenger at LAX. You mentioned a license plate. Can you give me the plate number?"

It wasn't easy for her to hide the disappointment that he wasn't calling for her, but for information. "Oh, so you need it for an article after all," she said. "I can call Muhammad to ask him for it." She looked at the clock. Not too late. "Right now, in fact."

"Great. Please call me as soon as you get it." The line went dead.

She looked at the phone in her hand, disappointed at his all-business tone. But knowing Richard as she did, she forgave him. There would be other chances.

* * *

When Muhammad answered his phone, she was still looking around the kitchen. Spotless. No paper in sight. "Are you sure you left it here?"

"Yes. I even came over last night, to pick it up when I realized I had left it. But you weren't home."

She winced. "Yes. I was ... busy."

"I posted my story on the FBI website as your sister suggested. But it didn't look like anyone was going to do anything about it. But then—"

Annoyed, she said quickly, "All right, I'll look for it. I'll talk to you later. Good night, Muhammad."

She hung up the phone, went to the cabinet under the sink and looked inside the trash can there. Only a clean plastic bag. Not even for Richard would she go diving into the trashcan outside.

Richard wasn't pleased. "But you said you had the number."

"I know. But I don't now. My housekeeper probably threw it away."

"Okay, thanks. I guess. But, I guess I can still go with the story. I can always slant it as an opinion piece."

And he hung up on her as abruptly as she'd blown Muhammad off.

She looked at the phone, muttered, "Men," and headed for bed.

Chapter 11

The SUV cruised down Olympic Boulevard. Its driver checked his rearview mirror frequently, looking for a following car. He stopped at a gas station, waited a few minutes, and continued driving. He did the same at the next two gas stations, watching for a car or motorcycle merging onto the road after he left each gas station. None did, at least that he could identify.

He turned left on Beverly Glen, then right onto Mississippi Avenue—a narrow, almost deserted street—and parked long enough to bring a follower out of his snake hole. After two songs finished playing on the car radio, he moved again, and merged onto Santa Monica Boulevard. A quick right into the Century City Shopping Mall, and Jacob parked and killed the engine, then retrieved a baseball cap from the glove compartment.

The escalator led to a level with numerous shops and department stores. Jacob hated the public's common tendency to view the escalator as an elevator they could passively stand on to lift them up or bring them down. To him, it was a disturbing symbol of laziness—one of this society's sicknesses. He even knew a gym whose access was from an escalator.

He set his foot onto the open floor and started walking, passing designer and famous brand-name stores. He stopped by a Macy's entrance, inserted two quarters into a vending machine and pulled out a *Los Angeles Times*. He passed the entrance and used the stairwell to exit onto the street.

Passing a modern building with mirrored windows, he

glanced at his reflection and was satisfied—just another white American male dressed in business casual, walking to his workplace with the morning newspaper folded under his arm. The large building's windows also verified that nobody was watching him.

Just past the corner of Constitution Avenue and Century Park East, he entered a building. Inside the elevator, he opened the newspaper. By looking busy, he deterred others from trying to talk to him on the short ride to the tenth floor. He used the time to think about the meeting scheduled for this evening, mentally rehearsing some caution-measures he needed to think about before the meeting.

The elevator arrived at the tenth floor. Its door slid open with an electronic beep. He exited, walked to Suite 1011 and opened the door. The surprised receptionist raised her head from the computer. "Good morning, Jack."

"Good morning, Rosemary," he said, walking to the corner office. "Any new messages?"

"No, nothing new," Rosemary said. "Have you seen our ad in the *Times*? It looks wonderful! I'm just certain it will bring in more donations...."

While Rosemary prattled on, Jacob bit back a sharp retort. The last thing he'd wanted was to hire a Jew to work for him. But the best cover for any operation was the most obvious one. And Rosemary Thornburg was a competent-enough employee. And what did it matter? She didn't suspect anything.

He held up the newspaper. "The new ad? I'm about to look it over right now."

Inside his office, behind the closed door, Jacob spread the paper out on the desk and started flipping the pages, scanning them for one of those poor cleft-lipped kids' images. Until his eyes rested on a different image. One of a familiar public venue. He immediately forgot his annoyance at Rosemary.

He sank into his thickly padded leather chair and started reading.

Adequate Technologies or Federal Cover-ups?

By Richard Miller

The threat elevation throughout our nation's infrastructures compelled me to look into our ways of dealing with those threats. What I found reminded me of Hans Christian Andersen's fable, "The Emperor's New Clothes." For those of you unfamiliar, this is the story of an emperor who is duped into wearing an invisible (i.e., non-existent) suit of clothes, believing they possess magical powers and are visible only to those noble enough to serve his court. The emperor dares not admit his own inability to see the clothes. However, walking through the crowd, his own subjects shout, "The Emperor has no clothes!" And the Emperor continues walking, pretending to be oblivious to the obvious.

The recent news about screening failures at major airports across the United States should have done more than merely ring bells and raise red flags—or threat levels. We should all scream, loud and long, that the Emperor is naked.

To be sure, technology provides the extra eyes, the x-ray vision, and the "super noses" we humans have yet to develop naturally. But it has also become our crutch. Right number or wrong? Good guy or bad? When the light is green, it's good; but what do we do when it's red? That's where our human judgment should have already been at work, but wasn't. And the consequences can be tragic.

So where have we gone wrong? The answer is in the process. We can't apply technology to predict someone's thoughts, so we can't apply technology to detect someone's intentions. The human mind, even if it only produces a gut feeling, is the best machine to detect suspicious indicators at our airports.

These recent screening failures are a wake-up call for us to realize that the most important security tool isn't the technology we buy, it is the procedures we apply. And those procedures include taking seriously those reports of suspicious behavior given by everyday citizens.

In this, I fear the FBI is sleeping on duty. Recent developments at our very own LAX, the place named as "the most vulnerable facility in California" by the Rand Corporation, shows the FBI doesn't pay careful attention to warning signals. In one of these cases, a citizen encountered an individual who wasn't a passenger, but tried to assume the behavior of one with suitcases and a weak story. However, the citizen's attempts to notify the FBI fell on the proverbial deaf ears....

Jacob dropped the newspaper from his hands as if it had burned him. He needed to think. He couldn't think. But most of all, he needed to act. The article was like a warning, a portent that he must move faster.

He pressed a button on his phone and said, "Rosemary, no phone calls or visitors for the next hour."

Rosemary also had imperative tasks—she had a guest

coming for a very important dinner, and was downloading recipes from a cooking website. She pressed the button and said, "Of course, Jack. No problem," then went back to her surfing.

Chapter 12

Joe entered his apartment, locked the door from the inside and turned the TV on, mostly from habit. In reality, he hated almost all American TV. The programs were excessively sexual, the commercials stupid and much too frequent. However, he knew what he needed to do to blend into the culture. In apartments made of thin drywall, he should play the same kind of music everybody else did. And the sound of the television would drown out his phone conversations and any discussions with visitors who came over ... just in case someone had managed to bug his apartment, or his neighbor's apartment, in a way he couldn't detect.

He confirmed the blinds were closed, and sat down at the desk and turned his Dell computer on. He watched the boot-up sequence carefully, as he usually did. The black screen blinked with a request: "Please enter your password." He followed the instructions and waited for all of the computer applications to awake from hibernation.

While Norton Antivirus looked for Trojan horses or other intruders, he went to make himself a cup of coffee. Instant coffee. He missed the strong black coffee with spicy cardamom he was used to, and didn't think shopping in one of the Persian markets for Turkish coffee would endanger the operation. But he couldn't, and didn't want to take any chances, however slight.

The coffee was ready as soon as he poured hot water into the cup. "That's why it's called instant coffee," he muttered. "Thank you, Sartori Kato," he added, in homage to the Japanese scientist who invented this form of cheap coffee in Chicago in 1901.

Cup in hand, he returned to the computer. Norton had finished 47% of the screening process. He placed the cup on the desk and went to his walk-in closet where the suitcases were stored. Pulling open one suitcase's side zipper, he pulled out the cell phone he'd hidden there. The screen display read, "1 Missed Call." He pressed the Details option and viewed his own cell phone number.

"Good," he muttered, and smiled in satisfaction, then deleted the phone's call log and connected it to a charger. He would need the phone again soon.

Back at the computer, he dismissed Norton Antivirus' declaration of the computer being clean and logged onto the Yahoo website. He quickly typed the username "noplacelikehome," and the password "Americanidol00." His Yahoo mailbox came up almost instantly. The inbox was empty. He clicked in the section marked Drafts. There was one draft email in the folder, and he opened it up to read the message.

The message was transliterated in Arabic: *"Fi'l Bachar, Al Joom'ah, when il maggannin bill'ab."* He read it again, translating in his head into English: *"At the sea, on Friday, where the crazy people play."* Their appointment was set for Friday afternoon at Venice Beach, by the place where the drummers always congregated.

"So soon?" he wondered aloud. It had only been a few weeks since their last encounter. Usually, much more time elapsed between their meetings.

Perhaps something had happened. Or perhaps not. Joe didn't need to consider these things. He simply had to show up.

Underneath the message were three letters: M, A, and J1. He placed his cursor next to J1, pressed Enter, and typed J2 as the last entry in the row. He clicked on the Save Draft option, closed the browser and disconnected from the Internet, still impressed at the inventiveness of using the Web-based email program's Draft folder to disseminate information. Nobody, including a federal agency, could interpret, intercept or pinpoint their messages. How could they? They weren't actually being sent anywhere or to anyone, simply being held as an email draft.

"Genius at work," he muttered, and headed for the kitchen to see if it would be an eat-in night, or another pizza delivery night.

Chapter 13

Holding the cup of hot tea gingerly, Agent Ethan Smith returned to his generic agency sedan, started the engine, shifted gears and merged onto Westwood Boulevard,. Minutes later, he eased up on the accelerator and pressed the brake pedal lightly as he turned left onto Veteran Avenue. Soon he was gliding into the Federal Building's underground parking garage. He climbed the stairs, reminded himself that he should really exercise more often, then swiped his security badge through the magnetic strip and entered the lobby. He greeted the guards on the first level, making sure not to be overly friendly. They were just guards, after all, and he was a special agent. Simple, just like every other aspect of Smith's world.

From the elevator, Smith stepped out at his floor and proceeded to his office cubicle, greeting two coworkers walking down the corridor with a polite "Good morning."

At his desk, he turned on his computer and typed in his password, clicked on the Send/Receive button in his mailbox and sipped his tea. The tea was his wife's idea; she'd read of tea's supposed health benefits, and decided that at his near-retirement age, he needed all the health benefits he could get.

Among the list of new emails on the screen was one with a red flag to its left. He looked at the sender's name: Amanda Lopez. He didn't recognize the name, but clicked on the link immediately; the email was addressed to him, but with a CC to his department head. The email read:

Subject: follow-up/ Case number A9032QA23

Please conduct full questioning on the subject. Get as many details as possible. Report directly to me.

It was signed, *Amanda Lopez, FTTTF*

"What the heck?" Smith rubbed his forehead, trying to recognize the case number. Tried to remember anything out of the ordinary he'd handled recently. He couldn't do either.

He started searching through the recent cases files and found it. Case number A9032QA23: Muhammad Abu Ali. The name finally jogged his memory. The conversation he had with the man, as well as his attempts to check out the guy's background. Clean, easy and simple. A taxi driver who got a little too paranoid about one of his fares.

So why am I getting an email about it from the Bureau's Foreign Terrorist Tracking Task Force?

He reviewed the brief report he'd filled out. Immaculate. Naturalized citizen, squeaky clean record. Even though he'd thought the guy was just a little overexcited, he'd even placed a request for the local PD to patrol the area Mr. Ali had described. He hadn't followed up, but there was no report from the Westwood precinct. No news, good news. That was Smith's motto.

But now, this message.

If it weren't so odd, he would've laughed. But what if the whole thing was some kind of test? He'd heard of an opening for a deputy director at the Department of Homeland Security's California office. A promotion for him. He didn't think he was qualified, so he never applied. But maybe someone else thought otherwise, and was testing him right now.

He logged onto the Bureau's intranet, typed "Amanda Lopez," and hit Enter. A picture of a middle-aged woman downloaded onto his screen. Underneath the picture was a short bio.

"Damn. She's the *head* of the task force?" Something odd *was* going on. But whatever it was, he had to handle it just right. As a long-time agent, he knew that anything that came out of DC was big stuff. If they wanted this guy interviewed, he wouldn't stop until he knew the guy's hat size and how many minutes he brushed his teeth every morning.

He printed out the case information and checked his day's schedule. Until he found out why the head of the FBI's terrorist task force had a bug up her behind about this, everything else could wait.

* * *

As he had countless times before, Muhammad waited in line for arriving passengers at the international terminal. As always, he mused on how the airport was a window in time. No, a *no*-time zone, where people arrived from all over the world on the same planes that carried people in and out of the United States every hour. A hectic place, but in a positive way.

His turn in line arrived, and he got out of his car to greet an elderly Asian couple. They bowed to him and said something like "How much?" The gentleman handed him a piece of paper. Muhammad looked at it as if it was written in Chinese. It was. On the other side, he saw an address in Santa Clarita.

Either they didn't understand the $80 price he quoted, or the amount didn't matter to them. Soon, he switched on the cab's meter and pulled away.

He would have preferred to chat, but his passengers seemed incapable of conversing in English. Not unusual, considering that he picked up fares from all over the world. With nothing better to do, he switched on the radio.

The familiar female voice said, "From NPR News, welcome to *All Things Considered.* I'm Michele Norris." The announcement was followed by a male voice that said, "And I'm Robert Siegel." Siegel's voice continued, "Following the disturbing article in the *LA Times* today, we invited the author of the article, Richard Miller, to shed some light on the subject of the Emperor's technology and federal cover-ups. Good afternoon, Mr. Miller."

Richard Miller's voice greeted them both, and Siegel began the interview. "In your article today, you criticized the policy of technology as a major step in the Homeland Security plan to diminish terrorist threats. Moreover, you compared that policy to the children's fable, 'The Emperor's New Clothes.' Do you think Americans *are* naked, Richard?"

"Absolutely, Bob. We buy extremely expensive tools we think will do everything for us—detect bombs, weapons, intentions of travelers—everything but make us coffee ... well, maybe that too .... But in fact, there are many gaps in what these machines can do. You and I might not know this, but the bad guys do."

Michele broke in. "By *the bad guys*, you mean terrorists, right?"

"Correct."

"And how do they find out about our security measures? Secret networks? Moles in our agencies?"

Richard laughed. "Hardly, Michele. All they, or you, have to do is log on to the manufacturers' websites. I've done that as part of my research. Those sites provide all the data for their products: their sensitivity, limitations and capabilities. Or if you really wanted to be thorough, you could purchase a machine under any phony pretense and check it out yourself."

"You mean that anyone can just go out and buy the same machines used at security checkpoints?" Siegel asked, clear astonishment in his voice—astonishment that Muhammad felt as well.

"Look, there are no federal regulations limiting these companies' markets or client profiles. Why would there be? They sell detectors, not explosives."

There was an awkward silence. The pause allowed Muhammad to acknowledge how satisfied he felt. Finally, to hear someone who shared his view that in spite of all the technology, it wasn't enough. He didn't read this man's article—didn't read the *LA Times* as a rule—but planned to as soon as he dropped off his fare.

"Since you contacted me about the interview," Richard continued, "I've been in touch with an expert in counterterrorism. He said I could quote him off the record. And he told me about one example of an inefficiency that almost blew my mind. Michele, do you know what a sniffer is?"

"Yes, I've got that right here."

Muhammad heard paper shuffling, then, "It's a device that ionizes material to detect vapors, right?"

"Right. A one-hundred-thousand-dollar machine that basically blows hot air onto materials to tell whether explosive materials are present. A databank is programmed into the machine to recognize explosives, narcotics, even some kinds of perfumes."

"Sounds like a good return on investment to me," Siegel said.

"Maybe," Richard replied. "But remember, it's just a databank connected to a sensor. Anyone can find out exactly what the machine's programmed to detect. And any material that *isn't* programmed into it would be missed."

"But why wouldn't *every* dangerous material be programmed into it?" Michele asked. "I mean, isn't that what a machine like that's for?"

Richard chuckled. "That's exactly what I asked the counterterrorism expert. But the problem is that many explosives are made of regular products that just about anyone can get their hands on. Take glycerin, for example. I—"

"Glycerin?" Michele said. "You mean, like the glycerin in things like, like hand lotion?"

"And lipstick, Michele, and my aftershave gel, and your sunblock, Bob. So almost any airplane passenger would check positive for glycerin. Those false-positive hits, as they call them, drove the TSA operators crazy. So they simply decided to take glycerin out of the databank. But, and here's the kicker ... that very same glycerin's a main component of nitroglycerin, the stuff used to make dynamite."

"What you're saying, then," Michele said, her voice hushed now, "is that if a substance is common enough, even when it's used in explosives, it isn't checked for?"

A young driver in a BMW convertible cut in front of Muhammad's cab and forced him to slam on his brakes. He didn't protest or curse. He didn't want to miss any part of this interview.

"So, does this mean someone can smuggle nitroglycerin through our airports?" Michele asked, her voice hesitant now.

"They could, but they wouldn't. Not as nitroglycerin, anyway. Sure, there's a slight chance they could slip it by—for example, during a busy travel time like Christmas. But a terrorist wouldn't bring nitroglycerin on his person, since there's a chance a sniffer would detect the 'nitro' in it. On the other hand, if *something else* substitutes for the other components—something not in the sniffer's database but could cause the same damage—the machine won't find it because it's not programmed to look for the glycerin component."

"That's a disturbing note," Siegel said with clear concern.

"I have one more piece of disturbing news for you, Bob. Aluminum foil, one of the most basic necessities in any American kitchen, can be used to deceive the sniffer."

"Aluminum foil?" Siegel asked in disbelief.

"Yeah, aluminum foil?" Muhammad asked too, and looked in his rearview mirror to make sure his passengers hadn't heard him, thinking he was crazy.

Richard replied, "Yes, plain old aluminum foil. Actually, it was the Israelis who found out about this. They asked people to find loopholes in their sniffers. Aluminum foil, kept clean enough, blocked vapors from the sniffer. Rendered it incapable of detecting a wide range of substances."

"Gee, I hope there are no bad guys listening to us right now," Michele said, only partly in jest.

Siegel announced a break. A loud sigh reverberated on the radio, followed by someone singing, "Mother do you think they'll drop the bomb...."

Muhammad recognized the Pink Floyd song, and nodded. His son, Ali, had played it numerous times, and even had a poster of the group on his wall. The song fit perfectly with what they were talking about.

Traffic on the I-405 Freeway was heavy. At least another forty minutes to get to Santa Clarita. But that was all right; he didn't want to get to their destination before the radio interview was over.

Aluminum foil? Hand lotion? Sunblock? I wonder what was in the article that caused so many ripples? he asked himself. He didn't read newspapers, nor did Fahima. But today, he would.

"Mother shall I run for President? Mother shall I trust the Government?" Pink Floyd went on. Muhammad was deep in thought when the break ended.

Siegel introduced Richard Miller again and said, "Before we went to a break, you told us about the inefficiency of detection technology. The second part of your article was about federal cover-ups. Can you elaborate more on this theory?"

"Certainly, Bob," Richard answered with confidence. "But first, I want to speak about one recent example of our dependency on technology. Actually, it ties in with what we in America always seem to want: the magic solution. In America, we call it 'plug and play.' So we count on technology, and neglect our common sense and intuition."

"I see," Michele said. "Is that why you think Americans aren't prepared to deal with terrorist threats?"

"Yes. And that's what my expert source spoke most strongly about when I interviewed him. In his opinion, the problem isn't technology, but the false sense of security it creates. And let's face it, we really don't know everything we need to know yet. We created the Department of Homeland Security overnight, and we assigned people who have no clue what their positions are about. I talked to one higher-up who's an *art* major. Never worked in anything security-related before being assigned to Homeland Security. Look, I'm not saying they're not good people. I'm just saying that what we've got right now is nowhere near enough."

Muhammad heard Siegel's frustrated sigh, then, "You might be right. We've had several terrorism experts on who've said similar things to what you're saying. But I'll ask you the same thing I asked them: What can we do about that, except use the best people we have and grow them into expert status?"

"Outsource them," Richard replied quickly. "There are experts around the world who've lived with these same threats for decades. Bring them here to teach us how. To teach us what we should be doing."

"Sounds like a good idea," Michele said. "But I'm sure our listeners are curious about what you said a few minutes ago—about a federal cover-up?"

"Well, that's a factor. But the main point: It wouldn't change anything for us to know who those nineteen operatives were on 9/11, if we weren't smart enough to catch them *before* they committed the crime. That's where information cover-ups can really hurt us—literally. But some of the problems came because certain people in our government ignored things they shouldn't have."

"That brings us back to your article," Michele said.

"Right. You see, the government asked the public to be vigilant. And the public *should*. The public can point out something our agencies might overlook. Yet when the public tries to give feedback ... well, that's exactly what I wrote about in that article. The taxi driver I mentioned saw something odd about one of his passengers, and when he tried to alert the authorities, he was dismissed, just like he was wasting the government's time."

"Taxi driver?" Muhammad said, loud enough for his passengers to begin babbling at him, thinking he was speaking to them. But he couldn't take his eyes off the radio. Somehow, he had no idea how, this reporter had found out what he'd told the FBI agent!

"You're not seriously suggesting that federal authorities have to follow *every* lead they get from the public, are you?" Siegel asked. "They must get thousands a day."

"That's the kind of mindset I was talking about, Bob. The tip made to the FBI described a scenario where someone tried to assume the profile of a passenger at LAX. Based on what I've learned, there are two types of people who'd do that. One, intelligence officers who use the airport for rendezvous—it's crowded, so it's a good spot for a secret meeting. But the other kind of person who'd pretend to be a passenger? A bad guy who's there to check out the airport for a future operation.

"But here's what worries me: Why do I, Mr. Average Citizen, know about this, and the officer who took the report doesn't?"

The silence in the studio was as awkward as it was in Muhammad's cab. Siegel regained his composure first and said, "We'll be right back."

John Lennon and Yoko Ono began singing, "Give peace a chance...."

"So he *was* a bad guy after all," Muhammad said aloud. He checked the rearview mirror. His passengers were sitting silently, staring at the Bel Air Crest views on their right.

Pride and fear seeped into his mind and body. He was glad that someone, anyone, had taken his concerns seriously. *But*, the alleged passenger knew his name. They even had a conversation about Muhammad Ali. According to what this Richard Miller had just said, the man might have been with some intelligence agency, doing a routine check of the airport's security. What if—?

His cell phone rang.

When he recognized the number on the screen, he forced himself to disengage from his thoughts and answer. Fahima almost never called him while he was at work.

"Muhammad?"

Something was wrong. On the rare occasions she did call him at work, she always started with "*Ayooni*" or "*Albi*," meaning "my eyes" or "my heart." The simple "Muhammad" increased his alarm.

He signaled and changed lanes in the heavy traffic, ready to stop on the road's shoulder if necessary. "What's wrong?"

"There are two men here. They said they were looking for you!"

His heart sank in his chest. His mysterious passenger knew his name. How easy it would be to find his house. Could the man have brought a companion with him?

"They say they're with the FBI," she said.

Every conspiracy movie he'd ever seen came to life in his head. "Did they show you badges?"

"No. And even if they did, how could I distinguish between a fake and a real badge?"

Her voice showed annoyance now, but his pumping heart didn't slow down. He tried a different approach. "What do they want?"

"They want you," she said. "I just got home and found them waiting in our driveway in a big car."

They found where I live and they want to get rid of the witness who saw one of them. He had to do something; they were there with his wife!

Trying to think, he touched her picture on his car's key chain.

"Muhammad?"

"Yes, Fahima, I'm here. I, I'm just trying to think."

"Why didn't you answer? They're asking me when you'll be home!"

"Who? Who asked?"

"The FBI. Who else?" Now her tone held outright anger.

He took a deep breath to calm himself. "Did they give their names by any chance?"

He heard her covering the receiver, and then muffled voices mixed in the background. He gritted his teeth, frustrated because he couldn't hear. Perhaps if he heard their voices, he could identify—

Fahima came back on the line. "The first one says his name is Special Agent.' The second one has the same first and middle name, but last name is Williams."

Blood began circulating through his body again, and he could feel his legs. "Yes, I recognize the name of the first one." He said with relief. "Oh, you really scared me. Tell them I'm on my way to Santa Clarita. I can make it there and be home in about two hours."

He heard the muffled voices again, and she came back on the line. "They'll return later tonight, so drive safely and come back soon. Meanwhile I'll cook some *fatayer* for you."

"No!" he boomed, scaring his passengers in the back seat.

"No? I thought you love *fatayer*," she said, disappointed. "And it's good for you." *Fatayer* was dough filled with beet leaves and herbs, a real delicacy.

"No," Muhammad said quickly, "I meant, no, I don't want you to stay by yourself at home. Where's Ali? I'll call him to come home—"

"Don't you remember? He was going to a concert tonight. The Hot Chili Peppers or something like that."

"Oh, yes, I forgot. Well ... go to one of your friends, go to Vicky's. Just don't stay by yourself."

"*Shoo Ma'Allak*—what's *wrong* with you? I'm here by myself every afternoon for years!"

If he told her his reasoning—if the FBI could find him so easily, his suspicious passenger could too—she'd panic. "Please Fahima, just do as I say," he pleaded.

"Okay. Call me on your way back home. I'll be either at Vicky's or at Zoheira's."

He confirmed and flipped his cell phone off, his mind eased only a bit by her assurance.

He looked into the rearview mirror and saw his passengers whispering to each other. He smiled and raised his thumb up. "Everything is okay."

At the word, "Okay," they both nodded and smiled. Muhammad thought they probably didn't want anything more than for this trip to end. He felt the same way.

Chapter 14

Even though the bohemian neighborhood had changed appearances a few times since it was formed in the 1930s, tourists swarmed the Venice Beach neighborhood. The most recent changes weren't good. Oil discovered nearby stained the horizon with petroleum drillers and clogged the canals with waste. Even so, the wide beach and famous sightseeing attractions remained magnets for tourists, artists and scores of eccentrics, including aging hippies who lived in multimillion-dollar homes along the beachfront and canals.

Joe had covered his hefty body with an oversized Hawaiian short-sleeved shirt and long khaki trousers, and sported open-toed sandals on his wide feet. He hid his eyes behind glasses darkened with clip-on lenses. Just the average early-middle-aged tourist out for a stroll.

When he arrived at the beach, his first sight was a young man on rollerblades playing an electric guitar and singing Jimmy Hendrix's "Foxy Lady." Power for the electric guitar came from batteries strapped to the man's waist on a leather belt.

Good idea, Joe thought, seeing that no one around thought anything odd about the bulge on the man's body. Making a mental note of this for later, he walked past the boardwalk, crossing over the sand toward a crowd of about a hundred men and women, most of them beating on drums. Some tapped African tam-tams, others pounded South American versions of drums. He recognized a few *darbookas*, the Middle Eastern drums. There were no patterns or rules; everyone performed as he or she desired in a cacophonous blend of sounds and rhythms in the marijuana-scented air.

He nodded with their beats, not because he enjoyed the tempo, but to nod approval of the area chosen as a rendezvous point. He also used his nods in a swinging arch to confirm, as best he could, that he hadn't been followed.

At the beach where the crazy people play. If there were cops around, they weren't in sight. Or perhaps they didn't care about the spontaneous fest. Otherwise, people in the crowd wouldn't have been smoking the green weed so freely.

The best place for a secret rendezvous, he decided. The best place for brainstorming too. Even more, this place represented everything rotten in this society, one of many examples why it should be annihilated.

The noise from the drums made any conversation covert. There was no chance anyone could overhear conversation, accidentally or otherwise. Still, they had to be careful. He saw Michael, who was clapping his hands in sync with the drums beating around him. When Michael caught a glimpse of Joe walking on the beach, he followed his movements, watching for their agreed-upon signal before approaching. When Joe moved his head up and around, in tune with the beat, Michael moved slowly toward him. He didn't stop clapping; this was his signal that everything was okay. They met near a cluster of palm trees, remaining silent until Michael lowered his head and said, "Underneath the tree on my right."

Joe glanced in that direction and noted the place where the grass kissed the sand. A few stubborn palm trees remained deep-rooted in the ground there, providing meager shade for those who chose to rest at their bases. He would never have recognized either Jacob or Abbed without Michael's help. Abbed was lying on his back, a cowboy hat covering his face. Jacob sat with his back against one of the palm trees, holding an issue of the *LA Times*. Unfolded, the newspaper concealed the slender man's entire upper body.

Joe coughed once, then again, faced the bluish-green ocean and stretched out his arms, then walked nonchalantly toward them, passing Jacob, who made no move to acknowledge his existence, and sat on the opposite side of the tree, leaning against its trunk.

Several watchful minutes later, Michael threw his backpack on the sand in the tree's shade, laid back and placed his head on the backpack.

Jacob opened the conversation while still holding the newspaper open. "How's it going, guys?"

Nobody answered until Michael said, "That's so *American.*"

Jacob sighed at the statement, delivered in Michael's clipped British accent. "All the better! As long as we are here, that's how it should be ... So what's going on with your projects?"

Michael sat up, pretended to stretch, and rummaged through his backpack while he said, "Everything's going as planned. I enrolled in the Advanced Chemistry class we talked about. As I text-messaged you, my dating is on track as well. I'm invited for Shabbat dinner tonight at her house."

"Shabbat?" Jacob fought to hide his surprise. "I though you were only supposed to date her, not join her religion!"

Now it was Michael's turn to sigh. "First of all, she's not Jewish, her stepfather is. And if I'd turned down her invitation, that would have looked odd, wouldn't it?"

A moment later, Jacob surrendered a reluctant nod.

"It's *just* a dinner. Let's move on," Michael peered into his backpack and pulled out a magazine, then handed it to Jacob. "Here's the latest issue of *scientific American*. Check out page 56."

Jacob flipped through the pages. "What do we have here?"

"It's an article about thwarting nuclear terrorism. Notice, there's a whole section about bomb making. Right down to a list of materials and instructions."

Jacob briefly read the subtitles. "It always amazes me how Americans can give all of their secrets away willingly, and through open media." He chuckled. "Saves us research time."

The three men around him smiled, and gave small but approving nods at the youngest member of their group.

Jacob kept flipping pages, but his interest was flagging. "In any case, obtaining uranium isn't something I want to deal with at the moment. We have better ways of showing them our sophistication. But thank you for the article, Michael. Keep your eyes open and concentrate on your chemistry class. And be careful with the girl ... especially going to that, that *dinner*!"

Michael nodded, took the magazine and returned it to his backpack. "You know I'll be careful. I'm always careful. And not that I have to depend so much on printed things anymore." He smiled. "Now that I'm signed up for chemistry, I have a bit more freedom on the Internet."

Jacob nodded at him before glancing at the man still lying on the ground, his head still covered with the cowboy hat. "Abbed? What's going on with our financing?"

The muscular man rose and placed the hat on his dark hair. Abbed looked Hispanic and had in fact adapted easily to the language. Whenever someone noted his accented Spanish and asked about his origin, he'd say he was from French Guyana. He didn't really know anyone from French Guyana, but he'd concluded there were few or no immigrants from France in Los Angeles. Over time, he'd even traveled to Guyana. After the trip, he decided his story would include a childhood in Saint Laurent Du Maroni, to better include his Spanish persona—some residents there were of Brazilian heritage. And now, he roughly knew the history of the place. It was a convenient cover.

"There are certain things you don't want to know about our ... fundraising," he said to Jacob's question. "Turned out to be highly profitable, though. We found a loophole in the Drug Enforcement Administration, the law enforcement procedures for Mexican exports heading through American airports. So many American corporations are relocating their manufacturing plants to Mexico. That made things much easier."

Joe's loud sigh was followed by Jacob rotating his finger in a hurry-it-up gesture.

Abbed did. "The distribution channels are still here, since this is still the biggest market. So the merchandise returns to California in huge shipments. A perfect access point to transport the drugs."

"You're doing *what*?" Jacob kept his voice low, yet it was as though he were screaming.

"Easy, Jacob, we're not getting involved. The 18th Street Gang is entirely cooperative. We're merely supplying the routes into the country. You might say that we engineer their access." Then he added, "As I said, the less you know, the better ... the *safer* it will be for the operation. Just know that I'll get you all the money you need for whatever plan we have in mind."

Nobody talked for the next minute, when the noise from the drums became almost deafening. Jacob kept his eyes on the newspaper, considering the options ahead. When the pounding faded and he spoke again, his voice was calm. "I want you to back off the drugs. The 18th Street will sell us for dimes to save their skin, or to get some credit at the feds. Get back to the nonprofit organizations and white-collar bypasses. I don't want any spotlights shining in our direction."

Abbed opened his mouth, but thought better of his first response. Instead, he replied, "Understood. But there's one computer motherboard shipment coming in for a large American company. If I back off now ... I don't want those maniacs to think I'm an undercover DEA agent. Once this operation is distributed to the 18th Street guys, we're done."

"Okay," Jacob replied, then turned to Joe. "What's going on with you?"

Joe took the clips off his glasses and said, "I rehearsed

the method three times already. It works just fine. There's full cell-phone coverage at the airport for the mechanism. None of the skycaps suspect anything. We'll have no problem launching when the time comes."

Jacob looked at him without saying a word. When Joe couldn't take the silence any longer, he said, "What is it, Jacob?"

Jacob picked up a section of the newspaper from the sand, thumbed through the pages, and then handed it to Joe. He read Richard Miller's article silently, then raised his eyes from the newspaper to meet Jacob's. The latter's eyes were harsh and unpleasant. Joe felt a knot growing in his throat, one that threatened to choke him.

"What went wrong?" Jacob asked quietly.

"That taxi driver. That has to be it. It turned out that I had the same driver for both legs of the trip. He recognized me from the first leg. But he believed my cover story—"

"Apparently not," Jacob barked softly. "The man must have passed information about you to the authorities."

"But the FBI always ignores—"

Jacob reached out and grabbed the newspaper from him. "They won't ignore it this time. After this article makes the rounds, the FBI *will* do something, if only to prove their glorified institution isn't useless. They might even be looking for you right now. Or watching the airport. All the time and money we invested in *your* plan, all down the drain now."

Michael and Abbed listened, but kept their eyes on the sand underneath them. Joe felt sweat dripping from his body, not from mere fear, but panic, and his mind searched for a getaway.

Finally, he mumbled, "Do you want me to ... well, take care of the taxi driver?"

Jacob smirked. "To *take care* of him, Joseph? *Dachillak*—Gimme a break! You watch too many TV shows and movies. You couldn't *take care* of someone if they handed you the gun and pointed it for you."

Hurt, Joe took off his thick glasses and wiped them with the edge of his Hawaiian shirt, then looked up and made a face that reminded Jacob of a grieving mole. Jacob couldn't suppress his laughter. "Listen," he said at last, wiping moisture from the corners of his eyes, "nothing fatal happened yet. Eliminating him won't do anything but raise more suspicion. If that changes, we can deal with him then. For now, keep away from the airport, *and* from the neighborhood where the taxi picked you up—at least until we're ready. Meanwhile, get yourself a driver's license. Buy a simple car—either Japanese or Korean, maybe a station wagon or even an SUV. Think of a different method of operation. And start preparing your relocation. A car might help you there."

He turned his attention to Michael. "Speaking of that ... Michael, get rid of your car in case someone saw the license plate. Park it somewhere in Inglewood, wipe it down. Leave your spare key in the ignition and call the police from UCLA to report it stolen."

Michael listened and nodded.

Jacob continued. "Say you just returned from a week's camping in Yosemite and can't find your car. You'll have to fill out some forms, but it shouldn't be a problem for you. Your papers are good. And if no one steals the car while it's parked there, sell it immediately and get another one. Don't spend too much time looking, but make sure it's reliable. I don't want you to get stuck somewhere, especially not on the way to the mission."

"Are we sticking to the original plan?" Abbed asked.

Jacob nodded. "We can't sacrifice years of preparation over stupidity. Joe will just have to change his part."

Joe thoroughly examined the sand below him.

"Why LAX?" Michael asked suddenly, slightly regretting asking the question aloud.

Jacob measured him for a long moment, considered whether he should say something sarcastic. Deciding the boy was speaking in ignorance, he chose a simple answer. "*They* made our choice for us, because *they* consider LAX the most threatened infrastructure in California. Why don't we give them what they want? They don't really *protect* the airport with all those guards and police officers. They just care about *looking* like they're actually doing something to protect travelers. Think about how disparaging it'll be, despite all of the 'security' measures they have in place, when we're still able to punch them hard where it hurt most."

    Michael studied Jacob. He didn't see a madman. Jacob was passionate and self-assured, just as any member of the group. But his plan wasn't meshing with Michael's rational thinking. *You always have options,* his father had always told him. *Try to avoid conflicts. Choose the main path whenever you can.*

    The end justifies the means, he thought. And as he had trusted Ibrahim in London, he had to trust Jacob now, and hope that his dream of honoring his father would be fulfilled.

Chapter 15

His Chinese customers had left the car quickly, as though running from something or someone. They didn't even wait for their change. But Muhammad had still bowed to their retreating backs before he returned to his place behind the steering wheel and allowed himself to revel in the euphoria he felt before Fahima's phone call. The FBI wanted to speak with him *personally*, not anything like that brief, frustrating call before that made him feel like a criminal.

He considered himself a modest man of modest means, and always tried to keep his ego in check. But now, unable to resist, he looked at the endless I-405 Freeway stretching in front of the cab's hood, picturing the front page of *Time* magazine with his face on it. For a few seconds, he debated whether Fahima and Ali should be in the frame as well, but decided against it. He was the man of the hour, after all. He'd found the bad guys, whomever they might be. He leaned his head back against the headrest, relishing in the image.

The program on NPR changed to *Fresh Air*, and soft music filled the air. Usually he didn't like this program. It featured songs he'd never heard before; most sounded grating to his ears. But today he tolerated even this cacophony, considering it his version of "Pomp and Circumstance."

The title in *Time* read "Muslim Patriot." The front-page colors were fire red and sky blue. In the cover picture, he wore a suit. This sudden image surprised him. He bought one just before the citizenship ceremony some thirty years back, but could count on one hand the number of times he'd worn it since. Still, it seemed fitting for his honored status. The article's subtitle read "An Arab Immigrant Leads to the Capture of a Dangerous Terrorist Cell in Los Angeles."

The article's author was, of course, Richard Miller. Muhammad had never read anything by the man, but the radio interview was enough for him to know this Miller fellow was the only one good enough to document the "man of the hour."

An 18-wheeler's horn brought him back to reality, and back to his own lane. He'd been inches away from being sideswiped by the truck.

"That would be such a waste," he said with a grin.

The traffic on his return trip seemed lighter, but he couldn't tell whether it was really so, or some kind of psychological illusion. Whatever the reason, his drive to the taxi station seemed shorter. He exchanged the taxi for his old Ford and drove back home.

The house was deserted. No cars were in the driveway, no lights were seen through the windows. Even though he knew Fahima wouldn't be there, he felt his heart accelerate as he parked the Ford and went to the front door.

He tried the knob. The door was locked. Also expected. Still, he couldn't rid himself of the uneasiness. As he used his keys to open the lock, he looked down to see Fahima's photo smile at him. Instead of the usual feeling he got looking at it, his body shook with a chill.

He entered the dark house. Rather than turning on a light, as he usually would have, he let his eyes adjust to the darkness as he searched each room. Two minutes later, he verified that nobody was there. Nothing was unusual in the house, in fact, except for the absence of his wife. So why did the chill deepen, invading his bones?

She said they were FBI agents. But what could be easier for a terrorist than disguising himself as federal law enforcement? *You don't need a special uniform or special car. All you need is a suit, even one as old as mine, and an authoritative tone.*

Without wanting to, he planted more doubts. *Why didn't I inquire about their car?*

"What if it was a white Toyota Camry?" he whispered. "What if they're outside somewhere, waiting for me?"

His brain froze, and panic almost took over. He inhaled deeply, trying to oxygenate as many brain cells as he could. Later, he realized that his mind was trying to break the magic circle in his thoughts. He heard that on NPR one day. The guest from the military spoke about the massacre of children in Beslan. He said there was a decision cycle where decision making occurs. Muhammad couldn't remember what it was called ... just that the first responders at the school in Beslan should have broken the magic circle. They should have intervened in the earliest stages of the terrorists' hostage taking. At that point, even crashing the police cruiser into the school's front door would have halted the chain of events. The outcome might have been far different.

"So what should I do now?" Muhammad asked himself, bothered at how loud the question sounded in the quiet house. The high spirits he'd felt on his way home were disseminated, now replaced by fear.

He decided to get outside and look for the Toyota. "Nobody will try to abduct me or kill me on the street," he assured himself, blocking any thoughts about such crimes happening daily in Southern California. And besides, he had to find Fahima.

He walked to the front door, his pace deliberately confident, placed his hand on the knob, inhaled deeply, exhaled, and pushed the knob down to open the door. He almost screamed, but managed to only say, "What are you doing here?" His voice betrayed him, though, climbing to an unbelievably high pitch by the end of the question.

"What am I doing here? It's my house too!"

"Where— ah, where were you?" he asked, struggling to regain his manly voice with only partial success.

"I went to Vicky's as you told me to. I heard your car in the driveway so I came back home." Fahima's expression turned curious. "Is that okay with you?"

"Oh. Yes, it's okay. And I'm sorry. I was just worried something happened to you." He wrapped his long arms around her petite body.

"And why are you so worried? I thought you actually *wanted* to talk to the FBI," she said when he released her. She passed him, dropped her keys on the dining table and walked toward the kitchen.

"And how do you know they *were* FBI?" he said. "Maybe they were the bad guys I saw, and they introduced themselves as FBI so you would let them in."

"You watch too much conspiracy stuff on TV, Muhammad. They didn't come in the house, although I did invite them. If they wanted to do something to me or to you so badly, they would have waited here for you, wouldn't they?"

"Yes. I guess you're right once again," he said.

He landed on the sofa, found the remote control and turned the television on. That was his escape at the end of the day. He smiled, remembering a study Ali once told him about. That a person alone in an empty room, with no visual stimulation whatsoever, uses approximately 12% of his brain capacity. The same person, while watching TV, uses only 8%. He embraced this relaxation now.

Then it hit him.

"Where is Ali?" he cried out.

Fahima entered the den, wiping her hands with a towel. "Will you stop it already? Ali's at a concert, remember? I'm here, and there is no one after you—"

Three strong knocks on the door caused them both to jump. He sprang to his feet, signaling for her to remain silent as he walked cautiously to the door and peered through the peephole. In spite of her chiding, instinct told him to stand to the left of the door before asking, "Who is it?"

"FBI. This is Special Agent Smith, Mr. Ali."

Muhammad thought he recognized the authoritative voice, even though he'd only heard it on the telephone once before. He wiped small beads of sweat from his forehead and opened the door. His view was blocked by two athletic-looking men in dark gray suits, neat ties and button-down shirts, a rare sight in this neighborhood.

"Good evening, gentlemen," he managed.

"Good evening, sir," said the man with the voice of Agent Smith. He introduced himself with a friendly smile, then said, "And this is Special Agent Williams." He turned to the bulky man who was examining the interior of Muhammad's house.

Muhammad invited them in. After the necessary introduction and Fahima's polite hospitality, he asked, "What can I do for you?" He found the remote control and switched the TV off before turning his full attention to the agents.

Smith cleared his throat. "We're following up on your tip. It's routine. That's why we're here."

Muhammad smiled. "Of course. So, what can I tell you?"

"The story you posted on our website. Can you please tell us the story again?" Agent Williams had opened his mouth for the first time.

Muhammad sighed, lowered himself into his recliner, and started. Both agents pulled notepads from their jackets and took notes. He wondered what had happened to the notes Agent Smith had from their first conversation, but decided the man was just being extra thorough. When he finished, he raised his eyebrows and said, "Any questions?"

The agents were still busy writing. Agent Williams raised his head and asked, "What about the license plate number you mentioned?"

"As I told Agent Smith, I took it with me to my neighbor to talk with Amanda, her sister. I forgot it at her house, and by the time I returned to get it, she wasn't at home, and—"

"I just returned from there," Fahima said. "She said her maid probably threw it away while cleaning yesterday."

Agent Smith heard Fahima, but was more interested in Muhammad's statement. "Amanda, you said, sir? Could that perhaps be Amanda Lopez, head of the FBI's antiterrorist task force?"

Muhammad shrugged. "I assume so. Yes, in fact, I believe our neighbor did say something like that."

"The maid threw away that slip of paper?"

Fahima nodded, her eyes narrowed in curiosity.

"I'll find it, then," Smith said. He glanced at his partner before pulling his cell phone from his jacket pocket, allowing Muhammad a glance at his gun's shoulder holster. He pressed two keys and said, "Hi, this is Smith. Please send me a unit, and also send Forensics."

He listened for a second, then replied, "Yes, I know. I'll include it in my report." He ended the call before asking Muhammad, "Would you be able to help our artist draw a composite portrait of your passenger?"

Muhammad thought for only a second. "Sure."

Smith stood up, pocketed his notepad and said to Williams, "Let's go have a talk with the neighbor." To Muhammad, he said, "Our agent will be here in a few minutes. You can open the door for her. She's one of the good ones." He winked, and both agents headed for the door.

As soon as Muhammad shut the door behind them, Fahima asked, "What was all *that* about?"

He smiled bitterly and turned the television on. *Counter Terrorism Agency* was on, one of his favorite shows. "What was that about? Someone published my story," he said. "And now they're all trying to prove they are doing something about it. But that's all it is—a show, just like this one."

By the time the doorbell rang again, his hero had already killed a dozen bad guys, saved the lives of a few dozen citizens, and almost died twice. It was obvious to Muhammad how the show would end, but it was entertaining anyway. He walked to the door and looked through the eyepiece. A nice-looking white female held her badge next to her face and said, "FBI."

When Muhammad opened the door to invite her in, he saw Agent Smith on his neighbor's lawn, talking loudly on his cell phone, excited or frustrated about something. Several times, he mentioned the term "Waste Management." Muhammad was familiar with the company; their trucks came each week to pick up the neighborhood's trash. He chuckled and said, "Good luck," over the woman's shoulder.

When the artist left, Muhammad was filled with euphoria again. His image on the cover of *Time* seemed assured, at least in his fantasy.

Chapter 16

Michael parked the rental car on the curb, got out and inspected the street for a long moment. His destination was still half a mile away, but now it was even more important to take precautionary measures. He didn't personally judge Joe's mistake as harshly as Jacob had, but since it was a possibility that Joe was recognized at the airport, someone might have also followed him to their meeting. And if that happened, even as careful as they'd been, someone might now be following all of them.

He placed his right foot on the car's bumper and tied his shoelaces. From this position, he was able to observe reflections behind him through the rear windshield, his own and anyone else's who might be overly interested in him. Next, he opened the trunk and leaned inside, tensing at the realization of how vulnerable he was at this moment. Anyone could easily push him into the trunk and lock him inside. Making a note to avoid doing that in the future, he scooped up the bouquet of calla lilies inside and closed the trunk, erasing the negative images in his head. He hadn't known whether a bottle of wine would be an appropriate hostess gift, so he decided on flowers. He knew alcohol was both a good and bad thing in American culture, and he didn't want to ask Dianne on his first meeting with her family if they were against alcohol in general, or wine in particular. *Flowers are always good*, he reassured himself. Besides, he'd always heard that mothers love flowers, even though fathers usually think they're a waste of money.

The bouquet shifted in his arms, and he struggled to keep from dropping it while he thought about the first day he'd seen Dianne in the library. Later, he told her he was attracted to her fair skin and blonde hair, such total contrast to his olive skin and dark hair, but was too shy to initiate any moves on her. The cover story convinced her. He'd visited the library frequently after that, and always in the evening, when Dianne was usually at work. She interpreted this, of course, as a clear declaration of his interest, and acted accordingly: She approached him and offered assistance. When he blushed and thanked her in his British accent, she was hooked.

At first, he was polite but distant, as if he didn't want any kind of relationship with her. She interpreted his laconic yes or no answers as a challenge. Later, she told him that had turned her on. When he finally offered to take her out for frozen yogurt, she was surprised, but accepted the offer with eagerness.

Even then, he didn't talk about himself at all, just asked questions about almost every aspect of her life. Although the conversation was more like a one-way interview, she said it made her feel special. "And unlike every other guy I've dated," she'd said after their first kiss, "you didn't try to get into my pants the first night." When they parted that night, she felt exactly as he wanted her to feel, as if it was the beginning of something special. And it was, just not in the way she thought.

He walked down the street, staying close to the edge of the sidewalk, checking the rear windshields of parked cars as he passed by. Nothing untoward appeared in their reflections, so he crossed the street and walked toward a bus stop, using the Plexiglas-covered advertisements on the side of the stop as a mirror to watch his back. The only thing he hadn't resolved yet was that he was beginning to grow fond of Dianne. When the time came, that would make it more difficult. From an early age, from Jacob now, but Ibrahim long before, he'd been taught that the Higher Cause mattered far more than any single human, including him.

Ibrahim and his friends had taught him many things. Every day since he came to America, especially recently, he'd seen the payoff of those difficult early lessons. He could still hear the voices of the men in the Central Mosque blessing him, and the proud look in Ibrahim's eyes.

Often, he resisted Ibrahim's goals for him. He didn't want to leave London, or travel at all for that matter, let alone to the United States, the core of the world's infidelity. They had long, sometimes heated conversations about the Higher Cause and the better world it promised. At first, the whole idea of leaving for America was irrational to him. His father had never been found, and Ibrahim blamed the involvement of Americans in Saddam's business in Kuwait for that.

"They killed all the key people in Iraq—*our* birthplace—and in Kuwait, to conquer the oil for themselves," he'd told Michael often.

Michael wasn't stupid. He knew Ibrahim tended to exaggerate when it came to the infidels. But the continued American presence in the Arab Peninsula proved to him there was much more to their presence than just assisting the poor people of Kuwait. That was just as clear to him now, hearing the news about Iraq—hundreds of thousands of innocent Iraqis killed while the Americans continued to say they'd "won the war."

But Ibrahim had laughed in Michael's face when he shared his epiphany with him, and said, "Why did I waste so much time lecturing to you about something you didn't even want to understand? It's for your father's memory, not for you or for me, that you must join the higher cause."

Michael didn't have an answer for him back then, but one single day changed it all. The day he woke up and felt the presence of someone in his room, and a strong hand covered his mouth, forcing him to breathe through his nose. He started to panic, making it even more difficult for precious air to move into his lungs. He tried to move his arms, but the heavy down comforter was wrapped tightly around him. Being only nine years old and light-framed didn't give him any advantage.

"Stop resisting and listen to me!"

The harsh whisper sounded familiar. It took Michael yet another second to comprehend that was Ibrahim's voice.

"We will now prepare you to recover your father's pride," Ibrahim said, and pulled him from the bed. He was led from the house, still in his pajamas, and into Ibrahim's car. They drove for an hour until they arrived at a rural area, a place Michael had never seen before. Ibrahim was silent the entire time, even when he parked the car at a deserted parking lot and killed the engine.

Michael raised his eyebrows in a confused and questioning gesture.

"Do you have money?" Ibrahim finally asked.

He couldn't understand the question, but blurted, "No." What he wanted to say was, *Why would I have money in my pajamas? That's silly!*

Ibrahim looked at his watch. "It's 3:00 am. I'll expect to see you at morning prayers. Now get out of the car."

"What?" He suddenly felt small and vulnerable.

"This is for your own good. Try to get home by dawn. You can't just cry for strangers to help you. They will call the police and put you and me in jail. That's not how your father would have wanted you to end up."

He leaned over and opened Michael's door, then brought the engine back to life. "You are wasting time."

Michael unbuckled his seat belt and stood outside, looking at Ibrahim's taillights disappearing into the darkness, crying like a baby. But he eventually stopped crying, wiped his face with his pajama sleeve and sought a solution. From the parking lot, he saw a sign that told him it was 59 miles to London.

"Fifty-nine miles?" he'd whispered. The impossible distance increased his desperation, and that desperation made him determined enough to attempt the impossible.

Headlights made him duck for cover, remembering

Ibrahim's warning. When the pickup truck passed, he saw boxes and wooden crates in the back of the truck. That gave him the idea. In the corner of the parking lot, he found two wooden crates. He dragged them onto the road and hid. When another truck stopped and the driver got out to investigate the boxes, Michael ran as fast as his small legs allowed and climbed into the rear of the truck. An eternity later, the sight of Big Ben over the Thames verified that he had arrived back in London.

He jumped from the truck at the first red light. Thanks to a sleeping homeless man in Piccadilly Square, his donations can forgotten in his drunken stupor, he was able to acquire enough for a subway token and a worn gray blanket to hide his pajamas, and for warmth. For anonymity as well: nobody on the train dared come close to him or even attempt to talk to him, since he looked and smelled like an indigent person.

He arrived home fifteen minutes before dawn. Ibrahim praised him the entire morning. At the Central Mosque later that day, Ibrahim told everyone that from now on Michael should be considered an "*Antar*." Michael's nine-year-old heart swelled. His mentor had introduced him as a man, or better yet, as a rooster. Even the *Imam* praised him, saying, "This child will reaffirm our faith in Allah."

The memory of that triumphant day buoyed him, and he assessed the neighborhood where he walked now, noting its single-family houses, its access points, and the proximity to emergency response crews.

The nearest police station was several miles away from here. *Good*, he thought with satisfaction. Not happiness, just satisfaction. Yet he was truly happy that day in London. A few years later, in a high school psychology class littered with infidel ideologies, he understood the transformation he went through that day. Learning about Abraham Maslow's Hierarchy of Needs theory made that day make perfect sense. He had his physical needs, which Ibrahim took care of. He could call Ibrahim's apartment "home" and really mean it. The congregation at the Central Mosque met his need for belonging. On the day he made his way back from the countryside on his own, his accomplishments and the accolades bestowed upon him planted the seeds for self esteem. The next and last stage he could hope to attain was self actualization, which would come very soon. Yet the final path to self actualization began in his last year of prep school, the day Ibrahim told him about his impending trip to America.

"Remember that day at the mosque when you became a rooster?" Ibrahim had said. "Just try to imagine what will happen on the day you become a *Shahid*. A martyr for the high cause! How proud your father would be!"

How proud would he be now? Michael wondered, and returned to practicing his countersurveillance measures, casually shifting the flowers from one arm to the other.

Half a block past the house where he was expected for dinner, he stopped on the curb, turned around and started walking back in the opposite direction. If there were anyone on his tail, this trick would confuse them. On his first pass, he'd determined the house was a one-story bungalow containing too much furniture—he could see the side of what appeared to be a headboard through one of the windows. There were no bars on the windows. The house also featured an attached two-car garage with access from the house. He wasn't sure if he'd ever need this information, but if he did, it would be ready in his memory.

He crossed the front yard, stood by the door, and rang the bell. A familiar female voice from inside called out, "Hang on, I'm coming."

Dianne opened the door and smiled broadly, then her eyes widened when she saw the flowers. "For me?" Her voice was a mixture of sweetness and coyness.

He didn't answer, measuring her with his eyes. Dianne was everything a young man could dream of. Gorgeous, funny, kind, sexy, and passionate. As well as naive and insecure. She was the best candidate they could have asked for.

Inside, while she rushed to find a vase for the flowers, he evaluated the house, finding it neither fancy in architecture nor luxuriously decorated, even though the neighborhood was upper middle-class. The entrance hall was spartan, its walls bare except for two photos in frames that looked expensive. The captions below told him the city scenes were of Los Angeles in the 1950s. An antique chandelier provided light.

When she returned, they entered the living room through the den. The latter was cozy and warm, and if he hadn't been so nervous, he would have been tempted to lie on the den's soft couch to watch a movie. The living room wasn't as sterile-looking as the entrance, but reflected little warmth in spite of the fireplace.

Dianne introduced her mother, who immediately insisted that he call her Rosemary, followed by, "Dianne didn't tell me you were so polite, and the flowers are beautiful, thank you. Lucky you, D." She gave her daughter a wide smile, then turned the smile at him and opened her mouth.

A man wearing an apron entered the room from the same doorway she had. He walked directly to Michael, gripped his hand, and with a forceful shake said, "I'm Allan, Dianne's stepfather. Glad you could make it to our Shabbat meal."

Michael smiled at him. "Judging by your apron, I guess you're the man I should stay close to, sir."

Allan laughed. "Where are you from, Michael?"

"I grew up in London. Can't get rid of the manners or the accent," he replied, still smiling.

"Oh, I *love* London," Rosemary said. "You *must* tell us all about life there."

To deflect her question, he asked quickly, "Is there anything I can help you with in the kitchen, Allan?"

Allan shook his head and clapped Michael on the shoulder. "No, I'm fine. Make yourself comfortable, I'll be right back." With a smile and wave, he disappeared back through the door.

Dianne showed him to his seat at the table in the dining

room, then sat down next to him. He could see both the main entrance and the door leading to the kitchen and garage. He couldn't have asked for a better vantage point.

"Dianne told me that you study at UCLA," Rosemary said.

"That's right. The best place to be," he said.

She nodded in approval, her eyes not quite sharing the light tone he had aimed for. "What's your major?"

"Science. Actually, I'm taking Advanced Chemistry this year."

"Oh, sounds interesting—"

"Voila!"

They all turned to see Allan enter, carrying a crock-pot, his hands protected with two kitchen towels. "Make some room for this, will you?"

He took his seat, and Rosemary spooned tiny potatoes and an unknown meat onto their dinner plates. Michael bit back a gasp. The meat was light in color. What would he do if it were pork? He remembered Dianne saying her stepfather was Jewish, but observing the values of religion in Los Angeles, he didn't trust anyone but himself when it came to food.

Dianne opened a bottle of white Zinfandel and filled four tall wine glasses. Michael watched, feeling the evening had already gotten off on the wrong foot. He hadn't expected them to serve alcohol; would they think it odd if he refused?

Rosemary placed a steaming plate in front of him. "I treated you to extra chicken, Michael."

Chicken! "Thank you very much," he said with a polite nod to hide his relief. It wasn't *halal* certified—the Islamic law approval. But at least it wasn't pig.

When they were all served and Rosemary took her chair, Dianne raised her glass. "Cheers!"

He raised the glass in the air with them, but returned it to the table. "I'm driving," he whispered in response to Dianne's questioning eyes.

"Oh, that's no problem," she whispered back, and

pointed to the water glass next to his wineglass. "If you'd rather have something else, say the word."

"No, thanks, water's fine," he replied, feeling as though he'd just dodged a bullet.

Before taking her first bite, Rosemary said, "Oh, Allan, guess what I found out? Michael studies science at UCLA."

"Excellent," Allan said between bites. "Do you intend to work in the semiconductor industry?"

"Possibly, sir," Michael replied, waiting for the next question, which came after Allan's very next bite.

"So how did you two meet?" Allan asked, pointing his fork toward Dianne, then him.

He opened his mouth, but needn't have bothered.

"Michael is *the* most devoted bookworm at the library," Dianne said proudly. "I don't think there's a science book or magazine he hasn't read!"

Rosemary smiled at both of them. "That's so sweet."

"So, where's your home, Michael?" Allan asked.

He was ready for the question. "I almost decided to live in the dorms, but I moved into an apartment instead." He forced a smile. "I'm glad I did. An apartment is much quieter than the dorms at the school, I've heard."

This brought laughter, after which they ate for a few minutes in blessed silence. Dianne put her left hand on his knee. He put his knife down, casually reached under the table and explored the texture and warmth of her thigh. Finally, it seemed the right time to bring up a question of his own.

"Do you like camping?" he asked her parents while rubbing her thigh under the table.

"We used to." Rosemary glanced at Allan. "But we don't anymore. Allan's so busy with work lately, and my job keeps me busy too. Lots of late nights for both of us."

"I'd like to take Dianne to Big Sur, to go camping sometime ... if it's okay with you, I mean. Maybe this weekend?" The tips of his fingers stroked lacy underwear. Out of the corner of his eye, he saw Dianne's smile.

"That's so lovely," Rosemary said, watching her daughter, and his hand stopped moving. Her eyes showed nothing but affection and approval, though.

Mission accomplished, he thought. As Jacob had hoped, Dianne and her clueless parents accepted him. The camping trip had been his idea, but Jacob okayed it, saying a weekend in the wilderness alone with Dianne would increase her absolute trust in him. For him, though, this weekend would be a sweet milestone on the path to a much different destiny.

Chapter 17

He stuffed the rental car with camping gear required for a fantastic weekend. He'd even splurged and bought a dome tent. *But not a large one,* he thought. A smaller tent would encourage greater intimacy. In fact, while at the sporting goods store, he'd also purchased a stove, one sleeping bag, a flashlight, and a cooler to add to his stock of camping gear. From the sporting goods store, he went to a grocery and purchased food, and didn't forget eggs, vegetables and condiments. He would spoil Dianne with a breakfast from heaven—or from nature, at least.

At Dianne's he was greeted by Rosemary and Allan, who were drinking their morning coffee and reading the weekend newspaper. Dianne appeared from her room wearing cargo pants and a tight-fitting t-shirt that exposed her navel piercing just below the edge of the shirt. "I'm ready," she said, and dropped a duffle bag by the door.

Between calls of "Drive safely" and "Behave!" Dianne hugged her mother and stepfather, laughing. Michael observed the exchange in silence. He'd long forgotten this kind of family warmth. Then, it was his turn for hugs and, in Allan's case, shoulder slaps. He promised to treat Dianne properly, to drive carefully, and to be aware of bears. Off they went.

* * *

The drive to Big Sur was long but beautiful, again reminding him of how different California was from his birthplace. When he arrived to the United States, it bothered him that American kids were so egocentric. He was sure Dianne couldn't put her finger on his *balad*—homeland—in a geographical atlas. It was equally certain he was more politically involved by age ten than any of his classmates by the time they attended college. He'd been judgmental of them for a long time. After awhile, though, his judgment was replaced by envy, a term that didn't exist in Arabic, at least as far as he knew; it wasn't the same as jealousy, which was associated with greed and therefore drew negative connotation. If he were forced to define the word to an Arabic speaker, he'd have said it was similar to *"I want to have that, too."* Similar, but not the same. Living in London, then California, he wanted that level of naiveté, wanted his youth to be filled with prosperity and numbness like most Americans he'd met.

He merged onto the 101 Freeway and drove north. The traffic was light and the weather perfect. The rental car's sound system played a new hip-hop band. He didn't recognize it, and didn't want to. There were a few things in the American culture he never wanted to adopt. He glanced at his passenger. Dianne seemed happy. Her window was half-open and the wind tousled her blonde hair. She'd placed her bare feet on the dashboard, admiring her nail polish, and seemed to enjoy every moment of the ride.

They traveled along the Pacific Coast Highway and stopped to refuel in Santa Barbara. He was impressed by the people he saw entering and leaving the gas station, calmer and friendlier than people living in LA, and less driven by money. Almost worth saving, if only they weren't infidels too.

They returned to the endless asphalt road and continued north, arriving at Big Sur as the sun began its descent into the ocean. He assembled the tent while she unloaded the car, and then they ate fried eggs cooked over an open fire. At one point, watching him tend the fire, she said, "Gosh, you're so knowledgeable about survival and camping."

He knew what made him good at it, but couldn't share it with her, he just watched her as she pulled marshmallows from her bag and pierced them on some twigs she'd found near their campsite.

When she saw his confusion, she asked, astonished, "You don't know what these are?"

"You don't want me to test you on *my* cuisines, do you?" he said quickly, and smiled.

"These are marshmallows. We scorch them over the open fire and eat them while they're hot."

"Okay. I can give it a shot." He tasted the hot marshmallow and grimaced. "It's so *sweet*. How can you eat it?"

"It's one of the sweetest American confections you'll find," she answered.

"Gotcha. Now, I'm going to brush my teeth and get this sweet glue off of them."

When he returned, he found her waiting inside the sleeping bag.

"Didn't you brush *your* beautiful teeth?" he said, and crouched near the waning fire.

"Of course I did, silly. But I didn't have to go anywhere. I did it right here with a bottle of water, just like a real Girl Scout."

"You'll have to explain that to me some day," he said, and spent a few minutes looking around. It amazed him how beautiful nature could be here. *If my people deserve the best, how come the infidels literally live in heaven, and my people must live in a desert? If Allah does exist, why does He care for the environment occupied by those who don't believe in Him? Why are they blessed with this perfect nature when they don't even have a religion?*

"Are you coming in?" Dianne asked him after awhile.

"What? Oh yeah, I'm coming." He undressed to his shorts and t-shirt and entered the sleeping bag with her. The warmth of her skin surprised him. He put his hand on the small of her back and realized she wasn't wearing a thing. She smiled at him, amused by his embarrassment, and placed her hand on his face. Her eyes rested on his lips and she moved to kiss them, gently at first, followed by kisses filled with wild abandonment.

She pulled his t-shirt over his head and reached to remove his boxer shorts. "Thank you for taking me on this trip," she whispered.

"No ... ah, thank *you*," he replied, drowning in a whirlpool of emotions and excitement.

She kissed him again, exploring his mouth with her tongue, then disappeared deeper into the sleeping bag to kiss his chest, then down. When he finally entered her, he bit his hand to make sure he wasn't dreaming. This was better than anything he could ever imagine....

After their lust was satisfied, she rested her head on his chest and he stroked her hair. It was a moment he wanted to savor forever. Yet the moment, and the pleasures that had led to it, did nothing to change his mind.

When she finally fell asleep, he slipped on his shorts and sat by the dying fire.

"You must never forget the higher cause," he could hear Ibrahim whispering from the darkness, almost seeing his serious face in the fire's embers. *"The infidels are evil. They don't deserve to live,"* the voice whispered. "Their punishment is the key to our glory and self-actualization." He heard the last words too. But this time, it was his voice whispering.

Chapter 18

Abbed awoke in his hotel room, but it took a few moments for him to realize that. When he confirmed that it was a Saturday morning in Mazatlan, he eased up to sit on the edge of the bed. The tequila from the night before pounded through his temples.

He entered the United States as a computer programmer, hired to work for a big hi-tech electronics firm, one of many that moved their manufacturing operations to Mexico in the wake of the dot-com disasters of the mid-1990s. Abbed actually had no knowledge of electronic manufacturing. But neither did the INS officer who granted Abbed the H-1 business visa approving his unencumbered travel to and from the United States.

So no, Abbed didn't have any special skills in technology. And he wasn't a nice guy by any definition. He was, however, excellent in getting things done, even if the accomplishments required dishonest methods and nerve-wracking situations. Shudy, the owner of the company that hired him, recognized Abbed's qualities, but preferred that Abbed use them to find ways to fund the Sacred Cause, rather than serve in management.

A rustle behind him made him jump to his feet and whirl his body around, his hands already forming into fists. He looked at the king-sized bed and saw a strawberry-blonde head resting on a pillow on the other side. Thanks to last night's party's major ingredients—alcohol and loud music—he couldn't remember who she was. Not that it would benefit him to remember her name. Even so, he shouldn't have lost his head last night. *There are important tasks to accomplish today*, he thought, and stumbled to the shower.

Moments later, he heard the shower door open and a female voice whispering, "You don't remember last night?"

He opened his eyes and saw the strawberry blonde standing next to him. Best not to give her the truth. Instead, he smiled and said, "Hi there."

She put her hands against his powerful chest. "Let me remind you ..." She kissed his neck and ears, her hands all over him.

"So, what was your name?" he managed to ask.

"As if you care," she replied.

They explored each other's body. For Abbed, since he didn't remember last night, it really was the first time with her. Later, he opened the room's curtains, revealing a calm Pacific Ocean, picked up the phone and called room service.

"Two breakfasts," he said, looking at his guest who nodded in approval. "And aspirin for two," he added. He went to the bathroom to shave.

The woman entered, still naked, leaned against the counter and asked, "So who are you, Mr. Tall, Dark and Handsome?"

"I'm just another computer geek, traveling for work."

"Computer geek, huh?" Giggling, she stroked his muscular arm. "Do you lift a lot of computers at work?"

It was Abbed's turn to laugh, but he wanted her to talk about herself, to discourage further questions. "Well, who are *you*? You haven't even told me your name."

She was about to reply when they heard a knock at the door. She covered herself with one of the hotel robes and headed for it, but he said, "No, no, I'll get it." Better that none of the hotel staff see her in his room.

They ate silently, Abbed because he had some errands to run and he was rehearsing them in his head. The woman was also deep in thought.

"When are you checking out?" she asked, swirling the last inch of orange juice in her glass.

He looked at his watch, feeling the nervousness grow, as he always felt before a dangerous job. "Two hours."

She drained the glass and placed it next to her plate, stretched lazily, stood and dropped her robe. "That leaves us 120 minutes, stranger."

* * *

He placed the unconsciousness woman, still in her bathrobe, on a bench outside his room. His one-night stand would wake up with a terrible headache and dizziness, but he'd had no other choice; after he drugged her, she still wouldn't reveal her name or her room number so he could leave her there. And being honest, he enjoyed his methods.

He retrieved his small suitcase and entered a waiting taxicab by the hotel entrance.

"*Buenos Dias. Acordos De Lusaka, por favor,*" he instructed the driver.

"*Vamos.*" The driver threw his cigarette butt out the window and started driving.

Mazatlán, one of the largest commercial and industrial centers of Western Mexico, is also one of Mexico's major Pacific seaports. The beautiful beaches of its southern neighbor, Acapulco, made Mazatlán *the* tourist landmark in Mexico. Which made Abbed's job even more pleasant. Today the city was filled with tourists who came to drink and have fun, and, like him, conduct a little business along the way.

He'd joined the operation right after the *Aleihoom*, the witch hunt the Americans started after the Sacred Cause's September 11th victory. Abbed always hated the Western presence in his country. Especially the one that began in the first Gulf War and never ended. The Americans explained their presence as foreign aid. Yet the mere fact armed troops sat on and spoiled his land was enough for him to protest them being there.

When he joined the Cause at age twenty, he was enamored by the idea of giving his life away. Being a *Shahid*—a martyr, was a fantasy of almost every Arab child. His parents' exultant praise of those young men spoke volumes, as did hearing the *Imams* and other spiritual leaders speak highly of the ultimate sacrifice. As a teenager with raging hormones, he was especially motivated by the promised reward of 72 virgins in paradise. It took some time to realize that one passionate, experienced woman was much better than any virgin could be. It took him longer to understand that if paradise *were* such a wonderful destination, those spiritual leaders would have gone there themselves.

He eventually did figure out their game. When he arrived to the United States, thoughts of paradise vanished. What incentive was there to get to an uncertain paradise, when he could get paradise in the present? While no one could convince him to commit suicide anymore, at any moment, his life could be taken by the authorities, his accomplices, or a work accident right here in Mazatlán.

After half an hour through heavy traffic, the driver stopped in front of a factory that appeared vacant. Abbed knew the man didn't understand the destination, but also that he wouldn't care as long as his fare paid, which he did, and well.

He waited for the taxi to disappear, then walked two blocks before he stopped in front of a small warehouse. He rang the bell and waited. After a moment, the door opened and he was greeted with a nod. "I hope the air conditioning is working," he said as he entered the building. It wasn't. The interior was dark and steaming hot. A few pallets stacked with boxes sat on the concrete floor. He wiped sweat from his forehead, reminding himself that this was the last time.

"Did you get the shipment, Miguel? Did the machine arrive?" he asked the man who'd let him in.

"Everything is here, *Señor*."

"*Bien*," he replied, and entered a small office, where he picked up a phone and dialed a number. He waited three rings before hanging up, then looked at the telephone as if trying to hypnotize it. After a minute the phone rang once, and he started to breathe again.

"*Bien*, we are ready," he told Miguel.

They went to the platform and opened one of the boxes. Abbed pulled out an empty white bag with the words "Silica Gel" stamped on the front and examined it. "Show me the machine," he said.

Miguel took him to a desk in one of the dark corners and switched on the light above them. The machine looked like a small printing press. Abbed filled the silica-gel bag in his hand with some sawdust left on the desk from another job. Next, he placed the edge of the small bag between the machine's two lips and pressed the green button on the machine's right side. A whistle sounded, followed by a mechanical click. The bag was instantly sealed.

He examined the bag closely. "Excellent," he said. Miguel nodded in agreement.

Three short honks from outside interrupted their assessment. By the time the overhead doors sealed the warehouse closed again, Miguel was directing the forklift to unload a pallet from the small truck that just arrived.

The driver jumped down and greeted Abbed. "I got your call, *essè*," he said, and then, "You don't look like a gringo."

"Neither do you. Just make the delivery," Abbed muttered from clenched teeth. "Your brothers at 18th Street will take care of the rest."

The driver shrugged and took one step backward. "Sure, Bro."

Miguel brought the pallet over and placed it gently next to the desk where Abbed now sat. They cautiously peeled the shipping labels off, cut the shrink-wrap, and opened the boxes inside. The boxes were filled with the same bags, but these were filled with amorphous silica—a material resembling white sand used as a drying and dehumidifying agent.

Abbed jerked his chin toward the boxes. "Let's get to work."

Miguel nodded and elevated the fork almost to its maximum height, then placed it under a pallet on a top shelf and brought it down again. These innocent-looking boxes were filled with what they'd all gathered together to pack for shipment.

Abbed pulled a plastic bag filled with whitish powder from one of the boxes, inserted it into the white paper bag and sealed it with the machine. He felt it from several angles. "Perfect," he announced. "Feels like the real thing. It won't protect electronic chips from humidity, but it will do the job for us," he added with a smirk.

They started a production line in which Miguel pulled the plastic bags from the boxes and inserted them into the silica gel bags, Abbed sealed them with the machine, and the driver placed them back in the silica gel boxes. Less than two hours later, the driver sealed the pallet with shrink-wrap, and Miguel placed the shipping labels on the pallet. Ten more minutes, and the pallet containing the whitish powder labeled as a silica gel shipment was loaded on the truck. The driver took his seat behind the wheel.

"Drive directly there," Abbed warned. "No lunch breaks, no tequilas, and no *mujeres. Entiende?*"

"Sure," the driver replied with a smirk. "And how will you know *these* bags and not others will get to *estados unidos?*"

"Don't worry," Abbed smiled, "Someone is waiting for *this* shipment."

The driver started the engine. Abbed turned to Miguel. "Bring your car. I want to follow this clown, and then I need a ride to the airport."

While Miguel went to retrieve his car keys, Abbed took

a last look around the hellishly hot warehouse. *Perfect. I'm one step away from early retirement. Life after the strike can't be sweeter than this moment. Los Angeles, here I come.*

Chapter 19

His face illuminated by the computer screen, Michael sat in his tiny bedroom with the curtains closed and the music turned on. He gave the keyboard a final tap before pressing the Save Draft option and logging out. As he'd done many times before, he next used the browser's Delete History function to wipe out the trail of where he'd been.

Dianne was his. Of this, he was totally confident. The camping weekend had been a success. It had been difficult to drop her off at her house. Several times, she hinted that if he let her come to his apartment instead, she'd happily stay there forever. Finally tiring of her inferences, he told her his roommate was introverted. She bought it, at least for now. After planting the seeds for his plan to take her to England soon, he was ready for the next step ... yet now, after having slept with her, the idea made him nauseous.

Jacob had warned him about getting too close, but he'd never said it would be such an internal struggle. And that struggle was keeping him from his task. He closed his eyes to eliminate outer stimuli and to focus. The blackness didn't bring relief. Instead, it flipped through his life-history pages in a dizzying pace.

"Where are we going?"

Michael could hear himself asking this, but the voice was different. Much younger.

"We aren't going anywhere," Ibrahim had replied. "We're doing homework. If someone approaches us, you don't speak English. Let me do the talking."

Michael nodded, and they entered London's Heathrow terminal. The bustling airport launched good memories of vacations with his father in the Gulf, but then the sad one, of the last time he'd seen his father.

Ibrahim began his instructions, his voice slightly above whisper. "What would be the biggest problem for us in a place like this?" He swung his chin toward the terminal.

Michael shrugged. "Police officers?"

"Very good. How many are there here? And remember, don't let them know you're counting them."

"Fourteen," Michael said after a while.

"Good. How many *undercover* officers are there here?"

Michael looked at him, confused.

Ibrahim explained what "undercover" means, then said, "Don't bother counting. In this place, there are no undercover officers. They usually stick out. They don't look like passengers, because they have no belongings. Or they stay at the same spot too long with no reason."

When Michael nodded, he continued. "But we do have people who might watch us here. Can you tell where they are?"

Michael carefully looked around, mulling over the question. "The airport employees?"

Ibrahim shook his head. "They expect the police to do all their watching for them. But ... look there, to the corner above that counter. Do you see the camera? That should be a problem, but it isn't."

Michael looked around and saw more cameras, many more cameras. He looked back at his mentor. "Why aren't they a problem? They can see everything we do."

"They're looking for bad people that they already know and have pictures of. They record everything, but they won't even bother to look at what they record until *after* our attack."

Michael continued. "Don't you try to avoid the cameras?"

"I do. But unless you're planning to blow the place up

now and want to get away, don't mind the cameras."

Michael opened his eyes and looked around at his tiny bedroom. *"Don't mind the cameras,"* Ibrahim said. But since Michael didn't have a solid plan yet, he had no idea how that advice would help him out. Jacob had directed each of them to develop their own plan and present it to him. Joe had a plan, which he'd ruined. Jacob had a plan too, which he wasn't sharing yet. And Abbed? Who knew what was going on in Abbed's quirky mind? Even though Jacob had been pressing him lately, Michael's plan still had obstacles that seemed insurmountable.

He abandoned his computer and retrieved a yoga mat from the closet. He spread it on the floor, went to his knees and prayed with all his heart, asking for energy and direction, for strength to keep doing what he needed to do, and to keep seeing the light at the end of the tunnel. Then, as he often did, he closed his eyes and concentrated until he saw Ibrahim standing next to him, felt Ibrahim's hand on his shoulder. He heard the entire congregation in London Central Mosque cheering for him and praising him. The image filled him with pride, and a renewed sense of belonging and purpose.

"They can't harm you," Ibrahim had whispered after Michael panicked when the police officer walked past them in the terminal. "Did we do something wrong?" Ibrahim asked him.

"We want to," Michael replied.

Ibrahim released a thundering laugh. One that caused the police officer to turn to them, but then continue walking away.

"They can't arrest us for *wanting* to do something, Michael. In that case, they'd have to arrest the entire country for *wanting* to harm the Queen, the prime minister, or even your infidel-history teacher. The most they can do is ask for your identification."

He smiled at Michael and gave him a tight hug. "You are so young, but you listen to everything I say. I know your father would be proud of you."

Would he really? Michael pressed his forehead to the yoga mat until its texture was painfully embedded into his skin. It didn't help. Memories of any kind always led back to his father, it seemed. And if he couldn't come up with a solid, low-risk plan, he would feel as though he had failed his father.

Eyes still closed, he rose up from his knees. Just before he opened his eyes, he saw his father sitting next to him at the kitchen table in Kuwait, a vision he'd held onto since he was five. But this time was different. This time, Habib was shaking his head in disapproval.

He opened his eyes, startled, and the image vanished. He tried shutting them again to bring his father back, but he'd disappeared, this time for good.

That night, unable to sleep, he rolled from side to side, threw his pillow to the floor, covered his head with the blanket, and meditated. His thoughts returned to Ibrahim.

"Our mission is to smuggle weapons into the gate area behind those checkpoints," he could hear Ibrahim's voice instructing. "You'll start with a small weapon, a pocket knife."

It took Michael two trips to Liverpool, but his accomplishment resulted in another Islamic Center ceremony. When they returned home, Ibrahim gave him a present—a carbon-made commando knife, metal-free. No metal detectors could detect it. *"Next step, you'll learn how to use it,"* Ibrahim *said with a smirk.*

And he did learn. That, and so much more.

When he awoke, he felt as if he was waking from a nightmare. He could barely drag himself to the shower, and wasn't much more refreshed when he emerged.

Mornings were chilly in Los Angeles, but he didn't care. To someone who'd grown up in a place as dreary and frigid as London, the temperatures in Southern California were an undreamed-of luxury. He embraced the cold breeze and started pedaling. Cycling was a great method for countersurveillance. Riders have no real traffic rules, so almost any violation was acceptable. Since he couldn't seem to shake the memories, he allowed them to occupy his mind while he pedaled to the library. The day Ibrahim showed him the significance of a laptop computer stood out.

"They examine laptops with the x-ray machine. What a joke," Ibrahim said while they crossed one checkpoint. The security operator heard Ibrahim, but simply handed back the computer after the required examination.

"It doesn't matter how thoroughly they look at the image," Ibrahim explained while they walked toward their plane. "The only two who can make sense of my laptop's image are the engineer who designed it and the technician who assembled it. There are no identical laptops unless they are the same model, brand, and components."

"Can't they see a weapon inside the computer?" Michael asked.

"Only if it's a gun or other significant metal. They can't see explosives. Explosives are organic material."

Ibrahim entered the restrooms. Michael followed, and watched while he pulled his laptop from its case and disassembled its battery. "Look," he said. Blue claylike material was visible in the place where one battery cell should be. Michael's heart stopped beating.

"Is this it? Is today the day?" he stuttered.

"It's just modeling clay today. I kept some of the battery cells in, though, so I can operate the computer if I'm asked to do so. But, very important ... nobody detected the clay, and it could just as easily be explosives."

"So why do they even check computers, then?" Michael asked.

"To show the public that they do something to protect them." Ibrahim chuckled. "A big surprise will await them someday."

At the time he spoke those words, he couldn't have imagined the world-shaking surprise of September 11. Or perhaps he did. Ibrahim was a big thinker.

For his sixteenth birthday, Michael was given a bicycle and a mission—to learn to shake off surveillance. Ibrahim and his friends followed him, and promised he'd become a *Shahid* instantly if they caught him. They didn't, so his reward of 72 virgins would have to wait a while longer.

"But then," he muttered, smiling, "one girl like Dianne is better than any number of virgins, I'd bet."

As soon as his smile came, it faded, and an uneasy melancholy fell over him, replacing the joy he'd felt only a second before. Was Jacob right? Would this conflicting set of emotions about using her continue like this? He hoped not.

A few moments of careful thought later, he attributed his nerves to lack of sleep, and his lack of enthusiasm on having to go to the library to gather information on the Internet. Jacob had assured him he could check the Internet in his apartment for anything he needed. *The authorities are incapable of enforcing any rules on open resources,* Jacob had said. Michael still thought it safer to do so from a public computer, though.

At the library, he learned that Dianne wouldn't be at work until the afternoon, at the same time he had a chemistry class. So he searched the magazine racks until he found what he was looking for: *Government Technology: the Technology and Security Information Magazine.* This magazine had been quoted in the *Scientific American* article he'd shown Jacob.

As he read the article about CTX machines, he made mental notes of names and brands he should look into. He didn't write down a thing. Ninety-nine percent of the time, his memory was excellent. And any information that could jeopardize the operation couldn't be written down anyway. The trick he used for his near-perfect recall was to associate new information with items he already knew.

He didn't even need to show his library card to use the library's free computers. All he had to do was fill out a sign-in sheet with a name. Any name. Less than ten minutes after his request, he sat at one of the stations, entering the General

Electric Corporation's security technology website. First, he searched the section on aviation security. With a few clicks, he was exactly where he wanted to be: the section on the CTX machines used at LAX and most every airport.

An image of one of the bulky machines appeared. Under it, he learned the machine uses technology derived from medical Computed Tomography (CT). The same methods used to diagnose illnesses helped locate and identify explosive devices in checked baggage.

The caption underneath the image read:

> As the conveyor moves each bag through the machine, the system produces a scan-projection x-ray image. Using sophisticated computer algorithms, the CTX system analyzes these sliced images and compares their properties with those of known threats. If a match is found, the system alarms and displays the object on the screen. An operator can determine whether a threat exists, and then follow established protocols for threat resolution.

"That's all good," Michael muttered, peering again at the image. "But now, show me how you wake up in the morning."

He froze. He hadn't thought of it in years, but that was one of his father's many pearls of wisdom. Laughing, his widowed father would say of a beautiful woman he'd met, "Only when she wakes up in the morning do you learn if she is really beautiful. That's when she doesn't wear makeup, wigs or accessories."

In fact, Habib had also used the saying when talking about things needing a more thorough inspection. He would also say," Not all that glitters is gold." Each time he did, Michael's heart lurched at hearing the basic moral his father had tried to instill in him.

He looked again at the image of the CTX machine, realizing that was how he felt about it: It was almost too good to be true. He closed his eyes, and was able to recapture the image of his father, this time waving goodbye to him at Kuwait International Airport.

A lone teardrop found its way from his eye and surfed down his cheek. He wiped it away immediately, then looked left and right to make sure nobody saw him, a full-grown man, crying. But it was early still, and the library was nearly deserted.

"So what is *your* loophole?" he asked the image of the CTX machine. "How do *you* wake up in the morning?"

No answer came. Not that he'd expected the answer to be easy. The time went by, and he digested huge amounts of information. He easily understood the algorithm system that checked the density of objects. And this is what helped him begin to understand.

Through his studies, he'd learned there were many objects in nature with similar densities. *So*, he thought, *the secret is to take the density of one object and compare it to another we already know exists in the computer's database as an explosive.*

"And then what?" he whispered. What would be identical to the density of an explosive?

Clicking on another link brought him a partial answer. Among the items listed were toothpastes, dried fruits, deodorants and dense metals.

So what happens when the machine meets a tube of Colgate?

He opened another page about standard features, and saw a disclaimer: *False alarm rates that exceed industry standards.*

"False alarms?" he muttered, and continued reading until he found another term he liked even more: *false positive.*

Could *this* be the concept he'd been looking for to complete his plan? He knew the term meant incorrectly detecting a condition. As one of his instructors used as an example, a false positive occurs if an intrusion-detection system generates an alarm when it finds a threat—a positive—but the threat turns out to be harmless, or false.

So finding the *right* false positive, one that would fool the CTX machine, could be the loophole he was seeking!

He stood and stretched, keeping his movements casual. One thing was certain. He didn't want to spend another minute at the library. The sleepless night was catching up with him, and in his excitement, he might have already drawn unnecessary attention. He needed time to digest what he'd just learned anyway, see how it might mesh with his plan. He cleared the computer's browser history and left, pedaling back to his apartment. Once there, he kicked off his sneakers and crawled back into his unmade bed. He was asleep within seconds.

His exhaustion was greater than he'd thought. Either that, or his subconscious didn't want to leave the dream he was having just before awakening. Or at least, the dream he thought he was having. Someone told him once that the subconscious protects one against their own dreams. He was almost sure his father had visited him in this dream, and his face was still disturbed.

But there was no time to recall or deconstruct the dream. The descending sun told him he'd almost missed a whole class. He put on his shoes again, grabbed his backpack and ran outside to his bike, figuring that would save the time he'd waste looking for a parking space for his car at school.

* * *

"One of the things we should keep in mind when composing two acidic particles together is how to stabilize them," Vinitzky was saying when Michael eased into the room and took his seat. "Do you all know the joke about one of the

Einsteins who claimed he'd invented an acid able to melt down any material known to mankind? The first question asked of this genius, by a child, was, 'In what container will you store this material?' I believe the moral is clear. Any questions?"

The students looked at him with doubtful eyes. Some of them were bored, others looked like they were afraid of earning a failing grade. Michael seemed to be the only one enthusiastic about the experiment.

As he spoke, Vinitzky walked from one side of the classroom to the other. "I want you to find a reactant stable enough to hold the experiment. What might this reactant be? You tell me."

He stopped by an Asian girl and asked, "What is a reactant, Joanne?"

The shy girl looked up at him. "A reactant is a substance participating in a chemical reaction, especially a directly reacting substance present at the start of the reaction."

"Bravo!" Vinitzky said. "Now get to work. Everyone!"

Michael eagerly searched the list of experiments Vinitzky had written on the board, then wrote down his theories with chemical connections, diagrams and equations.

He heard Vinitzky's footsteps stop behind him. "I noticed you were late, Michael. What are you working on?"

Michael bit back his nervousness and answered, "I'm trying to find a way in which reactants could undergo a large change in volume without releasing a large amount of heat. I'm not there yet."

"So you're trying to create something entropic."

Michael nodded in agreement.

"Why would this be of importance, Michael? Why would humanity in general, and this school in particular, invest in your research and not in others? What would make *your* research commercially valuable, if I may ask?"

While he waited, Vinitzky took his glasses off and cleaned them with his sleeve.

Michael showed him a drawing of two square plates

attached together with telescopic arms. "There are a lot of purposes for entropic energy. My idea is to build a tool. One that can be used by rescue teams. In structure demolitions, they need to lift heavy objects or wreckage at an emergency scene. If I can find a way to stabilize the substance, they'd have an instant jack—to assist in getting a wounded person from underneath a falling wall, for example. It might help emergency responders after earthquakes too."

He held his hands together horizontally, and then separated them to demonstrate what his design was supposed to do.

Vinitzky watched him closely, and leaned over him, his voice purposely low. "You must be kidding me. Had you really thought about this being of significant value when you started?"

Michael was puzzled by the professor's reaction, and alarmed. Of course he thought his purpose was great. Earthquakes were a big deal in Los Angeles. Surely a better, easier way to get people out of demolished buildings would find a supportive audience. But Vinitzky seemed so impressed by his idea, he was singling Michael out. Something he couldn't allow to happen.

"Significant value?" he said, keeping his tone light. "Nah, Professor. Actually, I had NASCAR races in mind. Something like this might save time in jacking up the car for tire changes. With my idea, you could build a ramp to lift the whole car instantly, and all four tires could be changed at once."

Vinitzky scratched his beard, processing Michael's idea. "Good. The idea of instant power *is* something that keeps a lot of minds busy. I hope you'll find something significant for us. How will you stabilize your mixture?"

Michael thought for a moment. "I don't know. I haven't thought about it yet."

"Okay. You should. You have to make sure it's stable enough. Otherwise, it could blow up in your face. Instead of rescuing people from wrecks, you'd end up creating them."

"Yes, sir," Michael answered, fighting to keep the awe out of his voice. As though Ibrahim's spirit from last night was still present, speaking through his chemistry professor, his plan was finally starting to come together.

Chapter 20

It seemed like an eternity until the voice on the other end of the line stopped. The man looked at his watch and brushed away an invisible stain from his clean uniform, his forehead furrowed with distress.

"Yes, I understand," he said softly and sadly. "But, honey, you know I can't just leave ... Let me finish my shift, and I'll be home as soon as I can."

He sighed heavily and replaced the receiver in the cradle.

"Problems at home, David?"

He looked up and saw his colleague, a nice-looking guy, recently divorced, and with no children to complicate matters. A lucky man.

As if you could even begin to understand, David wanted to say. Instead, he muttered "Yeah, with my kid at school."

He walked back to his post and sat there, supporting his head in his hands. His supervisor noticed, and approached.

David looked up, embarrassed. "Billy was caught at school with drugs. They took him downtown for some questioning. Helen's freaking out. Doesn't want to go down there by herself."

His supervisor sighed. "Look, I understand. But I can't make it today without you." He thought for a moment. "Look, as soon as we're done with the peak hours, you're free to go."

David nodded gratefully. "Thanks, Charlie."

"It's all right. Just don't forget your stamps before you

start work."

David looked at his empty desk. Thanks to Helen's call, he was already behind schedule. He quickly retrieved his toolbox and tried to wave off his worries, turned his post light on and signaled for the first man in line to approach him.

He inspected the document the man presented, tapped keys on his keyboard, and asked, "So you're from Italy. What are you going to do while in the United States, sir?"

The man's answer was correct and his papers checked out, so David stamped the passport and forced himself to smile at the man. "Welcome to the United States, sir, and enjoy your stay."

* * *

Once the captain instructed the passengers to prepare for landing, Abbed clicked his seatbelt closed, then looked out the window and saw the city spread below him.

"I hate flying," the woman beside him said.

"So do I," he replied without taking his eyes off the window. "At least we're almost there."

"Do you live in LA?"

"Yes, I do."

"So do I. So how come we've never met?"

This time, Abbed swiveled his head and looked at her for a long moment, sensing where she wanted this conversation to lead. But no. She was local. He was almost burned once by someone who became too possessive and obsessive about him. Even after she'd badgered him into marrying her, she tracked every step he made. As it turned out, she'd thought he was having an affair. But the truth would've only made her actions crazier. She might even have gone to the police. Finally, he called his accomplice at the time.

"Are you out of your mind?" George had said. "I warned you to keep it in your trousers. It would have saved us both a lot of unnecessary mess."

"Too late for that," Abbed replied. "Taking care of her is the only way out."

George patted him on the shoulder. "No, pal. Taking care of *you* is the only way out."

Abbed still remembered the wave of nausea he felt, hearing that. He fought the sudden urge to run and said casually, "What a lousy end it would be."

George patted him again and said, "Relax. We won't kill *you*. We need you. We'll just pretend you died."

It took them a week. With the Internet and the availability of high-quality printers, it wasn't a problem to fake a death certificate and police report. George even hired someone to wear a uniform and bring Abbed's spouse his personal effects. The poor girl was so upset, she didn't even want to see Abbed's wrecked car, or have anything to do with it.

In San Francisco, he found shelter at a comrade's house. His first visit was to a plastic surgeon to disguise his appearance. He dressed smartly for the appointment, and explained his decision for the change in a way unlikely to be questioned: that his boyfriend bought a nose job for him for their anniversary. This was perfectly acceptable to the doctor. It worked even better for Abbed. He liked his new nose as much as he liked the freedom his new appearance gave him. Both contributed to his sex appeal.

Which at times, was an annoyance. Yet that quickly prepared excuse came in handy once again on the airplane as he contemplated the enthusiastic woman sitting next to him. He affected a serious expression, leaned over to the woman and said, "My boyfriend doesn't like me to, ah ... meet other people."

"Oh," the woman said, and removed the entertainment magazine from the pocket of the seat in front of her. He smiled, worked like a charm.

Once the plane landed and passengers disembarked, he

ambled down the corridor leading to the passport check-and-arrival terminal, rehearsing his cover story in his head. As a programmer, he had nothing to do at the manufacturing and assembly plants in Mexico. He doubted the INS officers would even ask about his occupation, though. He scanned the INS posts and chose the one occupied by an officer who appeared to be there in body, but not spirit.

"What brings you to the US, sir?" the officer asked.

"I work here," Abbed said, and pointed out the H-1 visa in his passport.

The officer studied him, but his eyes were distant.

"Is there a problem?" Abbed asked after a long moment.

"No, sorry," the officer apologized, and stamped the passport, then handed it back. "Have a nice stay in California."

As Abbed walked away, David looked at his watch, then waved his hand at the woman standing behind the rope. "Next?"

Chapter 21

Joe started his day late, but that was intentional. He liked sleeping in, especially on weekends when his apartment building was quiet. After a long shower, total shave to rid himself of the goatee, and an impressive high-calorie breakfast, he walked to the shopping mall and purchased stylish new frames for his bifocals, purposely choosing frames that looked nothing like the previous ones. And then, he considered his next dilemma.

Los Angeles remained a city in which you couldn't get anywhere without your own wheels. A popular oil-and-lube franchise capitalized on the city's car culture by advertising "We make sure nobody walks in LA." When Joe saw the ad—and the reliance on cars in LA—he decided that worked for him, but also against him. The weather was perfect, the streets were wide and clean, but he was the only person in his neighborhood walking.

"And I'm worried about drawing attention to myself ... what a joke!" he muttered as he stood alone by the northbound bus stop.

The bus took almost ten minutes to arrive. He thought this was outrageous, but after all, buses weren't so busy in this city. Besides, bus-riders weren't the type of customers who complained. Sometimes they weren't the kind of customers who even pay.

It took him a few seconds to understand he couldn't pay the driver directly for the ride. Instead, he had to use a machine, which swallowed his money and produced a receipt. The driver remained distant, focused solely on driving.

The atmosphere smelled like body odors; he didn't dare sit on any of the seats. Most of the other passengers seemed one level above homelessness, with their worn-out clothes, mostly dirty, and their eyes that didn't reflect vitality or even any desire to get to their destinations. He felt malicious joy at detecting poverty in a prosperous American society, but even though it looked easy, he waved off the idea of targeting public buses. Nobody would care about these people, he concluded. Therefore, the impact wouldn't be as dramatic as he wanted it to be.

Too bad, he thought. *Buses work so well in other places.*

From a speaker somewhere in the bus, he heard a tinny-sounding bark: "Wilshire." He pressed the red button on the pole closest to him, reminding himself to wash his hands once he got to his destination.

He stepped off the bottom step and glanced to his right. The bulky gray structure of the Federal Building teased him with its power while he adjusted his new glasses and measured its seventeen stories.

After crossing the street, he walked underneath the ever-busy I-405 Freeway, crossed a grassy area and entered a gothic building that, with its gargoyles and ornate pillars, looked out of place in a post-war modern city like Los Angeles.

Two older ladies sat behind a desk, busy with paperwork. "Good morning, Sarah, good morning Rachael," he greeted them.

"Good morning, Joe," Rachael responded and added, "Oh, I just love your new glasses."

"Thank you. It's my new look. What can I do for you ladies today?"

"I think your usual will do, Joe," Sarah said. "The staff's really behind on folding laundry, I know they'll appreciate it."

Joe nodded and smiled, and Rachael walked out from behind the desk and led the way inside the building.

"God bless you for volunteering your time here," she said while they walked.

Allah will bless me, but not you, he thought. "Oh, I feel I get more than I give, Rachael. Everybody should give a hand to help this place."

"I've always meant to ask," she said, "what do you do for a living that you can afford to spend your weekends here?"

"Uh, I'm in real estate."

"Real estate?" She stopped walking and looked at him. "Don't you have to show properties on the weekends?"

Joe smiled. He didn't know whether he should kill her for prying into his life, or kill himself for producing such stupid answers. He tried again. "Oh, I'm in industrial real estate. No open houses on weekends."

"Oh," she said, and began walking again.

"That's how I find time to come here on weekends. I think the Veteran's Administration is a worthwhile place. We have to give something back to our vets for what they gave us."

"I know, and—" She turned to look at him with widened eyes. "I forgot. There's someone who'll help you today. His name's Tim, one of the residents here. He's a bit slow ... how shall I put it ... mentally disabled. I really can't say much, but ... he received a head injury in Iraq. A devastating one. Even now, he has to be extremely careful. No family, the poor thing. But a very nice fellow. And he gets so bored on the weekends—"

"Not a problem." Joe said, and opened the door to the laundry room, a vast space packed with mountains of towels and garments on stainless steel tables. Next to a table sat a young man about twenty-five years old, blond, slim, and bespectacled. There was a line in his scalp where hair was missing, replaced by a scar and a furrow-shaped depression.

"Hi, Tim, this is Joe," Rachael said. "He's a volunteer, and he'll help you today."

Tim walked toward Joe, his right hand extended. He lowered his head shyly and muttered, "Nice to meet you, Joe."

"Nice to meet you too, Tim," Joe said, and shook his hand.

"Since you guys have been introduced, I'll get back to my desk," Rachael said. "You know what to do, Joe. If anything comes up, Sarah or I will be at the desk." She left the room, closing the door behind her.

"So it's just you and me, Tim," Joe said, smiling. "We'll make great friends."

"Will we?" Tim raised his head, regarding Joe with shining eyes behind his eyeglasses.

"I assure you we will," Joe said, giving Tim a rare genuine smile. "You might even say God willed us to meet."

* * *

Joe entered the bicycle store. The docile Tim, already worshipful of him since their day in the laundry room, followed. Joe had concluded it would be wiser to avoid public transportation, and a bicycle seemed a reasonable way for him to get from one place to another. It might even help him lose some of the weight he'd gained since his arrival to America. And besides, based on Tim's obvious immaturity and knowing that most young boys are thrilled to own their own bicycle, purchasing one for him, too, would cement Joe's godlike status with him.

He read the store's biography on a small placard near the entrance. "Established in 1936?" he said in wonder. It amazed him that despite the huge depression at that time, Californians had still invested in leisure equipment—leisure, to Joe, was unnecessary waste. Yet what was once a wasteful pastime had become necessity for some.

"What do you think about this one, Tim?" he asked, pointing to one.

"Oh, I *love* red bikes!" Tim replied.

A short time later, a salesperson was extolling the features of two Marin hardtails. "It's a hardtail for its durability as much as for its lack of suspension. Shimano components, including LX shifters in front and XT in the rear. The best bicycle you can get for your money."

"And it's red, too," Tim said with an excited grin.

Within an hour, Joe and Tim climbed onto their new bikes and headed west toward the ocean. Joe had difficulty pedaling and managing the gearshift, but Tim was a natural-born cyclist. He laughed out loud and seemed to enjoy every moment.

Joe didn't. They stopped on San Vicente, and he sat on the grass and breathed heavily. Tim sat next to him and waited, watching the passing cars on the road.

"At least it's better than riding the bus," Joe said between breaths.

"Why don't you buy a car?" Tim asked.

"Soon," Joe muttered, and looked at him. Joe would have laughed at Tim guileless face, but the lack of oxygen in his lungs prevented it.

It took them two more breaks before reaching the beach-pier in Santa Monica. By then, Joe knew he wasn't a bike person. They walked with their bikes to the end of Wilshire where it joined Ocean Avenue. The Big Blue Bus, as it was named, stopped for them, and they secured the bikes onto a rack in front of the bus.

"America," Joe murmured when he sat down in the second row.

"Yeah," Tim said, and smirked. "It's great, isn't it?"

"Something like that."

They sat silently until they arrived at Federal Avenue. "This is our stop," he told Tim. But his companion seemed to be in a different world. Joe grabbed his shoulder and shook it once. "Tim?"

Tim looked strangely at him, as if seeing him for the

first time in his life.

"This is our stop," he repeated.

This time, Tim understood. They got off the bus and crossed the hectic street, and he escorted Tim back to his room at the VA rehab center. After he helped Tim settle his bike against one wall of the room, he said, "Take good care of the bike until tomorrow, will you?"

"Aren't you taking both of them with you?" Tim asked.

"No. I can barely handle one. I won't be able to deal with two," he explained, keeping his tone light.

"So I get to keep it here? Wow! Thanks, Joe! You are a true friend!"

"That's all right, Tim. I'll see you tomorrow."

He walked out of the room. In spite of his earlier difficulty, he felt light and powerful on the ride back to his apartment. The tiredness and shortness of breath had disappeared, replaced with something that felt almost like enthusiasm. And even if the bike didn't work out as a way to exercise, it had accomplished its main purpose: bonding Tim even closer to him, ensuring that when the time came, Tim would do anything he asked.

At his apartment building he checked his mailbox, threw away all junk mail and climbed the stairs. His apartment was untouched, at least by his check of the front door. The tiny piece of adhesive tape he'd left on the upper panel was still attached to the doorframe. Once inside, he checked the tape on the windows. Also undisturbed.

Once, the tape wasn't on the doorframe when he returned home. When he rushed down the stairs, beginning his getaway plan, the janitor saw him and casually mentioned that he'd finally got around to replacing the faucet handle in his shower. Living in an apartment complex had its disadvantages.

He began the process of booting up the computer, then heating the teakettle, needing a strong cup of coffee tonight. He took his sweaty shirt off and inspected his rotund figure in the full-length mirror on his bedroom door.

"In a month or two, I'll look like Abbed," he convinced himself, and opened a package of Oreo cookies. He took his full coffee cup and a handful of cookies back to the computer. After logging in, he opened his mail account. No messages in the inbox.

He opened a new mail message and wrote, *"Back in business. More information will follow soon. J2."* He saved the draft and logged out, then checked his watch. Another two hours to wait until *Counter Terrorism Agency* came on. But that was okay. Until it did, he could channel surf, perhaps check the news channels. He began searching for the television's remote control, whistling a tune he hadn't remembered since his childhood.

Chapter 22

The crowds around him led to Abbed's certainty that the shopping mall was an excellent choice for a rendezvous. Hollywood. No doubt, one of the most significant magnets in the entire world. Not even the Kaaba, the central stone structure covered by a black cloth within the Great Mosque in Mecca, was as popular as the giant Hollywood sign. The mall had been built and designed to be in view of the sign, to allow it to be packed with tourists who liked to take photographs of the sign and then shop for American couture.

There was no way anyone would overhear or even notice him among the thousands of people who amassed the place. He wore jeans and a blue pullover shirt. There were at least a thousand men dressed like him where he waited by the American Eagle store for his "date." He didn't have to wait long before the silhouette reflected in the display window in front of him.

"*Hola*," he said before the man approached him.

The man was a bit surprised, but said calmly, "How are you doing?"

"*Estoy bien*," he answered. "*Y tu*?"

"*Gracias a dios.*"

Abbed and his companion walked silently along the famous "Stars" sidewalk, where tourists were snapping pictures of celebrities' names embedded in the concrete. They climbed the escalator and walked on the shopping mall's upper balcony. To the northeast, Abbed was able to see the Hollywood sign.

Not a bad idea, he thought, but waved off the idea immediately. Getting to the sign was almost a "mission impossible." And after all the effort it would take to blow it up, California would simply build a new and better sign within days.

They chose the less-populated western side of the balcony. From there, he gazed down at the people walking from one star's name to another.

"So, *essè*, wassup?" the man asked.

Abbed looked at him, "Everything's good, Jose. It's nice to see you again." A lie. It wasn't nice at all. Between Jose's cruel narrow eyes and his black shirt collar, the tattoo of a serpent emerged and slithered from his neck. His gold watch and bulky onyx ring were equally tasteless.

"The last shipment was brilliant, man," Jose said. His voice didn't reflect enthusiasm, but it was as good a compliment as one would receive from him.

"Thank you," Abbed replied.

"I got the money. You should have it by now." The arrangement was to deposit the money into a small, family-owned bank in Trinidad and Tobago. The bankers, as middlemen, received five percent of the transactions for their efforts.

"Thank you again," Abbed said. "It's the last one, you know...."

Jose burst out laughing, an ugly laugh. "What do you mean, the last one?"

"I'm moving on, not doing *it* anymore," Abbed said, smiling. It wasn't as easy as he thought it would be.

"Do you want more money? Is that the thing?" Jose said, and his mean eyes turned crueler.

"I don't need money, Jose. I'm from Saudi Arabia, you know."

"Yeah, you told me. So why have you been doing it until now?" Jose pulled a cigarette from a gold case and lit it.

Abbed thought for a long moment, knowing he must

play it cautiously. The 18th Street Gang was best known for its members cruelty and efficiency. He couldn't let them think he might be a threat to them. Or worse, for them to suspect he was switching to one of the rival gangs.

He sighed and explained, "I don't care about the money. I did it to prove that I could. To challenge the authorities. Look how far we've gotten. LA is flooded with your shit, Jose. I'm ready to move on, find a different challenge."

Jose nodded and inhaled the smoke deeply. "You're returning to Saudi Arabia? Huh?"

It was Abbed's turn to laugh, "And give up all the fun here? No way." Then he decided it was time to shift the subject. "So, how's business?"

"Good, good. You know, one day dolce, the other ... not so much. We just had a fiasco in one of the schools. Some pushers were arrested by the pigs, and we don't make money there no more."

It was more information than Abbed wanted to know. "Can these, ah, pushers lead the authorities to you or me?" *Stupid question,* he thought as soon as the words left his mouth.

"No, no. They're kids, students. Good guys. One of them is a son of a pig. The other is a kid of someone from the INS. I don't give a damn, and they can't do nothin' to me because they don't know me."

Abbed nodded. "Okay. I just wanted to make sure they can't point their fingers at us. I don't need that kind of problem now."

Jose smiled. "Don't worry. If you do another job for us, I'll make sure those *muchachos* don't point their fingers anywhere...."

"But you just said they don't even know you," Abbed said. "So why should *I* be worried?"

"Well, one of those kids' fathers works for the INS. He'd love to know how his son was manipulated, and how the one who manipulated him got into his country. They were after me for some time.... They might be after you too, being our little helper and all that. Might not even want you in the country anymore."

He took his sunglasses off and peered into Jose's face. "Are you threatening me?"

"No, *essè*. But I need you, and when business turns out to be *dulce* good, you get *frio basa* and walk away."

Abbed sighed loudly at the mention of getting cold feet. Now, he almost wished he'd developed them sooner. "I don't like it, buddy," he said. "But I have some more important things to do now."

Jose smiled at him, but not a sincere smile. "So share with me, and I'll share with you, *cómo familia*."

He debated his response. Eventually, he replied, "I have to talk with the man in charge of business. I'll get back to you as soon as I can."

"Do you want me to get rid of that INS officer, *essè*? Just to show you how much I mean *business*?"

Abbed sighed. "No, I don't. I don't care. But if you want to, you'll do it anyway. Whatever makes you feel good, Jose."

Chapter 23

"Do you know why I called you here, Michael?"

"My professor said it's routine, that you do with most students, sir. That any student project that might be dangerous needs your approval." Yet when Vinitzky had told Michael this, he shifted his eyes away and wouldn't look at him. Like Michael was doing right now.

"Michael, look at me."

He raised his eyes to the man's intelligent green ones, and felt they were x-raying him.

"Do you know who I am?" the man asked.

"The sign outside says 'Public Safety Manager,' sir."

"Yes. And that's what I do here at the university. Is there anything you'd like to tell me?"

"Like what?"

"Like your interest in composing potentially harmful materials?" The man sitting behind the desk leaned back in his chair. "Tell me what your project's about."

Michael did his best to affect the expression of a disinterested college student. "I'm trying to figure out a way to instantly expand a device so it can push a heavy particle, sir. I had in mind a NASCAR racecar being maintained during a race. But such a device could also be used for lifting debris in demolition sites and things like—"

"You can call me McClain."

"Okay, Mr. McClain, what *am* I here for?" Michael asked, feeling his confidence return.

"Michael, I was in federal law enforcement for many years. I know when something smells fishy. I smell something strange about your project. Do you want to tell me what it is?"

Michael sighed. "I thought my idea might have both an audience and relevancy. It would be inexpensive, and can serve various functions. There's nothing wrong with having an idea, is there?"

"I'll tell you what's wrong with your *idea*. NASCAR races, you said? What's the advantage of your idea over what they use now to change tires? Those jacks are powerful enough to bounce a truck in the air. And if there was an earthquake here in LA, explain to me how you're gonna shove that *idea* of yours under all that debris in a rescue attempt?"

Michael was silent for a long moment. His father had taught him to avoid conflicts. Ibrahim had taught him about times when it was wise to force a conflict to a head. This, he decided, was one of those times. "Is there something you're accusing me of, sir?"

"Accusing you? Well, I talked to a few chemistry professors, and they all agree that your project doesn't make sense theoretically or operationally, nor does it fulfill the class assignment. I don't know what you're up to, *boy*, but you better quit now, because I'm not about to get off your back so easily."

Michael lowered his eyes to his lap, closed his eyes, and saw Jacob's disappointed face. The man's reaction was due to Michael's Middle Eastern descent. Michael knew it as surely as he knew that once, long ago, his name was Mustafa. But never before had he been treated like this at school.

Then, he remembered his father's lessons about disengaging from conflicts. He raised his head, looked McClain in the eye and said, "I think this was a matter of miscommunication; I might have failed to represent my project properly. To avoid any ... suspicion, I'll choose a completely different project."

"That's exactly what I wanted to hear, Michael."

"Yes, sir," Michael said, when what he wanted to say

was, *I know.*

"Good. We're done here. You can go back to your class." McClain smiled. "And be safe out there."

Michael left the office and headed toward the building's exit, both frustrated and relieved. They were smarter than he thought. He didn't think someone would question his idea or challenge the relevancy of his project. But they did. That was an unpredicted obstacle in his plan, and he should have had a plan B ready.

He started rehearsing his meeting with Jacob. He didn't want to let him down, especially after Joe's poor performance. He had to think of better ideas before the meeting, to provide Jacob with some options. Yet his head was empty.

Why did Professor Vinitzky have to go to the safety manager instead of confronting me with his concerns? He knew there was no simple answer except one. *We probably share similar qualities. I don't like conflicts either.*

The long corridor ended. He left the building and walked swiftly back to the chemistry lab. He didn't know why his legs took him there. He just obeyed and walked while debating whether he should confront Vinitzky.

He looked at his watch. Class had ended long ago. The lab would be deserted.

So what am I doing here? With no real answer but too restless to go home yet, he kept walking, entering the stairway to the lab in the basement. Perhaps a visit to the lab would give him some ideas for Jacob, or at least ease his restless mind.

He almost shrieked when he saw the man behind the stairwell door, his glasses shining under the neon lights. The man's already white face had turned completely pale under a glossy coat of sweat. In fact, Professor Vinitzky could have easily passed for a figure at Madame Tussaud's Museum just then, Michael thought when he finally collected himself. He flashed back to the first time Ibrahim took him there. Ibrahim had laughed at Michael when he saw how excited he was to see Michael Jackson standing there. "Billy Jean" was playing in the background.

"Can I ask him for an autograph?" Michael asked. He remembered Ibrahim laughing hard.

"Go ahead. Try it," he chuckled.

Michael still remembered how frustrated he was when the idol didn't accede, and even refused to look at him, just stood there with his gloved hand held up. "Why won't he look at me?" he asked Ibrahim.

"Maybe because you're an Arab, child," Ibrahim replied harshly. "It's not Michael Jackson, it's just a dummy. Now you see what the infidels do with their time and money. Let's go."

He remembered the look in Ibrahim's eyes. Not mirthful, but angry.

"Michael?"

He jerked himself back to the basement stairwell where they stood now. "Yes, Professor?"

"What are you doing here so late?" Vinitzky folded his arms across his chest and unfolded them again, allowing them to dangle against the sides of his body. But just a second later, he crossed his arms again, clearly uncomfortable.

"I'm ... not sure," he replied. "I just finished talking with Mr. McClain, and I guess I was still a little ... restless."

"Well, Michael, you know—"

A cell phone buzz echoed within the stairwell. Vinitzky reached into his pocket and dug out the electronic device as though he'd been literally saved by the bell. He wiped sweat from his forehead and pressed the answer button, then brought the phone to his ear and looked at the ceiling, presumably concentrating on the phone call. "This is Ed."

He listened for a moment and said, his tone formal, "All right, Melissa, what can I do for you? ... *CTA? Counter Terrorism Agency*? No, I'm not familiar with the series. Unfortunately, I barely have time to watch TV. How can *I* help you?"

At "*CTA*," Michael's hearing sharpened to the point

where he thought he could even hear the cell phone's binary codes communicating with the closest transmitting antenna.

Vinitzky repeated, "To tell you what? Are you serious? Are you sure you've got the right number? How did you find me?"

He listened for another moment, then said, "So what you need is something general, within the field of chemistry, that sounds and looks authentic? I think we can arrange that."

He glanced at Michael. "I think I can assign one of my students to help you. But first, I want to meet you. Can you get here during office hours so we can discuss this? Meanwhile, I'll find your candidate."

Again, he looked at Michael. This time, he didn't glance away, just continued talking, giving his office address and telling the caller to be there between one and three the next day.

When he ended the call, he smiled at Michael. Michael returned the smile with curiosity and said, "So?"

"Perhaps we can do something with your idea after all. That was Melissa Maddox, a director's assistant from Showtime. Welcome to Hollywood. If I understood that caller correctly, they're running a drama about terrorists. A series called *CTA*."

"I'm familiar with the series," he said. "But why did they call us? We're not in the film school here."

"Actually, they don't need film interns. They want information about our area—chemicals. Actually, the kind of chemicals that could be harmful."

His smile was so broad, it was almost a wink. "And since you're my best student this quarter, I thought of you. Think you can help?"

Michael remained silent, but the question of yes or no wasn't in his mind. On one hand, he'd just walked out of McClain's office. The phone call, and the professor's request, could be a setup to see if he really was into the explosives game. He didn't want to underestimate McClain's paranoia.

But he had to give the professor an answer he'd believe.

"I ... don't know, Professor. I'm not sure I can be of any help. I mean, I'm just here to learn. I don't want any prize named after me."

"Prize?"

"Nobel," Michael answered simply.

"Of course." Vinitzky chuckled. "In class, I could tell you're not the kind who wants attention. Even though just about anyone else your age would be jumping up and down at a chance like this." He thought a moment. "Tell you what, I'll ask McClain to join us in the meeting. If there's something fishy about it, he'll find out. And of course you won't sign anything until our department head okays it."

Michael nodded slowly, still feeling like the whole thing might be a trap. "There's another thing," he said, feeling his way. "I'm only undergrad. Some of the graduate students might be bet—"

"It's Hollywood, Michael," Vinitzky said, and turned back toward the lab door. "It doesn't *have* to be right, it just has to *look* right. For one thing, it could be fun. Second, it might bring some donations into our department. You can't even believe the money in that industry. And besides, if you get stuck on something, you can always call me."

Michael followed him, unsure what to say next. He glanced at the lab door. "Where are you going now, sir?"

"I want to check this *CTA* thing for myself."

While he watched Vinitzky enter the six-digit code to unlock the basement lab's door, he quickly associated those numbers with letters to make sure it stuck in his mind. He might never need it, but Ibrahim had taught him well.

Inside the lab, Vinitzky headed straight for one of the computer stations, opened the browser and typed, "Counter Terrorism Agency" into the search engine. He clicked on several of the links that appeared, and they both silently read the information.

"Melissa's name is listed here," Vinitzky said, then

swiveled his head to look up at Michael, his smile wide. "I'll meet you tomorrow in my office."

Chapter 24

Vicky replaced the phone in its cradle, turned to Richard, and smiled. "That was Fahima. Muhammad will be home in an hour. Have any suggestions about what we can do till then?"

Richard grinned at her, his blue eyes twinkling. "I'm sure you have something in mind."

"Oh yeah." She walked toward the bedroom, undressing on the way, dropping one garment, then another, on the floor.

He smiled and finished his drink in one gulp. It was evening, still a bit early for drinks, and this was his second one already. *But what the hell.* He stood, carefully unbuttoned his shirt, and followed her.

With Vicky, he knew exactly what buttons to push, literally. They would have continued enjoying each other if the annoying ring of the phone on the nightstand hadn't interrupted.

"I can't breathe. You answer," she muttered, gasping.

He rose to his knees, his chest shining with sweat, grabbed the phone from its cradle and barked hello.

"Hello. Is this Vicky's house? This is Muhammad, her neighbor." The voice was hesitant, almost shy.

"Oh, uh, hi, Muhammad. This is Richard Miller, Vicky's ... um, friend. How are you?"

"I know who you are, Mr. Miller. I listened to you on NPR the other day. Very interesting, the things you said. Did

Vicky want to talk to me?"

"Please, call me Richard. Actually, it was me. Can you come over here? There's something I'd like to discuss with you. Say, twenty minutes?"

Muhammad agreed, and Richard returned the receiver to the nightstand and smiled at the still-panting figure spread out on the bed under him.

"Twenty minutes to finish what we've started," she said, and wrapped her arms and legs around him again. His only choice was compliance. Not that he minded.

* * *

Twenty minutes later Muhammad entered the house, noting the reporter's shoeless, wet-haired state. The man didn't try to make excuses, just said, "How are you today?"

"Pretty well, and you?" Muhammad answered, still not understanding why he'd been summoned. Clearly, he'd interrupted something.

Richard offered him a drink. Muhammad accepted and followed Richard into Vicky's bright kitchen. He watched while Richard opened and closed cabinets holding kitchenware and canned goods, presumably looking for glasses. Just as he was starting to wonder where his neighbor was she appeared, dressed in an oversized red USC Trojans t-shirt and blue yoga pants. Her hair, too, was wet, and she had combed it back.

"Hi, neighbor," she greeted him, "how are you?"

"I'm fine. It's good to see you again," he said, and meant it, recalling her recent kindnesses. It wasn't her fault that her sister wasn't interested in his odd passenger.

She finally noticed Richard's struggles to find his way around her kitchen. "Are you hungry, Muhammad?" she said with a grin. "I'm sure Richard would love to cook something for us."

"I'm not sure he wants to compete with Fahima's

dishes," Muhammad replied. He saw the chagrin on Richard's face and couldn't resist smiling. Thankfully, Richard didn't seem offended.

Vicky led him to the living room. Soon after, Richard served their beverages. When she noted he held a cutting board instead of a tray, she raised her eyebrows but didn't say a word.

He accepted a glass and sipped his water, then said politely, "I really liked your interview on NPR. So ... what's going on?"

Richard put his glass on the cutting board, stood and reached for his briefcase, then drew a sheet of paper from one of its compartments. Muhammad recognized the drawing even before Richard returned to his seat and placed it on the table facing him.

"I want to talk to you about this sketch," he told Muhammad.

"How did you get that?" Muhammad said.

Richard was grinning. "I met with Agent Smith today."

Muhammad felt his last sip of water slide into his windpipe. He couldn't fight the reflex and choked, almost spilling water from his glass onto the sofa. "How did you get to *him*?" he asked when he caught his breath.

"Through Amanda," Richard said, nodding to Vicky who sat silently, amused by the order of events. "Amanda gave me Agent Smith's name."

Muhammad nodded. "So how can *I* help you?"

"Here's the thing." Richard leaned forward. "Smith was directed by Amanda to give this case top priority. I believe Amanda wasn't too enthusiastic about this—*until* I published the article."

Muhammad nodded. "I get it. And you mentioned me in the article."

Vicky said, "I hope you didn't mind that I told Richard—"

"No, it's all right," Muhammad told her, then chuckled. "I was thrilled that at least *somebody* was as bothered as I was."

She shared his laugh, then said, "Poor Amanda. I guess at the time we called, she was suffering from government-worker burnout."

"Or maybe it's a test."

Both of them turned at Richard's statement.

"Agent Smith didn't come right out and say it," he explained, "but I believe he thinks the whole episode's like a promotion test for him—to gain points. Main point, I believe he's eager to find out who your mystery passenger is. At least he is now."

Muhammad gave him a knowing nod, and Richard continued.

"He gave me the feeling they're looking into the Bentley Avenue connection now—what you saw—since the airport's in that general area. I don't know what it means yet, but ... I trust your intuition, Muhammad. The whole thing smells bad to me too. And I believe you when you say your passenger might never have intended to take that flight to Japan, as he claimed. That instead, he was up to no good."

He lifted the sketch in his hand. "But if I'm going to do anything about it, I'll need your help."

Muhammad nodded again, numerous thoughts demanding his attention. "I want to help, but ... I need to mention something first."

"I'm all yours," Richard said.

He took a sip of water, then began. "In truth, I would like to just forget what happened. Especially since the passenger knows my name."

Richard and Vicky's heads jerked simultaneously. "How could he have found out about that?" Richard asked.

Muhammad shrugged. "Easy. Think about it."

The light dawned in Vicky's eyes first. "Those ID cards you guys are required to have on the back of the front seat."

"Exactly. What if the passenger also read Richard's article and made the connection to me?"

Richard gave a low whistle. "Muhammad, I'm sorry ... I can't believe that didn't occur to me before."

"Please understand, I'm not saying no," Muhammad said, speaking quickly. "I just wanted you to understand that I have to consider my wife, my son. And ... the agents ... they were polite, but Agent Smith wasn't exactly friendly at first." He pointed to his dark-olive face. "Because of who I am. Where I come from."

Vicky didn't say anything, but her eyes showed her sympathy.

"On the other hand," he continued quickly, "I have to think about how something like this would have played out in Egypt. There, privacy was almost a dirty word. Egypt is a democracy, in that every Egyptian has the right to vote. But there's only one candidate for which to vote. Even when I was a soldier in the Egyptian infantry, freedom ... well, freedom was nonexistent for everyone. Still is."

Richard leaned forward, putting his notepad aside. "Muhammad, I wish I could say I could protect you. I can't. All I can do is report on things that matter to me. So if you say no to helping me, I'll understand."

Even in the late 1960s, when many Muslim organizations were formed in America, Muhammad didn't need anyone or any organization to get in the way of his freedom, or to grant it to him. But he was, and remained, a good, law-abiding citizen. *Maybe now, I have the chance to pay America back for the good house and shelter it's given me and Fahima and Ali. And the freedom. I definitely owe America for the freedom.*

He straightened up in the sofa and smiled at Richard. "Nonsense. What can I do to help?"

As he spoke, he felt his chest expand. He *was* an American citizen. It felt good.

Chapter 25

David waited impatiently for the employees' bus, which should have passed through the terminal five minutes ago. Today, it's lateness made him even angrier. He was on his way to the downtown LAPD station to bail his son out of jail. Billy was a minor, but the charges were for drug trafficking; the authorities wouldn't be lenient. He wished he and Helen didn't have to go through this nightmare. Most of all, he wished the frickin' bus could be on time for once.

Desperate, he waved down a white taxicab that was driving slowly on the road leading to the terminal entrance. When the driver balked at taking him such a short distance, David pulled a twenty from his wallet. Thirty seconds later, they passed under the famous Theme Building, the restaurant whose crossed concrete arcs looked like a big X from the air.

Exactly eight minutes later David was in his car, a simple Chevy sedan. He'd always dreamed of a sports car, but a government salary and his kid's school tuition didn't permit such luxury. Besides, the Chevy was reliable and got him to his destinations of choice.

He headed south and merged onto the I-105 Freeway. If traffic was reasonable, he should be in downtown in twenty-five minutes.

Where did we go wrong? he asked himself for the millionth time today. *Maybe he's just rebelling.* If it wasn't that, he couldn't understand Billy's motives for dealing drugs. When he first heard of the arrest, he'd been sure it was a setup—someone had used his naive son as a mule. But after he digested the news, his confidence slipped; Billy had actually confessed to all the charges. This nightmare was real. And it was just beginning.

The traffic was so bad, it took him almost an hour to get to the station. The next problem was in the lobby. After the officer scanned him from head to toe, he said, "Sorry, Mister Holman, you can't enter the building armed."

Not until the officer pointed to the gun in his holster did David understand. His gun was a part of his body, a part he never used. He once thought if anything happened at his immigration post, he'd rather *throw* the gun at a suspect than fire it. He was sure the results would be better.

"Can I leave it here?" he asked the officer.

"Nope. I can't take responsibility for it, sorry."

"I'm an INS officer."

The officer gave a snuffling laugh. "That makes you even more unwelcome with a gun inside this building. Sorry," he repeated, with a smile that wasn't meant.

David left the building and rushed back to his car, opened the trunk and threw the gun and holster inside, then returned to the station to face what seemed like a mountain of disclaimers and waivers. He didn't even know what he was signing, or care as long as they'd let him take his son home.

Billy was pale when he emerged from the detainees' section, and David couldn't help feeling sorry for him. On the way over, he'd rehearsed what to say when he saw Billy. But all he could manage was a weak "Billy" as he gathered him in his arms, and couldn't stop the river of tears down his cheeks. Neither could Billy, who wept like the child he was.

Billy got into the car and sat in silence, arms folded over his chest. David slid behind the wheel and glanced at him, decided not to engage with him just now, but after they got home.

They reached the intersection of Washington and La Cienega Boulevard, a mini-freeway in itself. The light turned red, and theirs was now the first car in line. He glanced at Billy again and felt useless. But Helen would know what to say. Seemed like she always did.

A sudden jarring and the sound of grinding metal interrupted his thoughts. It took him a full second to realize they'd been hit from behind. By the time he slammed down on the brakes, the Chevy was already in the middle of the lane. The truck driver tried to avoid the collision, but it was too late for the heavy eighteen-wheeler to stop. David never saw the truck that hit the Chevy, or the white Ford van that had pushed them in front of the truck, then turned right and disappeared through the northbound traffic.

The ambulance arrived in record time for rush hour. Two paramedics hurried to what was left of the Chevy. A flame was dancing from the rear of the car, but the paramedics took one glance and kept working to extract the victims, knowing that reality was much different from what's in the movies. A flame near the back of a car only meant there was a hole in the fuel tank, and the "candle" could burn as long as there was fuel inside the tank. An explosion occurred only when gasses from the burned fuel had nowhere to escape. That flame was actually less threatening than no flame at all.

The police arrived shortly after and blocked off two lanes, then one officer put out the tiny fire with an extinguisher he pulled from his cruiser. "You guys need a hand?" one asked.

"No, we lost 'em both," one of the paramedics said, and pointed to David. "When we got here, a witness said he was breathing, but he wasn't by the time we got here. No pulse. And his neck was broken, too. Right at the top of the spine. No chance."

"Bad luck," the officer said, and went back to directing traffic.

"Yeah," the paramedic agreed. "And oh, get this ... rubbernecking's definitely gone high-tech. When we pulled up, the witness was standing there taking pictures, and then he just ran off. Can you believe it?"

The officer gave a disgusted sigh and went back to work. His report cited the accident as a hit-and-run. Nothing unusual for LA County. By the time he filled out the report, he'd even forgotten about the picture-taking witness.

Chapter 26

Muhammad started work very early that morning, and had adjusted his schedule to be in Brentwood by noon. He was reliable. This was something no one could take away from him.

He observed the numbers on the curbs and braked. "House number 16330, here we are," he muttered, shifted into park, and pulled out his cell phone.

"I'm outside," he said when the connection was established, then hung up and put the phone aside. The door of 16330 opened, and Richard emerged wearing a striped button-down shirt and gray slacks. Moments later, Richard sat in the cab next to him. "I understand you're in the middle of your workday. So turn the meter on and let's get going."

"It's okay." Muhammad smiled weakly.

"No, it's not okay. And don't worry, I'll charge it to the *Times*. They want me to publish another article about the issue, they'll pay this expense. Turn the meter on."

Muhammad did, and off they went. Instead of returning to the ever-hectic 405, he chose the surface streets. Eventually they were at the airport, driving by the Terminal 3 building.

"I drove him over here," Muhammad said, waving a hand toward the entrance. "It was almost as crowded as it is now. I drove slowly, like this, trying to avoid getting a ticket. Every time they raise the threat level and bring extra officers to the airport, the city gets a lot more in revenue from handing out tickets. Look at them."

He pointed to a group of twelve uniformed officers

laughing together at the terminal's entrance.

Richard nodded. "Yeah, *now* I feel safe!"

He parked the cab curbside in front of Tom Bradley International Terminal. "This is where we stopped."

"Okay, let's park and snoop around here."

Muhammad's eyes widened in mock amazement. "Oh, *now* I get to see how you nosy reporters operate, huh?"

Richard bellowed laughter. "Yeah, nosy. But remember, a *real* journalist is always nosy for a higher purpose."

Chuckling, Muhammad parked in the multistory parking garage near the terminal and killed the engine. They crossed the road to the terminal, then stood on the curb. Muhammad pointed. "That's where he stood when I unloaded his luggage. He lit up a cigarette and just ... stood there."

Richard glanced at him. "Maybe waiting for an accomplice?"

He shrugged. "Perhaps."

"So you unloaded the luggage, and he lit a cigarette, and then he paid you? What did he do next? Get a cart for his luggage?"

"No. He was just standing there, smoking without really inhaling. That's what looked weird to me."

Richard mulled this over, then said, "When you met him again on the arrival level, did he have a cart then?"

When Muhammad nodded, he continued. "So either he got a cart after you left ..." He pointed toward the row of carts along the terminal's wall, "or he used one of the skycaps working here." His finger moved to one of the porters pulling a cart with two large black suitcases.

"Sorry. I took off by then, so I didn't see."

Richard heard Muhammad's regret, and turned to face him. "You're aware that without you, we wouldn't have gotten this far." Then he turned his attention back to the entrance. "I wonder what the FBI learned here. Agent Smith really clammed up when I asked him that. Or the TSA, maybe. There are hundreds of cameras around here. I'm curious about what they might've seen."

Muhammad's face showed surprise. "Cameras?"

"Oh, yes. Hundreds of closed-circuit cameras here. The FBI's probably still looking over the digital records."

Muhammad looked around, losing patience. "So why are we here, then, trying to solve a puzzle the good guys are about to solve anyway? Are you trying to get some Pulitzer Prize?"

Richard sighed, clearly frustrated, if for a different reason. "If Agent Smith said they covered the airport already, it means either they didn't find anything, or they missed something on the videotapes because they didn't know what to look for. Don't forget, this country still has problems dealing with terrorism. You might not remember, but I talked with a counterterrorism expert before I did that interview on NPR. He said all our methods are taken from law enforcement. That means no one's considered a criminal until he or she commits a crime.

"But that's part of the problem, a big part. The average person doesn't wake up in the morning and say, 'Hey, I think I'll blow up a building this afternoon.' A terrorist attack is huge, so it has to be planned in advance. So, those planning an attack aren't considered criminals until they actually *execute* the attack. By the time it happens, it's too late to stop it. Do you get it?"

Muhammad nodded. "Yes. Like that old American saying about closing the barn door after the horse ran away."

"So it's not just Agent Smith, or even the FBI. All law enforcement labors under that old doctrine, 'Unless something happens, nothing happens' They can't arrest or interrogate anyone just for having the *intention*. They have to have probable cause. That's how our legal system works."

Richard started walking toward the terminal entrance. "Do you like Tom Cruise?" he asked Muhammad, who was keeping up with him.

"Not as much as my wife does, but sure. Why?"

"Do you remember the movie *Minority Report*?"

"Yeah, it was a science fiction movie, wasn't it?"

"Right. Tom Cruise was a futuristic cop who could arrest criminals before they actually committed crimes. They relied on mediums to predict crimes before they happened. But do you know why that would never work in the real world?"

"Because Tom Cruise won't work for a cop's salary?" Muhammad offered, smiling.

Richard laughed. "On top of that, because you can't arrest someone just for wanting to commit a crime. Not even for planning to, unless you can prove it *before* the crime happens. Like the reason we're here today. I don't know if your passenger committed a crime. If he did, he can be brought to trial and convicted. But our federal and local law enforcement personnel are shorthanded, so if they don't find anything out of the ordinary, they'll write the incident down as closed. Understand?"

Muhammad nodded cautiously, "So what are we doing here? Are we trying to go around federal law enforcement?"

"No, we're trying to see whether they missed something," Richard answered. "Let's talk to the skycaps."

They walked over to one of the gray-uniformed skycaps, a man in his late fifties with tiny white hairs stuck desperately to his bald head. Deep wrinkles mapped his face. He was standing by a cart, his gray hat beneath his arm, counting one-dollar bills. Pinned to his breast pocket was a worn-out, gold-colored nametag that read "Henry."

At their approach, Henry folded the bills and stuffed them into his pants pocket, scanning Muhammad and Richard quickly, noting they weren't carrying luggage. "Hi, there," he said. "What can I do for you folks?"

Richard withdrew a sheet of paper from his pocket and unfolded it. "Have you ever seen this man, Henry?"

Smiling, Henry pushed his hat up and looked at the sketch the agent had drawn from Muhammad's description.

"You guys with the FBI?"

"No, we're not. I'm a reporter with the *LA Times*," Richard said, and presented his press card.

Henry glanced quickly at the ID, then back at the sketch. "I told them I thought I saw this guy almost a month ago. He had a full beard then, but I don't remember anything significant about him. He tipped me well with no problems."

Muhammad said to Richard, "Looks like luck is on your side today."

Richard nodded and asked Henry, "Did you see him again last Thursday?"

"No. The agent asked me that too. Didn't work on Thursday, so I can't tell you if it was the same person."

"Do you know who did work on Thursday?"

Henry raised his voice and shouted "Patrick, come here a second." A smaller skycap, whose uniform hung loosely from his slim frame, headed over.

Richard showed Patrick the sketch.

"Yeah, I served that jerk," Patrick said. "But the FBI guy said I shouldn't discuss it with anyone. Now if you'll excuse me—"

Richard took a ten-dollar bill from his wallet and handed it to him. "Let me buy five minutes of your time."

Patrick jammed the bill into his pocket. "I still can't talk about it, ya know."

This was a logjam, but Richard happened to be good at breaking up information logjams.

"You're not talking about anything," Richard assured him with a smile. "Can you just describe what he did or said when you helped him? By the way, Muhammad's the taxi driver who brought him to the airport," Richard added, pointing to Muhammad, who nodded and said, "It's okay to talk to this fellow. I did."

Patrick lowered his voice. "He lit a cigarette and waved me over. Then he asked me to take his luggage to Asiana's check-in counter. He was still smoking the cigarette, so he didn't enter the terminal with me. I ended up waiting inside like an idiot. That's it. He paid me and I left. But the jerk kept me waiting when I could've taken care of at least two other passengers."

"I get it," Richard said "but you didn't actually see him *doing* anything wrong, did you?"

"Now you sound like the FBI agent, pal," Patrick said, and smiled. "What I said is what I saw."

Richard thanked him, and Patrick raced off to help a family who'd just stepped off a shuttle.

Muhammad spoke up. "What do you think, Sherlock?"

Richard closed his eyes as if conjuring up a vision. He opened them and said, "I have no idea."

"You know, I have to take care of business here too," Henry said, and pointed his square chin at Patrick, who was already pulling a cart with suitcases into the terminal.

"Of course," Richard said, and handed him a ten-dollar bill. "When *you* assisted the man, did he go inside with you, to the counter? Do you remember what airline it was? Do you remember the suitcases?"

"Wow, one question at a time, pal! You got me all worked up and confused here."

"Sorry. Did he enter the terminal with you?"

"Yes. Walked maybe three yards behind me, but he was with me."

"Do you remember how he behaved?" Muhammad asked, remembering the man's careful behavior.

"Like any other passenger," Henry replied. Then, his eyes widened. "I just remembered. He tried his cell phone. I don't think he could see very well. He kept moving it back and forth, squinting at it."

"Do you remember what airline he was on?" Richard tried again.

Henry shrugged. "Sorry."

Richard thanked Henry, who rushed off to his next customer, then looked at Muhammad. "He wasn't flying to

Japan, or anywhere else. He was *practicing* something. Trying something out. I need to think. Let's get back to your cab."

They returned to the cab and pulled away. When they departed the airport, Richard broke the silence. "I think I know what he was trying to do. He was going to use the skycaps as mules. He wanted to deliver something inside, without actually delivering it himself. Something that would cause a lot of damage ... Something he could set off remotely, maybe with a few keystrokes of a cell phone ..."

"A cell phone," Muhammad muttered, remembering that strange behavior from the passenger too. "If you're right, there could definitely be trouble here someday ... and soon."

Chapter 27

The Nokia on Jacob's desk vibrated, and he jumped out of his skin. Well, almost. He *was* on edge, though. He stared at the vibrating cell phone, a simple, commonly used prepaid phone that cost him $100 cash when he bought it on craigslist.com. The seller was a young student, selling his belongings to pay debts. Another ludicrous behavior Jacob hated about Americans. Their obsessive consumption of material goods and eventual financial irresponsibility were disgusting.

Although he knew no one would associate him with the cell phone, even the fact that he carried something that would allow him to be tracked by GPS terrified him. Some might call it paranoia. He called it survival.

He scooped the phone into his hand and checked the display. He wasn't familiar with the number on the screen, a local number that ended with too many zeros. One that could have been dialed from any big facility. Such a facility could be a corporation; America had plenty of them. Or it could be a government office or agency, or even dialed from a public phone.

But *this* phone was for emergencies, and few had the number. So he assumed the worst. Rosemary and Helen were both working today, just outside his office door. He got up, still holding the phone as if it were a bad-tempered bear cub, crossed the room in two strides and closed the door. He covered the phone with the edge of his shirt and took a deep breath, pressed the talk button, and then said in his most feminine-sounding voice, "Hello?"

"Jay?"

He exhaled slowly. "This had better be good, Abbed."

"I'm on a pay phone, near you. Meet me whenever you can at the place where industry counts the most. It's important."

Jacob disconnected the call without replying, returned to his desk, put on his LA Lakers cap, and walked out of the office. As he passed the receptionist's desk, he told Rosemary, "I'll be back in an hour," and left.

Rosemary turned widened eyes to her coworker. "Wow, Helen, you'd think bees are after him."

Helen shrugged. "I don't think I've ever seen him move that fast. I hope nothing really bad happened."

* * *

Century City, a 200-acre commercial and residential district on the West Side of Los Angeles, was an important center for business, and many law firms, particularly those with ties to the film and television industries, had offices there. Its most well-known tower is Fox Plaza, a skyscraper used as the Nakatomi Plaza in the movie *Die Hard*. Jacob remembered how amused he was when he saw the actual building supposedly overtaken by terrorist criminals, and taken back by the tough Hollywood hero Bruce Willis. The movie was nonsensical to him, yet hilarious; he laughed until tears streamed down his face at the unbelievable plot, amazed that the American public actually believed heroes like the New York cop John McClane existed in reality.

Still chuckling at the memory, he walked on the Avenue of the Stars, crossed Century Park East and entered Century City Mall. He disliked shopping malls, not just for what they represented, but for their potential threat to him.

Security cameras and security personnel, and undercover loss-prevention officers were omnipresent. He'd never think of shoplifting, but the fact someone was secretly observing him gave him the chills.

The place where industry counts the most. Those were Abbed's instructions. Why couldn't things be as simple as "Meet you at Starbucks on Pico and Sepulveda." Yet caution was the most essential tool the team possessed. *I'm nearby,* means he's in Century City. And *the place where industry counts the most* must be the new multiplex cinema at the Century City Shopping Mall. This city revolves around the movie industry; this is Hollywood after all ....

Abbed was sitting in front of the cinema beneath an umbrella, checking out the women who passed on their way to the food court. Jacob entered the cinema and paid the admission price for a movie he thought nobody would be interested in seeing. His cap was low on his forehead, to prevent the cameras above the ticket counter from catching his face.

He walked toward the theatre and saw Abbed's reflection in the glassy advertisements for current movies, watched while Abbed walked to the cashier, bought an admission, purchased some popcorn, and walked toward the theatre. He made sure Abbed saw him entering one of the theatres, then stepped inside, walked to the far corner, and sat on a cushioned sofa-like blue seat. At this time of day, when fewer people were here, the dim theatre was a good place for a clandestine meeting.

Abbed arrived five minutes later, sat next to him and filled his mouth with buttered popcorn. Jacob wanted to choke him, but managed to control the urge.

"I'm listening," he said.

"We have a problem."

"*We?* What kind of problem do *we* have?"

"I think I got into some trouble with the 18th Street Gang." Abbed shoved a handful of popcorn into his mouth and looked straight at the screen, knowing Jacob's eyes were upon him.

Jacob remained silent for a while, digesting the information. When he spoke, his voice was empty and cold. "I'm listening."

Abbed sighed. "Look, I wouldn't have called unless I couldn't fix it myself. You know that. It was supposed to be the last job. Remember, I told you about it when we met last Friday? The job turned out unexpectedly well, and the guy wants me to keep working with them. They want in on the new job. I can't get out so easily.... It was made clear to me."

Jacob was silent for a long moment, then whispered, "I told you it was a bad idea."

"Not a bad idea. We made a lot of money in a short period of time. Much more profitable than your office gig. The problem is, I'm too good at what I do."

"That's always been your *problem*, hasn't it? You're so damn good, you don't know which *hazook* you should be sitting on." Jacob used a term he'd heard when he was a teenager. He thought a *hazook* was a flower bees would swarm around before they chose one to pollinate. When he grew older, he learned it referred to the male genitals. His mentor—Shudy—used this term to jokingly identify an ambivalent person.

Due to the circumstance at hand, this childhood memory wasn't a joyful one. "What do you want to do?" he asked nonchalantly, as if they were discussing the movie.

"Jose's the only one who knows me. If he's ... well ... removed, there'll be no one else to identify me, and I'll be off the hook." Abbed returned to chewing popcorn.

Jacob eventually replied, his voice lifeless, "Are you really stupid enough to believe that getting rid of one of them will do any good? All the people you were working with during your trips to Mexico, all the people you worked with here in LA ... don't you think they checked you out thoroughly before confiding in you?"

Abbed looked at him but didn't open his mouth. Clearly, the idiot hadn't considered this.

"You eliminate one of them, and you'll get all of the 18th Street Gang, the Mexican Mafia, and others I don't even know yet, after you," Jacob said.

Abbed's face showed fear, as he'd hoped for. They were comrades. However, with his analytic mind, he could see and analyze things Abbed couldn't even begin to understand. Their symbiosis was perfect. Jacob was the brain. Abbed was the muscle. Jacob the inventor, Abbed the executor. It had worked for a long time. Abbed had to trust him on this, too.

"What do you think we should do, Jay?" Abbed asked.

When Jacob finally spoke, his voice revealed real sadness. "I hate to tell you this, Abbed, especially after everything we've been through . . ."

"What? What?" Abbed, panicking, dropped the popcorn on the floor and turned his entire body to face him.

"I have no other choice. You've threatened the others now, and ... you can't continue with us here." This last sentence wasn't said with cruelty or anger, only pain and the beginnings of grief.

Abbed closed his eyes. Jacob knew he was trying to find some way to bargain for more time in the Disneyland of America. Finally, he opened his eyes.

"I'm sorry," Jacob said.

"So am I," Abbed replied with pain. And anger at what he was about to lose. Hurt in his eyes, he rose from his seat.

"I'll make sure you're deployed to Western Europe," Jacob said quietly. "Amsterdam's a good place for you. You can do good work and enjoy the lifestyle there."

Abbed didn't reply, just stood and turned to go. Without looking back, he exited the cinema. Jacob knew he'd head straight for his motorcycle, his pride and joy. One of the things Abbed loved most about America was owning one.

"But, they have motorcycles in Amsterdam too," he whispered, hoping that would be enough to salve Abbed's wounds.

Instead of his usual delay, he waited only a moment before exiting the cinema, wondering if he should go after Abbed. But he decided to return to his office. He'd let Abbed calm himself before he contacted him again.

Distracted by disappointment and anger, he failed to notice the waiter cleaning tables in the food court outside the cinema. The man looked like any other newly arrived Central American immigrant. He was actually following Abbed, but had just marked a new target. The waiter pulled a cell phone from his pocket, captured the view ahead as an image, and placed a call.

"*Cómo sea yendo, mano?*" was the fast reply.

"I just sent you a new description," the man said in Spanish. "I think he is *El Jefe*—the big fish."

Chapter 28

Dianne's beautiful face rested against his shoulder, her fingers entwined in his chest hairs while they lay on her bed. For a long time, Michael had hated his own maturation. Although Ibrahim supported and provided him with every material thing he possibly could, the few times he tried to talk to Ibrahim about his feelings and maturing physic, Ibrahim responded with, "Allah provides everything." Ibrahim didn't seek deeper explanations for anything; he simply drew on God's will as the answer to every question. As Michael was growing up, not having his father to talk to was tough and lonely, especially with personal questions that every teenager goes through. He spent hours in the school library reading books on puberty, but could never bring those books home; Ibrahim considered them the infidels' conspiracy doctrine.

Now, he looked at Dianne's magnificent curves, remembering the first time they'd really talked, on the bench outside the public library. They were having a conversation about sexuality in American TV commercials. Dianne was amused by his passionate objections. Teasing him, she asked, "But Michael, what's on television just reflects what Americans think and do. Haven't *you* ever had any sexual thoughts?"

He remembered how his cheeks burned with shame. Of course he had sexual thoughts. But as Ibrahim kept telling him for years, "The real hero is the one who suppresses his desires." How could he admit these thoughts plagued him while sleeping, while studying, and while talking to a lovely girl like her?

"What are you thinking?" she asked now, still playing with the hair on his chest.

"I had a very ... interesting day at school."

"Care to share?"

"Professor Vinitzky received a phone call from some Hollywood director. They want help with a television series called *CTA*. The professor wants me to meet with them, as a consultant, he said. To help them think of a new idea for harmful materials for their show."

She raised her head from his chest and read his eyes. "*CTA*? That's like the hottest show on television right now! Can you help them?"

"I ... don't know. I know some chemistry, but nothing about explosives or anything like that."

She thought a moment. "Did you check the Internet?"

He gave a disbelieving laugh he hoped sounded genuine. "Are you kidding? I don't need the FBI interrogating me for trying to cook up explosives. I mean, I appreciate the professor thinking of me, but I'm not even an American citizen." He caught himself and added, "Uh ... not yet, that is."

"Don't be silly, Michael. The FBI can't track everyone who searches for bombs on the Internet."

"They can't?" he asked, continuing to force a naive expression.

"Of course not. This country has, like, 300 million people or something, and maybe half of them use the Internet."

"But ... I heard someone say that they track those who log onto specific websites."

"True. But how can they know *why* someone's logging onto those sites? Do you remember the big news about the pedophiles a few years back?"

He shook his head. In truth, he hadn't.

"Well, the FBI tracked down some websites that had terrible child porn. They couldn't do anything about those who watched the disgusting things—'cause of all kinds of rules for freedom of speech and ... I don't know all the details. All I know is, they could only track down the website *operators*."

He nodded. "I see." And he did. But he also knew that the government could and did track the identities of users, not only to see what emails they sent and received, but what Internet sites they visited.

His thoughts were interrupted by her hand stroking his chest.

"And besides," she said, "*you* have a very good reason for visiting sites about ... like you said, about harmful materials. Heck, if anyone gets nosy about why you're on sites like that, your professor could back you up. Or hey," she nodded toward her computer on the desk next to the bed, "you could do it here."

Her idea had merit. Here, no one would peek over his shoulder. Or at least, no one who'd care. And records of visits to such sites from her computer might actually help with his plan.

He said quickly, "Do you mind?"

"No!" she replied, and giggled. "Anything I can do to help you in your new *television career*. But put your clothes on first. Don't want Mom and Dad catching you with your pants down." She winked at him and headed to her dresser.

"Okay, I'll do it," he said. "But, look ... let's keep it between you and me, okay?"

"Really? Why?" She was straightening her dresser now, so her back was to him.

"I ... I'd be embarrassed if anybody at *CTA* found out that I had to go to the Internet to find things out, just like they could have," he said. "That is, *if* I get the job."

He saw the back of her head bob up and down. "Sure, no problem. It'll be our secret."

I truly hope you mean that, he thought, feeling guilty already.

He dressed while looking at her naked body. Was it her

personality, or was it his lust that moved him so about her? He decided it was the latter, since lust was much less complicated to figure out. And placing the attraction on him, rather than her, seemed to make it a bit easier to keep his distance emotionally.

She dressed while he booted up her computer, then sat on his lap.

It was important she think this was the first time he'd ever searched on the subject. When he entered "explosives" into Google, and the results showed more than 40 million hits, he sighed dramatically. "It'll take me forever to check out all these."

"So narrow it down," she suggested. "Put 'explosives' *and* 'cookbook,'"

When he looked at her in surprise, she explained, "I heard that word on the news. They said the Oklahoma City Bomber had read some kind of cookbook for bombs."

Without replying, he typed this into the search field and hit enter. Now, only 100,000 hits showed matches. As he expected and hoped, the first result was a website called *The Anarchist Cookbook*.

"Told you," she said, her voice triumphant. "And wow, look at all that stuff! Recipes, instructions. Even excuses to use when purchasing bomb materials. Like a Dummies book for bombers!"

"Yeah," he said. "Amazing." And a page he'd always wanted to visit, but was afraid to—if the FBI watched any Internet users, they would surely give the visitors to this particular site close scrutiny, even though he'd heard that some of *The Anarchist Cookbook*'s methods were outdated.

After a while on his lap, she rose and started tidying her room. She made the bed again, but didn't change the sheets. Once, she'd told him she loved the scent of their sex to remain on her linens for a day or two. He didn't understand this, but it was her bed.

"You done yet?" she asked when she was finished.

He was busy memorizing the recipes' details. "In a

second," he said without raising his eyes.

"What do you want to do tonight ... except jump back into bed?"

"One second," he said again. He closed his eyes, using darkness to eliminate outer stimuli. He needed just a few more associations to tie up the entire story.

She stood by him, leaning forward so her face was horizontal to his, and asked, "What are you doing?"

He opened his eyes and stared softly into hers. "You have beautiful eyes. And I'm just trying to remember all the things I need to do tomorrow. Why?"

"You're so interested in that dumb website, you're neglecting me," she pouted, wrapping her arms around his neck and making herself comfortable in his lap again.

"Sorry. But here I am. Are you sure it's cool to surf here? The FBI won't knock on your door, will they?" he asked, and began kissing her neck.

"FBI knocking at *my* door? Yeah, right—"

Her answer was cut short by a soft chiming.

When she headed down the hall to answer the doorbell's call, Michael followed and grasped her arm to hold her back.

"What's going on with you?" she said. The doorbell rang again.

"Do you think it has anything to do with the websites?" Michael said. "I told you. I'm not an American citizen. It ... it will ruin everything!"

The hand on her arm was trembling now. "Relax. Nothing will ruin anything." She pulled gently away and started walking down the hall again.

Michael followed, but not into the living room. He stopped in the hallway, panicking, imagining agents waiting for him outside. He thought about Ibrahim and his attitude toward conflicts with the authorities. What would he say if he was caught? He thought about his father. What would he think about all this?

He heard the front door opening and tried to stop shaking. Impossible. From where he stood, he couldn't see who was there.

"Good evening, ma'am," he heard the authoritative voice say.

"Good evening, Officers," Dianne replied. Her voice held surprise now. And did he hear her say "Officers"?

His brain turned to full-emergency mode, shutting down his nervous system. He could stand here, or run away ... or he could face his fate.

He forced a casual expression and sauntered into the living room. Two men, dressed in black LAPD uniforms. One of the men was huge. The other was smaller and fair-haired, but still twice Michael's size. Both watched him curiously. He supported his weight on the back of a chair, fighting to keep his face normal.

"Are you all right, son?" the first cop asked, coming toward him.

Michael, embarrassed by his show of cowardice, moved around the chair and sat down. He couldn't look at them. He wished he could disappear under the seat. "I'm fine," he said in a voice he didn't recognize.

The officer nodded, then turned his attention back to Dianne and said quietly, "We brought the personal effects of David and William Holman. Is this the Holman residence?"

She gave a nervous but relieved laugh. "Oh, no. No, it isn't. The Holmans live two blocks down, on the other side of the street. This is 1196, they're at 1169. Sorry, wrong house."

"I'm truly sorry. It was our mistake," the officer said, signaling they should leave.

Her curiosity won over politeness. "You said 'personal effects.' What happened to the Holmans?"

"They ... were in an accident," he offered, and then they turned and left.

She stood by the door with her hand covering her mouth, not moving. Michael, who by now had collected himself, came over, shut the door and wrapped his arms around her.

"Who are David and William Holman?" he asked quietly, gently bringing her body close to his.

"My neighbors. Did you see their faces? They said they'd been in an accident. But their faces! They're dead! Poor Helen! I can't believe it."

She started to sob, and he continued to hold her. He also had tears in his eyes. However, his tears weren't of sorrow, but of relief. For now at least, he was off the hook.

Chapter 29

"Hey, wait up!" Joe managed to shout between labored breaths. Sweat covered his forehead. This whole bicycle thing was above his capability. Tim, it seemed, handled it much better. It was the third day they'd gone bicycling together, and for Joe, it was as hard today as the first time.

"Tim, wait up!" he called again.

Tim turned around and returned to where he was sitting. "What's wrong?"

"I'm finished," he gasped. "I need a break."

"There's a frozen yogurt place on Olympic and Westwood. The best frozen yogurt in the world. Please take me there, please Joe, please?"

Tim had annoyed him several times already with his childish behavior, and at times like these, he felt like he was Tim's babysitter. "Okay, okay, we'll go there. Stop whining and let me rest for a few moments, will you?"

Tim waited exactly two minutes before asking, "Can we go now?"

"Yes, but I'm walking. I can't ride anymore. My butt hurts."

"Okay," Tim agreed, and stood next to him, jiggling from one foot to the other.

They walked through the UCLA campus. Tim was surprisingly quiet now. Perhaps he was exhausted too, Joe mused. If anything could possibly exhaust him.

They crossed the tumultuous Wilshire and walked

along Westwood. "We're almost there," Tim said, his voice rising with excitement.

"Yeah, yeah," he replied. He just wanted the day to end already.

They continued on Westwood, Joe's neighborhood. He wanted to go straight home, but he had to escort Tim all the way back to the VA. He wished he could invite Tim to his apartment for a while, but he couldn't afford to reveal anything personal to this lunatic.

The line stretched all the way out the door of the small yogurt shop. Joe looked at it in disbelief. "Why is it so packed? Are they giving away free yogurt?"

"No. It's just the best yogurt in the world," Tim said, and licked his lips in anticipation.

"Whatever. Stand in line while I keep an eye on the bicycles," Joe said, a knot growing in his stomach. Frozen yogurt didn't even have nutritional value. It was simply a decadent pleasure for bored people. He thought about his childhood, when the ice cream truck would pass through his neighborhood in Lebanon. The truck's melody was heard only on Friday afternoons, after prayer. Only the kids whose parents could afford the ice cream waited eagerly on the side of the road. The memory filled Joe with both sadness and nostalgia. He thought about all the kids in his homeland who were forced to give up their childhood, going to work to help feed their families. Those children were never able to enjoy those treats. Joe knew this firsthand. He was one of those kids.

Tim finally came out of the store holding two huge cups of frozen yogurt and a smile to match his delight.

"I chose half peanut butter, half vanilla for you," he said and handed Joe his treat, then sat down and started licking his yogurt with apparent joy.

Joe didn't want it, but sat next to Tim and tasted it anyway. He had to admit it was delicious. The first spoonful flooded him with childhood memories. Memories of family values, poverty, superstition and religion—of home, where what was left of his heart would always remain.

He was so preoccupied with nostalgia, he failed to notice the police cruiser entering the parking lot until it was too late to get away without notice. Two uniformed officers got out of the car. The larger of the two stood in line while his partner, a fair-haired man, scanned the parking lot. His eyes fell on the odd couple sitting by the fence, eating yogurt. Joe took a casual bite, his eyes frozen to it.

But the line moved quickly, and it was the officers' turn. The blond one returned to the cruiser, took a spoonful of yogurt, then slowly, achingly slowly, placed the cup on the dashboard, spoke to his partner, and exited the cruiser. Even if Tim weren't with him to slow him, it was too late to flee.

"Good evening, fellas," the officer said, stuck his thumbs inside his belt and stood with his legs spread, waiting for a reply.

It's Tim, Joe realized suddenly. *That hole in his head. His hair—*

"Good evening, Officer," Joe said quickly.

"What's up, Officer?" Tim echoed.

"Not much. You have IDs with you?"

Joe felt as if a heavy weight had landed on his stomach along with the frozen yogurt he'd just eaten. Now, it was difficult to breathe.

"Hey, I have an ID," Tim said. "But what for?"

The officer smiled at him. Clearly, he'd already figured out that Tim wasn't quite right. "We've had some suspicious activity around here lately, and I'm just making a routine check. Show me your IDs, please."

Tim placed his cup on the fence and pulled his wallet from his pocket. He handed the officer his veteran's ID. The officer took the card and examined it, but only for a second. *So it's not Tim he's interested in?* Joe thought, watching, and his panic increased.

The officer kept the ID, but nodded at Tim. "Thank you for your service to our country."

Tim shrugged. "I didn't mind, at least until I got hurt. My head hurts a lot now." He lifted his free hand to the furrow in his scalp. "That's why I've got a hole here—to keep it from hurting too much when it gets all swelled up. But I was glad to help. That's what Americans are supposed to do."

The officer smiled at him and said, his voice a rasp, "Yeah, you're right. And ... thank you for helping."

The officer turned to Joe, and the sadness in his eyes changed to distrust. "What about you?"

Joe's efforts to remain calm were pointless. Cold sweat dripped from his armpits and covered his body now. He reached into his pocket for his ID, fully aware the officer was watching. The man's right hand rested next to his gun holster. Slowly, he handed the officer his passport. "Here you are."

The officer took the passport and said, "I'll be right back." Holding both IDs, he went to the police cruiser and took his seat. And there was absolutely nothing Joe could do about it except sit here, sweating, and try not to bolt. He tried to imagine what was happening in the car. First, they would type in Tim's name, even though the officer clearly wasn't interested in Tim, but in his companion.

Next, they would notice Joe's passport was from Belize, and spend a few seconds viewing the few US visa stamps inside. They wouldn't be familiar with the codes, though, so rather than trying to interpret them, they'd go ahead and enter the bearer's name into the computer—Joseph Banuas.

Joe assured himself they wouldn't find anything. His passport record was clean. They would have to let him go. He hoped with all his heart.

The fair-haired officer got out of the cruiser car and returned their documents. "Sorry for the inconvenience. Just checking." He saw Joe's sweating red face. "Everything all right?"

"Yes, Officer. I just couldn't keep up with Tim on the bike." He laughed and added, "Thank you for asking."

Still, the officer wouldn't leave. "I noticed you're from Central America," he said. "What are you doing in the States?"

"I'm with the missionary delegation of St. Joseph's Church," he replied promptly. The golden cross around his neck was intended to refute any suspicion about his cover story. Not only was he not from the Middle East, he was a Christian missionary to boot. To ward off any lingering doubts, he nodded quickly toward Tim. "This is part of our mission."

"Well, have a nice day," the officer replied, and finally, he appeared to lose interest and returned to his car. It took a moment for him to catch his breath.

It was close, but his passport had gotten him off the hook. And why wouldn't it? When he was in Canada three years earlier, looking into new ways of smuggling operatives into America, he happened across a magazine titled *Best Life*. A magazine targeting the upper middle class male, full of advertisements for luxury items. But further into the magazine, he saw an advertisement that showed an image of sandy beaches and palm trees. It said:

"PROTECT YOUR ASSETS.

COME TO BELIZE AND ENJOY YOUR RETIREMENT IN OUR TROPICAL PARADISE!"

And below that, in smaller print:

BECOME A PERMANENT RESIDENT OF BELIZE

OBTAIN A BELIZEAN PASSPORT!

He was amazed to discover that if a foreigner bought a piece of land in Belize, they were entitled permanent residency status, including becoming the bearer of an authentic, clean, Belizean passport.

Pursuing this led him to meeting Jacob for the first time, through a mutual contact in Vancouver. Jacob was skeptical, but went along after Joe said, "One year of residency, even if you don't live there, entitles you to a passport. They might do a background check, but what can they do—ask my teachers in Hermel how I behaved in high school?"

What clinched the idea in Jacob's mind was that Lebanese passports weren't welcome in the United States ... but Belizean passports were.

The process was much easier, faster, and cheaper than they anticipated. Joe's association with the Catholic congregation in Belize was almost as easy. Within a year, he had an R-1 passport—a religious worker's visa. He could get in and out of the United States without any problem. And no INS officer checking passports knew the bearer's place of birth—in Joe's case, a Muslim fundamentalist enclave in Lebanon.

The first part of his plan was accomplished perfectly, and so was the next. They infiltrated operatives into the United States, also equipped with genuine legal documents. When he later met with Jacob, he laughed about the ease of the plan. "Like a commercial for MasterCard," he said. "One acre in the Caribbean: $200,000. Government fee for residency: $19. Government fee for issuing a passport: $170. Getting into the United States legally: priceless!"

Jacob congratulated him, saying, "You have good ideas and creative thinking. I wish I could say the same about Abbed."

Having never met Abbed, Joe had no idea who he was talking about. Then. But he would learn. As Abbed would abruptly discover that Jacob was the kind of man who kept his promises.

Chapter 30

Abbed's absconding of the shopping mall was easy. His motorcycle's high-revving, muscle-car-inspired 16-valve V-4 engine produced power and momentum beyond his wildest dreams, exploding from 0 to 60 miles per hour faster than the time it took him to exhale. Even though at that moment, it felt as though he was driving a suicide mission. He passed Overland Avenue as if it were the racetrack at Daytona, aware of the speed trap just by Notre Dame High School but not caring. He was about to be forced to leave the country. Why should he care about a traffic ticket?

He merged onto the I-10 Freeway. Startled drivers cleared the lanes for him. Seeing their anxious glances, his ego soared. Soon, he maneuvered his bike along Venice Beach and parked on the road leading to the Venice pier. He took off his jacket and gloves and stored them, with his helmet, in the bike's storage compartment, then removed his shirt. He hated working out, but enjoyed the payoff: the attention and compliments from women, the jealous glances of less-muscular men. And now, it was showtime.

Selling the bike wouldn't be a problem. One phone call, and the broker who'd been salivating over it for months would meet him, cash in hand, no questions asked. But first, he needed a drink. Looking hip in his black shades, he walked confidently along the beach, nodding at people who looked familiar. Just across Muscle Beach, he chose a table on the outdoor balcony of a bar and ordered a Scotch on the rocks. He gulped it down, and ordered another.

He'd already pulled out his cell phone when a tall young woman on roller blades wearing skin-tight spandex rolled by on the sidewalk. Blonde, attractive, early twenties, and apparently eager to have some fun—exactly what he wanted. He returned the cell phone to his pocket and slipped his sunglasses to the edge of his nose for a better view. She sensed his stare, turned her head toward him and smiled provocatively. Still smiling, she glided past him, circled around and returned to where he was seated. He continued to gape at her without embarrassment, remembering to tighten his biceps. She was local, but what was the harm if he was leaving soon?

She slid smoothly to his table and sat beside him.

"What a wonderful surprise," he said and drained his glass, as though surprises like this happened to him all the time.

"My name's Karla."

Lovely accent. Most important, she revealed her name first. He wasn't sure anymore who was the predator and who was the prey. Not that it mattered.

"What would you like to drink?" he asked, pretending to be a gentleman. The end justified the means. And right now, the end was wrapped in tight spandex and needed a boost to loosen up.

"I'll have Gatorade, doesn't matter what flavor," Karla told the waitress.

"Another for you?" the waitress asked Abbed, pointing to his empty glass.

"Sure, why not?" he said, still smiling even though his mind was conflicted. *The perfect life is right here and now,* he thought in a mental pout. *And I have to leave it.* Even his mother wouldn't recognize him—his new look, his fondness for alcohol, and his attraction for hot, non-Muslim women. Like Karla, who was running her fingers through her hair. Just what he needed to recover from that awful encounter with Jacob.

"Where are you from, Karla?"

"Norway. Why? Can you tell by my accent?" She giggled.

"Only that you're from Scandinavia," he replied. *Perhaps Amsterdam won't be a bad place to live after all.*

"What's your name?" she asked.

"Abe."

"Like Abraham Lincoln?" she asked, still smiling.

"Yeah, something like that." He laughed and added, "But not as honorable."

Their beverages arrived. "So, what do you do?" he asked, feigning interest.

"I'm a student at Santa Monica College," she answered. "Photography."

"That's nice." He was a bit tipsy, and wasn't in the mood for a long flirtation. Time to move things along. "What type of photography?"

"Mainly artistic black and white," she answered. "Why? Do you have any experience with photography?"

"I have experience, but not with photography. Do you want to play photography?"

"Play photography? What do you mean?" she taunted, amused.

"We can go into your darkroom and see what we can develop." He winked at her.

She laughed openly. "That's a good one! And what if I told you I'm afraid of dark places?"

"I'll hold you close, don't worry." The entrapment was set, and the prey had walked willingly into it.

Three minutes later, he pulled some bills from the roll he extracted from his pocket, placed them on the table beneath his glass, and took her hand.

"Wow!" she exclaimed when she saw the bike—exactly the reaction he expected. From experience, he knew women got excited by a motorcycle, but didn't necessarily want to ride with him. Appreciating a wild animal like this was one thing.

Trying to conquer it was something different.

* * *

Her apartment's walls were covered with black and white photographs. One of them was of Karla, her back to the camera, naked. She had perfect buttocks, he noticed.

She was removing her roller blades, but noticed him noticing. "That's one of my favorites."

He turned to her. "That's mine too."

She laughed, went to the window and closed the curtains, then came over to him and whispered, "Are you ready to hold me close now?"

* * *

When he climbed onto his motorcycle again, it was dark outside. As always, he left his prey panting and exhausted, captivated and satisfied, the soul-sustenance he needed to prove he was worthy. Fleeting feelings, but enough to boost his ego. Now he rode his bike cautiously, no longer needing the adrenaline high it had given him before. The well-being he felt now—a feeling worth dying for. Worth living for.

He laughed when he remembered Karla's request. Especially how she had expressed it. She watched him get dressed, and asked in a sweet voice, "So, Abe, how can you help me buy photo supplies?"

Confused, he asked, "Help you do what?"

She gestured toward her nude photograph. "It costs a lot of money to develop those things."

Initially, her straightforwardness shocked him, but he admired self-confidence that was so much like his. "You *are* good," he said and reached into his pocket.

"I know," she replied, and her innocent expression

triggered another laugh from him.

He placed some bills on the dresser. Still smiling, he said, "You deserve it ..." and walked to the door, turning around to ask her for her phone number "... in case, um, we feel like playing in the darkroom again."

* * *

He didn't rent an apartment, but instead lived in a suite at the Holiday Inn. His cover as a foreign computer engineer employed by an American company was believable. Just in case, every three months he switched hotels to avoid suspicion.

He pressed the button for the 14th floor—really the 13th floor, but Americans, advanced as they seemed to be, were still superstitious. He had no problem walking underneath a ladder, and didn't spit when he saw a black cat. He didn't like cats, but had no problem with their existence. Dogs were a different story. Muslims all over the world regarded a dog as a dirty animal that, when touched, would give you impurity. "Dog" in Arabic—*kalb*, became a common nickname for the evil and corrupted.

The elevator arrived with a soft whoosh and an electronic chime, and he walked down the long corridor to his room. He stood before the door and studied the electronic card key that would grant access to it, smiling, thinking of the James Bond movies he'd seen. Of Secret Agent 007 attaching a hair from his head to the doorframe with his own saliva, to know whether anyone entered his room while he was out. Wouldn't work for him, of course. How would the housekeeper get into his room to clean? So he never kept anything suspicious in his room. Except for his laptop computer, on which he'd installed multiple security nets and features. Like Bond's trick with the single hair, no one could access his computer without him knowing.

He slid his card key into the reader. When the green

light blinked, he turned the handle and stepped inside. The room was dark. No surprise. The housekeepers closed the curtains after tidying. Even so, he sensed something wrong even before reaching for the light switch.

He closed his eyes, waiting. He'd always thought his demise would be something heroic, something that ended in a booming noise and flashing lights. A martyr's end. He didn't want to die, not when life offered him so many pleasures. But if someone were here, ready to take his life, he'd make sure it was special for both of them.

Keeping his eyes closed, he listened for the sound of a knife slicing the air on its way to his throat, or the sickening metallic sound of a gun releasing a deadly bullet. When neither came, he slowly outstretched a finger to turn the light on, but stopped. The light bulb might be a bomb that exploded once the light was switched on. He had used the technique himself.

Leaving the light switch alone, he stepped into the dark room, touching the wall to his left to become acclimated, passed the short distance from the door to the kitchen and switched on the kitchen light. The pupillary reflex made him blink several times to help his eyes adjust to the sudden brightness.

He scanned the small kitchen. Everything seemed in order.

Maybe the whole thing was just in my head. The encounters of the day influenced my lucidity, perhaps. Or perhaps too much alcohol and sex playing tricks on my mind.

Smiling at the last, he dropped his bike keys, on the small kitchen table, then placed the card key beside it.

"It's about time."

The rapid drop in his blood pressure caused the hair all over his body to bristle, and his bladder suddenly felt full. The quiet voice had come from the living room, behind him.

He eased his body around. Jacob sat on the sofa in the corner, his legs crossed, his back straight. His hands rested in his lap. "Where've you been?" he said. "Did you go to boost your ego between some woman's legs?"

Abbed made it to the sofa and sank down next to Jacob, and stared at him, confused. Certainly, he was relieved the intruder turned out to be Jacob. Yet he was angry too, that Jacob had put him through such a harrowing moment.

"What's going on, Jay?"

"Since I smell alcohol on your breath, is it possible you've forgotten what we discussed at our meeting this afternoon?" Jacob's tone was sharp, angry.

"No, I didn't forget. I haven't. How could I?" He leaned back on the sofa. "But I wish for my personal life to remain personal."

"That's where you're wrong, Abbed." Jacob pierced him with burning eyes, his jaw tensed and the veins at his temples prominent. "It's not about you and me. We're nothing in the Higher Cause. Just pawns of the game. Do you understand?"

Not waiting for Abbed's reply, he continued. "We should be ready to sacrifice our lives for the success of this operation. Remember?"

Abbed nodded unwillingly, waiting for the lecture to be over, and focused on an invisible spot on the floor.

"You were *brought* here. You didn't just arrive by yourself, you were brought here! You should've done anything to help *me and the others* achieve our ultimate goal. Do you even remember that goal, Abbed?"

Abbed nodded again, his eyes never leaving the invisible spot on the floor.

"Do you? When you came here, I was told you'd be *my* special operations man. That you'd be the one who pulled the trigger, even if the muzzle were aimed at your own head. Yet, what happened? You created your own objectives."

Abbed could stand it no longer. "Are you jealous? Do you envy my lifestyle?"

Jacob held his hand up. "It's not about me. It's about making sure our next generation won't be infected by *their* lifestyle. It's about *their* attempts to suppress Islam. It's about *their* ethnocentrism, and the duty *they* imposed upon themselves to dictate *their* order. And you needlessly aligned yourself with *them*, and put us all at risk!"

Jacob seemed finished, and calmer, but Abbed didn't reply. They'd been comrades for more than two years. No, longer than that. Yet he felt like a little child who'd been caught in mischievous attempts to gain attention.

Jacob was waiting for him to respond. That, he knew. And nothing he could say would make a difference. Yet he had to at least try. "No one could have accomplished what I have in such a short period of time. You know that."

"True. But it goes both ways. Time's an advantage we have, one the infidels don't. We needed another year or two to gather the intelligence, we need to have the greatest impact since 9/11. No one would've spotted us raising funds slowly and secretly. But now, we have someone who thinks we're pissing in their swimming pool, and they're demanding their share of our profits. I still can't believe you got involved with the 18th Street Gang. What were you *thinking*?"

"It was the best way to get a lot of money fast," he replied, unsure whether he was trying to convince Jacob or himself.

"And why did we need money *fast*?" Jacob's voice was angry again as he waved his hand toward the furnished room. "For this? Your ostentatious bike, your flashy wardrobe? Or was it simply enough to ensure you get laid regularly?"

"*Bikafi*—Enough!" Abbed said. "I did my best for the operation. I can't turn back the clock. And just to let you know, I think I may have discovered another way to meet our objectives. I—"

"You received something today," Jacob said as if he didn't hear Abbed's last sentence. He jerked his chin toward the coffee table, at the brown manila envelope he'd laid there. "Slid underneath the door. It's safe. I already saw what's inside."

Abbed opened the envelope and removed the two eight-by-ten photographs it contained. The photos showed a domestic car, or what was left of it, and the bodies of a young boy and an older man wearing a blue uniform—a uniform he recognized. Both bodies were covered in blood, both men clearly dead. On one of the photos someone had written, "I told you how much I mean business. Now it's your turn, *essè*!"

"*Allah Yistor*—Oh my god," he whispered, but couldn't pull his eyes away.

"They know where you live," Jacob said quietly. "How long before they find out what you do—if they haven't already? Now, we have to move fast. You placed us all at risk. It might be too risky for you as well."

He looked up at Jacob. "Are you ... threatening me?"

Jacob smiled unhappily and gestured toward the photos. "Do I really need to? And don't you think you've earned some ... threats?"

He swallowed heavily, decided his best chance was to try to mollify him. "Look, here's my idea. I'll move to Miami and chill a bit. Then we'll continue what we started here in LA. You need me to stay in the country, you know that."

"Miami? No. That, that *gang* would find you there too. You have to leave the country, disappear for a while." A long moment passed before he added, "I'm afraid if you're too stubborn about this, you might disappear for good."

Then he stood, pulled something from his back pocket and dropped it onto the coffee table. "Your ticket to Amsterdam. Tomorrow, 6:00 p.m. Business class, of course. Someone'll meet you at Schiphol. You'll love the women there. We'll take care of your belongings here. Except the bike. Get rid of it before you leave. Take a taxi to the airport. Call me once you're there. I need you to do something at the terminal before you leave."

He looked at Abbed for his reaction, found none. "Don't try to be a smartass. This isn't personal. Once we accomplish what we've started, you'll get credit for all you've done."

Abbed nodded and stood, sighed loudly and walked to the door. He opened it, turned around, and leaned on the wall beside it.

Jacob rose and made to leave, but stopped next to him without looking at him. "I'm sorry, Abbed. *Allah Ma'ak*—May God be with you."

He exited the open door just as Abbed replied, "*WuMa'ak Kaman*—And with you too," and slammed the door behind him.

Chapter 31

He felt uneasy when he placed the call—he was calmer by the time he left her house, but he'd still left abruptly. But when he heard her voice inquiring about his wellbeing, he forgot everything else.

"I'm fine, I guess," he said in reply, and fiddled with the rental car's steering wheel. "More important, are *you* all right?"

"I ... don't know," Dianne replied. "I knew Billy from high school, but not really well—he was a freshman when I was a senior. So I guess I'm okay. But Mom and Dad were shocked last night when I told them about the Holmans. Especially Mom. I never mentioned it, but she and Helen—Billy's mom—work at the same place. Helen helped her get the job at the charity where they work. So Mom took it really hard, and she's trying to help Helen, but ... I can't even imagine losing a husband and my only child at the same time like that, can you?"

"I'm sorry. I wish there was something I could do."

"As a matter of fact, there is. Tell me what happened to you yesterday."

Her voice had changed, become ... cautious. He eventually replied, "I don't know. I was so scared everything would blow up in my face and all my plans would go down the drain, you know. My plans to become a citizen," he added quickly. "And maybe even getting that job with *CTA*."

"I understand, I guess. But ... it's not like you're doing

something wrong.... Are you?"

"Umm, no."

He heard her sigh. "Michael, there's nothing more important to me than honesty. I don't want to live my life like my parents did. By the time they got divorced, they had so many secrets, you couldn't tell what was true or bullshit with them. Promise me ... no matter what, you'll always tell me the truth, even if you know I won't like it."

"Sure."

"No! Think about it, *and then* answer."

He counted to five, then said, "Sure. I will."

"Now, back to my question. You were so freaked out by those police officers. And that freaked me out. I need to know why."

When he spoke again, he was able to make his voice calm and steady. "There's nothing you don't already know. I'm simply a foreigner in this country. And as one, I need to avoid getting into trouble. I'm sorry for the way I acted yesterday." *And can we change the subject already?*

He heard her sigh, this time in relief. "I'm glad we talked it over. So what are you doing today?"

"I have a meeting with my professor and the director from Showtime. Do you want to meet later on?"

"Sure. Call me when you're through."

"I'll give you a ring when I get out of school."

"Give me a ring?" she replied, laughing. "It's easy to tell you're British. Bye, honey bun."

"Goodbye," he said and switched off his cell phone, shaking his head. It was only in America where people twisted phrases so badly, nobody knew what they meant anymore. He'd lived in America for almost four years, but still had to ask people about the idioms they uttered. When he asked one teacher about the origin of "goodbye," the befuddled reply was, "I don't know. It's been used for years."

Later, he learned that "goodbye" actually came from "God be with ye." This lack of awareness, even amongst his teachers, convinced him that Ibrahim was right all along. Westerners were shallow, with no heritage or culture, and that showed in their language. Each phrase of the Arabic language was full of heritage, history, and meaning—all of which every schoolchild was taught along with their grammar lessons.

He walked from his car to a 7-Eleven on Westwood, feeling the superiority Ibrahim had worked so hard to instill in him. The Lebanese man at the counter was busy helping another customer. Michael was tempted to start a rare conversation in his native tongue, but decided not to. Instead, he pulled out a roll of bills and asked to purchase a money order. When he first arrived in the country, lacking a Social Security number, he couldn't open a bank account. So, he'd rented his apartment with a money order. When he signed the lease agreement, he noticed the landlord had written "Michael Sloan" instead of "Michael Siluan." Realizing it was a lucky break, he never corrected it. So, five years later, he still paid his rent with a money order, and received his mail at a nearby Mail Boxes Etc., leaving no way to track him down under his real name.

He returned to his car and thought of Dianne, and a pang of guilt hit him. He hadn't wanted to lie to her. She was the only woman he'd ever respected. When he first met her, Abbed insisted on giving him advice, and Jacob encouraged him because he thought it would work well into their mission. Yet both men's attitudes toward women were degrading, to the point where Abbed often referred to Dianne as *sharlilla*—slut.

Even then Michael was able to stay detached, both emotionally and mentally. Jacob's idea made perfect sense, and whatever Jacob approved was Michael's guiding principle. When the relationship began to evolve, though, he found there were many more traits to the person they'd called *sharlilla*. Sometimes, like now, he wished that hadn't happened. Seeing the good in her made what he must do someday that much more difficult.

* * *

The long distance from UCLA's parking lot to the faculty offices allowed him to compose his thoughts about Dianne and her easygoing lifestyle. With Ibrahim's influence, Michael was programmed to criticize her way of life. However, as he spent more and more time with her, he learned some important lessons. Although she wasn't ambitious and didn't wish to expand her horizons—well, any more than those illustrated in *InStyle* magazine—she wasn't unkind, and didn't have cruel intentions toward anyone. He found it hard to admit, but he'd learned to appreciate the lifestyle she shared with his fellow students. But although it bothered him to keep secrets from them, he didn't dare share this changed attitude with Jacob, Abbed or Joe.

He climbed the stairs two at a time, arriving at Young Hall ten minutes early, and walked down the corridor to Professor Vinitzky's office. He'd raised his hand to knock when he saw the door open a crack, and pushed slightly on the door. He distinguished Professor Vinitzky's plump shape, and recognized UCLA's head of security. He'd known McClain would be there, but unaccountable alarm bells sounded in his head, remembering the hard time McClain gave him before. He thought of all the years he'd spent preparing for the operation, and how frustrating defeat would be now, when they were so close to finishing.

Instinct took over. They were by the window, looking out. What were they looking at? Perhaps a backup team waiting outside? He looked left, toward the end of the hallway. A sign read "Emergency Exit" and led to the emergency stairway. No. Too easy. Too predictable.

The young woman bumped into him before he realized she was even there. He caught her outstretched arms as she collapsed to the floor, her briefcase tumbling open to release a stream of papers that scattered around her.

"I'm so sorry," he mumbled, and stooped to help her

collect the papers, which turned out to be glossy, full-color brochures. He stacked them and started to hand them to her, but stopped. On each cover was the title, "Counter Terrorism Agency," with photographs of an exploding car.

He glanced at the woman. Modestly dressed in a navy suit and matching shoes, around her neck dangled a red lanyard with a plastic identification card. The red and white card showed her picture and, in large letters, "Showtime."

He apologized again and asked, "Melissa?"

Her eyes narrowed. "Do we know each other?" Then she sighed and picked up her picture ID. "Oh, you saw my name. No, I've never met you before, and we don't know each other. And now, if you'll excuse me, I'm running late for a meeting."

"It's the same meeting I'm going to," he said. "I'm supposed to assist you and my professor ... Professor Vinitzky?"

"Oh, sorry. Can you show me to his office?"

"Of course." He gestured toward the door.

Professor Vinitzky was sitting at his desk now; McClain still stood by the window.

Melissa shook hands with them after being introduced, then handed each of them her business card before spreading the brochures on a small conference table. "*CTA*'s scriptwriters have many ideas on how terrorists might attack the nation, and our episodes unfold these plans and plots. But, after several successful years, the writers are looking for new ideas." She smiled at Michael. "Young ideas."

Vinitzky took one of the brochures and placed it on the pile of papers on his desk. "It sounds interesting. What do you want from us, though?"

"An upcoming story line has a group of students who basically concoct a bomb. We want you to help us create a chemical composition that would act as improvised explosives. In other words, generate something the viewers would see and say, 'Why didn't we think of this before?' The writers will also want Michael's input on setting up the scenes where the students actually make the bomb. In exchange, we'll include a credit with special thanks to UCLA for their cooperation and conception."

She crossed her legs and waited for their reply.

Professor Vinitzky arched his brows at McClain, who nodded vaguely. Then he said, "Mr. McClain is in charge of public safety here at the school. I'd like to hear what he has to say."

McClain said, "In the interest of protecting UCLA, my duty is to ensure the ideas we give you won't be used by ... undesirables. I don't want to make a terrorist's life easy by giving out instructions for their next *event*."

Melissa nodded. "Okay. Although I'm not sure why you're so concerned about that. Everything a terrorist needs to know is on the Internet nowadays. And of course our legal people vet anything that goes into the script for each and every episode."

McClain leaned forward. "What I mean to say is, we'll watch this project closely with Professor Vinitzky and the student he assigns."

"Totally understood," she said, dismissing him, then turned to Professor Vinitzky, who removed his glasses and wiped them clean with a tissue before speaking. "Michael will be your contact. I'll guide him and supervise the process. Mr. McClain will monitor *all* of us."

She turned hard eyes on him. "How old are you, Michael?"

"Almost twenty-two," he answered.

"Perfect age," she said, smiling. "Call me when you have an idea. I don't want to pressure you, but I need you to cook something up as soon as possible."

So do I, Melissa, Michael wanted to say. *So do I. And your request has essentially given me the key to the bank vault.*

Chapter 32

As soon as Melissa left, Michael turned to Vinitzky. "So, Professor, what shall I do to satisfy this lady?"

Vinitzky adjusted his glasses. "Check the Internet and see what looks flashy. You can use one of the computers in the lab. We'll try to compose something harmless that will still sound and look good to TV viewers. I even thought about your project, the one we . . ." he looked at McClain, "disapproved. It might work for her. Whatever you come up with, email me and copy McClain. We'll check it out and handle it from there. Agreed?"

"Sure," Michael said, and shrugged. *Free access to hazmat in the lab? I surely can use that.*

McClain misinterpreted his shrug. "Look, son, my duty here at school isn't easy. And I have to admit, I have some concerns about this project. I told Ed here I want to watch things closely. After all, you're not even an American citizen."

Despite his racing heart, Michael felt the blood draining from his face. *He'll watch it closely, all right.* "How do you want to work it, then?"

McClain smiled broadly, then stood. "Leave the details to me. We'll be in touch," said and left.

Michael turned to Vinitzky after the door closed behind McClain.

"There are two aspects here," the professor began. "First, the ingredients should be easily available. We don't want Showtime's viewers to ask where the heck a terrorist could obtain C-4. Second, you should look into the detection technology available. And we need to make whatever we come up with a step short—so there are no avenues terrorists can follow for an actual attack. Questions?"

Michael thought for a moment. "Isn't that what McClain warned us about? Giving ideas to bad guys? I don't want to mess this up with him, you know. I'm not a *citizen*."

Vinitzky ignored the sarcasm. "Whatever you discover, we'll filter it in a way nobody can copy a harmful process. Email updates to me as you progress. I recommend you try the Mentos-and-Coke experiment as a start. You might get some ideas there."

"Will do," Michael said, and stood. "I'd better get going. I'll give you an update as soon as I can."

He walked quickly to the chemistry lab and sat at one of the computer stations. He had no hesitation or fear now. He was doing this on behalf of his school and professor. His activities on the computer would be monitored by McClain, but dovetailed perfectly with his part of the mission. Better than the best cover story he could invent. Jacob would be pleased.

And now, he could try an idea he'd had ever since the day he'd read about CTX machines in *Scientific American*.

He typed his student username and password onto the computer and waited. When the UCLA homepage appeared, he clicked on it, opened Google, and typed "security" and "technology" into the search field.

The screen filled with thousands of hits. Some were security companies, others the pages for security consultants. Remembering it from the public library, he clicked on the General Electric website, then the link to their flagship security device, the Automated Explosives Detection Machine.

Thirty minutes later, he'd learned a great deal more about explosives detection technology, and the process in which the machine showed positive hits. But now, he needed to learn the machine's limitations. For once, there wasn't enough on a Web page to answer the questions rolling in his mind. But he'd spent so much time wishing he could do this, he felt prepared.

He wrote questions he thought of in bullet points, then logged off the computer and left, heading for the teaching assistants' office, normally occupied by Ph.D.-candidates but deserted at this time of day. He sat at the TAs' desk and picked up the phone, dialed 8 to get an outside line, then the long number on the sheet of paper.

"Good afternoon, General Electric, this is Brian speaking. How may I direct your call?"

The first step, he decided, was to use language impressive enough to confuse. "Hi, Brian, my name is Michael, and I'm working on a project in the Science Department at UCLA. We're conducting an experiment using improvised substances that react with sublimation or rapid changes in status from solid into gas. We need to check the market for detection of such substances, and therefore need a further description of your automated explosives detection machine's capabilities. In particular, the substances it can detect ... and the ones most likely to show false positives."

The tactic worked beautifully. "Uh ... That's not really my area, Michael, but ... what I can do is mail or fax a brochure with all of the information about the explosives detectors we have—some things that aren't on the Web page. All the information a prospective buyer would want. Do you want me to mail it to you, or fax it?"

Could it really be this easy? He glanced at the nearby fax machine. "I'd appreciate a fax."

When the call ended, he returned the receiver to the cradle. Moments later, the fax machine began to hum. He removed the printed sheets and read them in amazement.

Finally I see how you wake up in the morning, he thought. *And from what I see, there'll be a lot of people in LA County who won't wake up anymore—*

His cell phone buzzed once, indicating a text message. It read, "Meet me by the cafeteria."

The message wasn't a concern. But the messenger's name shocked him. *He never comes here! Something's happened!* He quickly shredded the papers and headed for the cafeteria.

He almost reached his destination when the familiar, calm voice greeted him from a bench to the left of the entrance. Jacob kept his newspaper in front of his face. Michael took one of the school's newspapers from a metal rack in the cafeteria entrance and sat on the bench beside him.

"We've had a change, and I wanted to let you know as soon as possible," Jacob said from behind his paper. He explained Abbed's sudden relocation, then said, "And now, tell me what's happening with you. Thanks to Abbed's stupidity, and Joe's, we might be depending solely on your plan now."

Michael glanced over the newspaper to see whether anyone was watching, and started explaining the new development with Showtime. As he did, he noted that Jacob constantly glanced over the newspaper at the activity beyond it, as if he were starring in an old spy movie. The only thing missing, he thought, were two holes in the center of the newspaper through which Jacob's eyes could observe the surroundings without lifting his head. It was difficult not to chuckle at that, but he managed.

Once he finished, Jacob said, "*CTA?* I've been watching it. You never know what you can learn from shows like that. In my opinion, they just complicate matters, though. A plan should never have to be as complicated as they make it."

Michael nodded. "So, knowing what you know, do we really want to launch a TV script?"

To Jacob's confused expression, he explained, "It's like *Debt of Honor*, a book I read back in England. The author used an aircraft to blow up a place. I guess that's why I wasn't surprised when someone eventually followed the instructions in that book. So again, do we really want to launch in reality what they show on TV?"

Jacob shook his head almost violently. "No way. All we need to give them is something that ends in a big boom. Something sophisticated, yet not too complex. We don't care for ratings, you know."

"So we'll use high explosives," Michael half asked, half stated.

"And where will you obtain standard high explosives?" Jacob asked, then caught himself. "I suppose that's why you're spending a fortune at UCLA, isn't it? I'm sure you'll learn how to create the best and most lethal substance. Hollywood will shoot a film about you a few years from now." Jacob's words were light, but his tone held no humor.

"I don't need the exposure," Michael replied quickly. "I'm committed to our cause, nothing else." Then, after a moment, he asked, "Jacob ... do you ever fear the authorities might capture us?"

Jacob gave a short laugh. "They aim so high, they never see the simple things under their noses. Do you know what it reminds me of? The beginning of the space era. The American astronauts had problems filling out reports in space. Their ballpoint pens didn't work—no gravity. So NASA invested a few million dollars and their best engineers to invent the space pen. It could write upside down and in almost any atmosphere or condition."

Michael waited for the punch-line, but it never came. "So?"

"So the Russians kept using a pencil, like they always had."

He had to grin at Jacob's rare joke. "That was a good one."

Jacob gave a small shake of his head. Michael carefully looked around at the students who passed through the cafeteria. A janitor cleaning the floor was almost within hearing distance from the corner table where they sat. Jacob waited patiently until she went in another direction. Michael looked at his watch. Dianne was waiting for him.

"So what's next?" he asked.

"I think the new development at school is a good one," Jacob said. "But don't neglect your relationship with your *sharlila*. It'll pay back eventually."

He nodded. There were so many things he wanted to say about his '*sharlila*,' but preferred not to.

"We should shift into higher gear," Jacob continued. "We'll have to outline our mission and targets soon. There've been too many ... failures. We need to finalize a plan, likely the plan I hope you'll have soon."

Michael thought about what Jacob said, nervousness growing in his stomach. He looked at Jacob, trying to find answers in his dark eyes. Jacob noticed.

"Michael, the only difference between us is, I've been here longer. I don't have all the answers, and we both know you're smarter. What do *you* think that plan should be?"

He didn't know whether Jacob praised him just to encourage, or whether he really believed Michael was smarter. Still, he was given an opportunity to offer and idea. "I think we should target a school. Look at this university. Look how many people are here. Even the cafeteria ... or better yet, a Bruins game. Either can be a great target."

Jacob nodded. "I wouldn't attack this yuppie school, though. Might give the wrong impression that we're some kind of modern Robin Hoods, punishing the wealthy. On the other hand, if an attack happened in, say, a rural area where there were no Special Forces or federal law enforcement, the consequences would be horrific. No doubt, there's a group planning an operation like that. Schools, especially elementary schools. Hospitals. Places like that would be targets.

"But, I still think an airport the size of LAX makes a terrific target. For the economic impact alone. I know there were several other targets marked. But let other groups take them. Better for everyone. Compartmentalization can help us keep working, and not defeat any other group."

"So we're staying with LAX," Michael said. "Even

though Joe failed his rehearsal and Abbed won't help?"

Jacob sighed. "In spite of Joe's failure, the best inventions are always the simplest. The ones where you ask, 'Why didn't we think about this before?' In the end, Abbed only contributed to the funding, not ideas. Joe's idea was good, it just needs shifting. Your idea's even better. And I have an idea of my own."

He smiled and added, "And I'm sure all these TV shows can give us even more. People are fed movies and TV shows—fantasies—while the government won't even supply the right information. So we'll let them look for a needle in a haystack while *we* see the big picture."

Jacob flipped the newspaper he was holding, making a rustling noise. "*They* wait for intelligence to bring them suspects. If we continue being careful, we'll never be in their intelligence databases, not even after we strike. So stay optimistic and creative. And don't forget, keep it simple."

"But what makes a plan *simple*?" Michael said. "It seems like every idea we've considered seems simple, but it really isn't."

"By sticking to basics. The element of surprise. Using available resources. Combined, it'll be like burying them in the pothole they dug themselves."

"What would the ... the *pothole* be at LAX?"

"I don't know. I'm depending on you for the idea."

Michael gave him a smile he hoped looked confident. "Well, I'd better get going. I have something cooking...."

"Be careful out there, Chuck Tower," Jacob said, and winked.

Chapter 33

"We're on the road to nowhere..."

Talking Heads sang through the car's amplified sound system while the dense urban environment changed to a green tree-lined upper-class suburban landscape. Vicky shifted gears and cruised along the road effortlessly. She could still smell the seductive perfume scent she'd applied generously before dressing. There was no underwear under the dress she wore, and she enjoyed the feel of cool cotton against her skin.

She picked up the cell phone from her purse on the passenger seat, pushed a button and read the latest text message. She smiled and felt a familiar flush spread over her face. The message came just after lunch, when her level of energy was at its lowest point and she was in the middle of a session with a client: "Will Rogers, sunset, lustful, R."

She rehearsed multiple scenarios in her mind for the rest of the session. They kept her awake. Will Rogers Park at sunset. Yet she had sharp words ready for him. Asking her to come lustful, as if there was any other choice!

She closed her office early and drove home. Once there, she looked for the sexiest outfit appropriate for an outdoor activity. She didn't know what plans Richard had in mind. A hike through the Backbone Trail, perhaps? She shivered, thinking of him making love to her on top of Santa Monica Mountain beneath a "lucky" tree. Or, there might be a gathering in the polo field she wasn't aware of. So she couldn't show up in cargo pants and a t-shirt, her first choice. She decided on a plain greenish-turquoise cotton dress to match her eyes and comfortable sandals. Now she was ready for any occasion. "As long as it involves sex in the outdoors," she whispered, smiling.

The parking lot at Will Rogers was unmanned at this time of day, and sparsely occupied except for a few scattered cars. She easily spotted Richard's car and pulled in next to it, then checked her face in the rearview mirror, popped a Mentos into her mouth, took her purse and locked her car.

She looked around, hoping to see his silhouette on the grassy area, but didn't. She'd just pulled her cell phone from her purse when she saw the folded note flapping underneath his windshield wipers.

"Oh, Inspiration Point." She nodded, smiling. "Appropriate."

She started walking up the marked trail, cursing herself now for choosing sandals instead of sneakers. The trail was beautiful, though. She inhaled the smell of the gigantic eucalyptus planted along the way. Two riders on horses maneuvered their great animals gracefully down the hill, looking at her with admiration as they passed.

"Okay, so maybe sandals were a better choice than sneakers," she whispered to herself, flattered.

By the time she climbed the hill to Inspiration Point, the sun had nearly vanished over the Pacific Ocean, replaced by a perfect blend of purples and pinks. On top of the hill, she saw a wooden picnic table. On the table were a picnic basket and two lit candles. Richard sat on the bench, holding a glass of red wine in his hand. But for the first time since she'd met him, he wasn't grinning from his first sight of her.

She decided not to push to find out why right now, just leaned forward to kiss him and said, "Hey, stranger."

"Hey, gorgeous." He handed her a glass of wine. They toasted, drank, and she placed her glass on the table and peered into the picnic basket. "What do we have here?"

"Some good stuff." He placed his glass next to hers and

started emptying the basket. A fine baguette sliced into thin discs, assorted pickles, raw vegetables arranged on a large plate by color, and goat cheese. The soft, creamy cheese was variously flavored with olives, herbs, and sun-dried tomatoes. There was also a wooden plate covered with slices of cheddar, Swiss, French, and Italian cheeses.

"Luckily, I love cheese," she said, dipping her finger in one of the pickle containers, then licking it.

He was quiet as they ate. Again, she decided not to probe for what was bothering him. And besides, she'd learned that just about anything bad in life could be fixed with a good roll in the hay. So when they finished eating, eager for dessert, she took the paper plates and wrappers to the nearby trash bin.

She returned hugging herself. The ocean breeze, though sensuous, was a bit chilly now. He smiled at her and stood, collected her into his arms, turned her around and hugged her so her back was pressed tight to his chest and his hands over her belly.

She grinned. "You have an appetite already? You just ate."

"No, I'm just trying to warm you up."

"You mean to turn me on, don't you? My hands are cold, not my belly."

"Oh, I do feel warmer, but it isn't spreading from my back."

She sent her hands backward and gripped his waist, pressing him tighter to her body. "I don't know about warming up, but I think I'm ready," she whispered.

He lowered his face to the back of her neck and his teeth pinched her white skin. A squeal of pain and pleasure escaped her throat.

The atmosphere, the spreading darkness, the dancing candlelight, the lingering taste of fine cheese in her mouth, the ease of their meeting, the longing she felt for the man who was behind her, even the thought of getting caught by the park ranger drove her to overwhelming pleasure. Their climax was spontaneous and timed perfectly together as she melted into his arms.

When they caught their breath, he sat at the picnic table, she curled up in his lap. Her greenish dress looked as if she'd worn it three days straight. Her hair was a tousled mess, too, and he didn't help it when he massaged her scalp gently with his fingers. Her obligations at work seemed like weak and distant memories.

"How was your day?" he asked.

"Routine. Nothing very exciting. Till now. And now, tell me about yours."

"You knew?"

"I didn't *know* anything, just that you weren't smiling when you saw me, and you've been far too quiet. So spill it."

"It's ... more than one thing. But mostly, it's about the conference I attended today. On terrorism."

"Oh. I think I'm beginning to understand it. Be a good patient and continue please."

At least he chuckled this time. But it seemed as though the longer he spoke, the more it seemed he'd forgotten the pleasure they'd just shared.

"We're totally off track, Vick," he said after describing the conference. "We invest fortunes in research, and nothing in the people who *can* make changes. And when they're playing games like that with terrorism, it scares the hell out of me. The police officers at that conference ... they're scared too. And that scares me even more.

"Not only is it scary, but it is frustrating too. They are focusing on the wrong thing. Most of the conference was dedicated to technology. Do you get it? They're trying to find tools to fix the problem. I'm not an expert, but it seems to me that they're missing the point. Not only is it impossible to solve the problem of terrorism with tools, no matter how sophisticated the technology, but the researchers are so removed from the front-liners—they might by missing the target completely."

He briefly told her about his encounter with an arts major who was somehow supposed to suddenly become a counterterrorism expert, then said, "And those front-line people think like me—if the policy people don't change their thinking, someone's gonna get hurt. Many someones."

Hearing the frustration in his voice, instinct compelled her to put her therapist hat a little tighter on her head. "What, in this situation, makes you feel frustrated?"

He played with her hair while mulling over her question. "I think it's the realization they're barking up the wrong trees. And that perhaps hundreds of thousands of people could die because of that. Think about it. We all know what a nuclear bomb can do, how many people it can hurt. But what if some terrorist group attacked something simple, like a refinery? A power plant? A water treatment plant? Or even some food processing plant? I—"

He stopped because she was patting his arm.

"You're right," she said. "But you know as well as I do that we can't change the policymakers. So what can you do *yourself* to change the mindset? Can't you write an article about it?"

He didn't respond right away, just continued running his fingertips over her scalp and through her hair. When he spoke, his voice sounded tired. "An article? Yeah, that's an idea. *If* they'll run it. But ... who am I fooling? It doesn't matter what *I* feel. I don't want to publish something just so *I* can feel good about it. I won't get to the decision makers, because they don't pay attention to anything except research. Decision makers don't even comprehend the fundamentals of what I'd write about, so how will they design the right policy for frontline people? The people who work at the airport, or the water treatment plants, or—"

"Okay." She shifted around in his lap to face him. "I think I need an explanation. Tell me what you'd say to, I don't know, a researcher if you had the chance. Someone who's done a lot of research, and thinks they know how to prevent terrorism." She smiled at him. "Hey, I'm a Ph.D. I'll play the researcher, you play the ace reporter."

He didn't even smile at her joke. "Terror ... what is it? If you had one word to describe terrorism, what would it be?"

She frowned. "Fear?"

"Bingo. Let's talk about fear, Doctor. What's the association between fear and the populace? Why is terrorism such a powerful phenomenon? Because 'one man willing to throw away his life is enough to terrorize a thousand.' That's Sun Tzu, *The Art of War*. Meaning that a small incident can get a huge impact. The butterfly effect. How many people are killed every day in car accidents in this country?"

She shook her head. "I don't know. A few dozen?"

"Would you read about all of them in the newspapers?"

She shrugged. "Only if it were an extraordinary accident, I suppose. Lots of people killed, or something about it that made it different from the average accident."

"Okay. Now consider this. If someone walked into LAX tomorrow and shot two passengers to death in an act of terror, would you hear or read about it somewhere?"

"I would *definitely* hear about it everywhere," she said, gripping his waistband and pulling him closer.

"So what's the difference between a man who dies in a car accident and a man who's killed in a terrorist attack?" he asked, his hands resting on her shoulders. "*That's* where fear comes into play."

She'd been trying to unbuckle his belt, but stopped. "So you're saying we fear dying by terrorist bullets more than a car collision. Either way, we're dead. But fear sells more newspapers and gets more ratings."

"Right. Ever heard of the Mall of America in Minnesota?"

She nodded. "One of the biggest shopping malls in the country. They even have a theme park in the middle of it."

"If you were a terrorist, would you attack that shopping mall?"

Her eyes went wide. "Uh ... I never thought about it before, but ... yes. I suppose I would. Crowded. Lots of people. And oh, the name. Mall of America. It represents American culture. And there'd be a chain reaction. If something goes wrong at one big mall, it would affect every mall in the country."

He leaned forward and kissed her on the lips. "You *are* brilliant. So it doesn't matter where it happens, it would be enough to terrorize an entire population who wouldn't know if they were next. The butterfly effect *and* the fear impact."

She frowned. "Psychological warfare."

"And the researchers would draw the same conclusions, only theirs would be bound in four-inch-thick reports. But what they'd failed to do—what they're failing to do right now—is help the first-line officers convert that knowledge into practice. So, as a reporter, what can *I* do about it? How can *I* contribute?"

"In a lot of ways," she replied, and returned her hands to his zipper. "Let me show you.... Well, in a little bit—"

He placed his hand over hers. "No, I mean it. If I just write an article, I'm doing nothing."

She thought a moment. "You keep saying 'the frontline.' So why not focus on that? Visit the frontline people, maybe even at LAX. They'll talk to you. It'll look bad if they won't talk to the media. And then maybe you can write an article from *that* angle?"

He nodded and removed his hand, remembering the visit he'd made there with Muhammad. If he could learn that much from the skycaps, what might he be able to learn from the people who manned the security checkpoints?

He smiled at her. "I'll give it some thought. Later. Now, back to what you were doing ..."

* * *

Only a few stars stained the dark velvet blanket above them with dots of brightness. In the distance, the skylines of Santa Monica and West LA converged with the evening sky, and they watched aircraft ascending from LAX in the distance until she rubbed her arms with her hands. He caught the hint, packed up the picnic basket, and then they began the walk down the trail to their cars.

"Are we finished talking about terrorist scenarios?" she asked as she took his hand in hers.

"No. I'm still waiting for your pearls of wisdom. This place is called Inspiration Point, isn't it?"

"Hey, I recall reaching my point of inspiration earlier this evening," she mentioned with a wink. They passed the old stable once occupied by Will Rogers' horses. Then she said, "We have an approach in therapy where we try to reflect what the patient feels. To analyze what he or she feels. Step into their shoes."

"All right, I give up. Go ahead and get into my shoes. God knows you were in all my other garments already."

She laughed. "It's not *your* shoes I'm talking about. It's the terrorists'. I guess if you needed an on-the-record opinion for your article, a forensic psychologist would probably be your best bet. No doubt, that's a big interest for those guys. Me, I'm a clinical. But I have to admit, ever since September 11, I've been interested in forensic psychology. Even thought about taking more training to specialize in it. But ... and remember, this isn't an expert opinion ... you explained how terrorists choose their targets. It makes perfect sense. What I mean is, by reflection, maybe you can predict how they work. Do you get what I'm saying? If you can really get into the terrorists' shoes, you can predict what they're up to. And if you know that, you'll know what would deter them from doing ... whatever they're planning."

"Reverse psychology," he murmured.

They were at their cars now, and she searched for her keys. "Isn't that what we've been talking about the whole evening?"

He mulled over what she'd just said. "Could you ... I mean, someone like you, a psychologist ... could you apply something like that to predicting terrorist behavior?" Like on what happened at LAX last week, maybe. What you think the bad guy, if he were a bad guy, aimed to do at LAX?"

"Well, it's not an exact science, but I can try," she said, handing him her keys. While he unlocked her door, she said, "You can explain to the skycaps the method you just explained to me. Tell them not to carry anything in, like luggage, without the owners. By the same token, you could alert security to watch for a skycap with a full cart and no passenger along. Things like that. Because those are things terrorist would do."

He handed her the keys, then took her in his arms. "Meanwhile, you didn't tell me what you thought about dinner tonight. And how about breakfast, then?"

"I loved dinner tonight. If breakfast includes the same dessert, I won't refuse. Let's just get out of here, I'm freezing."

"I'll meet you at my place," he said, and entered his car. When he saw her blinking taillights, he flipped his cell phone open, searched its phonebook and dialed a number.

Chapter 34

The cabin light was switched off and the pilot's voice came across the speakers in a heavy Scandinavian accent, wishing passengers a good night's rest for the remainder of the flight. Abbed agreed to another glass of champagne and drank it while he scanned photos of fitness models in the *Men's Health* he'd purchased at the airport. The champagne was good. The fact that it was forbidden made it taste even better.

The magazine's cover photo of a well-built man led to a piece inside the magazine about what would turn the reader's anatomy into the perfect athlete's. Below the table of schedules, weightlifting sets, and nutrition advice were blank boxes for the reader to fill in. While waiting in the LAX lounge, Abbed had filled them in. Now, he reviewed what he'd written. The "T9" in one box indicated only nine TSA personnel in Terminal #2, where KLM flights to Amsterdam departed. In another box, he noted "P5"—the number of police officers visible at Terminal 2. All of them at the same place, talking.

Next to the letter "C" was "~250." It had been hard to get an accurate count of the passengers passing through the terminal. Certain there were no undercover security people in the terminal, next to the letters "UC," he'd written "0."

Jacob hadn't asked him to do this, but Abbed still stung from his comrade's rebuke. "In spite of what you think, Jay," he whispered, "I care about our success."

And what better way to prove that than to do something

he wasn't asked to do?

Back in the terminal, while he'd written these things, he wondered how he could send this surveillance report to the guys in LA. Then, he remembered that he didn't get a chance to tell Jacob something in their last meeting.

Karla was a bit surprised by his phone call, but pleased, then excited when he told her what he'd called about. "Don't pack yet," he'd said. "I'll call you tomorrow at 8:00 p.m. your time, and we'll take it from there."

"Okay, handsome. Have a safe flight."

He hung up the phone smiling. Usually for a call like that, he used public phones. His cell phone, a prepaid cellular he'd purchased from a tourist, was for emergencies only, and rarely used. But public phones, especially at an airport, were ... well ... too public. And he was about to leave the country for an indefinite period. What could go wrong by him using the cell phone now?

His last task before boarding, the one Jacob asked him to do, was simple. He stood in a corner by the restrooms, positioned himself between one of the structure poles and an artificial plant, then leaned on the wall next to a door marked "Fire Extinguisher" and "Hose Reel." He opened the phone again, probably for the last time in America, and dialed a number.

"Are you at the spot?" was the quick reply.

"I am. I have four bars."

"Good. I'll contact you over there. Bon voyage," the voice said, and the line went dead.

Abbed wished he'd had longer to talk. There were many things he wanted to tell the person on the other end. Especially about his new, brilliant idea. After all, one didn't find someone like Karla every day.

***

Twelve miles from LAX, in an air-conditioned call center, Orlando Gallegos wrote something on a sticky note, turned on his encrypted screen saver, then said to the technician in the neighboring cubicle, "I'm going to take a leak, bro."

Orlando went toward the restroom, but entered the cafeteria instead and headed straight for the payphone there. He swiftly dialed a number and then waited for an answer, looking nervously out the window to make sure nobody was approaching.

"Hallo?" the voice on the other end of the line barked.

"Jose?"

"*Si mano*," Jose replied, much friendlier now. "What do you have for me?"

"I just triangulated the phone by the number you gave me. It used the transmission antenna at LAX about an hour ago. I got just two phone numbers, both dialed in the last twenty-four hours. I have them. Can you copy?"

At Jose's go-ahead, Orlando read the numbers he'd written on the sticky note. After ending the call, he ripped the note into several pieces before throwing it into the trashcan and heading back to his desk. There were advantages to working for a big cellular telephone company. For Orlando, one of them was access to confidential information—information that, if requested by the right people, had a price tag worth double his salary most years. Among his extra-income providers were private investigators in need of scandalous or incriminating evidence for their work. Jose was an exception; he never said why he needed what Orlando passed him from time to time. But, as well as he paid, he didn't need to explain.

Almost always, Jose wanted to know who owned a cell phone number. But a few times, he also wanted the user's location, like today. Not a problem. Cell phones were the most popular electronic device in the country. And thanks to the same towers that stained the landscape with ugly, radiation-polluting antennas, each cell phone was also a GPS.

It was easy for Orlando, or any tech like him, to locate a cell phone's user by the signal from phone to antenna.

He had to admit he was curious about this one user. Most users have twenty or thirty calls a day from their phone. This one only had two. He toyed with the idea of finding out what Jose *hadn't* asked for—the owner of the phone. But by the time he returned to his desk, he scrubbed the idea. Jose didn't ask for it, so it was none of his business. To go snooping where he hadn't been asked was like playing with matches. And as his mother told him more than once, those who play with matches get burned.

Chapter 35

If there could be an image of happiness, it was Dianne's face when Michael arrived at her parents' house with a pint of ice cream in one hand and an envelope in the other.

"What a lovely surprise," she said when she opened the door. Her arms spontaneously wrapped around his neck.

"But I called you and told you I was coming," he said.

"You and your British sense of humor. I meant the ice cream." She took his shoulders and hauled him inside the house, then slammed the door behind them with her leg.

"Where are your parents?"

"Mom dragged Allen out shopping. He hates it, but didn't have much choice. The house is ours for the next couple of hours."

"Great," he said, enhancing his British accent.

They walked to her room. He felt the same nervousness he always did when he wasn't sure what to do. Not a fear of rejection, simply because he'd never encountered one with her. It was that he never knew when she wanted only to cuddle, when she wanted to make out, or when she wanted to lose her inhibitions. Although he was supposed to be in control and lead her where he wanted her to go, when it came to what happened between the sheets, he was helpless.

Ibrahim had taught him that feminism was a westernized illness—a regression in superiority of the Prophet's heirs. But since his original mixed feelings subsided, he wasn't offended, as his mentor had been, by an assertive woman. Especially when that assertive woman was Dianne, who knew how to please him in ways he didn't believe possible, and without apparent fear that God would punish her. Dianne didn't practice any religion at all, in fact. He recalled one conversation where he asked her whether she was Jewish like her stepfather. When she said no, he said, "So, you're Christian then."

"Actually, Michael, I'm neither Christian nor Jewish nor Muslim," she said. "Not since I learned that religion brought a lot of good things to humanity, but it also brought so much bad to the world."

He nodded and didn't say a word. How could he? She spoke the truth.

"Look at the so-called Christian Crusaders," she said. "They killed everyone who wouldn't convert. And the Holocaust—people exterminated just because they were Jewish. As if being Jewish was some deadly contagious disease." She leveled half-teasing eyes on him. "Shall I continue about Muslim fundamentalists?"

He shook his head, not surprised by Dianne's response, except that it reminded him that she wasn't the airhead he thought she was at first.

Later, after they'd made love, he decided that it was hard to dislike her, especially when his head rested on her breasts and his arms wrapped under the small of her back. She represented the typical American young adult, clueless, ethnocentric, narrow-minded, indolent and lacking in motivation. Exactly as Ibrahim described during their long conversations in London. But Ibrahim failed to explain, perhaps because he didn't know, that young adults in LA, like the one he now held in his arms, had much good to them. Ibrahim failed to mention the sensitivity, passion, easygoingness, and their simple view of life. Ibrahim didn't interpret American flatness or hollowness correctly. These were the advantages of people who could concentrate on their hobbies, fields of interest, and leisure, something only dreamed of everywhere else in the world.

But no matter how it turned out, he cared for her ... and it was the last thing he wanted or needed. He missed her when they weren't together, and was excited just by the idea of seeing her. *I just wish that caring about her didn't distract me sometimes from the Cause, and—*

"Do you want to eat the ice cream *before* it melts? For the *second* time?"

"Yeah," he said, disengaged himself from her and rolled over, then grabbed the ice cream from the floor where he'd dropped it when she threw him on the bed. He opened the carton and fed her the first bite, then took a bite, after which he kissed her lips.

"What's in the envelope?" she asked. "The one you brought in with the ice cream?"

"That's a surprise," he replied around a mouthful of melting ice cream.

"Oh, I love surprises!" she said, sprang from the bed, knocking him back on the pillow as she did, and retrieved the envelope from the floor on his side.

He nodded, chuckling. "Go ahead. You will anyway."

She tore it open and looked at the contents, then up at him, wide-eyed. "Is this what I think it is? I ... I don't know what to say."

"Say you'll be ready on time tomorrow. And pack light. You won't need more than your swimsuit outside," he smiled, "and you won't need *any* clothes inside."

Chapter 36

Richard found the old airport control tower easily, parked his car and waited. At 6:15 a.m., the lot was almost deserted. The LAX police chief arrived at exactly 6:20.

Jonathan Stewart was African American, a big man in his mid-fifties, a college football player before beginning his impressive law enforcement career, most recently with the Santa Monica PD. When Richard heard of Stewart's appointment, he'd wholeheartedly approved in his very next column for the *Times*. With over 60,000 direct employees, LAX was a city in itself, and the man's familiarity with LA County was, to him, an asset to managing law enforcement for it. Best of all, while Stewart was coy about the question in their last interview, the rumor mill said the new chief was eager to employ modern procedures. Before he left this morning, Richard intended to find out if those rumors were true.

When he said "Good morning, sir," and offered his hand, the chief took it in a firm handshake that made Richard's knuckles pop.

"My apologies in advance," Stewart said as he released Richard's hand. "But as I mentioned on the phone last night, I'm in a bit of a rush this morning."

They crossed the street to an office building while Richard answered, rubbing his knuckles, "Understood, Chief, and I'll get right to the point. You're aware of the incident the FBI investigated last week."

Stewart's serious face turned grim. "I am. I think they

missed something, and after reading your column, I know you thought so too. And unfortunately, the investigation's the FBI's baby, so there's nothing I can do about it." He smiled. "You didn't spare your tongue, did you?"

They entered the building, and soon arrived at a door on the first floor.

"Coffee?" Stewart went to the percolator behind his desk.

"Sure. Black, please. No cream or sugar." Richard had slept only four hours. Vicky went back to sleep after he left for the meeting. She didn't get the breakfast he'd alluded to the night before, but seemed satisfied with her morning dessert. The memory made him grin.

Stewart handed a cup to Richard, then sat in the chair behind his desk. "So what do you have in mind?"

"I have to tell you, Chief, I'm not police or military. Don't even have a law enforcement background. The only clearance I have is the six feet two inches you see here. But a psychologist friend gave me an idea to try to help prevent terrorists from doing what they want to do in places like this."

Stewart folded his hands on the desk and locked eyes with Richard. "Law enforcement appreciates all the help we can get. From the public, and from keen observers like you."

Encouraged, Richard began, "No doubt, this theory's being floated around the FBI too, but ... I can't help but think the incident I wrote about last week had something to do with terrorism."

Stewart nodded. "After reading your piece, the thought occurred to me as well. My contacts at the FBI said the case is closed, though." He fixed Richard with a long gaze. "What do *you* think?"

Richard cleared his throat, hoping for the best. "I hope you don't mind, Chief—I didn't seek permission first. But after I spoke with the taxi driver, I interviewed the skycaps. I understand that the FBI thinks no criminal activity was involved. I think otherwise."

Stewart concentrated on Richard's face while he repeated the theory he'd assembled with Vicky, then added, "I firmly believe that strange passenger was part of some plan for an attack on the airport. And I think there's a way we can prevent it. Or at least try to prevent it."

Stewart removed a cell phone from his belt clip. "Where are you?" he asked the person who answered. "Get your butt in my office."

He hung up and looked at Richard's questioning face. "Captain Perez is my chief of security here. I'd like you to brief him with your suggestions too. Fair?"

"Fair," Richard agreed. *Gee, the wheels turn fast here. But then, they have a lot to lose if I'm right.*

When the deep voice behind him barked, "Good morning, Gentlemen," Richard turned around and measured a bulky, dark-featured man, dressed in a black business suit with a bulge in his jacket. Stewart introduced them, then summarized what Richard had told him so far. Then, he nodded at Richard.

"It's really a simple idea," Richard said quickly. "When that taxi driver saw someone acting odd, he didn't know what to do. Sure, he suspected the guy might be up to no good— *after the fact*. But what if he'd made the connection sooner? He's not a law enforcement officer. The most he could've done was find one of your officers and tell him. By then, the guy would've known someone made him and been long gone. In fact, if a police officer had been anywhere near the guy, the guy would've been very careful not to do anything suspicious in the first place."

He leaned forward and put his elbows on his knees. "And that, I think, is part of the problem. Terrorists know exactly where the police are inside the terminal. So when they see one, they're extra-careful. But what if a terrorist *wasn't* so certain?"

"What you're saying is that we need undercover officers in the terminals," Stewart said.

"Exactly, Chief. When we spoke before, you mentioned that the security cameras were intended to substitute for plainclothes officers. But you also mentioned that the cameras aren't manned. They're just for recordkeeping, you might say."

Both Perez and Stewart nodded. "With hundreds of cameras, there's no way we'd have the manpower to watch all of them fulltime."

"I understand," Richard said. "But ... well, I won't ever presume to do your job," he chuckled, "but it occurred to me that not having plainclothes people inside the terminal might work against what you're trying to do here."

"Well, Chief, I won't waste our time here," Perez said. "I can see undercover on the planes. The sky marshals program works, partly because none of the passengers knows they're there. And if something happens, the sky marshals are right there, and can act quickly. But in as big a space as the terminals? We're talking miles of space all together. But my biggest objection? For every officer we take out of uniform, that's one less officer the public sees. I think it would affect our public perception. Negatively."

Stewart considered this. "But the main issue is to create obstacles for terrorists. If they can't tell the police from the passengers, they'll feel free to do their planning—and be more likely to be noticed by one of us. Since political correctness won't allow us to profile, this might be the next-best option—their profile won't matter, but their behavior will."

With that, Stewart rose from his seat. "You'll have to forgive me, fellows. I have another meeting. Perez, do a feasibility study on Richard's suggestions."

Perez glared at Richard. "Look, Richard, I know you mean well. But it's difficult enough maintaining security with visible officers."

"This might sound weird, so bear with me," Richard said and started to explain.

* * *

"Call it politics if you want," Richard said while following Perez into the terminal. "But that's where I'd be one step ahead—because I can predict what the bad guys will do. Once you see the suspicious behavior, engage with the suspicious individual. What do you think?"

Perez stopped walking and turned to Richard with a frustrated smile. "Do you know what a police officer's worst nightmare is?"

Richard grinned. "A snooping reporter like me?"

"Don't give yourself so much credit. Even worse than you. The ACLU."

"The American Civil Liberties Union?" Richard said. "*That's* your worst nightmare?"

"Believe it or not. Those bleeding-heart attorneys will do everything they can to convict a police officer simply for being too rude, using too much force, or anything else that makes them feel righteous. They say they do it on behalf of our Constitution, and for the sake of the public." Perez chuckled. "Yeah, right."

"But ... if an officer's following procedure, I don't get where there's a problem," Richard said.

Perez took a deep breath. "ACLU versus Logan Airport Police, 2004. As you might know, some of the 9/11 terrorists used Boston Logan to launch their attack. After that, Massachusetts invested a huge amount of money training their airport police. One day, an officer saw someone who wore a suit, placed a call at a public phone, and seemed to be monitoring all the arrivals. Exactly the kinds of things the officer was trained to look for. So he approached him."

"So the officer was doing what he was supposed to do," Richard said. "So what was the problem?"

"The *problem* came when the officer approached the man and asked for ID. The man refused. By the end of it, the man pulled out his ACLU ID and threatened to sue for racial profiling. He did sue, and he won. *Now* do you understand why your *engagement plan* might bring the ACLU down on us?"

Richard remained silent. He could hear Vicky saying *"Get into their heads!"* She was talking about the terrorists. But first, he realized, he had to get into the head of a frontline security person.

"It was pointless for that officer to demand that man's ID," he said.

Perez's forehead furrowed. "What the hell are you talking about?"

"Think about it. Until the terrorist actually carries out his plan, it's a psychological game. Do you really think any terrorist is going to involve someone with a record in their operation? Highly unlikely. So instead of saying 'Stop and show me your ID,' that's where engagement comes in—in the prevention phase."

Perez shook his head. "Engagement. Exactly what the police officer did at Logan. And got his butt sued off!"

"Uh, uh. It wasn't engagement, it was confrontation. By treating the man as though he were already guilty of a crime, the police officer *did* intrude on his Constitutional rights."

Perez sighed. "Now *you* sound like an attorney."

Richard gave him a smile he hoped was calming. "Try a psychologist. Based on what my psychologist friend's theory ... okay, here's a scenario. You're a terrorist, and I approach you and just start chatting with you about, say, your destination. What would you do?

The man's surprise was evident. "I ... I guess I'd get nervous as hell. And the more you talked, the more I'd want to run, or at least try harder to get away. Maybe even do it."

"And *that's* where I'd have probable cause to stop you and interrogate you."

Perez let go of his arm.

Richard carefully pointed toward a man standing nearby and said quietly, "That man is suspicious. Mid-thirties, loitering around with a small suitcase. But do you see what else

I see? The way he's swinging it around?"

It took Perez a moment to understand. When he did, he said, "Let's go."

"Let me do the talking," Richard whispered. Perez didn't argue, just stood behind him.

The man, casually dressed, apparently not in a hurry, looked at his watch. His suitcase was outstretched from his arm.

Richard passed by him, then stopped and ambled back to him. "Hey, that's a cool watch," he said, leaning to get a better look. "What's the brand?"

"Seiko," the man said.

"It looks great," Richard said, then pointed at the man's suitcase and added, "I bet you'll be in another time zone soon. Which one?"

The man looked at him. Not nervous, just curious. "What?"

"Where are you flying?" Richard asked casually.

"I'm not. Just bringing my wife. She's the one flying. Going to see her cousin."

Richard smiled and gestured toward the suitcase. "Oh, I just thought—"

"Oh, no. Our scale at home's broken, and she was afraid they'd try to charge her extra for the weight. So she brought an empty suitcase. In case she had to offload some stuff for me to take home." The man chuckled. "You know women."

Richard shared the man's smile, then said, "Boy do I. Did she fly already? You off the hook yet?"

"Nah, she's at the counter." The man pointed toward an older brunette woman and waved. The woman waved back and smiled.

Richard patted the man's arm. "Tell your wife to enjoy her trip."

"Yeah, I will. Thanks."

* * *

"The guy's explanation checked out," Perez said as they walked away. "But actually, I'd be more concerned if the suitcase had looked heavy. That might mean it's full of explosives."

"Get into the terrorist's head," Richard said. "If you wanted to observe the place before you bring the suitcase *full*, wouldn't a passenger profile be the best to assume?"

"Sure. Less obvious that way."

"And what makes someone look like a typical passenger? A suitcase. But would you bring your entire closet in it for the surveillance?"

Perez nodded, and his swarthy face broke into a grin. "I noticed how slick you were with your questions. Definitely something a police officer could learn from. We're not exactly wired to be that nice, but I see the advantage."

"Exactly my point," Richard said. "Engagement first, then confrontation only if you need it. Doing it that way, you don't have to worry about ACLU attorneys."

"Too bad God sends rain for the wicked, too," Perez said with a sigh.

Richard's eyebrows arched at him. "Rain for the wicked?"

"It's from the Holy Bible." Perez touched the cross on his necklace. "Book of Matthew. It says God sends sun and rain to the righteous *and* the unrighteous, the good *and* the evil. That's why I'm willing to take your suggestions—so we might be able to cut their supply of rain before it's too late…"

Richard nodded, wondering whether the wicked already have all the rain they needed.

Chapter 37

The Ford Expedition roared smoothly in the south lane of I-405 Freeway. The Expedition's light-green paint was the most common in Southern California, exactly the reason Jacob had purchased the vehicle. Well, not the only reason. As manager of one of the biggest nonprofit organizations for cleft-lip treatment in Third World countries, his cover didn't require anything but a bank account, an office, and an advertising budget. Yet like what Abbed's souped-up motorcycle did for him, Jacob liked the feeling the big SUV gave him. It made him feel ... superior. And the power American-made engines produced! A wonder. He knew Joe would envy him if he saw what vehicle he was driving. Chuck Tower, Joe's hero in *CTA*, drove the same car. *Except I don't carry weapons in my car,* he thought, chuckling.

The objective must be tangible. That was on his mind while he was looking for a source of money. Michael's mentor had been generous, and Abbed's funding source was lucrative, though problematic. Even so, Jacob wanted to diversify the group's funding as much as he could.

The solution came to him on a long flight. With nothing better to do, he flipped through the pages of a *Time* magazine, but stopped as one advertisement caught his attention. The ad had a picture of a young boy who had a cleft lip. He read every word of the ad, noting with surprise the amount of donations required to help these poor kids. Then he knew he'd found his tangible object—a need he could point to, whenever required, to justify a donor's generous funding.

Forming a nonprofit was as easy as going to the grocery store and buying milk. He was soon head of a tax-free goldmine with constant cash flow. A minuscule amount went toward the organization's public objective and to logistics like salaries. The rest, he shuttled through a confusing channel only he could trace to its end.

When he saw the Bellflower Avenue sign, he took the first left turn off the exit. Passing several warehouses, he stopped in front of a plain-looking building where a simple red sign stated, "Emergency Response Supply."

He parked in a crowded parking lot behind a truck, where the SUV would be hidden from the main road. Even so, he felt exposed. He walked fast, entering the warehouse from the shipping deck, and knocked on a door. A familiar face looked at him through a window and buzzed him in.

The spacious warehouse was netted with corridors of shelves filled with cartons and boxes, all labeled with the "ERS" flame design logo. There were no workers inside right now. Jacob didn't want to see or to be seen by anyone, so that was a condition of his agreement to visit.

He said, casually, to the man who'd let him inside, "So Shudy. How are things going? And remember, I want to get this done and get the hell out of here."

Shudy climbed onto a forklift. "Come, I'll show you."

Shudy stacked a pallet of boxes onto the fork and blocked the corridor so nobody could see them, and pointed to the shelves behind Jacob. Like all the others, they were filled with cartons with the ERS logo. But these cartons, Shudy pointed out, contained additional labels, bearing the name: "LAX."

Jacob nodded in approval, and Shudy opened one of the labeled cartons that looked new. Jacob looked around nervously, almost counting the seconds being here. It made him feel ... vulnerable ... not a good feeling for a man who lived by caution. Caution always helped him develop a better plan, get better accomplices, and avoid defeat or entrapment. Caution, and patience. To date, Abbed was his only failure.

He lived by the Irish Republican Army's credo: Those on the side of law and order have to be lucky all the time. Freedom fighters need be lucky only once. Even if the threat level remained high, security would eventually break somewhere and provide them a loophole. Patience would pay off. And it seemed it finally had.

Unlike the others, he was born in this country, in Irvine, California, the son of Albanian refugees. Albania was a vague and uncertain place to most of his classmates and their parents. Albania's environment was Balkan, the culture a mixture of Greek and Roman, the language Albanian, the role Russian, the religion Islam. So his background was obscure. Just the way he liked it, down to his innocuous appearance, tall and light-skinned with dark hair. Only his eyes hinted at his ancestor: dark and piercing, a dramatic contrast to his pale skin. Otherwise, he looked like any typical mid-thirties suburban American.

His looks came from his parents, and he still recalled their stories of the problems they had settling into the country. The Muslim congregation they joined was suspicious at first, but took them in. Jacob was still attending the center, out of boredom, when Shudy found him.

Shudy, or as he pronounced his name, *Shaa-dy*, was a young charismatic member of the congregation: not a permanent member, but one who came and went. So the young Jacob didn't notice Shudy until he noticed Jacob. And when he did, he displayed an intense interest in Jacob. At first, Jacob didn't know why Shudy, rumored to be a successful businessman, showed up more frequently to the evening prayers and insisted on sitting next to him. Yet there was nothing sexual about this closeness, only intellectual, and eventually Jacob's defense melted. Shudy instilled in him his knowledge of Islam, the Arabic language and heritage, and a deep hatred of America's hollow culture—the same one that had made him a very rich man. The same culture that forced Jacob's parents to work long hours so he could have a better life than they did.

Jacob took his mentor's lessons seriously, but never considered any actual revenge against the United States. He wasn't a hero or a *Shahid* type. Yet the "war on terrorism" led Jacob to join what Shudy had been harping on all along—the Cause. Since then, Jacob had devoted his talent, brains, and most importantly, his American appearance to the Cause. After their attack, Shudy assured him, they would eventually enjoy the fruits they'd harvest from the American economy. All it took was caution, and patience, until the right time came.

Yet if the authorities discovered him in this warehouse, and with what he was looking at right now, how could he possibly explain his reasons for being here. He looked at Shudy and said, "I want to finish this business as soon as I can."

"Soon, my friend, soon," Shudy replied. He took a red-painted object from the carton and placed it on one of the shelves. Jacob gingerly patted the bulky metal cylinder, then tapped on the gauge and asked, "So what's the trick? How does it work?"

"The mechanism is the same as any other brand on the market. Look." Shudy pressed the lever and released a white foamy cloud to the warehouse floor. Jacob jumped to the other side in response.

"Blanketing the fire with an inert gas—which chokes it for lack of oxygen," Shudy explained, amused by his friend's reaction.

Jacob drew in a careful breath and blew it out in a slow, ragged rush. "I don't care how *that* works. How does it help *us*?"

Shudy looked at him with warm fatherly eyes. "*Akbar minac biyom, bearef annac bsini.*"

Jacob nodded. "Older than you one day, wiser than you one year. You're right. I'm sorry. I just feel nervous even being here."

Shudy chuckled. "Don't worry. You came to collect a big donation from a respected businessman. A lot of cleft-lipped kids will be able to smile again due to your visit."

He removed his hand from Jacob's shoulder and gripped the cylinder. "A regular ten-pound fire extinguisher. The difference is in here." He pointed to the gauge.

Jacob nodded, for the first time seeing something odd about it, something he should have noticed instantly, but didn't. Above the round display indicating the container's internal pressure, there was an additional square display with two LED lights—green and red. Both lights were currently off.

"This device is a new patent, now pending in the Patents and Trademarks Office," Shudy explained. "Basically, it converts the analog pressure gauge into a digital one. You see here?" He pointed at the square display. "That's where the digital reading is shown. And here . . ." He pointed at the LEDs. "That's where it transmits the status to the command center."

"How does it transmit it?" Jacob asked.

Shudy twisted the head of the fire extinguisher and opened a small hollow compartment. "See those? Lithium ion batteries. They last for two years of daily transmissions to the command center. The transmission only takes a split second, so it doesn't consume much electricity. But the *patent* is for using only one cellular cell for a venue the size of ... well, the size of a terminal at LAX." He chuckled. "The idea is, each one of these devices has its own ESN and—

"Whoa, slow down," Jacob said. "What's that?"

"Oh, sorry. That stands for 'Electronic Serial Number.' A unique fingerprint for each cellular cell that indicates the status of each fire extinguisher. An easy way to maintain emergency equipment. Whenever the fire extinguisher has a problem—not enough pressure, for example—the cell sends an automatic signal to the command center in its daily transmission. And there's also the old analog gauge as a backup."

"And you have a patent pending on it, huh?" Jacob said, his face showing mirth now.

"If I can make a couple of bucks from it, why shouldn't I? And next week, a group of buyers is coming here to negotiate for the patent. When the time comes, the company won't even be mine anymore."

Jacob gave an approving nod. "That would take the heat off you. Away from *us*. Now tell me, how do we use your patented device?"

"Carbon dioxide should be stored in here," Shudy pointed at the bottom of the cylinder. "But we need this space for the good stuff. So *these* fire extinguishers have a compartment at the bottom."

He waved his hand across the cartons with the LAX labels on them. "This compartment is for carbon tetrachloride—CCl_4. Much better than carbon dioxide to put out a fire. But, it's toxic. Prohibited for use indoors."

Jacob shrugged. "Why would we care?"

"Exactly. If someone needs the fire extinguisher for its real purpose, it'll work fine." He grinned. "As long as they don't leave the empty tank close to a source of heat. Main point, the rest of the space is for you."

"This is a great idea," Jacob said. "But what will detonate it?"

"That's the beauty of it. The transmission system can receive signals as well. We didn't write a patent on it—there's no need to *send* a fire extinguisher a signal. But the receiving signal works the same way—with the ESN and the cellular cell. Once they come together, the electric circuit closes and the power from the battery goes to the detonator in here."

Shudy pointed to the bottom of the gauge structure. Jacob saw an electric lighter, the kind available in automobiles.

"The, ah, materials you put inside will be isolated with two layers," Shudy explained. "The first one is this gel." Shudy pulled a casing from the container that looked like an icepack. "It will protect the interior from heat. We don't want it to blow up prematurely, do we?"

Jacob shook his head, thrilled, impressed, and amused at the same time by the proud expression on his friend's face.

Shudy continued. "The outer layer is a cotton insulation filled with black pepper and coffee beans." He raised his eyebrows, waiting for Jacob to figure out its purpose.

"The dogs," Jacob whispered.

"Exactly! The K-9 dogs shouldn't be able to sniff anything suspicious if they happen to walk by."

"Good idea. How many people know about this?" He gestured toward the cartons.

"Only you and I. These fire extinguishers were engineered as a pilot-design to contain a mixture of materials that need to be stored separately. Despite the failure, the engineering and template remain. The rest was done due to the Czechs' ingenuity."

"*Rubota*?" Jacob answered with a smile.

"I'm impressed you know the original name for 'robot'. In any case, all I had to do was label the extinguishers and add the improvised detonator and sleeves. As you know, I'm just replacing the manager while he's on vacation. Before he returns, this merchandise will be gone from the warehouse."

Jacob thought a moment. "How did you sell them to LAX?"

"I didn't. I offered them as a marketing campaign. Said I'd give them the fire extinguishers if I could use LAX as a referral. LAX responded as Centinella Hospital did," his eyes fell, "and a few other places, it's better you don't know the names. They accepted the offer gratefully."

"Brilliant," Jacob murmured. "Simply brilliant!" Centinella Hospital was the closest hospital to the airport. In case something went wrong at the airport, many casualties would be directed to that hospital.

Shudy's eyes were fixated on the ground, but his proud smile was undeniable. "We'll give the Americans a totally different perspective on the term 'emergency response,'" he added, chuckling. His eyes burned with a mix of enthusiasm and evil.

Chapter 38

There wasn't much to pack into the small rolling suitcase for a two-day trip. Michael packed enough clothes for three, and it still closed easily. He glanced at the other suitcase on his bed, checked his watch, turned the lights off, and exited the apartment with both suitcases, fighting to untie the big knot forming in his stomach.

"Do you understand you'll be a part of Jihad in America?" Ibrahim had stated, excited. They both wore black uniforms and stood outside the catering facility at Heathrow. Years of preparation gave Michael everything he needed to know. And besides, it was a simple plan. Get in, find a catering cart that goes onboard an aircraft, and place the half-pound bomb disguised as a sandwich in the space between the wheels' axles. And get out, of course. A walk in the park. If the dry run worked, they could mark the operation feasible. Most important, success tonight meant he was ready for the operation next year in America. He didn't know the details of that one yet, but Ibrahim had assured him it was huge, bigger than anything the Cause had ever done.

Ibrahim patted him on his back, startling him. It had started raining again, but Michael didn't feel it. Adrenaline kept him warm. *No turning back,* he thought, and ran toward the short fence surrounding the facility, Ibrahim in tow.

The catering onloading area was guarded by one security guard, no police officers. *Sophisticated but not complex,* as Ibrahim described it. *"Why would we try to smuggle a bomb through their security, when we can just as easily deliver it through the catering? Much less complicated."*

Ibrahim had almost been right. Should have been right. After loading the suitcases into his trunk, Michael rested his head on the steering wheel. A minute later, he forced himself to crank the car and head out. Although the air conditioner was working fine, the air in the car felt thick, like his sadness was physically choking him. The last time he could recall feeling that way, he was waving goodbye to his father at the Kuwait airport over a decade earlier.

A disturbing buzz sent him leaping out of his skin. When he realized it was his cell phone, he knew he had to calm himself.

"I have everything laid out and ready," Dianne announced. "I tried to keep it as light as possible, but, oh, don't forget that suitcase!"

He didn't respond. His muscles felt paralyzed.

"Michael?"

"I'm sorry ... bad reception. What did you say?" He fought to keep his tone casual.

"Never mind, just bring your cute butt over here."

He ended the call and tried to clear his mind while he crossed two junctions and one green light, and pulled into a shopping center. Minutes later, he walked into the supermarket and stood in the health food section. The long aisle offered an incomparable variety of cereals, energy drinks, powders, gels, and power bars. So many power bars, far more than he expected.

He peered at them for a moment, awestricken, then forced himself to start checking labels. Most of them contained grains of some sort, sugar, and other ingredients he didn't care for. Most contained a certain level of protein—exactly what he was looking for. He checked a dozen different brands, looking at their protein levels, having to squint at the tiny print on the nutrition labels. When he found what he wanted, he almost laughed at the silliness of its simplicity. And its obviousness.

"Right on the front of the box in great big letters," he muttered. "'Highest protein of any nutrition bar!' Of course. Why didn't I think of checking the *front* of the boxes first?"

He turned it over. The label didn't lie. This brand offered an extraordinary 36 grams of protein per bar. He noted the bar's weight. Seventy-five grams. Almost half of the bar contained protein.

He remembered when he tasted power bars before, they were chewy and tasted pretty much like flavored cement. But that's exactly what he was looking for now. The density of the power bars resembled the same density as high explosives.

Chapter 39

"You want to help us in the storeroom today?" Rachael asked, surprised. "I appreciate the offer, but it's so dusty in there."

"Sure, why not?" Joe said with a shrug. "I'll even have Tim help me, if necessary."

"All right then, you know where it is. If there's anything you think should be disposed of, throw it in the bin outside and mark it on the log by the door. Tell me if you need anything." She smiled at him with shining eyes. "I'm so impressed you're devoting your time in the middle of the week this way. God bless you."

He gripped the gold cross around his neck, brought it to his lips and kissed it. "God bless you too, Rachael."

First, he walked around the warehouse from the outside. Then, using the key Rachael gave him, he entered a large space that contained everything from household supplies to hospital necessities. As Rachael had painstakingly explained, everything was stored on racks labeled with detailed descriptions. Joe's task was to make sure the racks' contents were labeled properly, with no shortages or jumbles. That task, and one other.

His checks revealed no closed-circuit television cameras. But then, why would there be a need? It was only a supply warehouse, not even used to store drugs. He found the back door and looked outside. Nothing but the parking lot and the trash bin. Perfect.

At the section where paint was stored, he scanned the racks, wiping sweat from his brow. There were fans, but they didn't help cool the place. He saw every imaginable type of paint: for walls, oil paint for outdoor use, for wood, for metals, and even for patients who used them during therapy treatments. But paint wasn't what he was looking for.

He passed the paint racks and found the label for paint removers. He picked up a square container, held it so he could read the label through his bifocals. The main ingredient was acetone, 80% by volume. *A bit lower than what I already purchased. I wonder—*

"Hey Joe!"

He turned around at the familiar bellow to see Tim standing at the far end of the room, waving. He waved back, then waved again to signal to Tim to come closer, suppressing his sigh. He wasn't in the mood to baby-sit Tim, but had to keep him close. Soon, he would need him.

Tim looked around in wonder. "Wow, look at all the paint! It's almost like Home Depot, isn't it? What are you doing here? Rachael said you're here for the whole day."

Joe smiled at him. "I'm trying to organize some things here. Want to help?"

"Sure," Tim replied, and stuck his hands in his pockets. "But Sarah said I had to be careful in here ... because of my head." He giggled. "I heard one of the orderlies say if I ever bump it too hard, it'll crack like an egg. Funny, huh?"

Joe didn't think so, but nodded agreeably. "Don't worry about that. What I'm doing here isn't dangerous." *Yet.*

When he tired of Tim watching him, he said, "Tell you what. Can you help me find the shelves holding the hydrogen peroxide?"

Tim gasped. "Why? Did you cut yourself?"

"No, Tim. It's some of the things I need to check. Can you help me?"

"Sure. Maybe it's over there." Tim pulled one hand from his pocket and pointed to the general direction of the medical supplies. Then his finger swung in an arc. Within seconds, he was spinning around, laughing, finger still pointed, saying, "Or there.... Or there!"

"Thank you," Joe said, already regretting asking.

"Look, I'll go with you."

Actually, Tim's first idea was good, since hydrogen peroxide is a common skin disinfectant. Yet while there were plenty of antibacterial products, bandaging supplies, and other first-aid necessities organized on the shelves, Joe couldn't see any bottles of hydrogen peroxide. *It must be somewhere else. Perhaps cleaning supplies?*

He looked up to see Tim, now at the other end of the warehouse, facing the wall, staring straight ahead ... at a wall that was completely bare.

He shook his head and continued his search, and soon realized why he couldn't find the bottles on the shelf. Among the antiseptics was a tower of boxes. A dozen plastic bottles of hydrogen peroxide were packed in each box.

Hydrogen peroxide was easy to buy at almost any store. But it would take an eternity to obtain this much that way. Judging by this cluttered room, nobody would notice the shortage until it was too late anyway. He opened one of the boxes and pulled out a bottle, adjusted his bifocals and peered at the tiny letters.

"Stabilized liquid hydrogen," he muttered. "All we need now is to help you to regain your instability."

He checked the last place he saw Tim; the young man still faced the wall, like an electric toy whose batteries had died. He walked to the cleaning-supply rack, removed a box of black industrial trash bags and returned to the antiseptics rack. He placed two boxes of the hydrogen peroxide into a trash bag, as much as he could comfortably carry at a time, and went outside. Beside the trash bin was a small parking lot for patient visitors. Only a few cars were parked there, as usual. He looked around to make sure he wasn't being observed, and then crossed the small lot in four long steps.

Ten minutes later, the tight space between the trash bin and wall held six of the bags. Once that was done, he returned to where Tim was still staring at the white wall. He stood next to him and tried to see what he was looking at. A plain white wall, no marks or stains. It meant either Tim had an extremely vivid imagination and saw a fascinating picture there, or he was hallucinating.

"Tim?" He waved his hand in front of Tim's eyes. There was no response.

"Tim!" He shook his shoulder firmly.

"What? What?" Tim cried out, and looked at him with empty eyes—eyes Joe was relieved to see finally start filling with vitality.

Perhaps he has low blood sugar or something?

Joe said quickly "Do you want to eat anything?"

Tim rubbed his eyes. "Yeah, sure. Are we done here?"

"No, we aren't, but we need to eat. Let's go."

Okay, I'll go get my bike—"

"Ah, no, you won't need to." Joe gave him a sheepish smile. "I decided to bring different transportation today."

He locked the door behind them and returned the key to Rachael. "We're going to grab something to eat. Do you want anything?"

"No, thank you. Did you finish what you started in there?" she asked.

"No. Unfortunately, I was sneezing half of the time. My dust allergies are kicking up again. Of course, if you want me to come back—"

"No, it's okay. Thank you for your effort," she said. "And oh, I hope you feel better."

Joe managed to smile and thank her before they left.

In the employee parking lot, he used his key remote to unlock the door, then said, "Get in. We'll go find something to eat."

Tim looked with childish amazement at the white 4Runner. "Wow, Joe. Is this new?"

"No, it's used. But it's new to me."

"Do you have a driver's license? Was it expensive? Why did you pick a white one?" Tim asked the questions while he strapped the seatbelt around his chest.

"I don't know why I chose white," he replied, amused by Tim's excitement. "What color would you have chosen?"

Tim shrugged. "Yellow?"

He winced. "Yellow? Yellow is the most visible color for a car on the road. That's why all of the taxi cabs in New York are yellow."

Tim looked at him, confused. "What's wrong with that?"

"Never mind," Joe muttered, shifted into drive, and off they went.

He chose a fast-food Mexican restaurant on Wilshire for their lunch. Once inside, he pointed to a vacant table. While Tim settled in, he ordered a chicken burrito for himself and fish tacos for Tim, plus beverages, guacamole and tortilla chips for both of them. As always, he paid cash, and then took the receipt with his pickup number and two empty paper cups. One reason he liked this place was the free refills. Another American extravagance he'd become fond of.

He looked toward Tim, to ask him what he wanted to drink. Now, Tim was staring at a spot on the table. He gave up and filled their glasses with Dr. Pepper. When he brought the food and drinks, Tim's vacant downward stare didn't change until Joe sat across from him and touched his hand. At this, he looked up, his eyes wild and searching.

"What's wrong?" Joe asked.

"I ... don't know."

"Okay. You can eat now. Then I'll take you back so you can rest in your room."

They ate silently. When they were finished, Joe cleared the table and took Tim back to the car. There'd been no more staring episodes, but he was worried nonetheless. He'd spent much time setting up this part of the plan. If something happened to Tim, there would be a big cog in the wheel to either replace or work around.

"I have a present for you," he said, and opened the back door.

Tim woke up at once. "For me?"

Joe handed him a shopping bag. "For you."

Tim opened the bag and cried out, "Wow, it's beautiful." He pulled out a multi-pocket vest, the type photographers wore, and tried it on. It fit perfectly. "Thank you so much, Joe!"

"You're so welcome," Joe replied and got into the car, relieved to see Tim so alert, and hoping that alertness held a while longer. He debated whether he should notify anyone of Tim's condition, but decided not to. Alerting the staff might add some unwelcome variables to his plan.

* * *

Tim had obediently stretched out on the bed in his room before Joe closed the door behind him. No one was in the parking lot when he returned, so he moved the trash bags from their hiding place and into the back of the SUV. Another half hour, and he was merging from the I-405 to the I-105, heading west. Soon he was on the narrow, dead-end Redwood Avenue, allowing the garage door, like the mouth of a gigantic monster, to swallow the white SUV inside it. He waited to emerge from the 4Runner until after the mouth closed.

Two dozen cans of paint and thinner were stacked against the wall in the living room, purchased at the local Home Depot two days earlier. He had no interest in painting anything, but needed the thinner; it was 90% acetone in volume. He'd bought the paint, along with rollers and brushes, to avoid suspicion.

The house on Redwood Avenue was a lucky find. There were no neighbors in the adjacent houses—all were for rent or for sale—and the rent was better than what even Jacob could have hoped for. Even better, the absurdly low rent was due to the living room view of the Hyperion Sewage Treatment Plant's outer fence. Curtains took care of the view, but the smell ... Despite the odor-control facilities at the plant, the neighborhood frequently smelled like a public lavatory. Exactly what he'd needed: an isolated place, close to the airport, where residents were used to unpleasant odors: odors exactly like those improvised explosives being cooked might create.

Chapter 40

Michael knew her parents were at work, so after circling the neighborhood several times, he dared to park his car in their driveway.

The door was unlocked. He walked on silent sneakered feet down the long hallway linking the living room to the bedrooms. At her closed door, he listened a moment, heard music inside. Instead of knocking, he pushed the door open slowly and peered inside.

The television was tuned to a music channel. It was difficult for him to watch; the scenes flickered rapidly. Blinking, he shifted his vision to the center of the room. She was dancing, but not just dancing. Her thong panties were visible through the transparent fabric of a scarf she'd tied around her waist. Her long bare legs danced across the floor in tune with the music, her eyes closed and her hands fluttering gracefully like a Middle Eastern belly dancer.

He walked to her and put his hand around her wrist. She jumped instinctively, her mouth open to scream, when her eyes recognized the intruder.

"Honey bun!"

"You are beautiful," he said. "I'm not sure you can fly wearing only a scarf, though."

She giggled. "Oh, I can't? Then take it off me."

"We don't have time for that."

His conscience pulled at him. How could he be with her in that way, knowing he was about to use her, and cruelly, later? He said, hoping his voice wouldn't betray him, "We should get going."

"Shower first." She touched his lips with hers. He kissed her back. But then he drew back and put his fingers on her lips. "We really have to go."

She gestured to the stuffed suitcase, then the clothes still on her bed. "Please tell me you remembered the suitcase."

"Sure. I'll bring it in. Get into the shower already." He walked outside to his car, wondering what if, after all his planning and preparation, it went badly, like it had in London?

Was it Ibrahim's fault or mine? He asked himself that question a thousand times since that night. Jumping over the fence at Heathrow Airport was easy. Getting inside the catering area, even easier. Only a few food service employees were scattered in the big facility, too busy to notice anything but their deadlines. There was a guard, but he sat at the entrance at least thirty feet away, looking at something on his desk. Even so, and despite the cold weather, Michael's body felt slick with sweat.

Ibrahim pointed to one of the British Airways carts. "That one. Go!"

Michael did as he'd practiced so often; he put the small bundle, wrapped to look like a deli sandwich, in the wheel well underneath the heavy cart. Mission accomplished.

"*Yallah*, let's go," he whispered as he stood. But Ibrahim's eyes were now focused elsewhere.

"Come," his mentor said. But then he started walking in the wrong direction, inside the facility.

What are you doing? Michael's mind screamed, but he followed.

Ibrahim stood in front of a room labeled "Kosher" and peered inside. Michael joined him, fearing his pounding heart would alert the guard.

The knife in Ibrahim's hand surprised him. *"Your test, Mustafa,"* Ibrahim had hissed, and opened the metal door wide. *"You have to kill this infidel!"*

The sun on his back was warm, so different from that horrible raining night. He opened the trunk and looked at the suitcase inside, but remained in the same position, staring, until he turned and collapsed onto the rear bumper, feeling as though he was attending his own funeral.

The old man was sitting low in his chair, his head on his chest. He softly snored. *Is he a rabbi?* Michael remembered thinking. Behind him was a rack of pots, pans and kitchenware.

Ibrahim shoved the knife into his hand. Michael remembered the uncontrollable shiver. How terribly his hands shook. How his gaze switched from Ibrahim to the sleeping man, then back. Ibrahim's encouraging nod. He could still remember the old man's smell, a mix of food and fading cologne.

Placing the bomb wasn't the same. The bomb would kill and maim, but not while he watched. But this?

"I—I can't!" he murmured, and lowered the knife.

"You must!" Ibrahim said harshly.

The old man shifted in his chair, causing both of them to freeze. He then continued snoring.

"It's the only way for you to join the Higher Cause," Ibrahim rasped. When Michael didn't move, he added, "The only way to honor your father. To take revenge for your father's death."

Michael nodded. With aching heart, he knew what he had to do. His father was gone, and the only thing he had left was Ibrahim. And the Cause. Yet his only desire at that moment was to flee, to go away and pretend this never happened.

"*Allah u-Akba,*" he whispered. The plea came out as a sob as he turned to a rack of kitchenware and ran straight into it, causing it to fall down with an awful crashing sound.

But instead of that long-ago sound, he only heard a buzzing now. He opened his eyes and looked left, then right. The street was still deserted. After a moment, he realized the buzzing was coming from his cell phone.

"Hey, did you get lost?" A nervous giggle. "Where are you?"

"Sorry, baby, I'm coming right back in," he said, and hung up without waiting for a reply.

He wiped his eyes, then pulled the suitcase from the trunk. The distance seemed the longest he'd ever walked in his life. Longer than the impossible sixty miles he'd had to traverse, at nine years old, so he could get back home to London. Longer than the distance from the catering facility to the welcoming darkness beyond the fence, with Ibrahim hissing, then shouting, *"Why did you do that?"* all the way.

As he ran, Ibrahim held his arm close to his body. His arm had been sliced through by a heavy cleaver that fell from the rack. At the same instant, a heavy pot had crashed onto the old man's head. Blood was all over the place, but Michael couldn't tell if it was Ibrahim's or the poor old man's. Blood stained the man's clothes, though, and he was motionless.

Mission accomplished, Michael thought, numb. *Now, run! Run! Run!*

He remembered grabbing Ibrahim, leading him away. He remembered whispering, "Just a few more steps and we're out."

A few more steps ... He dragged the suitcase, now a chunk of cement, beside him toward the front door, every step burdened by hesitation and regret. This time, there would be no lucky breaks. This time, instead of carrying the fear of the unknown, he must walk each step with his heart breaking.

"There you are," she said when he finally got inside. "What happened?"

"I just had to check something in the car," he said, and handed her the small suitcase.

"Hey, what's this?" she said after unzipping the bag. "Power bars?"

He shrugged. "You never know what kind of food they'll serve there, do you."

She rolled her eyes, but giggled. "You guys. Always

thinking of food."

Exactly as he planned, she quickly finished packing and he took the bag to the car while she locked the house.

He didn't exceed the speed limit even once. Even if he wanted to, it was already morning rush hour. When they reached LAX, he parked in the short-term parking garage.

She looked at him, took in his distracted, weary face. "Why not long-term parking? It'll cost a fortune here."

He leaned forward and kissed her. "We don't have time. We've got a plane to catch."

Chapter 41

"Good morning, Ms. Aldheim, My name is Artillio, and I represent your cellular phone provider. I must inform you this call is absolutely free," Orlando said with ease.

"Please, call me Karla. What can I do for you, Artillio?"

From the way her sweet voice sounded, there were a lot of things Orlando wanted her to do for him. Instead, he said, "We're conducting a short survey. For your cooperation, I'll give you five hundred minutes free. Do you have three minutes to participate?"

"Sure, go ahead," Karla said, and giggled.

He verified her address and occupation. When she answered "That's correct" to both, he said, "Your English is perfect. Where are you from originally?"

"Oh, thank you. I'm from Norway."

"That's great. Now, Karla, what is your main purpose for using your cell phone? Generally speaking, do you use it for professional reasons, talking to friends, things like that?"

As he expected, she didn't answer right away, likely because of confusion.

"I can be more specific," he added quickly. "I can tell you the phone numbers you called, or which ones called you. Then, you can tell me the purpose of the call. We try to determine the profile of our customers, and if I haven't thanked you yet for your participation, I'd like to do so now. In fact, I'm even authorized to add three hundred free text messages to compensate you for your time."

"Oh, ah, it's ... that's great. What did you want to ask?"

Perfect. He read a random phone number from the list of numbers she called, a twelve-minute conversation she initiated two days earlier. "What was this phone number used for?" he asked.

"Oh, that's Nicole, my friend from school." Accompanied by another of those delicious-sounding giggle.

"Okay. I labeled it as 'friends' rather than 'colleagues'," he said after a short laugh he thought was required. "Let's look at a different one now." He read a few more phone numbers, and then, the only one he was actually interested in.

"Hummm," she said. "It doesn't sound familiar to me. When was it?"

He paused for two seconds, as if searching for the date and time. "Yesterday afternoon, at 4:12 p.m. to be precise."

"Oh. That's Abe, then."

"Abe?" He repeated the name while writing it down. *Close enough to the name Jose mentioned.* "So, what was it?" he asked.

"What *was* it?" She laughed. "It *was* a fling. Definitely personal. Abe is his name." She giggled, this time in embarrassment.

"A fling, you say?" he asked, his voice raising a notch. "As far as I can remember, flings don't call back."

"Unless you were so good it requires a second one."

He laughed freely. "And will you give him a second chance?" he asked, still laughing.

"I don't know. He went to Europe to recover. He'll call me tomorrow to tell me when and where we'll meet. Does that make him a friend? I don't know. I'd consider him more a colleague though."

"A scheduled conversation with a fling? That's a good one," he said. "Well, will you fly to him, or will he come here?"

Orlando knew he was walking on thin ice with that one, but he wanted to close the loop. And besides, he enjoyed his specialty—instead of breaking into a vault or security system, he maneuvered others to reveal whatever he wanted to know just by chatting with them.

"You know what?" she said, "I'm not sure how to answer that last question. You can call me tomorrow after 8:00 p.m., and I'll let you know who is going and who is coming." She released a rolling laugh at her own joke, clearly a double message.

"Maybe I will," he said, laughing too. "Maybe I will. Meanwhile, I want to wish you a great day, and to thank you once again for participating in our survey. The features I offered you will be active at the beginning of your next billing cycle. "Thank you very much, Karla. It was a pleasure talking to you."

He hung up and sighed, then studied the information he'd written and smiled while he turned to the keyboard and typed into the system, *Customer called to talk about reception problems she's been having with her cell phone.* Then he entered the standard explanation he gave to such a request, and closed the customer profile.

Karla would never suspect a thing.

He looked at the next number Jose asked him to check, and scowled. Prepaid phones were always more complicated. He wouldn't have the advantage of knowing the user's background prior to the conversation.

"What the heck," he muttered. *Jose will repay me big time. It's worth trying.* He keyed in the number.

Chapter 42

Chief Stewart entered the terminal, spotted Richard and Perez and joined them. "I didn't mention this before, but I won't be able to stay long."

Perez met his eyes. "The funeral this afternoon?"

Steward nodded and explained to Richard, "One of our INS officers. And his son. Terrible accident, both were killed instantly. I'll attend, Perez will stay here and mind the shop."

He let his eyes roam over the terminal, then back to them. "So, what are you guys doing now? Find any security loopholes?"

Richard smiled back. "If you were a terrorist, Chief, how would you attack the airport?"

Stewart measured Richard through wary eyes. Eventually he said, "Depends on what I want to achieve: killing people, attacking the terminal or aircraft, or all of the above. Demolishing aircrafts or structures? Horrible, but they can be rebuilt. Human beings? Killing creates panic, and the impact would be devastating."

"Can you think of a method for your attack?" Richard asked.

"Oh, of course, I've given a lot of thought to that. Since there *are* police officers in view, I'm not sure I'd come through the main doors. I'd go after the airplane, plant a bomb. But not through the terminal and checkpoints. Instead, I'd use a vendor. Perhaps a baggage handler. Perhaps even one of the caterers. Or I'd insert the bomb into something—say, a cigarette pack.

When a customer purchased it, the merchandise wouldn't go through security. And since the airport's smoke-free, nobody would open the pack by accident."

"So how could you make it less desirable for a terrorist to try that?" Richard asked. While he spoke, he kept his eyes roving around the busy terminal. Something was making him uneasy. Edgy. He couldn't determine what.

He forced his mind back to Perez and said, "What you said about the cigarette pack reminded me ... from that taxi driver's account, maybe that passenger came here to rehearse a crime. To judge how feasible it would be to use a mule to leave a bomb at the terminal."

Perez scratched his ear. "The man's behavior was odd, but a lot of people in this place act peculiar."

"I'm sure that's true," Richard said. "But ... what I mean is, why don't you use the employees as force multipliers? Turn them into your eyes and ears?"

Perez shrugged. "Do you know what it'd take to train every employee here?"

"Maybe not as much as you think," Richard persisted. "Maybe you could just explain to the skycaps that they shouldn't enter the terminal with luggage when the passenger isn't present. And tell the employees at the outer perimeters something similar. That shouldn't take that long."

The feeling that something was wrong stayed strong, and he wondered if it was because they were talking about terrorists. Determined that the other two men would assume precisely that, he decided not to mention it.

"Tell you what," Stewart said. "I think Richard's right. And what do we have to lose except a little time? I think we should start now, at least with the skycaps."

* * *

Richard was happy to get outside, where the strange

feeling subsided a bit. He remembered Henry and Patrick from his last visit, and suppressed a grin. With the airport police authorities present, he didn't need to buy their time this time. They all listened carefully to what Perez had to say, and all agreed to the new rule.

Moments after they reentered the terminal, while they chatted about the cameras and other deterrence measures, they heard someone calling them. They turned to see Patrick racing in their direction.

"You said to let you know, Chief ... there's a young couple who wants Henry to take in their luggage while they wait outside."

They walked to the entrance, and Perez asked Patrick, "The blonde young woman and the slim man? Them?"

Patrick nodded. "They're the ones."

The strange uneasiness in Richard's stomach returned.

Chapter 43

The mailman rang the bell again, and Joe's usually steel-like nerves sang with rising panic. It had to be the wrong address. It had to be! Yet the mailman was still standing at his door, blocking the peephole. Despite the chilling temperatures inside the house, Joe's blood gushed hot in his veins.

He swiveled his head to see what the man would see if he opened the door right now. The rental house's curtains were closed, shielding his work from prying eyes, but the air conditioner outside worked at its full capacity, indicating that someone was in. Joe didn't move, tried to avoid even breathing as he scanned the frigid living room, checking for anything suspicious. The ice-filled bathtub in the bathroom was visible from the house door. The ice cubes in it shouldn't be a problem; they were level with the tub's rim, hence hard to see at a distance. Even if the man noticed, nobody suspected ice could be used for anything devious. But the basin full of chemicals nestled in the ice and the containers of hydrogen peroxide and acetone beside the tub could suggest otherwise.

He tried to think. How much time had passed since the doorbell first rang? Thirty seconds? A full minute? Time mattered more than anything now; a steady temperature, like the constant stirring of the chemicals inside the basin, was critical.

Just as he placed his hand on the doorknob, he remembered the gasmask on his face and yanked his hand back. He didn't dare take the gasmask off. No, his only option seemed to open the door, grab the man, and subdue him until the fumes did their work. And if they didn't, he would have to take more drastic action.

He reached for the doorknob again. But, as though the man finally sensed the danger inside, he turned and walked away, dragging a small wheeled cart with the USPS logo on it.

There was no time for hesitation or sighs of relief. Joe hurried back to the bathroom.

The process he'd begun wasn't new, nor did it improve much since its first incarnation a century ago, when chemists shelved the idea because the result was highly unstable, being heat, friction, and shock-sensitive. But then "Mother of Satan" was rediscovered accidentally, and the mixture of hydrogen peroxide and acetone was renamed to triacetone triperoxide, or TATP. Having seen it many times, Joe knew what the results were, even though he didn't care to know that the process creates an open monomer and dimer—a mix of chemicals that form cyclic dimer. No, Joe's only concern was that the primary product, if produced under the proper conditions, formed the cyclic trimer, a polymer formed from three molecules of a monomer.

Thankfully, the reaction from combining those chemicals was much slower under certain conditions. In a certain room temperature and with a strong acid catalyst, the reaction produced more monomeric organic peroxide than the reaction. Under those conditions the trimeric form slowly refined, becoming the less-stable dimer that was much more sensitive to shock, heat, and friction.

"And which makes everything go boom," Joe whispered while checking the thermometer inside the solution. The reading caused him to risk a low whistle behind the gasmask. *Another minute at the door, and we would all have witnessed how powerful this shit is.*

He checked the mask to make sure it had kept a tight seal, then continued stirring the chemicals that, in reaction, converted into a crystalline solid. Once finished with that phase, it was safe enough for him to return to the door. The mailman was still gone. For now.

Returning to the bathroom, he contemplated his next steps. Joe knew many ways to convert innocent materials into explosives. He wasn't a chemist, but he didn't have to be one to know what made good ingredients of the exploding kind. All he had to do was turn to a page in some of the many history books he'd pored over in his research. There were so many examples from which to choose. The Belarusian guerillas against the Nazis during World War II. The IRA in 1979. Afghan Mujahideens against the USSR in 1977. Hezbollah in Lebanon against the Israelis in 1982. Chechnya's guerillas in the USSR in 1984. All the way from 2003 to the present day, when the Iraqi insurgents used these same methods against Americans.

In all of these conflicts, insurgents converted available materials into deadly weapons. What Joe was producing was the outcome of lessons learned in bombing strikes all over the world, for different causes against different enemies.

And in every case, caution is the key to avoiding an accident. He knew this basic rule, and also how much was at stake.

That caution made him peer at his face in the bathroom mirror. His eyes looked irritated. *Not good,* he thought, and readjusted the mask.

He'd examined the case of Ahmed Ressam, the Millennium Bomber who was caught at the Canadian border in 1999. Ressam was pulled over at the peaceful border checkpoint because he appeared sick. And he was. Inhaling the toxic vapors from the explosives he'd cooked a few days earlier made him look pale. That, combined with his runny nose and bloodshot eyes, prompted the US Customs agent to pull him over. When he was unable to produce the right answers, the agent searched his trunk, and the explosives were found.

The mix became thicker. Joe gradually added a fixative.

Stabilizing the crystals was imperative since a spark or wobble, or even heat could set it off at this point.

He packed the end product into aluminum bags, which he placed into Tupperware containers. He carried them cautiously, one by one, to the freezer and placed them inside before returning to the icy bathtub.

He was anxious to leave, even more eager to take the mask off and to breathe fresh air outside. He couldn't. Not yet. There were more ingredients to be shaped into deadly crystals. So much yet to accomplish, and so many things that could still go wrong.

Chapter 44

She couldn't figure out why his behavior had changed so suddenly, just that it had. He'd been morose since before they left her house—and that was *after* that strange disappearing act while he was getting the extra suitcase. But now, she was *convinced* something wasn't right. His gloominess disappeared as soon they were inside the airport. Now, he was as uptight as she'd ever seen him.

Except that day ... The memory came back in a rush. When the police came to her house by mistake to return the poor Holmans' stuff. He'd said his nerves were because he wasn't a citizen. But that couldn't be the reason he was acting that way now. He said he had a valid passport. And heck, probably half the people at this airport were born somewhere else!

But while he parked the car, she could swear she saw goose bumps on his forearms. And when he pulled their luggage from the trunk just now, his hands were shaking.

A more logical reason occurred to her while he closed the car's trunk.

"Michael ...?" she said.

He slammed the trunk and looked at her. "What?" His eyes were wild, disoriented.

"Are you okay? I mean ... is something bothering you? Like ... I don't know ... maybe you're nervous about flying?"

"*Tammam.*"

Even weirder. "Huh?"

"What? Oh, nothing. Everything's fine." He gave her a weak smile. "But yes, I'll admit it. I'm one of those white-knuckle flyers."

She reached out and patted his shoulder. "Don't worry. Mom's the same way." With a giggle, she added, "Her cure's a couple of bourbon-and-waters before a flight. Don't guess you want to go there, huh?"

He tried to match her giggle with a convincing laugh. "Ah, no. I usually just white-knuckle it. Maybe this time, you'll be able to distract me."

"Guaranteed."

He shifted his eyes ahead, toward the building ahead of them. "Let's go. I don't want to miss the flight."

They crossed the road to the terminal entrance. When his steps abruptly slowed, she looked at him, about to ask him if everything was all right.

"The *CTA* director's assistant said she might be flying with us today," he said, his tone deliberately nonchalant, and stepped up on the curb. "Forgot to mention it."

"Really? You didn't tell me."

He was watching the passing cars now, so all she could see was the side of his face, which revealed nothing.

"Yes," he said. "That's what she told me anyway."

She touched his chin and turned his face to hers, trying but failing to lock eyes with him. "Michael, what's going on here? Why didn't you tell me something like that?" She forced a laugh. "You planning something with her, and I'm standing in your way?"

Jolted, he reached out and grabbed her up in a hug. "Are you out of your mind? It's *our* vacation. And besides, there is no comparison. She couldn't even get as high as your ankles." He kissed her, then added, "I just need to see whether she's coming or not."

She shook her head, befuddled. "But ... didn't you say a minute ago we were running late?"

"Yes. Yes, that's right." He looked around, saw one of

the skycaps. "Tell you what. I'll send the porter inside with our luggage while we wait here for Melissa."

Melissa. So that's her name. The name of the girl who's suddenly so important, he's willing to risk missing our flight. Something's definitely creepy here.

"No, it's okay. You wait here, I'll go in. I can check us in while you do ... whatever."

"Nonsense. Hang on." He waved to one of the porters.

* * *

"What can I do for you folks?" the man asked. A much slimmer colleague of his stood several paces behind and watched them.

Michael glanced down at the two small suitcases he and Dianne carried, then back up at the men. "Can you please take our luggage to Mexicana's counter? We'll be right in. We'll be waiting for someone outside."

"Sorry folks, it's against airport rules," Henry said, repeating Captain Perez's mandate. He smiled. "Once your friend arrives, I'll be more than happy to take you *and* your luggage inside."

Michael was confused. Nothing Joe reported told him to expect this response.

He saw the slimmer skycap turn and walk back to the terminal. Did he walk too fast? Michael wasn't sure. Perhaps it was his natural pace. Perhaps he always walked fast because of his job, like some taxi drivers always drove fast. But he didn't have a better story, and his rising panic wouldn't allow him to try to construct a better one.

He turned to Dianne. "Let's wait here for a couple of minutes."

"Perhaps *Mellissa* is already inside," Dianne suggested.

He fought a wince. Her customary sweetness had disappeared, and there was nothing he could do about that either.

"Just a couple of minutes," he repeated, feeling like an old record. His hands began to tremble again so he clasped them into fists, wanting nothing more than to return to the wild outdoors of Northern California, away from civilization, away from police officers, away from what he was about to do at this airport.

* * *

Perez approached the couple, who were standing with their backs to the terminal. He wondered why they didn't just enter the terminal after Henry refused their request. Remembering what Richard had advised about a pleasant approach, he mentally rehearsed several possible greetings, picked one, and walked to stand behind them. Even from behind, the woman was young and attractive. The young man beside her seemed harmless. But Perez had encountered more than a few meek-looking persons who still attempted to stab him or pull a gun. The amicable greeting he'd chosen left his mind, and he pulled the badge from his jacket and cleared his throat. When the couple reacted and turned around, he placed the badge at eye level.

"Good afternoon. I'm Captain Perez with airport police. May I ask what you're doing here?"

"We're flying to Cancun," the blonde girl said. In spite of his authoritative tone, her eyes met his head-on. Yet the man seemed to shrink at the question. Perez could swear his olive skin, as dark as his, had lightened a few shades.

"May I see your travel documents?" he asked, returning his badge to the jacket.

She gave him her passport. The young man reached for his backpack and pulled out a manila envelope. It seemed almost as though he surrendered his tickets and passport.

Perez checked the papers, giving the burgundy passport

a closer look and noting the name inside. "You're British, Mr. Siluan?"

Silence. Perez tried again. "How long have you been in the United States?"

This time, he got an answer. "Five years, sir."

"Doing what?"

"A student. At UCLA. Sir. My F-1 student visa's inside."

Perez examined both their documents, looked around, and asked, "Are you waiting for someone, Mr. Siluan?"

"Ah, yes sir. Someone I work with on a research project. But it seems she stood us up."

The man's delayed answer bothered him. Apparently, it bothered the girl, too. She glanced at the side of his face as he replied, but then looked away without adding anything to his answer.

Yet he couldn't detain them on a gut feeling. He rested his hands on his waist and said, "Enjoy your flight."

"We can go now, Michael," Dianne said quietly, and took his arm with her free hand. His response was to retrieve his suitcase and walk silently beside her into the terminal.

Chapter 45

"So how did it go? What was your gut feeling?" Richard asked when Perez approached.

"You see how that guy acted?" Perez said. "I'm sure he was lying. Maybe not about who he is ... his papers looked okay ... but something."

Richard chuckled. "Look, I couldn't hear what was going on, but I saw your face. With all due respect, if you were coming down on me like you did on those two poor kids, I'm not sure *I* wouldn't be shaking. Somehow, I don't think that ACLU attorney was in your mind when you questioned them."

The smile on Perez's face faded and he looked at Chief Stewart, searching for criticism or approval and finding neither.

"We can discuss your strategy later," Stewart said. "Did you find out why they wanted to use the skycaps in the first place? They had so little luggage. To me, that seemed odder than the way the man was acting."

Perez clearly hadn't noticed their scant luggage. "Maybe they were—"

"Waiting for someone," Stewart said, closing the issue. He looked at his watch. "I think we're done for the day. And I have a funeral to attend."

* * *

Mexicana Airlines' offered flights to multiple

destinations, including Cancun, so the line at the counters stretched like a snake between the ropes and posts. Michael watched the people in front of him, boxes and bulging suitcases surrounding most of them, and wondered if they were all moving back to Mexico. Of course, they might be bringing gifts to relatives back home. Or, after being indoctrinated by the American urge to have far more possessions than they really needed, perhaps they just brought what they thought they needed for their trip.

No matter what the reason, he was glad to have something else to occupy his mind. The encounter with the police officer left him dangerously off balance. Worse, Joe's method was going down the tubes. Dianne was still distant, and constantly scowled toward the terminal doors, no doubt waiting for Showtime's director's assistant. This confirmed to him how fragile their relationship still was, and how painful it was to hurt her. His hastily conceived cover story was a mistake.

But it was too late to back out now—another hard lesson learned that day in London's Heathrow Airport. On that rainy night, backing out meant running away, and fast. He would never run away again, no matter how high the stakes.

At least the line moved fast. An overstressed ground attendant gave them a fake smile and took their tickets and passports. She didn't even ask if they preferred aisle or window seats, just clicked a few buttons on her computer and handed them their boarding passes, then tagged their luggage, pointed behind them and said, "Go to the CTX area, get your luggage scanned, and have a nice flight."

He couldn't follow the woman's lightning-quick speech and turned to Dianne, who said, "We should get our luggage scanned."

The real test began, and he felt his heart rate accelerating. *No matter what, no backing out!* he reminded himself.

The silence between them grew too great; he had to say something. "If I forget to say this before the end of our trip, I thank you for joining me."

She looked at him for a long moment, her stare hard at the beginning, but then a smile sparkled across her face. "I believe I should thank *you*, but ... are you disappointed Melissa didn't show up?"

He grasped her hand and locked his eyes on hers. "There's nothing I want to do and nobody I want to be with more than you."

Her smile returned. "I'm glad I'm here."

"I'm glad you're here too," he said, not letting go of her hand. It helped him to focus and restrain the nervousness threatening to tear him apart.

The line for the CTX machine was slower than at the ticket counter, and he had a chance to watch the process in action. A few TSA officers took luggage from passengers and instructed them to wait on the far side of the machine, then loaded the luggage onto the belt, inspected the machine's determination for threats inside the luggage, and then released the luggage to another agent, who carried it to the counter. The whole process lasted a few minutes. Unless there was a problem. But so far, there had been no delays he could see.

When it was their turn, a tall man wearing a white uniform with a TSA patch on the sleeve approached. "I'll take it from here, folks. You can wait for your luggage over there."

He pointed to the exit area, beyond the small perimeter. Michael nodded, then he and Dianne walked to the other side to wait.

The first bag, Michael's, moved over the conveyor and entered the machine. Smooth sounds of an accelerating jet engine accompanied the scanner's projection. From his reading, he already knew how the scan projection worked, understood what the conveyors inside the machine did with the luggage, and what the algorithms did with the results it produced. And he was certain his bladder was about to explode.

His suitcase was ejected forcefully, and Dianne's two

suitcases entered, sliding smoothly on the belt. As they moved, a TSA officer placed a colorful stamp on each luggage tag and a porter verified their destination. He felt his nerves stretch to the danger point. Was it taking longer for her luggage to be checked than his?

He listened to the conveyors moving inside the big machine, and wanted to chew his nails to their roots. His bladder signaled he was gambling that it would hold until this was over.

Dianne's luggage was ejected with the same force as his. But then, the TSA officer lifted her suitcase from the conveyor and placed it on a metal table, unzipped it and peered inside. Both of them watched the officer shifting Dianne's garments, then pausing when he apparently found what he was looking for and pulled it out. Michael held his breath and willed his bladder to hold.

The officer made the obvious inference: the box was a container of power bars. He showed it to the officer behind the machine screens, who looked at it and nodded once. The first officer returned the box into the suitcase, closed the latch, and zipped the luggage again.

A false positive, Michael thought, his brain stuttering with his recall of what he'd read. *Something marked by the machine as threatening—positive—but in fact, it proves harmless—false. And I fooled them into thinking that's exactly what the box is—harmless.*

He started breathing again. The restrooms were right behind them.

"I have to take a leak," he whispered. "I'll be right back."

"I'll be right back." The same thing he'd said to Ibrahim as he laid him on the muddy ground and told him to wait, that he would get their car and drive back to where he lay. Even though Michael feared their escape route had been noted in the rain and darkness, it seemed the only way at that moment to get Ibrahim to the car. Weak from blood loss, Ibrahim kept

falling, slowing them too much. But in spite of the older man's entreaties, Michael refused to leave his mentor behind.

Ibrahim had been the first to hear the sirens. "Police," he muttered.

It wouldn't have mattered if Ibrahim had announced the Easter Bunny's arrival. Michael was already beyond panic. His responses were instincts only. The car was there, unlocked and beckoning, and closer with each hurried footstep.

Then there was the sound, the one breaking the rhythm of the rain. Once, twice, like the uncorking of two bottles. *Gunshots,* his brain told him, but it didn't register at that instant. All that mattered was making it to the car and getting away.

Chapter 46

Unbelievable as it seemed, the first batch was done. Now, the freezer and refrigerator were filled with small packs of the next American disaster. Joe took the gasmask off his face and rubbed his eyes, which became instantly irritated by toxic vapors that just as quickly threatened to choke him. He didn't dare go outside the freezing-cold house. Not yet. It would be an invitation to get the flu or a cold, something he couldn't afford at this stage. Instead, he entered the bathtub, used only minutes ago for the final batch, and showered. He needed the water to wash off the chemicals that had permeated through his clothing and the gas mask.

Once he toweled off, he dressed casually in blue jeans and a black button-down shirt. Cotton decreased the chance of static electricity as he moved. Already feeling terrible, he popped two Advils for the rapidly worsening headache and a Dramamine tablet to ease the nausea. He was eager to leave the now-toxic house, but knew his best accomplice at this point was caution. Even a spark inside the house could blow up half the block.

With the explosives contained within the side-by-side American refrigerator, ventilating the house was no longer as much of a danger. He opened the tiny bathroom window and placed two industrial fans inside the living room, hoping the constant stream would refresh the air quickly.

In the garage, he allowed caution to continue driving his movements. He locked the kitchen door behind him and tried the knob to make sure it was secure. A burglar breaking in now would be catastrophic to the entire city of El Segundo. *To our plans as well,* he thought, and hissed.

He opened the 4Runner's door and inserted the key into the ignition, but didn't get inside. Instead, he reached over, shifted the gear into neutral, then released the handbrake. Only then did he press the remote clicker and opened the garage door. As it rose, he pressed his body weight against the SUV's frame and pushed.

He wasn't strong, but his extra weight was enough to make the SUV roll. When the rear wheels passed the garage's doorframe and merged with the down-sloping driveway, he climbed in and closed the driver's door. He waited until the SUV was at the end of the driveway before braking, and then pressed the remote clicker to close the garage. At that point, he felt confident enough to start the engine.

While he listened to the smooth sound of the cylinders kicking under the hood, he wiped sweat from his hot forehead. The sweat surprised him. Was it rolling the car out of the garage? Possibly. Or might it be from inhaling the air inside the house.

"Or, perhaps it's just the adrenaline rush, as they say," he muttered with a weak smile.

He merged onto the Pacific Coast Highway and headed north, letting the cool ocean breeze clear his mind. He turned on the radio and enjoyed the ride and the wind blowing through his thinning hair. On the radio, the Eagles sang "Hotel California."

"But you just can't kill the beast..."

The infidel singer couldn't have known that three decades after he recorded those words Joe would be listening, constructing his own meaning to them. Before then, Joe didn't know or care that the song was a metaphor for the dark, surreal world of dissipation, the group's expression of the pessimistic 1970s.

But when the song concluded with, *"You can check out*

any time you like, but you can never leave," Joe couldn't agree more.

He pulled onto Santa Monica, parked the SUV, fed the parking meter, and walked west toward the 3rd Street Promenade. The pedestrian-only street lined with prosperous shops was everything he hated about this country's ridiculous consumer-driven behavior. Bizarre-looking people performed street shows in the middle of the street, and the atmosphere they created was of a crowded festival. Visitors ambled from store to store as if they were bees in a blossoming field.

While he walked, he looked around. Two uniformed cops directed traffic where the promenade intersected with Santa Monica Boulevard, but that was the only police presence he could see. At the end of the promenade—or at the beginning of it, depending where you started your tour—was the shopping mall.

Perhaps a better target than the airport? He played with the idea in his head. But no. After his failure, he wouldn't confront Jacob with a change-of-plan idea.

He entered the mall and headed straight for the gigantic Macy's. On his way to the men's section, he was forced to walk through the cosmetic department. A yellow-haired older woman attacked him from behind one of the booths and tried to interest him in perfume.

"Women will drop dead around you," she said and produced a huge fake smile.

I already have that power, he wanted to say, but simply muttered, "No, thank you."

Ten minutes later, he exited with shopping bags in hand, their contents paid for in cash. The price had been outrageous, but the object's purpose was worth any price.

* * *

I accomplished more in one day than any of you

accomplish in a year, Joe thought while driving down Wilshire. Heading east, reveling in his triumph, he could see the rise of Beverly Hills and Hollywood in the distance. The sign was still visible, but starting to fade as evening darkness covered the polluted metropolitan area. Santa Monica would bring him to West Hollywood, where homosexuals walked hand-in-hand. But that was a sight he didn't want to view. Instead, he decided to treat himself the way he liked most.

He headed for prosperous Beverly Hills, where he turned right into Century City Shopping Mall. A sign on the building beckoned: Houston's Restaurant. He felt he wasn't walking from his car to the restaurant, but gliding.

Perhaps it's the vapors I breathed, he thought, amused by his atypical good mood. *Perhaps there* is *commercial value to my TATP. I might be the inventor of the new Prozac. Ha!*

He played with the thought and immediately regretted it, decided it meant he was becoming materialistic, like the infidels around him. He refused to let such thoughts change his excellent mood, though. The first half of this day was his most dangerous since his arrival in North America, yet a symbolic day. He'd stopped being just a conspirator, something the American law system couldn't easily prove, and was now a terrorist operative, someone who had illegal explosives in his possession.

No turning back, he thought with a chuckle. *Either way, something will blow up.*

The meeting with Tim had been, as predicted, successful, if a bit more troubling than usual. They'd walked to the gelato place on Federal Avenue and Joe treated them to a pint of assorted-flavor ice cream. Tim was cheerful and grateful as always, but something was fading in his eyes. His vitality seemed to have dissipated, his confusion deeper. Joe wasn't happy with the regression in Tim's mental state, but at least everything was ticking now. The game would be over before the sand depleted in Tim's hourglass.

On their way back to Tim's room, they passed by Joe's

car as he had planned, and Joe gave him the contents of the two shopping bags from Macy's.

"A present?" Tim had cried out. "But it's not even my birthday yet."

"When is your birthday, Tim?" Joe asked. When Tim didn't reply, Joe regretted broaching the subject, but relaxed when Tim reached into one of his new vest's many pockets, found his wallet and handed Joe his veteran's ID.

"You see?" Joe proclaimed. "Your birthday is next week. I got you an early birthday present."

"Oh, okay," Tim said, then pulled the long coat from the bigger shopping bag and tried it on. "Wow, cool! Thank you so much, Joe. It even matches the vest color!"

Tim looked inside the second, smaller bag and said, "Cologne? It's too much, Joe. Why did you buy me five different kinds?"

"I wasn't sure what scent you like," Joe had said. "Besides, five is a lucky number. In any case, since you have so many pockets now, you can store all five bottles in your new vest. You can wear any cologne you like, whenever and wherever you want."

"Thank you. You are the best friend ever!" Tim said, and hugged Joe, then allowed Joe to take him back to his room.

Inside Houston's, the smiling hostess led Joe toward a table, saying, "How are you this evening?" Joe didn't answer. The hostess only wanted his money, nothing more, nothing less. She wouldn't have given him a second look outside this upscale restaurant.

He walked behind her, casting around occasional sideways glances. The place was packed, mostly with couples. There was just one other single diner besides him, and he almost regretted choosing this restaurant. Abnormality could make him look suspicious to the trained eye. Yet, after the accomplishments of the day, he deserved to spoil himself, and Houston's seemed a good enough place for that.

When the server arrived to take his order, he said, "I'll

start with an order of foie gras with berries, and zucchini stuffed with goat cheese and herbs. Make sure it's creamed with extra cheese, please. For the main course, I'd like the filet mignon, medium well, mashed sweet and blue potatoes, and a garden salad with bleu cheese dressing. I'll drink San Pellegrino and a fruit shake of strawberries and bananas."

"Would you like to see the wine selection?" asked the impressed server.

"No." His sudden annoyance caused him to almost bark the word. But, when the server left and he looked around, nobody seemed to have noticed. Either the structure's acoustics prevented noises from echoing back, or the restaurant's guests were polite enough to ignore his one-word rebuke.

The waitress brought the drinks and Joe enjoyed the sweet taste of banana mixed with the semi-sour strawberries. When the first course arrived, he forgot about the people around him, the city he had to endure, the comrades he worked with, and their plans in the making. The tender goose liver melted in his mouth, its flavor emphasized by the tang of the berry sauce.

"Voila, here is your entrée," the waitress announced as if actually born and raised in the Palais de-l′Ělysěe. He didn't think her statement was amusing. Only in North America did "entrée" mean the main dish. In Europe, it simply meant the starter. The anticipation of the food, however, suppressed any criticism he might have given her.

While he ate, he tried to eavesdrop on some of the hollow conversations of people around him. The couple next to his table caught his attention. What really drew him were the woman's eyes. They were sparkling pools of ocean green, the color of the San Pellegrino bottle on his table. Her jade-green dress complemented her eyes and flame-colored hair, and her makeup emphasized, not disguised, her facial features—features that tightened with worry whenever she pulled her cell phone from her purse, dialed a number, and waited for an answer that apparently never came.

Across from her sat a tall, handsome man who didn't look like an athlete, but something in his face expressed power. Neither of them wore wedding rings, but they seemed to share a similar intimacy. She called him "Rich," and that is exactly how he looked. He wore a fine watch, a man's status symbol, but Joe looked at his feet. The shoes were what mattered. The black loafers looked almost new, and expensive.

He has style, Joe admitted. Two yuppies in their mid-thirties or forties, fit, probably professionals of some sort. He wanted to hear more of what they were saying, at least to find out whom the woman kept calling. He couldn't. But thankfully, acute hearing wasn't required for explosives-cooking: mystery skills gained in the mountains of Eastern Turkey, a paradise for people who didn't want to be found.

The waitress appeared again. "Would you like to see our dessert menu?"

He shook his head, impatient to resume his listening. "I'll have the crème brulee and a large cappuccino."

The less-than-perfect hearing that frustrated him now was received in one of his few failed tests. He'd filled a keg with fertilizer and poured petroleum gas into it. ANFO, Ammonium Nitrate combined with Fuel Gas creates a powerful improvised explosive. He then sealed the keg to prevent oxygen from getting inside—necessary to create enough pressure for the explosion. He'd chosen a flashlight bulb as the catalyst, and a massive boulder in a deserted Turkish valley as the test site. He stood 500 yards away, shielding himself with another boulder, before he released the donkey that hauled the materials to the location. Plenty of distance, he thought. As soon as his index finger press the switch attached to the electrical cords the shockwave threw him hard against the boulder. He didn't hear the blast. Actually, he didn't hear a thing. It was not like any movie he ever seen. He couldn't run away from the blast and the thousands of ricochets that found his within spilt second. His body was pierced as if it was a sieve. The dust chocked him down but he couldn't move. He lay there until evening, when a friend came looking for him because he didn't show up for his English class.

His injuries eventually healed, his field tests definitely improved, but his hearing never recovered. So he could only hear partial sentences while the attractive woman, a doctor of some kind, talked about a patient of hers. While the man held the woman's hand, she spoke of a car accident, and he tried to fill in the words he couldn't hear. While he did, he swallowed the sweet crème brulee and sipped coffee that wasn't strong enough to his taste.

He'd pulled money from his pocket and was ready to leave when he overheard the woman saying something about loss of life and the way people deal with it. He smirked inside. *Soon enough,* all *of you will be forced to "deal with it."*

Chapter 47

"I told you!" Ibrahim's voice boomed inside his head, *"I told you!"*

The memory, Michael reasoned, brought back what he'd felt long ago, and what he felt right now. The adrenaline-racing fear of getting caught at the airport had rubbed off, replaced by exhilaration. Throughout the world, martyrs were given a day of pleasure prior to their execution. For some of them the pleasure was women, for others the gratification was luxury items or money. For him, it would be a trip to a luxurious Mexican resort.

How stupid some people are! he thought while washing his hands. *To get one indulgence this world can offer by having to give up life the very next day.* Yet while he didn't want to consider this vacation as his reward for the sacrifice he was about to make, he couldn't avoid the coincidence.

"This is for you, Ibrahim," he said to his reflection in the mirror. "And for my father."

New relief surged through him when they boarded the airplane, a formal end to his successful test run. Dianne sensed the change in him too; her anger gave way to affection and excitement. Even the flight attendants were pleasant, their actions showing a buoyant mood that seemed to affect the passengers too.

"Sujete su correa de asiento. Estamos aterrizando." The message was followed by one in English, but due to the pilot's heavy accent, it sounded exactly like the previous one to

him. He turned to Dianne, who was flipping through a women's magazine, and asked, "What did he say? The pilot, I mean."

"*Yo no hablo español,*" she said with a shrug.

"But you studied Spanish in school, didn't you?"

She lowered the magazine and said, as if explaining to a child, "I was registered for classes. It doesn't mean I studied. *Etiendo?*"

He shook his head, his annoyance deepening. No matter how much he cared for her, and he did, nothing could bridge the gaps between them—their cultures, values, and particularly their religions. Yet there was a reason for being there, and he would do everything he could to accomplish the task.

At the hotel, the beautiful panorama of the Mexican Gulf from their bedroom window and the sensual atmosphere of the hotel took his mind away from his earlier annoyance at her, and Americans in general. Especially when she wrapped her arms around his waist from behind and said, "It's lovely. Thank you."

He drew his arms back and grasped her buttocks, pressing her body to his back. "No, thank *you*," he said. An alert segment of his mind suggested her forwardness was part of the low values American girls adopt. The rest of his body muted that idea immediately when she whispered in his ear, "What do you want to do now?"

He turned around, took her in his arms, stroked her blonde hair. "We can grab some dinner."

"Nah." She smiled. "If we get hungry, we have tons of power bars we can't take back with us to LA. I just want to be with you."

There is no passion as symbolic as one of the flesh, he thought with the euphoria he always experienced when physically aroused. He pulled back and searched her eyes, wanting to gaze through her soul, to verify that she carried the evil look of a woman who seduced him to betray his values, religion and heritage.

What he actually saw shocked him. Caring. Passion. The intent to please him. She didn't care for herself; she was there only for him. The realization threw him off balance. He hated being ambivalent. It was so much easier to take sides and to stick to them. But she made it ... difficult.

She smiled at him and pressed her lovely head onto his chest, tears moistening his shoulders. He felt his own tears start, tears from a far different source than hers, they began flooding his face.

Chapter 48

The oversized clock on the wall didn't have small hands or big hands, or any hands at all. In America's advanced society, anything that *could* be digitalized, was. The company Orlando worked for wasn't spared. Everything was digital, from the encrypted card readers in various departments, to the massive equipment throughout the entire building. And of course, to the clocks on the walls above the workers' cubicles.

With no second hand on the clock, Orlando had to count to sixty for a minute to pass. Finally, it was 8:03 p.m. He checked Karla's account again, and saw that the line wasn't in use anymore. But still, he had to wait. It might look suspicious if he called her as soon as she ended her call.

While he waited, he thought of what had happened since he received the assignment from Jose. Jose was really keen about that stranger's number, but not forthcoming about why he wanted it. And that offer was unlikely to happen. Just as unlikely as Orlando getting up the nerve to ask Jose who Abe was, or what he meant to Jose.

He had succeeded in locating another phone number the mysterious Abe frequently called. Although it was a prepaid phone, it worked the same as any other cell phone. The only difference was the billing method. The triangulation of the phone number and ESN indicated that the phone was somewhere in Century City. Yesterday, Orlando risked trying that number. The phone rang four times before a female voice answered, "Hello?"

This pleased him; it was much easier for him to apply his charm on females. Unless she was another *fling* Abe had encountered prior to his departure to Europe. "Good evening, madam, my name is Artillio," he'd said. "I'm a customer service—"

"Not interested, thank you," the voice replied, and hung up.

Orlando sat for a moment, bewildered. The second voice sounded much lower, like there was more than one person on the other line, or that the speaker changed voices entirely, going from a high soprano to a very low alto in their second answer.

No, he decided. The second response was made by a male. Of that, he was certain.

So did a man snatch the phone from the female who answered, or was the female who answered that same man, but imitating a female voice? If his second guess was correct, why did the man do that? Orlando had no idea.

Unless, the idea blinked in his head, *he didn't want to reveal himself, then felt at ease enough to be himself when shaking off an annoying customer service representative.*

"Humm." He checked the phone transmission again to find out if the bearer had left Century City. But the phone was dead, no signal at all, as though someone had turned it off.

So he's cautious, Orlando thought. *By nature, or for a specific reason?*

If he could determine that reason, Jose might reward him with a substantial bonus for his efforts. That thought charged him with new energy.

Before his meal break, he checked for the peculiar phone's signal. It was on now. The triangulation showed the phone was in the Long Beach area, but moving. A bit later, he checked again. The phone signaled to the Inglewood antenna that it was nearby, and holding in stand-by mode in case someone called its number. Five minutes later, the antenna at Culver City signaled that the phone was now in its jurisdiction.

"Again, the end of the journey is in Century City," he muttered, and peered up at the clock again, trying to focus his thoughts.

In contrast to what most people thought, there were very few cellular frequencies. The conversations were carried on radio frequency, like any radio broadcast. One single-antenna transmitter could produce 999 combinations. This meant that 999 phone numbers can release or receive a signal from a phone by the antenna coverage. In his training, Orlando learned that this structure was, in part, the reason for system failure. In certain places or events, when a large number of people try to use their cell phones at the same time, the system collapses. For the same reason, skyscrapers and populated venues have multiple receptors and transmitters, sometimes one on each floor of a skyscraper.

All this made his task of tracing the cell phone's movements easy, even to the point of knowing it was on the 10th floor of the skyscraper in Century City. He wrote down the address from where the phone transmitted, then called Jose to check whether it was important to him or not.

"El Diablo," Jose had said, indicating the information was, in fact, critical.

When Orlando told him how cautious the cell phone user seemed, Jose promised him a large bonus, exactly as he predicted. Enthused, Orlando's curiosity had surged. Thanks to the World Wide Web, he was able to determine that only four companies shared the 10th floor of that building.

But that was as far as he'd gotten before his shift ended. Before he could pick up his search anew, now he had to follow through on Jose's other request—to find out if Karla spoke with Abe, the one Jose seemed to want so badly.

The digital clock showed 8:08 p.m. now, and Karla answered on the first ring.

"Hello," she said, accentuating the word as long as she could. She sounded amused by something. He couldn't have expected a better opening.

"Good evening, Karla, this is Artillio, your customer service representative."

"What? Who? ... Oh, yeah, you. How are you?"

"I'm great. I promised yesterday I'd call, so I just wanted to show you I keep my word."

"Good," she replied, but not with enthusiasm. He decided to turn up the charm.

"I wanted to inform you we checked your account, and decided to give you an additional 500 minutes free for the next month also." He lowered his voice to a whisper and said, "I pulled some strings because you were so cooperative yesterday."

"Thank you, uhh ... Artillio, right?"

"You're welcome. And yes, I'm Artillio. So, did your 'fling' call?"

She laughed, her earlier disinterest gone. "Oh yeah, he did."

"And ...?"

"And I'm going to visit him next week in Amsterdam!"

"Wow, that's excellent! Amsterdam? I've heard that Amsterdam is the best place for partying. When're you going?"

"Next Wednesday. Why?"

Bingo! "Oh, just asking," he said. "Have fun, okay? And once again, thank you for using our services." *And for making my day!*

* * *

As soon as he could take a break, he borrowed a random phone from the pile on the shift manager's station, then went into the restroom. He stood by the sink and dialed the number.

"Si?"

"It's me," he said.

"I'll call you at this number," was the reply.

Orlando waited three seconds before the phone rang. He described all of his findings. Jose was quiet and didn't interrupt his report.

"You did a great job, *essè*. You just entitled yourself to a really nice bonus."

"Do you want me to send a technician to find exactly where this guy is in Century City?" Orlando asked, excited to help some more.

"No," Jose simply said, and hung up.

* * *

Jose looked at the low-resolution picture in front of him. "I think I just found you, *Jefe*." His voice was a victorious murmur. With luck, not only would he find out what Abbed was now into, but perhaps find a way to involve the 18th Street in it. And if Abbed wouldn't go along? Well, there were options, including catching a big fish.

Chapter 49

"I have a suggestion for you for extra income," Michael said while stroking her hair. Dianne relaxed on the king-sized bed facedown, eyes closed, her back to the ceiling, the ceiling fan drying the sweat from her back. In reply, she giggled. "A part-time job? I wonder what that would be."

"You have the perfect skin to be a cosmetics model," he said, and ran his fingers from the base of her scalp down to the hills of her magnificent backside.

"Thank you, my love. But there's no cosmetics here. Just a lot of hydration and no smoking." She smiled at him, then yawned. "And a lot of sleep, of course."

My love? He managed to mutter "But of course" as he withdrew his hand, dumbstruck. She said *love* as if that were an ordinary word, a word they used all the time. It wasn't. And he suddenly felt the same betraying anguish he felt every time the endorphins in his brain settled down after their sexual engagements.

She had called him *My love.*

He watched her breathing softly, in a constant rhythm, until she was asleep. He rose from the bed, careful not to wake her, and dressed quickly, wrote a short note on hotel stationery and left the room, eventually ending up on the now-quiet beach.

Why am I doing this?

He knew exactly why, but in such a weak moment, logic wasn't enough.

"Checklist," he whispered. "Think about the checklist!"

Searching for sources for improvised nitric acid and nitroglycerin hadn't been a problem. He'd read about the Ostwald process, the principal commercial process for the manufacture of nitric acid, even before he'd felt okay with deeper searching on Dianne's and the school's computers. Even readily available propane could be nitrated in relatively large amounts, and the result would still be the heavy, colorless, oily, explosive liquid called nitroglycerin—a substance he'd just proved the airport's detection equipment couldn't distinguish from similar materials, like the power bars. Glycerin—anything containing glycerin—was too widely used by the public, and would cause too many false positive alarms.

Finding equivalent substances for the nitric and sulfuric acids to mix with the glycerin was easy as well. Thanks to UCLA's labs, he could test all kinds of substances. He'd cooled the mixed acid to room temperature before adding the glycerin, recalling that if he didn't, they would exotherm significantly when combined.

Exotherm. This made him smile. Professor Vinitzky would have been proud that he knew the term—the heat produced when two substances were mixed—and horrified to know that his student used the school's labs to create it. The process of making the explosives required great care, but was doable. Brilliantly, he used the chemistry lab for both Showtime's *CTA* show and for his improvised nitroglycerin. *Killing two birds with one stone ...*

His operational research was complete, and this helped him quell the mental tangle in his mind. And his test of the airport security had gone perfectly. But, he still needed to test the material he created. Thanks to Showtime, he even had a cover story for that. *"Check out the Mentos-and-Coke experiment,"* Professor Vinitzky had said. Michael easily understood that chemical reaction, a break-up of attractive forces between water molecules. With the introduction of the chemicals in the Mentos, the Coke's bubbles expanded, sometimes hundreds of times their original size, in mini-explosions that caused the carbonated gas to erupt from the bottle like a superheated geyser.

None of his explosive preparations were difficult, it was his mental anguish that was unbearable.

Will it help? he thought while pacing the shoreline, the sand still warm under his feet. *Will it accomplish anything? Will it bring Father back? Or Ibrahim?*

"*Il'Anna!*—Damn it!" Ibrahim cried out, and Michael guessed the worst; his mentor had been shot. Instinct forced him to drag Ibrahim to the car and pull him inside, into the total darkness. By the time he was behind the wheel, shivering from both cold and fear, he heard more sirens in the background. But no lights. Praise be to Allah, there were no lights as he drove into the dark, the windshield spattered with raindrops, his eyes with tears, and Ibrahim gurgling something about the Higher Cause behind him.

A police cruiser emerged from a side road, not seeing their lightless car. The driver slammed on the brakes and the cruiser spun a few times before ending up in a ditch. Michael drove on, not knowing or caring where he was going or what he should do.

A tourist couple was making out on the beach, as if they were there by themselves. Americans, by their easy confidence and scanty dress. He fixed his eyes on them, but no longer saw them.

But now I know what to do. Now, I know exactly where I came from and where I'm going. And more than that, I know there is no turning back.

Chapter 50

"Everyone seems so ... intimidated in an elevator," Richard said with a grin. "People don't engage with each other in them, just stare at the numbers above the doors."

As he spoke, the elevator, unaffected by Richard's poor assessment, moved quickly toward their floor.

"Well, no matter what you think about them, I'd rather take an elevator than climb stairs all the way to the 10th floor—especially after eating that huge meal." Vicky's face showed renewed worry. "I just hope Helen's all right. She's a new patient, so when I couldn't get her on the phone to tell her I needed to reschedule her next appointment, I thought I might have gotten her number wrong."

Richard shrugged. "We were in the area anyway. And everything's probably fine."

"Maybe. But for some crazy reason, my sixth sense keeps telling me everything's not fine with her. If I'm wrong, I'll be happy to eat crow about it."

He smiled and said, "That straight line's so easy, I won't even touch it."

She grinned, reached up and patted his cheek.

At the 10th floor, the doors opened into a wide hall. Moments later, she was pointing out Suite 1010. On the right side of the hall, a man in a blue uniform was operating a vacuum cleaner. He wore headphones, and didn't give them more than a glance.

Vicky knocked gently on the door. When there was no

answer, she grabbed the doorknob and swiveled it from side to side. "It's locked," she said, and pounded on the door again. "But Helen said she'd come here after the funeral and keep herself busy with work."

She reached up and gently pounded on the door with her open palms.

Richard crooked his index finger at her, said, "Look," and pressed the button next to the door. A loud ring sounded from within the office.

She rolled her eyes at him. He returned with a grin, then idly shifted his eyes to the janitor, scanned him from headphones to toes without being obvious. The man still refused to pay attention to them ... strange, considering the way Vicky was dressed and the way she was pounding on the door. But, perhaps he came from one of the many cultures where people minded their own business, or considered it a sin to look at a beautiful woman.

At least in public, he thought with a smile. He turned to the door and idly turned the doorknob.

"No, I told you it was locked—"

The door opened a few inches. He glanced at her with a puzzled look, and she shook her head. "I ... I swear I turned it all the way and—"

"No biggie. Maybe it's got a quirk to it. A lot of doors do, you know."

Inside the suite, she called out her patient's name. Then, without waiting for the echo in the room to fade, she cried again, "Helen!"

They quickly scanned the four small offices and one larger cubicle area. "Nice place," he said while they checked each room. "What do they do here?"

"Oh, I forgot to mention, it's a not-for-profit. Raises funds for cleft-lipped children in poor countries." She returned to the reception area and stood, hands on hips, looking at him. "I don't know what to think, Rich. It's just ... too weird. I don't think I'm breaking confidentiality about this, but ... in our session, she said how proud she was of her work, never missed a day. And now," she waved her hands around, "now this. Something bad's happened, I just know it."

He glanced at the coffee table in front of the small room's sofa, saw the fundraising brochures. "We've got the right place. But are you sure she'd be here this late, and on the day of the funeral?"

She looked around again, as though doing so would make Helen magically appear. "I'm certain. She said they all tended to work late. And that people were in and out of the office at all hours, because they were always on the phone to other countries. But that's what's even weirder ... look at all these desks. *Nobody's* here."

Richard thought a moment. "Do you have a cell phone number for her? Maybe she left the office and forgot to lock up."

"Oh," she gasped as she reached for her purse. She keyed numbers into the phone and listened. Two seconds later, an electronic ring echoed from one of the small offices at the far end of the suit. Both of them hurried to the source, and saw a cell phone on the desk. Vicky stared at it silently, her mouth open as if she needed to gasp for air.

He took the phone from her and closed it. The ringing stopped. Next, he went to the window. In the distance, a light aimed toward the sky sporadically circled through the darkness from one of the nightclubs on Sunset Boulevard.

"Window's bolted tight," he said. "She wouldn't be able to bolt the window if she'd jumped out."

"No shit, Sherlock! She wasn't the suicidal type."

She thought hard, trying to recall Helen's exact words. "I want to squeeze the most from life, as if there were no tomorrow."

She turned, wide-eyed. "*As if there were no tomorrow.*"

"Call her home phone number," he said quietly.

She nodded and keyed in the call, then said, "Let's get out of here. Maybe some of the other businesses are still here.

We can ask them."

They walked toward the suite's entrance. As Richard put his hand on the doorknob, she gave up. "No answer."

Richard turned the handle to open the door for her, but had to stifle a surprised yelp when he bumped into the tall figure trying to enter. Everything happened so quickly, neither one managed to stop before the inevitable collision.

"I'm sorry. Are you all right?" he said quickly, his hands reaching to stabilize the man, who looked even more surprised than him.

"Who are you?" the man asked, rubbing his shoulder.

"I'm Richard Miller, and this is Vicky Woodman."

"We're friends of Helen Holman," Vicky added.

"She's in the ladies room," he said. "She's been in there for over an hour. By the way, I'm her employer."

He pointed to a door in the hallway they hadn't seen, and said to Vicky, "I'm sorry to impose, but I'm very worried about her, and I—"

"Of course," Vicky said, and hurried down the hallway.

Richard wasn't so easily put off by the symbol of a woman on the door. A moment later, he eased open the door and called out, "Everything all right? Just checking."

The women emerged from the restroom, and Vicky introduced them.

"I'm sorry we have to meet under these conditions," Helen said, wiping her face with a paper towel. Vicky immediately pulled tissues from her purse and handed them to her.

Helen blew her nose, wiped her tears, and said, "I wanted to work late ... didn't want to be by myself tonight." She gave them a puffy-eyed grin. "Bad idea, I guess. Did you meet Jack? He's my boss. He should be in his office."

"We did," Richard said. "Do you want me to tell him you're leaving?"

She shook her head and smoothed her crumpled blouse with her hands. "That's okay. I need to get my purse from the office anyway."

Out of the corner of his eye, Richard saw the janitor, who stopped vacuuming and was standing by his vacuum cleaner. Then it occurred to him that every time he'd seen the man, he was cleaning around the same spot. A tiny red flag raised in his head.

As they walked the short distance to the office, Richard said, "You know ... it's funny, but I keep thinking I know Jack from somewhere. Perhaps when I gathered information for an article on not-for-profit orgs?"

"He's very active in charitable circles," Helen said. "And he's also very wise. And so very smart with our bookkeeping here. Why, I can barely keep track of the finances myself, and he just tells me to let him handle the tough stuff— I'm sorry, I shouldn't have been blabbing. So, what do you do, Richard?"

"I'm a journalist." He gave her a reassuring smile. "But don't worry. I don't really look for white-collar crimes to write about. Gee, this is LA. I could question the entire city about that."

The three of them laughed at his joke. Helen's laughter was less hearty, but enough to tell him she was okay about accidentally letting private information slip.

At the door to the office, she said, "Come on in, I'll only be a minute," then went to the corner office and peered inside. "Jack, I better go home," she said, and sniffled. Clearly, for her, the word "home" wasn't a good association.

Vicky immediately went to her and interjected, "We'll see her out, Jack. And it was nice meeting you. Good night."

"It's all right, Jack," Helen quickly added. "I know these people." She punctuated the last with a nervous giggle.

Partly to be polite, but partly to get another look at the man, Richard also peeked into the office and said "Good night, nice meeting you." But Jack's eyes were already on some papers on his desk, and he only lifted his hand and mumbled goodbye.

As they went toward the door, Richard glanced at the receptionist's desk and saw a picture of a beautiful young blonde. He recognized her instantly, but from where? Frustrated, he decided to try to get a bit more out of Helen.

"So, Helen, how long have you worked here? Helping disadvantaged children. Sounds like a job easy to love."

The janitor continued to push the vacuum back and forth. He'd moved, but not far. Richard pressed the elevator button. While they waited for it to arrive to the 10th floor, he examined the janitor's reflection behind him. He continued vacuuming, but Richard noticed that he gave them a couple of careful-but-quick glances. Finally, he decided he was just being paranoid, because of all the terrorist-talk at the airport earlier that day. Or perhaps it was because he couldn't remember where, or if, he'd seen Jack before?

The elevator arrived. They entered, and as the doors slid shut, they turned as one to watch the electronic display. He smiled at Vicky, then asked Helen, "Did you know Jack before you started working for him?"

"No. Actually, the job was a lucky find. Found it in the classifieds."

He sighed. "I really feel I know your boss somehow. Just can't figure out from where." After a moment, he smiled. "It's probably the six degrees of separation theory. So I think I know everybody."

Vicky smiled at him. "In your case, I wouldn't be surprised if it took only three degrees."

They walked from the elevator through the lobby, then headed for the adjacent parking garage. Once there, they escorted Helen to her car and waited for her to get in. And Richard felt he had to try one last time.

"Helen, forgive me for asking, but given my occupation, I tend to take liberties. I understand the hit-and-run was caused by a stolen van. But ... do you know whether someone might have wanted to harm your husband or son?"

Vicky pierced Richard with harsh eyes, but Richard had

purposely used an approach intended to soothe, and Helen's reaction was one of surprise, followed by serious consideration.

"You know, the police never asked me that question," she said at last. "Not once. But ... I can't think of anyone who might want to hurt David because of his job with the INS. Or Billy either. Even though he was hanging out with some ... unsavory types."

She looked at Richard, her eyes turned to saucers now. "Do you think what happened might not have been an accident? Is that what you're saying?"

"I don't know," he said truthfully. "Likely, it was simply a tragic accident. I'm sorry for bringing it up."

Helen touched his arm. "Don't be sorry. Billy was arrested for being involved in drug trafficking at his school. David went downtown to get him released. Could ... Could that have had something to do with their deaths? Maybe someone was following them?"

She turned to Vicky. "I didn't tell you about that. I was so embarrassed...."

Vicky reached out to Helen. "It's okay. Really, I understand."

Wiping tears, Helen told them about Billy's arrest just before the accident. Richard leaned against her car and listened, but suddenly stood straight again. "Does your boss live nearby?"

Helen raised her head in confusion. "I ... don't know. Why?"

"I just saw him leave the building, but he didn't come inside to get his car. He just walked around behind the building. And I wondered."

After a moment, Helen said, "Actually, I've never seen his car."

"Maybe he lives within walking distance," Vicky said. She turned her caring eyes to Helen. "Do you need anything from me tonight?"

Helen shook her head as she unlocked the car and got

in, then lowered her window. "No, I'll be fine. My sister's staying for a few days. But thank you both so much."

When she drove away, they headed for Richard's car. Their first stop would be the shopping mall so Vicky could get her car.

"Poor Helen," she said while Richard maneuvered out of the garage. "But I can't believe you asked her all those questions. You know I wasn't even supposed to tell you about her, it violates my professional—"

"Sorry, I couldn't help it. And I truly do mean it, I'm sorry."

He drove slowly, his head preoccupied with Helen's boss and the janitor's just-short-of-strange behavior. As though his thoughts had turned into reality, as they passed by the building's entrance, he saw the janitor emerge. The headphones now hung around his neck; a cell phone attached to his ear was in their place.

"The shoes," Richard murmured, and maneuvered the car onto Century Park East.

She smiled and gently touched his face. "That reminds me, I didn't tell you about the shoes I bought today. Three-inch stilettos, in the most amazing color." She giggled. "The saleswoman called it 'whorehouse red.' Just because you mentioned it, I'll perform a show for you, with or without the shoes...."

He smiled and nodded, but his mind was in a different place. The janitor's Nikes were brand new and spotless. Not the kind of shoes a minimum-wage worker could afford.

Chapter 51

One of the greatest advantages of the rented house was its isolation. Half of the houses on the street were unoccupied. In those occupied, neighbors were never visible. Who could blame them? Few people could bear to sit in their gardens or balconies or barbecue outdoors, where the smell was reminiscent of a not-very-hygienic public toilet. So no one saw the red truck slowing, then stopping in front of Joe's house.

He glanced at his watch. As always, Shudy was on time. He opened the garage door and waited for Shudy to back the truck in, and then watched while Shudy maneuvered the automatic lift on the truck's back end to lower a shrink-wrapped pallet.

"You have about three hours," Shudy told him. "I've just unloaded some stuff to my employees on Imperial Avenue. They have three buildings there to set up the fire extinguishers. By the time they go to lunch, I need to come and get the pallet."

"*Allah Ma'ak*—may God be with you," Joe said. "And don't worry, I'll be out this afternoon. I have to try out something." He wrinkled his nose and chuckled. "And besides, this place stinks."

"It was an excellent selection, Joe," Shudy said, and climbed into the driver's cab. While the truck pulled away he closed the garage door, swallowing him and his disastrous components inside.

He removed the shrink-wrap from the pallet, opened the

boxes and brought them into the living room one by one. Then he disassembled each of the fire extinguishers inside the boxes. He had to be very careful, because the bottom of the cylinders connected to the sprinklers with small hoses, and he couldn't risk disrupting that part of them. If someone had to put out a fire, the toxic material in the small compartment would do the job, with injurious aftereffects nonetheless. The midsection, however, was hollow and empty, awaiting Joe's attention.

The near-freezing temperature in the house kept him from perspiring profusely, replacing it with a cold sweat. Even so, he felt nervousness seeking a way out. And he already felt the stirrings of hunger. Since he didn't dare use the stove or microwave, he'd only had one of those worthless power bars for breakfast. Yet he had to keep his mind on his work. The task ahead was crucial, and dangerous.

The packs in the freezer looked harmless, he thought with pride. No special signs on them, no warnings to indicate their catastrophic potential. "But that's all right," he muttered, viewing his handiwork. "The proof is in the pudding, as the infidels say."

He walked slowly, carrying a pack in both hands, placed the pack inside a heat-protection sleeve and wrapped it with another. Then he inserted the sleeved pack into its compartment and pierced it with the electric match head. When the cellular signal caused the electric circuit to close, the ion-lithium battery would produce the required current to set off the match head and create the spark required for detonation.

He cautiously reassembled the fire extinguisher, checked the electronic gauge on top. It worked. He looked up. One was done, another bunch to go.

The work was monotonous, but he progressed with caution. When the hunger became too great, he drank an energy drink to keep his strength. Within two and a half hours, the pallet was shrink-wrapped again and awaiting pick-up, and he could check mark another task off the virtual checklist in his head.

He didn't have time to celebrate just yet. Ignoring his hunger, he took a shower, shaved, and dressed in a fresh set of clothes and shoes. By the time Shudy arrived and picked up the pallet, he was ready for his next accomplishment. But first, lunch.

* * *

When he entered Tim's room at the VA, Tim was sprawled on his bed, staring at the ceiling. *One of those days,* Joe concluded, instantly wary.

Tim was happy to see him; he sat up, rubbed his eyes, and smiled. Tim's glasses magnified an indistinct misery behind his blue eyes. Joe smiled. *Exactly what I need.*

"Come on Timmy, let's have some fun," he said. "It's a beautiful day outside."

Tim looked at him for a long moment until his stare focused, then shook his head as if trying to shake off demons inside. "I need to take a shower," he said.

"Go ahead, I'll wait."

When Tim returned from the shower, dressed in only underwear and pants, his new clothes were waiting for him on the bed. He studied his newly purchased coat with a questioning glance. "Isn't it too hot outside for a coat?"

"The place we're going is air-conditioned, so the coat'll keep you warm. And besides that, you look so good in it."

He handed him the vest, then the coat, and Tim dressed silently. No staring episode. This reassured Joe.

Their first stop was a family-owned Italian restaurant about a mile from the airport. Joe gorged himself. Tim also seemed to enjoy his lunch. He'd removed his coat but the vest remained on. The cologne bottles made it heavy. Joe complimented him often during their ride to the restaurant, so he agreed when asked to keep it on, just for Joe.

The waiter appeared, collected the empty plates and

refilled their water glasses. Tim drained his immediately

Joe refused the dessert menu and offer of coffee, pulled out his wallet and paid for the meal in cash; he never over or under-tipped for service. A waiter wouldn't remember him, as the cheapest diner or the most generous one.

He helped Tim into his coat and they entered the car, buckling up. "So, we had Italian food," he said cheerfully. "Let's get some good ice cream. Hey, do you know where there's a Häagen-Dazs around here?"

Tim shook his head.

He pretended to think, then snapped his fingers. "Oh, I remember. Someone told me there's one at the airport. At Tom Bradley International Terminal, I believe. Let's go."

After a careful drive into LAX, he pulled over by the terminal and handed Tim a twenty-dollar bill. "Please go to the food court and buy us two large cups of Häagen-Dazs ice cream," he said. "I'll be waiting for you here."

Tim looked confused, but regained his self-control and left the car. He looked out-of-place in the long heavy coat and vest, but as Joe suspected, nobody paid much attention to the blond young man, even though his head was somewhat misshapen.

He immediately pulled away and continued on to Terminal 4, the American Airlines terminal, parked the car in the parking garage and walked to the lot adjacent to the international terminal. At the elevators, he peered between the third and the fourth floors, surveying the terminal entrance. He'd found it to be an excellent observation point without being noticed.

He checked his watch. Ten minutes since he sent Tim inside. The Häagen-Dazs counter was busy at times, and it was lunchtime after all. People were probably standing in line to get their treat.

An additional five minutes passed. A thin line of perspiration surfed down his back, and his mouth started to go dry. He rehearsed his getaway plan, to walk fast through the parking garage's second floor and exit from the lowest floor, where parking spots were used for arrivals. It would take the authorities a long time before they understood what was going on.

Then, he saw Tim's blond head glancing about the terminal, holding two Häagen-Dazs cups, confusion showed on his face while he looked for Joe's 4Runner. Once he was certain no one else was watching Tim, he descended the stairs to the second floor, the departure level. As he did, Tim walked the few steps toward Terminal 3. Not finding Joe's car, he returned to the international terminal's entrance.

Joe stood at the entrance to the parking garage and called, "Tim."

Tim looked up. Behind his glasses, Joe could see fear. But when his stare locked onto Joe, he smiled broadly and began crossing the street, almost getting run over by one of the hotel shuttles. That was bad. Someone might remember the near miss.

Joe turned and started walking, fearing someone from the airport might be watching Tim to see whom he met.

"Hey, wait up!" Tim called. Joe could hear his footsteps pounding on the concrete.

"Don't you want your ice cream?" Tim said, raising his voice.

Joe looked beyond his right shoulder. Nobody was watching them as far as he could see. He turned toward Tim and said, "There you are! It took so long."

"There was a looooong line in there. Where are we going next?"

"I couldn't wait for you at the curb," he explained. "I had to park the car."

"Oh, man, sorry," Tim said with a crestfallen face.

Joe reached out and patted his arm, hearing the cologne bottles tinkling. "It's all right, Tim, you did just fine."

They walked silently for a while, each of them concentrating on their ice cream. Finally, Joe said, "Did anyone stop you or ask you anything in the terminal?"

Tim shook his head. "No. Oh, wait ... except for the ice cream flavors. Why?"

"Just a question. Nothing special."

"Thank you for lunch and dessert, Joe. You're a really good friend. I hope we can do it again someday soon."

"Oh, yeah, we will," he said. He opened the car, sat behind the wheel and smirked. It was easier than he expected. The only variable, of course, was Tim's impulsiveness. Yet when the time came, he was certain Tim's trust in him would allow him enough control to do what needed to be done.

Chapter 52

The drive to Death Valley National Park was like an inspiring anthropologic drama. As the road headed east, the luxury and sports cars of Los Angeles were gradually replaced by trucks, utility vans, and heavy-duty vehicles, and the concrete buildings and downtown towers were replaced by open fields and farms. A great time for Michael to think everything over.

The team had a meeting set for the next day in Apple Valley, in the San Bernardino Mountains. He'd told Dianne he was going to a conference at the UC-Davis campus, and would be in the labs most of the time ... which meant he wouldn't have good reception and couldn't be reached on his cell phone. Her spirits still high from the trip to Cancun, she accepted his story easily, told him she'd see him when he returned.

But before tomorrow's meeting, there were things he had to do.

Once certain he was in the most remote place possible, he parked his car, carefully donned his backpack and walked for an additional hour in the desert. When he felt certain there was no one within a few miles of him, he removed what he'd brought with him from the backpack: a minute quantity, not more than three ounces. He placed the substance inside the metal case he retrieved from the backpack, then placed the case in a small burrow and stretched a fifty-foot cord from it. One end of the cord was attached to an electric match head. The other connected to the set of batteries he held in his hand. He held his breath, lowered his head to the ground, and turned the switch on.

Nothing happened.

He looked at the wires and the way they were connected to the battery ends, couldn't see anything wrong, and gritted his teeth. If the problem wasn't here, it was in the improvised bomb he'd hidden in the burrow. He recalled the lessons Ibrahim had taught him in Lancaster's countryside about this kind of "accident." The stories of people who lost fingers, legs, eyes, and even their lives during testing of improvised explosives.

Is it a sign I should withdraw from the whole thing? But what would I tell the others? Abbed won't let me off so easily. Should I just run away? Where to? How? What about Dianne?

He sighed. *Why do I think so much about Dianne? I mustn't care what she thinks!*

Confusion paralyzed him. *Think!* he ordered himself. And then, as though a switch turned on in his brain, *What would Ibrahim have done...?*

No one seemed to be chasing them, but after the near collision with the police cruiser, Michael drove as if there was. All he heard from the backseat now was Ibrahim's occasional strangling breath.

He applied everything he'd learned to shake off tails until he was at the safe house in the countryside. Ibrahim's friend took him in and gave him medical aid, and Michael's relief was great at first. Yet the memory did nothing to offset Michael's sense of failure while staring in the distance at the unexploded bomb.

What would Father do?

This last question brought self-disgust. *Father would never get into this situation. So how did* I *get this far?*

He spread out on the California desert sand, mumbling questions to himself. It was the first time in his life he felt ... well, he just didn't care anymore. He was tired of the struggles. He wanted to die. He *should* die for failing now, and back then.

"And what better way to go?" he mumbled bitterly.

In despair he got up, walked to the metal case in the small burrow and opened it, looked at the glass jar containing the dangerous liquid he had formulated, and unscrewed the cap.

He closed his eyes and waited for the explosion. That would be the best way to finish it, he decided. To stop hoping for acceptance from comrades whose hatred he tried to, but couldn't fully share. To reunite with his father, whom Ibrahim had told him died years ago in Kuwait. To stop lying to innocent Dianne. Mostly, to either live his own life or meet his own death. Even without the *Shuhada,* even if he didn't enter heaven, death would still bring comfort.

"Am I in Shuhada?*"* Ibrahim had asked when he finally opened his eyes.

"Not yet," his friend said, cleaning the ugly wound in his chest. He went out to bring more bandages.

Ibrahim turned fevered eyes to Michael. "Mustafa, it's time to move on."

The words were rasped at Michael, who fought back tears he didn't want his mentor to see.

Ibrahim gave him halting instructions. "Take the money from my drawer. Use your new British passport and fly to America. You are almost ready for the Jihad." He coughed wetly; foamy blood appeared on his lips. "If you feel you're ready, contact Muhammad Atta ... in Miami. He's preparing an operation. If you're not ready, contact Shudy Tarif ... Los Angeles. You'll find both numbers in my drawer ... in my desk."

He coughed again. *"Allah ma'ak.* Now go!"

"Allah ma'ak," Michael had whispered back, and managed to make it outside the safe house before breaking down....

Willing tears away, he allowed himself to open his eyes and look down. The contents of the jar, the colorless jelly-like liquid, could easily be mistaken for hair gel.

The desert sun seared the back of his neck while he examined the electric cord. He quickly found the problem: one of the match-head ends had slipped loose of its connection to the electric wire. A simple fix, but he hesitated. Was this a sign for him to back off? Was his father, perhaps, telling him to abandon the plan, the mission he'd prepared for since that day of triumph and adulation in the London mosque?

No matter. He reattached the cord to the improvised detonator, inserted it into the thick liquid and closed the case's latch, then replaced the container in the burrow and watched it for a moment, waiting. It didn't explode. He almost wished it had.

Too many what-ifs crossed his mind while he returned to where he'd stood before. What if Ibrahim could have understood the advantages of living in western society, rather than fearing and hating westerners? What if, as his father had taught him, Michael could stand up for his principles and still avoid the conflicts between his culture and that of his new home? What if his father had gone with him to England? What if Saddam hadn't invaded Kuwait?

"Too many questions," he muttered, and pushed any further ones away.

He reassembled the set of batteries, his hands moving in a pattern he'd practiced so often, it required no thought. He saw Ibrahim's head nodding in agreement, the malevolent smile that had blotted his face just before he returned his soul to Allah.

Just as he reconnected the wire to the battery pin, he saw his father's image. His features expressed the familiar weariness ... and great sadness. His hands shook.

The powerful explosion jerked him away from any thoughts. A cloud of sand and dust rose through the air, blanketing him and blocking his air passages. He remained standing but coughed fiercely, his lungs and nostrils fighting to remove sand particles lodged in them. It took a long while before the sky became blue again.

He eased down to the hard ground, brushed sand from his shoulders and hair and tried to direct his thoughts back to where they needed to be, where they must be.

A few minutes passed before he pulled himself to his feet and went to examine the results. The metal case had shattered. Large pieces of it were scattered on the ground in a wide radius. The narrow burrow had collapsed, requiring him to dig handfuls of sandy soil from where the device had been. Nothing was left of the jar, the wires, or the detonator.

It had worked. It worked even better than he expected. And if a mere three ounces of the gel was powerful enough to demolish a metal crate, a larger amount could easily pierce an aircraft's fuselage.

And this, it seemed, was the sign he'd been seeking. So why did his heart still feel so leaden?

Chapter 53

Their foreman didn't show up. No reason, no explanation. And even weirder, the company's owner, a white-collar rich man, had picked them up for work that morning in the truck their foreman usually drove. When lunchtime came, the owner just drove up to the closest shopping center, handed them each a twenty-dollar bill, and promised to pick them up an hour later.

Earning nearly minimum wage, they always had to spend wisely. They decided on a sandwich and a cup of water each, their usual lunch. As for the change, they'd surprise their wives and children with later. "And besides," one of them said as they ate, "it's not like the owner can't afford it."

His buddy nodded at that. Business was flourishing for the company; they'd never had so many deliveries before. They'd overheard rumors of ERS being bought out by another company, but didn't dare ask their boss.

"I just wonder why he's actin' so nervous," he said. "We aren't behind schedule or nothing like that."

His colleague swallowed the bite he'd been chewing and said, "Shudy's into so many businesses, maybe one of 'em's got him jumpy. You saw how he was on the cell phone from the minute he picked us up."

When they finished eating, they climbed back into the truck cabin and Shudy started driving toward the airport. As before, his eyes shifted from side to side. But instead of talking on his cell phone, he kept changing the stations on the radio.

When they were almost at the airport, Shudy handed one of them a piece of paper and his phone and said, "Call our airport administration contact and tell him we're five minutes away, and you'll meet him at the entrance."

The man took the phone, glanced at his buddy, who shrugged, and then did as he was told. Whatever the boss wanted, the boss got.

They arrived at the terminal and Shudy pulled up, close to the curbside, then jumped out before they could, flew to the back of the truck, and quickly off-loaded a pallet of boxes with labels that had "LAX" stamped on them.

"Man, shouldn't we be doing that?" one man whispered.

"He's the boss. If he wants our help, he knows how to ask for it."

There was someone waiting at the terminal entrance, an administrator-type holding a clipboard. He noticed them and started walking in their direction. Distracted by his approach, the men didn't see Shudy pulling the truck away from the curb, leaving them by themselves.

"Let me show you in," the man said, then turned around and started walking toward the terminal entrance. With no other option, they followed, dragging the pallet behind them with a dolly.

Chapter 54

The sound of twigs snapping and crackling in the bonfire usually signaled relaxation, but it didn't work for Michael this time. Joe, apparently amused by something he was pondering, poured Turkish coffee with cardamom into tiny clear glasses and passed them around. Jacob appeared to be deep in thought, and didn't say much; neither were abnormal for their leader. What *was* unusual was that Abbed wasn't there—and Shudy, whom Michael hadn't seen since he was recruited into the cell, was.

Shudy was talking about the impact their act would have on millions of suffering Muslims throughout the world, and the morals these American infidels would learn from their inevitable punishment in their own nation. Words Michael had heard many times in his life, but now they seemed ... absurd.

When he finished, Shudy demanded that each of them state if they were ready for the next level. At Shudy's order, Michael told them about his experiment, then added, "We found a loophole in their detection system. The CTX machine detects materials based on their density—*if* there is more than a pound of the material. But I don't need a whole pound. And even if the machine detects it, it will fall into their false positive category."

Despite the feeling of heaviness in his stomach he kept a positive tone. He explained, "They already know commodities such as power bars, deodorants, and dried fruits are similar to explosives in terms of density. But the components of my bomb won't set the sniffers off, because they took glycerin out of the databank because it's so common. So my ingredients aren't in their databank, and should pass through their sniffers with ease."

"Good, Michael," Jacob said. "Abbed's in Europe now, but before he left, he gave us another good idea. I know someone who's going to visit him. She'll deliver some of the ... merchandise you created. I'll contact you tomorrow to arrange the delivery. I think that an economy pack of deodorants will do."

Michael nodded, and Jacob turned to Joe. "So what are *you* up to?"

Joe smiled. "I want to terrify the Americans in more ways than one. I think I have the right way to do just that."

He didn't offer any more details. Curious, Michael asked for more, but Shudy said, "It doesn't matter. The less details we know, the better our chances are of success. The important fact is that we have four simultaneous attacks with multiple targets." His face nearly glowed with a dark smile and piercing eyes. "And we're about to make history."

Michael recalled one of Ibrahim's favorite phrases: *"For people who don't remember their past, their present is weak, and their future is dim in the fog."*

He remembered his past, but his present seemed weak. And his future was certainly dim. *May not be from the fog, may be from dust caused by my explosion ... still, this phrase doesn't seem to fit.*

Before he could continue exploring his thoughts, the meeting ended.

Chapter 55

"I'm happy to see you here on such short notice, Jose."

"Don't mention it, *essè*," Jose replied, his words rushed. "This woman is the link to someone who tried to screw me. What do you have for me?"

The man pointed toward the simple Spanish-style apartment complex. "I'm not sure, but I think the *chica* has a lot of boyfriends. Know what I mean?"

Jose shrugged. "Si. So what's new today?"

"Her last visitor was *El Jefe*—your out-of-country friend's big fish. He went in with a shopping bag. Stayed there for about ten minutes. When he left, he didn't have the shopping bag. I think it was *endroga*—drugs."

"Interesting. Why didn't you follow him?"

"I couldn't. He's a pro, I'm sure of it." The man smiled. "He even looked at me, but nobody pays attention to the gardener."

"And? Has she been out since then?" Jose jerked his chin toward the building.

The man shook his head.

"Good job, hombre. She's flying tomorrow, so this shopping bag is the delivery, and she is the courier." Jose gave him the same smile that had frightened Abbed. "I ought to pay her a visit."

"Shame to get rid of her," the man mused, and gave Jose a leering smile. "But she looks good, the bitch."

"An interesting idea, I'll consider it," Jose said, and

displayed the smile again.

He climbed the stairs two at a time and knocked on the door. When Karla opened it he said "*Hola, senorita*, I'm your last boyfriend."

Chapter 56

Joe's fingers tapped on the steering wheel to the beat of song playing on the radio, only his beat was quicker, in sync with his jumpy nerves. The traffic lights seemed to be against him; all of them were red.

A strong soap-scent lingered in the car like a cloud, coming from the antiperspirant that covered his entire body. The aluminum-based complexes reacted with the electrolytes in his sweat to form a gel plug in the duct of each sweat gland, preventing the glands from excreting liquid. He knew the perspiration had to go somewhere, but preferred it to go into his shoes, where it was unnoticeable. He didn't need to drink any coffee this morning or to eat anything sweet. In fact, he couldn't eat anything at all. His adrenaline pumped his blood pressure to a dangerous point all by itself.

He knocked on Tim's door, thinking that the ordinary sounds of the facility and surrounding areas were mellower than usual, even muted. A sharp pain went through his temples, shielding his vision with a black curtain. He inhaled deeply, allowing oxygen to clear his mind. The curtain faded.

After what seemed an eternity Tim opened the door with a wide smile and a towel covering his waist. "Morning, Joe. Come on in."

He returned a weak smile of his own and entered, immediately scanned the room. When he found what he was looking for, he returned to breathing normally.

Tim went in the bathroom, humming and talking to

himself. Joe assumed he was shaving, almost ready to dress, so he hurried to the only chair, covered right now with clothes, towels, and the vest he'd bought him. He opened the bag he carried and withdrew an identical vest, lowered it cautiously onto the chair, grabbed Tim's vest up and stashed it in his bag, and sat on the edge of his bed.

"What are we doing today, Joe?" Tim asked, his head peering out from the bathroom.

"What would you like to do, Tim?" he asked in reply, directing all the energy he could to lower his heart rate. Without success.

Tim emerged from the bathroom wearing jeans and a white t-shirt that said "I Love California," headed straight to his chair and put the vest on. While slipping his glasses onto his nose, he sniffed the air and asked, "Do you smell coffee?"

"I drank some before coming over," he lied. "What would you like to do today?"

Tim grinned, sensing only fun now. "Is it, like, a special day?"

Actually, it is, he wanted to say. "Every day is a special day," he actually said. "The kind of day where you'd ask yourself, 'What would you do if this were the last day of your life?'"

Chapter 57

Fahima finished ironing, slid the shirt from the ironing board and held it like a matador awaiting the bull.

"Whooo, it's hot," Muhammad complained when he shoved his arms inside the shirt's sleeves.

"You have to suffer a bit if you want to look good," Fahima said, and gave his buttocks a loving spank.

"Sometimes I think you forget I'm a taxi driver, not a lawyer or a businessman," Muhammad said, and began packing his lunchbox with the goodies she'd prepared.

She smiled. "Since you're not handing out business cards, you have no choice. The way you look *is* your business card. Blame me if you want."

Still lingering over how she spoiled him, he left the house and drove to the cab station, where he exchanged his car with his plain yellow cab, cleaned the backseats and windows, sprayed a nice fragrance inside, and drove off to begin his work day.

The first customer was a woman who sought transportation from Culver City to Canoga Park. Although only thirty miles, the ride could take an hour or more. A good way to start the day.

The next customers also requested long rides. The fifth was someone from Valley Village who wanted to get to LAX, a one-hour fare. The day had certainly smiled at him thus far.

"What airline are you flying with, sir?" he asked while the customer made himself comfortable in the backseat.

"Lufthansa," the man replied. "I think it's in the international terminal."

"Yes, it is," Muhammad confirmed. "We'll be there in an hour."

Chapter 58

Orlando hated morning shifts, and anything else related to mornings. When he was younger, his mother used to pour cold water on his face and scream, "*Despiértese ya*—wake up already!" to get him up on time for school. Waking up was still torment to him. But while he didn't know what was so special about this particular morning, he did as his best customer had just requested.

Since starting his shift, he'd searched the technical reception system for one phone number, the same prepaid-phone number for which he couldn't find the owner ... the one that had transmitted its signal from Century City all morning, from the same building and floor each time.

Finally, he yawned and stretched his arms. He had to boost his energy somehow, or he wouldn't survive the day. In the cafeteria, he put an overflowing spoonful of instant coffee into a Styrofoam cup, added hot water, stirred the muddy black liquid, and sipped. More bitter than absinthe, but it pumped his veins with some vitality.

Back at his station, he logged onto his computer again. The screen displayed the last customer profile he'd searched. He pressed the Refresh button, and the screen blinked and changed. Even before the pixels made the image clear enough to easily read, he'd grabbed up his phone and dialed a number.

"Jose? Hi, it's Orlando. He's moving. Toward Olympic Boulevard, probably walking.... Hey, I'm getting a strong signal from the antenna at Ralph's on Olympic ... he's probably in the parking lot now."

"Let me know if he heads south toward the airport," Jose said, and hung up.

Orlando looked at the bitter coffee in disgust. He didn't need it anymore. The day had suddenly become interesting.

Chapter 59

They sat at her parents' dining table and ate silently. Michael chewed his food and swallowed it with difficulty.

"Are you ready for today?" she asked. "I'm so excited!"

"What?" He raised his eyes from his food long enough to say, "Ready? Yes, I think so."

Dianne lifted a forkful of scrambled eggs to her mouth, but then lowered it back to her plate. "I swear, I'm even too excited to eat. You probably wouldn't believe me, but I've never been so excited in my entire life! The first time in my life I'll leave this continent."

Then, her exuberance left. "I just wish there'd been a way we could take the same flight."

He sighed. "I know, I know. But I have to take my final. And there were no more tickets available for my flight. Your 1 o'clock flight and my 7 o'clock flight was the only way I could swing it. But like I said, you can just wait for me at the hotel. Take a bath, tour the city. Just a few hours, that's all."

Her wistful face wrenched his heart, and he looked down. If she only knew ...

"Hey ... honey bun."

He felt her warm hands on his shoulder and turned around in the chair. "You're right," she said. "I don't know why I'm being such a baby about it. And I'm going to be with the man I love. How could that ever, ever be bad?"

He stood, and she kissed him, and he closed his eyes tight. Her sweet breath covered him in tranquility and something else, something that made him feel so alive. *Was* it love, like she'd said? The word terrified him.

The what-if questions returned, screaming at him. He wanted to scream back.

No ... he wanted to cry.

She rose from the breakfast table and picked up her plate and glass. "If I'm gonna to make my flight, I'd better hit the shower."

"Take your time," he called after her, and waited until he heard the bathroom door close to hurry to his backpack and remove the small shopping bag that held the box of power bars. He checked the watch inside the box—to the casual inspection a simple Casio, but this one had a built-in GPS. The coordinates were set for Nuuk, the capital of Greenland.

A study of flight routes told him that flights go north before continuing to Europe, since the distance is shorter than flying along the horizontal latitude routes. During the sleepless night before, he programmed the GPS to beep when it crossed Nuuk's longitude. At that instant, when the aircraft crossed the virtual longitude of Greenland's capitol, the device would send an electronic signal to the watch's twitterer. Which was no longer there. He'd replaced it with one of his electric match heads. When the aircraft reached that longitude in the middle of the Atlantic, the match head would set off the improvised nitroglycerin he'd hidden in the power bar package. Even if an attempt was made to retrieve the plane's debris from the cold North Atlantic, what would be the rush? No one can survive an explosion 30,000 feet above the earth.

Willing his hands to stop shaking, he placed the box in Dianne's suitcase, nestling it under a stack of sweaters.

The sandglass started its countdown.

Chapter 60

At this time of day, Ralph's Grocery was mostly occupied by senior citizens, whom Jacob didn't care for. They moved their carts between the wide aisles, too slowly, creating a constant battle for him to get up or down an aisle. He'd come here because he needed something to calm him—today was *the* day. But his frustration only increased while he chose a bottle of chamomile iced tea, then stood in the short line at one of two open registers. He scanned the parking lot through the store's front windows, checking for any overly interested passersby, but found none.

"Do you have a Ralph's card, sir?" the cashier asked him.

"No, I don't," he said, and handed her five dollars. He didn't want to wait for his change, but forced himself to, to avoid being obvious. Then he returned to his Expedition, which had been waiting for him there since morning, started the engine and drove to the parking lot's exit. At the curb were two men in their early thirties. Most likely Central American immigrants, he decided. Probably waiting for a construction developer to pick them up for a day's work.

He sipped his tea, turned the wheel and merged onto Olympic Boulevard.

It would be nice to pack the SUV with the fire extinguishers, but he didn't want to chance being stopped at the airport entrance and questioned about the number of fire extinguishers in his vehicle. Too risky at this point.

He looked into the passenger's seat at the portable device with the multiple green lights on it, and gently patted it with his fingers. *Soon ... very soon.*

* * *

The men at the curb watched the SUV leave and returned their attention to the road. Jacob had guessed right: they were, in fact, day workers. But they were already working on their first job of the day. One of them pulled a cell phone from his pocket and dialed.

"Jose, he just left Ralph's in a light-green Ford Expedition. Heading west."

He hung up and muttered, "If we don't get work today, at least we'll get something from Jose."

His friend nodded in agreement, and they continued their vigil.

Chapter 61

Michael maneuvered the car mechanically, since there was no other way he could drive. Every single breath seemed a gasp for air, and his fingers gripped the steering wheel so hard his knuckles had turned white. Dianne snuggled against his shoulder, and this made his actions even more difficult.

"So, when's your final?" she asked.

"When is what?" he asked in a voice he didn't recognize. *Final? What's she talking about?*

"The final you have to take ... the one keeping you from going with me on this stupid flight." She sighed against his chest. The movement made the knot in his stomach grow larger.

"Oh, *that* one! In just a couple of hours... I just need to show up." The lie was physically painful to give. His tongue felt like sandpaper, lifeless, like something dead inside his mouth. Only then did he realize he'd been chewing on it the entire drive.

Another sigh, then she said, "Mom said you're the sweetest man. She wanted to tell you that herself, but she's too busy with our neighbor. Helen. You remember? The one who lost her husband and son."

"I remember," he said. *How could I forget the day I almost had my first heart attack?*

The LAX sign was visible now, and he was certain his tongue was bleeding from all the biting he'd done.

"Have I told you that I love you?" she whispered,

reached up and ran her fingers through his hair.

He nodded, but couldn't manage to say anything while he pulled into the parking garage and found a spot close to the entrance, parked the car and killed the engine. "It's showtime," he whispered, and got out of the car.

"What did you say?"

She'd followed him to the trunk, where he was carefully offloading the small suitcase, and now stood, one hand on her hip.

"I thought I heard you say *showtime*," she said, worry crossing her face. "And you seem so stressed out. I hope you'll be more relaxed when you get to the hotel tonight. You did fine on the flight to Mexico, so try not to worry about this one, okay?"

"I'll try," he said. "But I was just reminding myself to call my supervisors about the Showtime project." This time, he didn't lie. To the extent he could, he needed to tie up that loose end with Mellissa. One never knew when he might need that again. And to fail to complete the assignment might get him in hot water at school.

They walked toward the terminal with him holding her suitcase and her hands wrapped around his free arm. He dragged his feet. It was showtime indeed, and his stage fright was immense.

* * *

The airport officers gathered around them seemed attentive. Richard presumed the attention had something to do with the way Vicky looked. *But that's all right. Whatever works.* He had introduced Vicky as a psychologist with an interest in the terrorist mind. That was true enough. But his real reason was curiosity: to see if what he and Perez talked about the other day made it to the front ranks yet.

"I really appreciate you guys talking with me," Vicky

said. "What I'm trying to do is learn from people like you, who deal with preventing terrorism every day. So ... pretend I'm a terrorist. Before I even decide to attack, what should I do?"

"Get information about the place first," a tall, red-haired officer said. "Case it out. Pretend to be a passenger, walk around to see what's going on, check out the security in the place, things like that. That's what we always watch for around here."

"The other day," Richard said, "your captain and I ran into a guy who was holding what looked like an empty suitcase. Turned out, he wasn't a terrorist checking out the place, just someone whose wife had brought an empty suitcase, just in case she had to get rid of some stuff to avoid getting charged extra."

The officers chuckled just as Vicky said, "See the man over there? The one who's walking with his head down? He looks like he's heading toward the exit. But ... what if he's casing the place, like you said?"

"Thanks to your friend here," the officer said, nodding at Richard, "here's what we do nowadays. Watch and learn." Without saying anything else, he ambled toward the man.

* * *

Michael rammed his head against the steering wheel once, then twice. But it didn't take his mind off his roiling gut. Being questioned yet again was terrifying. Even though this officer was nicer than the last one, it was all he could do to come up with the right answers. But other than that, everything went perfectly. Just as he'd dreamed it would.

He'd escorted Dianne to the Lufthansa counter. He'd managed to distract her during the screening, so she wouldn't notice the box she didn't pack. Her luggage was scanned and, as he'd hoped, the TSA personnel decided her box of power bars was only giving the machine a false positive. But then, before she left for the gate, when he said he had to rush to his final at school, she kissed his lips for the last time....

For the last time ...

He couldn't look back, not even when she called after him and reminded him to call Showtime. She didn't know she was the final episode.

He was shivering now. Desperate to deflect his thoughts, to keep him from racing back into the airport, screaming there was a bomb, someone stop the flight, he pulled his cell phone from his pocket and dialed a number.

"This is Ed Vinitzky," was the quick response.

"Hi ... Professor? It's Michael. I, ah, wanted to know what you thought of the experiment I did for Showtime."

He heard his voice echo in the closed car, not normal-sounding to him, but close enough. He hoped.

"It was very good, Michael. I was impressed. Oh, and it's good you called. McClain requested you call him right away. Do you have his number?"

What does McClain want? What does he want? He quelled the screaming in his head and said only, "No," then wrote the number Vinitzky called out. Then he dialed again, fighting to make his quivering fingertips touch the right buttons.

"McClain here." The voice boomed in his head.

"Hi, sir, uh ... this is Michael Siluan. I understand you're looking for me?" He turned the car's air conditioner to a lower temperature. The shivering had stopped, now he was soaking wet.

"I was briefed about your idea for Showtime," McClain said. "Very imaginative."

The man's voice lowered, became almost contrite. "I ... I also wanted to apologize for ... our harsh conversation a while back. It took me a while to discover who you really are. Now I know."

"Know, sir? What do you know?" He held his breath.

"I know you're the son of Habib Siluan, a man who

assisted our country enormously. I was a veteran of the first Gulf War. I'm just sorry we didn't get to your father before the Iraqis did. He was a great friend to America. But you probably knew it already."

Michael dropped the phone and let it bounce on the car's floor mat. *My father, a friend of this country? But Ibrahim always said ... He told me himself!*

What was this man talking about? *What the hell is going on here?*

Through the curtain blanketing him, he could hear McClain say, "Hello? Michael? You still there?"

Chapter 62

Joe counted exactly sixty seconds before the numbers changed again. No, the car's digital clock hadn't failed. Just in case, he checked his wristwatch.

"What are we waiting for?" Tim asked, bored.

Joe looked at him in disgust, tired of the man's prattling. Since the rest of his pores were blocked with the antiperspirant, only his scalp was sweating. And his feet, which were making squishy puddles in his shoes.

"I'm just waiting for someone," he said.

Another moment passed. He turned the engine off and opened his door. "Are you coming, Tim?"

Tim exited the car immediately, a bit too fast in Joe's opinion.

"Be careful," he called through the open passenger door.

Tim turned and stuck his head back in the open door, befuddlement in his blue eyes. "What?"

"Can you see the terminal entrance over there?" Joe pointed to the entrance. "We have to meet someone who's joining us for lunch. I just need to do something else before that. Wait for me there until I get back, okay? And if you see him before I do, say hello."

Tim looked at where Joe pointed, then back at him. "Okay. How will he recognize me? Do I know him?"

"No, you don't. But he knows you're wearing a long coat, so don't take it off, okay?" Joe searched his eyes. "Tim, did you hear what I said?"

The last thing he needed now was one of Tim's blackouts. When Tim didn't reply, he leaned over and gently jostled his shoulder. To his great relief, the gentle shaking was enough to bring Tim back. He repeated his instructions, made Tim repeat them back.

"Are we clear?" he asked when he finished.

Tim nodded. "And then we eat?"

"As much as you want," Joe said, and sent him on his way.

The show was about to begin.

Chapter 63

"Jacob, I can't do it!" Michael pleaded into the receiver. "It was a mistake! I can't send her off with this bomb! I can't!" Tears covered his face, his hands, and the cell phone pressed firmly against his cheek. "I ... I just can't!"

"I know," Jacob said.

He ignored Michael's gasp and continued. "I've already notified authorities about the threat that someone might bring a bomb onto a Lufthansa flight. They'll stop all departing flights soon." He chuckled. "It's going to be hectic there today. If I were you, I'd leave now."

"Wh— What did you just say?"

"Go get your *sharlila* and live your life. You already contributed to the operation more than you know. Goodbye, Michael."

The line went dead.

Michael gasped at the silent cell phone, trying to fathom what was wrong. How could Jacob give up so easily on an operation they'd worked so long to bring to fruition? *How did he know I'd back off? How could he possibly have known that?*

He tried to put himself into Jacob's mind. Was Jacob's easy acquiescence—no, his outright *prediction* of Michael's plea supposed to make him relax, make him only *think* he didn't have to do anything else?

If that guess was correct, Dianne and who knew how many people on that plane were still in grave danger. If he'd guessed wrong ... if he was wrong ...

It didn't matter. He had to be sure.

He opened the car door, not knowing what to do next. His only certainty was that he couldn't trust Jacob's words. If her flight were grounded, as Jacob just said it would be, how would he know?

The timetable. The scrolling, ever-changing lists of today's flights and each one's status. If there were a problem, it would be noted there.

But I can't go back inside! He looked at the cell phone in his hand and debated only a second before he flipped it open, scrolled down the menu, and placed a call to the woman who'd just changed his life's purpose.

It didn't ring.

What if they've already found the bomb, and they took her phone? He pictured her beautiful face, tearstained and horrified, telling them the truth—that she had nothing to do with any bomb! The picture coalesced in his mind with others: harsh interrogation, a rough-handed strip-search, even torture until she gave them the answers they wanted—measures that, at one time or another, Abbed had gleefully described from his time in the training camps.

He locked the car and hurried into the terminal. The entrance seemed busy, with countless passengers bustling in and out. On his way to the terminal entrance, he had to sidestep to avoid running into a man in a long trench coat who smelled strongly of coffee.

The timetable displayed the day's flights ... and the blinking message "Delayed" after each one.

The clamor inside the terminal was deafening over his rushing heart. He hastened to the Lufthansa counter and tried to locate Dianne among the myriad blonde women nearby. What was she wearing? He tried, but couldn't remember.

Finally, he was able to determine she wasn't by the counter. He proceeded toward the gates, but was stopped by a uniformed officer.

"Sorry, pal, only passengers can come through here. And *nobody's* going through right now."

"Is something wrong?" Michael babbled, trying to glimpse beyond the checkpoint. "Can ... Can you tell me what's wrong?"

The officer shrugged. "I don't know, except that passengers from the gates have been instructed to exit through here."

Michael searched the gates, scanned the faces of those waiting. Thoughts, so many thoughts crossed his mind at once. *My father was an American ally? Why didn't Ibrahim ever tell me? Or was corrupting my mind Ibrahim's sweet revenge against Father—to use his only son against the infidels Ibrahim so abhorred, but that Father supported?*

And why did Jacob give up so easily on our operation? If that was the plan all along, why did he need the explosives I made in the first place?

"My love," she had said. Except for his father, no one in his life had ever cared about him the way she did. She never turned off her cell phone, yet it didn't ring when he tried to call her. What if they'd already found the bomb in her luggage?

When he thought of what he'd almost done to her, what might still happen if he couldn't find her, his gut twisted harder, and he felt himself becoming faint. The dizziness worsened, made him wobble on his feet.

No! He couldn't pass out. Not now. He had created this horrible nightmare. It must be he who ended it. If it meant his life to spare hers, he was willing to make that sacrifice.

Fighting nausea, he scrubbed at his eyes and forced his vision to clear. Waves of passengers, the confusion on their faces matching his, hastened outside. He searched their features, trying to recognize one face. The only face that mattered.

Finally, he saw her, and couldn't see anyone else. Tears he'd held back for well over a decade flooded his cheeks.

Chapter 64

Jacob left the public phone at the strip shopping center, just a few hundreds yards from the airport entrance. The threat call had gone perfectly. He didn't need to see the explosions, didn't need to be physically present when justice finally came to the infidels. Even so, he wanted to be close enough to view the screaming people, hear the whine of emergency vehicles, revel in the catastrophe in the western United States' most prominent city. Later, he would celebrate with Shudy. Now, he wanted the victory to be only his.

He ambled into a diner he'd spotted across the street, found a booth across from a TV mounted above the counter, placed his briefcase beside him and checked the menu. It would take news channels several minutes to get there. He might as well have something while he waited ... and while anyone inside the diner still cared about eating and drinking.

An elderly waitress approached. "I'm waiting for someone," he said. "Just coffee for now."

She nodded and left, and he watched the show playing just then. The psychologist-host dealt with people willing to expose their problems to the entire nation. He watched while a mother blamed her daughter's boyfriend for her own shoplifting habit. *Very soon, nobody will care about your so-called priorities!* he wanted to shout at the agitated people on the screen.

The waitress brought his coffee, and he shifted his gaze to the turbid liquid that reflected a face showing both amusement and disgust. His personal cell phone rang. As he anticipated, the boy broke down and copped out. That didn't matter. Even in failure, Michael's part of the plan would still create an initial panic, one that would still distract airport security from the much bigger plans to come. And Shudy might still give the boy another chance someday.

He hung up and looked outside in time to see a blue van, an antenna on its roof and "FOX News" on its side, racing toward the airport.

"Media, the best collaborator ever," he whispered, leaned back in the seat, and sipped the tasteless coffee.

Quickly bored with waiting for the breaking news to interrupt the stupid TV show, he opened the briefcase and examined the portable device, scanning his eyes over its multiple green lights. *Just a press of a button.* But not yet. Not until every news channel arrived.

* * *

Across from the diner, in the strip mall's parking lot, two Hispanic males sat in a well-equipped Honda Accord and listened to a popular Latino song booming from the car's sophisticated sound system. A cell phone rang. The man in the passenger seat switched off the music and answered.

"*Si. Si Mano.* He went to a diner across the street. His car is here."

He listened and said, "He has a briefcase." A moment later, he clicked off with a chuckle, then nodded to the other man. They both got out of the car.

Chapter 65

"I can't tell you how impressed I was by the way your officer engaged that passenger," Vicky said while she buttered her roll. She and Richard had bumped into Chief Stewart, who invited them to lunch at Encounter, the X-shaped restaurant at LAX.

Stewart nodded at her compliment. "I'm glad it turned out to be nothing. But of course, that's what I always hope for—"

The pleasant atmosphere was shattered when his cell phone and pager beckoned at the same moment. He smiled politely at them while pushing the button on his cell phone and checking the pager.

"Feed me," he said calmly into the receiver, listened for a few seconds, nodded, and stood. "I'll be right there." As he switched the phone off, his shoulder radio awoke with orders and commands.

He lowered the volume and gave Vicky an apologetic smile. "As I was saying, I always hope that a suspicion turns out to be nothing. Not this time, unfortunately. There was a threatening call regarding a bomb inside luggage on one of the flights. That means I have to go."

"Oh, my goodness!" Vicky muttered. Concern was visible across her face. Or was it fear? Richard wasn't sure of anything, except this could be the story of his career.

"Where are you going now?" he asked when they rose from their chairs.

Stewart pushed in his chair and shifted on his feet, a rare show of impatience. "The FBI takes control of an ... event like this. I'll be doing my department's thing from a command center right behind the checkpoint. Unfortunately, you're not authorized there."

He started walking, but stopped and turned. "You know, I don't see any reason why you can't be. And I'm the boss. Come on."

Richard grabbed Vicky's hand and hurried after Stewart, who was moving in a loping half-run now.

They entered the command room behind the checkpoints in what Stewart had hastily described as the sterile area. The room was covered with plasma screens and packed with both airport security personnel and people in the classic blue suits of the FBI.

One agent approached Stewart. "It's the real thing, Chief. The dogs found a bomb made of improvised explosives in the baggage area. Made it through security somehow. We shut the airport down, and we're checking all passenger luggage now.... As you know, it'll take some time."

Richard gazed across the room to the plasma screens of images from the CCTV cameras. Most showed people moving in the stiffened gait of those trying to quell panic. One showed an officer accompanied by a bomb-sniffing dog, going through piles of baggage.

"The real thing," he murmured. And he was the only reporter at the right place and right time to cover it. This was his walk on the moon—what would make him a household word.

He headed back to where Vicky and Stewart stood. The chief talked on the phone with the LAPD

"So we have terrorists at the airport after all," Vicky whispered.

And then it registered in Richard's mind. Something the counterterrorism expert told him, casually, while they chatted that day.

"I have to talk to you, Chief," he said, anxiety breaking his voice.

Stewart cut his call short and looked at Richard.

"Terrorists don't deliver just one bomb, Chief, do they?"

Stewart gave an impatient wave of his hand and pointed to the screen showing the bomb-sniffing dog. "Of course not. But you heard the agent. They're checking each piece of luggage right now."

Richard shook his head. "They informed you there's a bomb on an airplane for a reason. Get into the terrorist's head. If you were the terrorist, where would you place the next bomb?" He gestured toward one bank of screens.

Stewart followed his pointing finger and whispered, "The terminal ..."

Chapter 66

"*Hola mi amigo bueno. cómo es usted?*"

When he heard the friendly greeting above the television's blathering, Jacob didn't look up. The screen finally showed an airport official, talking to a reporter. The speaker hadn't addressed him, and no one could possibly know he was here.

He was wrong. "I'm talking to you, *essè*."

This time, the statement was followed by a tap on his shoulder.

He inserted his hand into his pocket and found some cash. He didn't check the bill, just handed the money above and over his shoulder. "Keep the change," he said, and kept his eyes on the screen, where an excited reporter was now talking about a threat found in one of the suitcases on its way aboard an airplane.

"What do you have in *your* briefcase, *essè*?"

The same annoying voice. This time it sounded right across from him in the booth. He lowered his eyes from the television screen and faced a man he wouldn't want to meet in the proverbial dark alley.

He blinked a few times, measuring the repulsive presence of the tattooed, nasty-looking man. "Do I know you?" he asked quietly.

Jose grinned and chuckled. "You might know this."

He placed a package on the table, and gave it a shove that sent it across the table and into Jacob's lap. Jacob had recognized the deodorant six-pack the moment Jose placed it on the table. It took his brain a split second to send a refusal order, though. By the time he sent his hands to stop the package, it was already in his lap. He jumped as if he'd been bitten by a snake, his hands barely able to scoop up the package and place it back on the table.

The realization sent shockwaves through his brain. Had his well-planned masterpiece blown up in his face? What did this man want? He glanced around. None of the other diners was looking at him. All eyes were frozen to the screen. Except for his, and the man's across from him.

"I wanted to consider myself Abbed's associate, but he decided to turn his back on me. That's not appropriate in this business." Jose's small, cruel eyes never left Jacob's as he spoke.

Abbed, Jacob thought. *Abbed led you to me.* If he could only put his hands on Abbed's throat right now, he would squeeze the life from him. If he only could ...

That was no longer relevant. The immediate problem, and danger, was seated across from him, grinning.

"What do you want?" he asked, his voice no louder than a whisper.

"I want to know what this contains." Jose pointed to the deodorant pack on the table. "I want to know what you're up to at the airport." He nodded toward the television screen. "And last but not least, I want my fair share." Jose ended with a malevolent smile that showed broken yellow teeth.

Jacob bit his lip and closed his eyes, the first intuitive acts he could think of. It was a mistake. When he opened his eyes again, he couldn't see his visitor's unpleasant face. A gun's muzzle blocked his view.

"I want your briefcase," the man behind the gun said quietly.

Jacob thought he might talk his way out of this, but couldn't argue with a gun. He raised his hands. "Why? There's nothing in it that would benefit you."

"So *you* say. *I* say give it to me."

"It's yours."

Jose snapped his fingers. Someone behind Jacob lifted the briefcase from the seat.

"I'm not done with you, *essè*," Jose said, and stood, still holding the gun on Jacob's forehead. "Think of my offer. We'll be in touch soon." He turned to leave.

The blow came from somewhere behind him. Something hard, like the butt of a gun. Then the diner began spinning around him. That was all he had time to think before losing consciousness.

Chapter 67

Richard flipped his cell phone closed and looked at Vicky. "Yours the same?"

She nodded. "Same thing. System failure. Never seen that message before."

"Too many people here using cell phones at the same time, I guess," he said. "Looks like the cell system collapsed." *And no way to call in the story. Damn!*

They followed Chief Stewart up the escalator and to the second floor, through the packed food court and to the balcony to look at the terminal below. "What a mess!" he murmured, then barked into his radio, "Perez, where's the K-9 unit?"

"On its way," the muffled voice replied.

"Shouldn't you evacuate the food court just in case, Chief?" Richard asked.

Stewart shook his head. "The panic would cause more casualties than any real strike, if there is one." He held the radio to his mouth again. "At least we can stop people from getting in."

"Here Roxey, here boy!"

The dog quickly came toward his handler, and followed him to the food court.

Stewart pointed toward the dog. "These dogs are being trained to detect explosives. In most cases, they do an even better job than the machines. But we can't operate the dog for more than an hour. They wear out. And we can't know exactly when the dogs operate efficiently and when they don't. But neither can the terrorists, at least."

Minutes later, the handler emerged from the food court and signaled a thumbs-up to Stewart before moving on. Unless he wore out, Roxey would sniff three kitchens and four storage rooms full of food and supplies.

Stewart, Vicky and Richard kept their second-floor vigil until Roxey and his handler emerged from the food-service area. Another thumbs-up, and Roxey headed toward the escalator. Right after they stepped off, they passed a wall. Roxey stopped dead and sniffed the air, then slowly approached the wall, his nostrils wide open, inhaling big gasps of air. The handler watched.

"Amazing," Stewart muttered. "The dog has to be exhausted, but he's smelled something there."

"Like what?" Vicky said. Stewart shrugged, and they kept watching.

Roxey sniffed for a few more moments, then sat perfectly still, pointing his sharp nose toward the compartment on the wall that read "Fire Extinguisher."

Stewart, watching, said, "Might be nothing, but ... let's head down there."

* * *

"Is it new technology, maybe?" Richard asked Stewart while they examined the fire extinguisher. "I mean, I can't say I've seen a million of these things up close. But I don't think I've ever seen one with a green light on top—"

Richard had the realization at the same instant Stewart did, and both men began walking backward, trying not to think about what would happen if the green light on the fire extinguisher suddenly turned red.

Stewart turned to Perez and barked, "Get the bomb squad here and check all these bastards."

"And?"

At Richard's question, Stewart turned hard eyes on him. "And *what*?"

"What will they do with them? The bomb squad can't do anything with all these people around." Richard gestured toward the crowd. "Someone might be watching and waiting for the right moment."

Stewart removed his jacket, covered the fire extinguisher with it, and hurried to the first airline counter on the departure level. He pressed the luggage conveyor button behind the counter and placed the bundle on its belt, following its disappearance with his eyes. The whole process took less than a minute, and with pandemonium breaking around the terminal, few noticed his actions.

"Brilliant," Richard whispered to Vicky. "The baggage area's solid concrete. Bombs won't do much damage in there."

Stewart raced back and spoke to Perez, "Make sure there's nobody in the luggage area. Then send your plainclothes people to do the same thing I did. Plainclothes, not uniform. I don't want the public to panic, and I don't want the bad guys to see what we're doing if they're still here."

He grabbed some duffel bags left by the conveyor belt and emptied them. "Use these. We're walking on thin ice, so let's do it right."

Perez didn't hear the last sentence. He was already on the radio, quietly barking orders.

Richard was just close enough to hear Stewart's statement about plainclothes officers. Stewart saw him smiling and grinned back. "Yes, Richard ... even though you're not an *expert*, you had a pretty damn good idea. And in my line of work, the best plans are the simple ones ... and the ones nobody knows about."

Chapter 68

Why is it taking so long? Joe wondered.

As he'd feared, Tim was getting restless. Standing under the hot sun, wearing the heavy vest and long wool trench coat, contributed to his obvious discomfort. By now, he was probably hungry too.

From the opposite side of the road, Joe waited for the explosion inside the terminal that would frighten the crowd into running outside, in Tim's direction. Joe held the remote control that was his responsibility, obscured by the crowd outside the building.

Tim was losing patience, but it was too late to cross the street and calm him. *It should end soon, Tim. Soon, no more hunger, no more worries—*

He saw Tim give a frustrated gasp, then walk toward the curb, as if he intended to cross the street to find Joe. Something he couldn't let happen.

* * *

As he passed into the airport, Muhammad saw two police officers in his rearview mirror. He slowed the cab and watched while they stopped their cruisers on the road and blocked the airport entrance he'd just driven through. Unusual. Although this crazy airport had witnessed stranger events. Still, he drove his cab cautiously through the huge complex. Just before he turned the curve between Terminal 3 and the international terminal, he saw numerous vehicles that meant only one thing—the media. Lots and lots of media.

"Probably another celebrity flying somewhere," the passenger in the backseat said.

"Not likely," Muhammad replied. "Celebrities use the private gate on Imperial Highway."

With the taxi creeping along, he surveyed the entrance, then the parking garage on his left, then turned his head toward the terminal. The face was familiar. In a very bad way. The glasses weren't the same and there was no beard, but Muhammad knew it was the same person: the passenger who'd sent Muhammad begging to the FBI. And this time, the man was watching the terminal entrance as though it was his last sight on earth. His head still turned, instinctive panic made Muhammad's foot hit the gas, trying to get away.

A snapping sound followed by his passenger's scream made him face forward in time to see his windshield obstructed by an unthinkable sight. The mix of red blood stained with grayish specks spread across the window, and he slammed on the brakes.

* * *

Tim's blue eyes were open and fixed, and turned in his direction. Joe didn't have to be a paramedic to know those eyes didn't comprehend anything. And he didn't have to be near him to see that Tim's head was cracked open; the dreadful grayish tissues of what could only be his brain bulged through the opening caused by his missing skull.

Joe remained on the sidewalk across the street, his back ramrod straight, unmoving. Muhammad and a group of passersby surrounded the body; he could hear their horrified, panic-filled shouts and cries for help. More people swarmed away from the terminal to the outside. Some noticed the small crowd gathered on the road and moved for a closer look.

It's time, he thought, pressed the remote control button and ducked.

Nothing happened.

He pressed the button again, but with no success this time either. He struck the remote's battery housing, thinking the batteries might have shifted. The mechanism still didn't respond.

He walked down the stairwell to the arrival level, trying to think of how he could possibly explain this, his second failure, to Jacob.

* * *

Darkness. Until he sensed the waitress standing above him, coffeepot in hand.

"Are you all right, birthday boy?" she said, and chuckled while she refilled his cup, then headed to the next booth.

"Sure," he muttered, not listening, busy trying to determine how long since he was struck.

He looked at the TV; the news he'd waited his whole life to hear was still going on. They were still talking about the terrorist threat, but also a car accident, it seemed. The image of a yellow taxicab was visible now, crowds around it.

Rising from his seat was difficult at first. When he eventually did and looked outside the window, he realized his SUV was gone. He understood why. They'd taken his vehicle and briefcase, not his life, because they could still use him.

He collapsed into the booth and did a fast damage-check. A painful swelling emerged from the back of his head, stiffening his neck. His wallet was missing. But they'd left his cell phone. He pulled it from a pocket, dialed a number, listened, and said, "Change of plans. Operate it from your end. I'll explain later."

He shook his head again, trying to clear it. When his focus sharpened more, he saw the waitress returning, this time with a plate holding a slice of cream pie. Atop it was a lit sparkler, its colors flashing gaily.

"The gentleman said it's your birthday," she said, and began lowering the plate to the table.

He looked at his lap. The package Jose had thrown at him was there. Instinct propelled him from his seat, the package in his hand.

The waitress jumped back, surprised by Jacob's unexpected movement. The plate left her hand. The cake and the sparkler met with Jacob's body. The package wrapping was set immediately in flames.

Michael had done a good job. A commendable job. The substance was solid, hence not too sensitive. One could carry it around with relative confidence. There was only one thing the substance was vulnerable to—flame.

Sublimation. The substance instantly multiplied itself 50,000 times in volume, pushing aside everything in its way. The explosion sent Jacob's and the waitress' body parts to the diner's big windows, shattering them.

The diner would be closed for renovations for a month. The authorities would mark the event as particularly inventive episode in LA's perpetual gang wars.

Chapter 69

Three-quarters of the crowd inside the terminal had been evacuated. Most of them now occupied the area designated for parking. Not wanting to take any chances, Perez directed them farther, to the lower levels, in case the vehicles parked nearest the entrance held any more surprises.

Roxey led his handler between the parked cars. The German Sheppard was surely tapped out, or nearly so. *Probably a miracle he smelled that fire extinguisher*, his handler thought.

He looked down and smiled at his friend. "Roxey the Wonder Dog. How's that sound, bro?"

Roxey gave a tired nod and wag of his tail and continued plodding ahead, unaware of how many lives he'd saved that day.

* * *

Inside the terminal, an officer signaled Stewart with a thumbs-up and called out, "Already done, Chief."

Stewart nodded, then pointed toward a man wearing a blue uniform. "Our head of maintenance. The last fire extinguisher's on its way downstairs through one of the baggage conveyors."

"Big relief," Richard said.

"Bigger than you even know," Stewart added. A smile

twinkled across his face. "The guy supervised the installation of those fire extinguishers. Says their mechanism works on a cellular system. And there's absolutely no cell reception in the baggage area."

Richard allowed himself a smile that faded when he saw the chief's face.

"I keep feeling like we're forgetting something," Stewart said.

Richard pondered that for a moment, his mind rolling over all his research. "Disguising the bombs that way was brilliant, Chief. If I'd thought it up, I wouldn't stop at just one target. Maybe check into the vendor's clientele to see who else had them delivered?"

Stewart nodded. "That might not be what I missed, but it's an excellent idea. You're just full of 'em, aren't you?"

Richard sighed. "Chief, I suspect that no matter how many ideas you or I or anyone else thinks up, the bad guys will already be one inspiration ahead."

Chapter 70

In downtown LA, in one of the city's tallest buildings, Christopher Adams the Third arrived at his luxurious office. The board chairman wasn't impressed with the beautiful panorama below his office window, or the Hollywood sign to the northwest. He was preoccupied with the media's blackout of the event at LAX. After initial reports, it was as though the media forgot about the bomb threat and moved on to other stories.

All those years of preparation! he thought in frustration. It should have been his triumphant moment now, with endless orders for the latest equipment his company offered. Fear should have opened the American wallet seeking Galaxy's outrageously expensive electronic solutions. And Adams would be the one to supply those solutions, raking in profits for years to come.

He picked up the newspaper his secretary left on his desk, sat in his soft leather chair and mulled over the return on investment that just disappeared, despite his brilliant plan. Millions down the drain. Not that he couldn't afford it, but ...

Should he contact those good-for-nothing Muslims and try again? Or search for a different way? He flipped through the paper, and an article by Richard Miller caught his eye. Richard Miller, a man Adams had come to hate. Yet Miller's enigmatic force led him time and time again to the articles he wrote. Today's article actually made him groan....

Learning the methods in which

terrorists act increases the chance of stopping an attack before it's carried out. To do this requires thinking like a terrorist, to the smallest detail. However, such strategies are only valid if based in reality. Sci-fi scenarios, while good for novels, are of little value in real environments and situations.

Contrary to popular belief, terrorists aren't crazy. Their acts are calculated, sophisticated—and well planned. Nobody wakes up in the morning and decides to conduct a bombing on a whim. Such acts as what almost happened at LAX require preparation not unlike a military operation's.

Regardless of the type of attack, terrorists usually take a year or much longer to plan it. In most cases, the attack itself is the shortest stage of the mission. Split seconds for the detonation of a bomb, a few hours at most to begin a hijacking or sabotage. In most cases, as soon as explosives, arms or other means are introduced, it's too late for law enforcement to prevent anything....

Adams squirmed in his plush chair at one line and muttered, "Most terrorists take a year or more to plan a single attack." He shook his head, retrieved his secured cell phone from his pocket. Richard Miller was right. It was never too soon to get started. And he'd been too stingy last time, too quick to pinch pennies. This time, he would ensure success, even if it cost twice as much. His bottom line would only benefit.

<END>

For more information about the creation of this book visit
www.rainforthewicked.net

Made in the USA